DUPLICITY

A Jon Steadman Thriller

Nellie Neeman

ISBN: 978-1-7351505-9-8 (Paperback)
ISBN: 978-1-7351505-8-1 (E-Book)

Author Photo: Elan Sachs
Library of Congress Control Number:
Printed in the United States of America

To all those gone but not forgotten
May your memory be a blessing

PROLOGUE

Rainbow Falls Trail
Maui, Hawaii

Jennifer Cartwright searched the sky for the island's distinctive rainbows. She breathed in deeply, allowing the pristine air to fill her lungs, forcing away the momentary nausea. In the distance, she spotted the emerging colors, a blurring mist, slowly forming into a defined spectrum far above the earthly paradise.

Jennifer kept her pace steady, acutely aware of each planted step. Glancing down at her sky-blue hiking boots, she was gratified to see them coated in mud. The ground was soft and pliable, creating short-lived imprints of her shoes' treads.

Despite the current circumstances, this trail would remain one of her all-time favorites. An explorer's dream, it snaked through the dense rainforest, ending at the hundred-foot cascading falls. Right up her alley.

Jennifer was utterly flummoxed at the seismic shift that had destabilized her life in recent weeks. If things had gone as originally planned she'd now be on a plane back to the mainland.

She turned around to see Makoa a few strides behind, a watchful look on his handsome face. A mix of Polynesian and Caucasian, Makoa seemed to win the genetic lottery with thick black hair, soulful eyes and a square jaw. Sweat beaded on the deeply tanned muscles bulging beneath his USMA tank top, reminding Jennifer of the Hulk. Primal, masculine.

Snap out of it, Jen. This isn't a date. Far from it. They had come here for a purpose and she was prepared.

They'd hiked for nearly two miles. Not long till they'd reach the falls.

Every few minutes, Jennifer stopped to take a picture of the scenery. The cell reception was poor but holding the device skyward, she managed to upload the photos onto social media. Several hundred people would see the posts in their feed. Thoughts of her sister infiltrated. She pushed the disquiet aside.

Jennifer removed her laden backpack, grateful for the reprieve, and took out her water bottle, nearly draining it. Makoa did the same. He was a quiet one. Only spoke when he had something of value to say. She respected that.

Makoa took her hand. Due to the earlier rains, they were alone. As expected.

"Hungry?" he asked.

"A little."

Makoa pulled out a granola bar and handed it to her, letting his hand linger on hers, his piercing gaze mirroring her own desire. She could drown in his beautiful eyes. Determined not to be distracted, she looked away. An awkward moment passed and he let go of her hand.

Jennifer had met Makoa weeks before, their mutual attraction growing with each passing day. Under other circumstances the time alone together would be welcome. But not today.

They continued on in silence, the unmistakable sound of rushing water soon confirming their arrival at the top of the falls. From this vantage point, the view was magical, an Eden nestled amid tropical foliage. Makoa moved past her, mere feet from the cliff's edge.

He waited for Jennifer to unpack her gear, then

extended a hand. "Trust me." Framed by the picturesque backdrop, he looked otherworldly.

Jennifer took his hand, gripping hard, the adrenaline spiking as he brought her close. She could smell the musky scent of his cologne. Their faces were inches apart. Time stood still.

Makoa wrapped his arms around her. His body was like a brick wall. All muscle. It was dizzying. Exhilarating.

"Ready?" he asked.

A mix of passion and trepidation as she nodded.

She felt his breath on her neck. "A hui hou," he whispered.

"What's that?"

Makoa's grip tightened on her waist. Swiftly, he pushed her, the momentum propelling them apart. Jennifer let out a cry, instinctively reaching out to Makoa for stability, the ground vanishing beneath her feet.

"It means, until we meet again," he said, as Jennifer plummeted toward the glistening rocks below.

CHAPTER 1

S ienna Lamont sat at the edge of Jon Steadman's sofa, her
legs crossed, her eyes cast downward as if studying the
glaring black specks on her white leather Jimmy Choo
sneakers.

Jon was still reeling from the woman showing up on his
doorstep, claiming his partner had sent her. His dead partner.

"Sorry to mess with your run," Sienna said. "I didn't
know who else to turn to."

Jon grabbed a sweatshirt from the front closet and put
it on over his faded UNT t-shirt, noting stray flurries swirling
lazily outside his kitchen window. "Looks like I wouldn't have
gone far. It's snowing." The weather had been wacky of late,
rapidly changing from unseasonably warm to bitingly cold in
a matter of hours. He sat on a chair across from Sienna. "You
knew Carrie?"

Sienna spoke to the floor. "We grew up together,
roaming around Europe with our parents. Our fathers were
military men. She and I stayed in touch for years. But over the
last twelve months or so, we sort of drifted apart. I gathered
she had a lot on her plate between being a single parent and
managing a demanding career."

Jon didn't fill in the gaps, namely, the job that Carrie
Santiago once held with the CIA. Carrie and Jon had worked
together for a short time, much of it overseas. She died in

the line of duty, leaving behind her four-year-old son, Randy. Jon was hyper-protective of the boy, having taken on an unexpected uncle-like role.

Sienna raised her gaze to meet Jon's. As if reading his mind, she said, "I know what she did for a living, Agent Steadman."

Jon raised a brow.

"Like I said, we were close. She didn't tell me the details, but I knew she worked in American intelligence. It must have been really tough for her to leave Randy behind to go on assignment."

"It was." He left it at that.

Sienna seemed to sense something in his tone. "Were you two . . .?"

"No." Aware he was coming off as abrupt, Jon added, "Maybe under different circumstances things would have been different."

"The story of my life." Sienna reached for the chamomile tea Jon had poured for her after escorting her up to his apartment. Her hands were well-manicured. She took a sip, quickly placing it back on the small table beside her, the remnants surely cooled by now.

Jon took in his guest's attire, her bearing. The peacoat Sienna had worn into his apartment was now draped over the back of his kitchen chair, its black and gold Dolce and Gabbana label visible. He took note of the stylish cut of her light hair, edgy but refined; the jeweled choker around her throat that to his untrained eye appeared authentic. He estimated Sienna was at least five years his senior.

There was something about her Jon couldn't quite put his finger on. Perhaps it was the odd resemblance she bore to the fair-skinned, green-eyed model he'd seen on one of Times Square's iconic jumbotrons. He recalled the fashion ad. *Posh*. It was impossible to miss the scrolling glittery script the size of a full-size car shining down on 42nd Street.

Sienna had money. Of that Jon was certain. Apparently,

she'd come a long way since her army brat upbringing.

Jon stood, cleared the mugs, placing them in the kitchen sink. Sienna came up beside him. She had the petite, lithe physique of a gymnast, the top of her head barely reaching his shoulder. She smelled of fresh-picked roses.

Jon said, "Why don't you tell me what brought you to my door."

Sienna stared out the window at the stray flakes, seemingly trying to organize her thoughts, then turned to face him, her green eyes studying him. "Do you really work for the FBI? You look so young."

Jon pursed his lips, made the effort to remain amiable. And patient. "I've been with the New York office for over a year."

Sienna took a deep breath, blew it out. "I have a genetic disorder."

It wasn't what Jon was expecting to hear. "Oh?"

"I was twenty-three, engaged to my college sweetheart, when I learned about it." She cleared her throat. "The gene passes down exclusively to boys. I wasn't willing to take a gender gamble and risk subjecting a child to a debilitating illness." Her eyes watered. "My fiancé couldn't bear having no biological children of his own." She paused. "He broke off the engagement."

"I'm sorry," Jon said. He meant it. It must have been bad enough learning she was a carrier of a hereditary disease. Topping it off with losing her fiancé would have been devastating. He knew what *that* felt like.

Sienna said, "Since then, I just assumed I wouldn't have children." She turned away, extracting a tissue from her jeans pocket.

Jon guided her back to the sofa. "Go on."

She sat, her mascara now smudged. "About nine months ago, I learned about a fertility clinic that could help me." Her eyes flicked to his, then away. "You've probably heard the term, designer babies. Parents select the gender, eye color."

Jon nodded. "Only embryos with the desirable genetic markers are selected for implantation, right?" Noting Sienna's surprise, he added, "I studied forensic criminology. I read about it in one of my science journals. Sounds like science fiction."

Sienna shrugged. "Maybe it was at one point, but today gene therapy is becoming increasingly popular." Sienna shifted in her seat, bit her lip. "This particular clinic specializes in gene editing."

"What's that?"

"It's a procedure where the DNA associated with the disorder is edited out of the embryos and then implanted into the mother. Or carrier. It corrects genetic variants of reproductive cells."

Sienna's unease was starting to make more sense.

"Isn't that illegal?"

Sienna exhaled, her shoulders slumping. "It's a gray area. In the U.S., federal funds cannot be used to research gene editing but there's no legislation yet regarding genetic engineering in humans. In any case, the facility I heard of is private. They conduct clinical trials."

Either she's deluding herself or rationalizing. Jon didn't care for either option. "Messing with Mother Nature never ends well." He had learned that lesson on more than one occasion.

Sienna said, "Maybe so, but put it this way, if you had the option to remove the gene for diabetes or Alzheimer's from your child, would you?"

Jon couldn't deny her point. "Of course."

Sienna held out her hands, palms up. "You see? Once we peel away the layers, the right thing to do is not so obvious. Needless to say, for me, the prospect of editing out my disorder was like finding gold. I jumped on it. I've always wanted to be a mom, have a large, noisy family. The chance to have that, was without exaggeration, life changing. I began to see the future differently, one with new purpose."

She spoke faster, her eyes brightening with the talk of motherhood.

"You signed up for the procedure?" he asked.

Sienna nodded, broke eye contact. "I'm using a surrogate."

Jon didn't comment. It was none of his business.

Perhaps she read his silence as confusion. "The procedure has a low rate of success to begin with, not to mention an exorbitant price tag. My doctor thought I'd have the best chance of success with a surrogate to carry my child."

Jon suspected there was more but didn't press the issue. There were lots of reasons for surrogacy. "Can I ask who the father is?"

Sienna said, "Most clinics allow you to either use sperm you acquire independently or choose from a catalogue. This facility has an unusual policy. Clients are required to select a donor from their exclusive catalogue. I assume the protocol increases the odds of success with their highly desirable pool of donors. Which was fine with me. I'm not in a relationship and would have done so anyway."

Jon wondered if like him she was commitment-shy given the trauma she went through in her past relationship. Still, he was enthralled with the advances in reproductive technology. He leaned back in his chair, put his feet up on the coffee table. "What happened?"

"It worked. Probably the best day of my life. Jennifer was scheduled for a gynecological exam two days ago but she didn't show up. I tried reaching her to no avail. She doesn't answer her phone or emails. I called the clinic and they claimed not to have heard from her."

"That's it?" Jon regretted the words the moment they left his lips. "I mean, is there something more? Maybe her phone isn't working. Maybe she was under the weather. There are countless reasons . . ."

Sienna must have sensed where he was heading. "She didn't back out of our surrogacy deal," she said, crossing her arms like a brooding child.

When Jon didn't respond, impatience crept into her tone. "If it weren't for her last voice message, I'd think nothing of it."

She pulled out her phone, tapping the screen. A young woman's breathless voice came through the speaker. "Sienna, call me asap." She spoke in a rapid whisper. "Something awful is going on at the clinic. Watch your back." In the background, Jon heard a knock. "I-I'm sorry."

Jon asked Sienna to play it again. There was no denying the fear in her words.

"That call was from yesterday. I'm kicking myself for missing it. I tried to call back but it goes straight to voicemail. Something's happened."

"Did you call the police?"

Sienna nodded. "They took the info but said there isn't much they can do at this point. That she probably turned off her phone or is out of range. Whatever. But I know her. She'd never go this long without a word."

"She did sound scared of something . . . or someone."

A groan escaped Sienna's lips.

Jon felt awkward. A woman was in his kitchen confiding in him and crying. Despite being a so-called friend of Carrie's, to him Sienna was a stranger. And something felt off. "What am I missing?" he asked, looking her square in the eye.

A flood of tears broke through, freely running down her cheeks. Between sobs Jon deciphered Sienna's heartbreaking words.

"Jennifer is more than my surrogate. She's my big sister. And she's carrying my baby."

CHAPTER 2

Isle of Palms, South Carolina

It was a long night for Dr. Terry Lavi. After the heated argument with her fiancé, Gabe, she'd left the beach house in a huff, taking a lonesome seaside walk to blow off some steam. There, on the blustery beach, Terry had felt the weight of her relationship with a man who lived thousands of miles away from her homeland. A man who knew little about her job as a 'consultant' for the Mossad, Israel's intelligence service.

A man she loved with every beat of her heart.

In the heat of the moment, she'd left her phone behind, letting her guard down for only a few minutes. And was approached by Charlotte Colbert. Terry had spent long and frustrating weeks in pursuit of one of the world's most hunted black market brokers. Until she was unceremoniously pulled off the case. The appearance of the matronly, white-haired businesswoman on the South Carolina beach—a woman she'd met briefly at a New York conference—served to reveal her true identity as the White Knight.

Charlotte had offered a helping hand, inviting her to a cottage a mile up the beach. The modest sand-colored one-story house wouldn't warrant a second glance. The interior had the expected amenities but little in the way of luxury. Given its prime location, it wouldn't be long before some Atlanta hotshot gutted it, turning the property into another seaside gem.

Terry sat on the threadbare sofa, trying to slow her heart rate. The initial shock had not yet worn away. Being privy to the true identity of one of the most wanted international criminals was terribly dangerous. No matter what she looked like.

Twice, Terry spotted a large man in a bulky windbreaker pass outside the window. His voice was muffled as he spoke firmly into his earpiece. Terry pulled the chenille throw more tightly around her.

Charlotte followed Terry's gaze, pouring herself a glass of Merlot. "That's Simon, my head of security. He's nothing to be concerned about. As you can imagine, I need to protect my identity at all costs. That's why I've taken precautions."

A likeable woman in her seventies, Charlotte had been overlooked by both the Mossad and CIA. She'd never even been a suspect. "My greatest protection is my appearance," Charlotte had told her on the way to the cottage.

Charlotte placed the wine glass on the kitchen counter. "I gather you've had a bad row with your fiancé."

How does she know that?

As if reading her mind, Charlotte said, "I have no surveillance on Mr. Lewis's home. It was merely a deduction, my dear. A despondent woman sitting alone on a beach typically adds up to matters of the heart."

Charlotte took a seat opposite her and made her pitch. Terry listened quietly. The proposal was nothing short of jaw-dropping. Charlotte would provide Terry's genetics lab with a sizeable endowment, clearing the way for the experiments and research she'd been unable to conduct due to the financial constraints.

The problem lay with the quid pro quo.

"I've been patient, waiting for the ideal opportunity to approach you, privately. Now that we've met, I'm eager to proceed. However, if you decide to decline my proposal, no harm done. I'll have Simon bring you back to the beach where we met or anywhere else you'd prefer to go."

By two a.m., Terry couldn't keep her eyes open. They agreed she'd sleep on it, Charlotte making it clear that until things were ironed out Terry could not return to Gabe's house. Or contact him.

If Terry agreed to the terms, she would need to remain off the grid for several days as a security measure. Otherwise, there was no way they'd move forward.

Terry *needed* to move forward. International security depended on it.

***

New York City

Jon waited for Sienna to calm down. He passed her a box of tissues.

"Thanks." Sienna wiped her eyes. "Jen is my older sister. She knew my deal and offered to act as my surrogate. I couldn't believe it. I was over the moon."

Jon was still stuck on Sienna's earlier evasiveness, wondering why she'd initially hidden the fact that the surrogate was her sister. He wasn't sure what it meant but made a mental note.

Sienna said, "I was going to sit in on Jen's doctor visits. But then she fell off the radar. Now Jennifer—and my baby— are gone."

Jon felt awful for the woman. He'd suffered so many losses himself over the years. But he didn't see why she'd come to him.

Sienna said, "I made a terrible mistake."

"What do you mean?"

"From the beginning, I sensed there was something about the procedure that was too good to be true. The degree of exclusivity, the NDA I needed to sign. I talked myself into believing it was all legit. I wanted a child so badly I refused to look too closely. There's something shady going on at that clinic, Jon. I need to find my sister."

"Why didn't you tell me it was a family matter from the outset?"

"Would it have mattered?"

Jon didn't care for the response but restrained himself from saying so.

Sienna said, "I'm praying she's all right. Either way, I want to get my other embryos out of there and move them to a traditional facility."

Feeling a strong pull to get outside, Jon glanced out the window. The snow hadn't let up. "What's keeping you from doing that?"

"I had to sign a waiver. It requires they maintain supervision of all embryos created with their technology until implantation. I thought nothing of it at the time."

"This sounds more like a lawyer issue than something I can assist you with."

"I wish that were true. But there's trouble there. I know it. The police won't help me locate Jen. I need protection and someone to help me find her. I'd like to hire you for both."

"Protection?"

"You heard her message."

Jon intuited there was far more to the story. "Ms. Lamont, I feel for you. I really do. But . . ."

He stood.

She didn't.

She said, "It should only take a few days."

"What if it doesn't?"

"Then you're off the hook. I'll pay you and find someone else. But I don't think that will be necessary."

The conversation was taking an odd turn. "I already have a job." He eased his way to the door, hoping she'd pick up on the hint. When she didn't budge, he added, "No offense but I'm pretty sure intuition and that voicemail don't warrant all this." His words sounded insensitive even to his own ear.

Sienna frowned. "Look, I get it. You don't know me. I show up here with what sounds like a crazy overreaction. This isn't making a lot of sense to you. But Carrie told me if I ever needed help—*real* help—I should turn to you. I guess she overstated that." Sienna finally stood, walked to the door. "Thanks for hearing me out."

Jon held the door open for her, irritated that she brought up Carrie again. *She's playing me. Let her go.*

He watched as Sienna walked down the hall toward the elevator. As she turned the corner, he cursed under his breath, then heard himself call out, "Wait."

She faced him, a question in her eyes.

Jon said, "What exactly would you want me to do?"

Without a moment's hesitation, Sienna replied, "Come with me to Maui. Help me find Jen."

***

Isle of Palms, South Carolina

Terry was jolted awake by a knock on the door. Opening her eyes, she was momentarily disoriented, startled at her surroundings and the unfamiliar bed. She sat up, her head spinning with all that happened over the last few hours.

Thoughts of Gabe accosted her. If only she could call him to say she was all right.

Another knock. This time the door opened a crack, a halo of white hair visible. "Good morning." Charlotte was carrying a tray.

Terry found it bizarre that a woman of her means was handling things personally. "Come in." It felt like when her grandmother, Savti, woke her up on summer mornings with tea and sugar cookies.

Maybe Charlotte knows that.

The thought that the White Knight was privy to that tiny detail about her and was exploiting it, was both odd and disturbing.

"I brought you morning tea." Charlotte placed the tray on the bedside table, sitting on the edge of the bed. "Have you had a chance to consider my offer?"

Terry took a sip from the teacup. *Peppermint. My favorite.*

There was only one way to play this. Only one chance she'd be given to infiltrate the criminal's lair and learn all she could in the hopes of somehow informing Kahn. "Yes, I have."

Charlotte looked at her expectantly. "And?"

Terry looked into Charlotte's light blue eyes and smiled. "I've always wanted to visit the American West."

***

Gabe Lewis spent the night scouring the beach. After calling Terry's phone only to find it in her purse by the front door, he called the few neighbors he knew, waking several. No one had seen Terry. He then drove to the local precinct, thinking his presence would warrant more urgent action. They told him what he expected. It sounded like they'd had a lover's quarrel and Terry went somewhere to cool down. It didn't warrant using their valuable resources to search for her.

Gabe knew better.

Terry had important work in Israel's prestigious Technion genetics lab. She would never leave for an extended period without her phone. And as much as she was a hothead, she wouldn't leave without an explanation.

Terry was in trouble. Gabe was certain of it.

Since their premature departure from their vacation in Eilat, Israel's southernmost city on the banks of the Red Sea, Gabe understood Terry was at Yosef Kahn's beck and call. He'd assumed by the time they reunited on the Isle of Palms to assess Gabe's family's vacation home as a potential wedding venue, whatever work she'd been doing for the Mossad chief had been resolved.

Perhaps he'd been wrong. Perhaps she was still working for Kahn. It would explain her foul mood. Gabe ran a hand through his hair in frustration. He couldn't think clearly. What should he do next? Who would Terry call if she was distraught?

Out of obvious options, he glanced at his watch. It was two in the afternoon in Haifa. He picked up the phone and dialed Dr. Hannah Lavi, Terry's mother.

CHAPTER 3

New York City

J on ran across the Brooklyn Bridge at what he deemed to be an impressive speed. The snow had stopped, the emerging sun burning the dusting away. The weather in the city was all over the map. Still, it was probably the last day for a while that he'd be able to go for a run without freezing.

He had just spent two hours at his apartment speaking with Sienna Lamont and couldn't shake the feeling he was being played. But in the end, Carrie won out. He was convinced the two women had indeed been close friends. Sienna knew more about Carrie than most people. More than he did. Randy's birthday, and even Carrie's parents'—Esther and Raúl's —anniversary.

With so little in the way of family, Jon's friends became his chosen kin. Carrie among them. He had no choice but to help Sienna, even if she was holding things close to the vest.

The problem was how far to go to help her. He glanced at his smart watch, turned south. He had an appointment and the timing couldn't be better.

***

South Street
Lower Manhattan

"How have you been, Jon?" the shrink asked, closing the door behind her and settling into the tan leather chair, her iPad in hand.

Jon looked out the second story window. The cobblestone street offered a glimpse of 1800s New York. "Fine."

The therapist tilted her head. "Really? You seem preoccupied."

"A lot on my mind."

"Care to share?"

Silence. Then, Jon said, "I suppose that's what I'm here for, right?" A tinge of sarcasm crept in.

The shrink didn't take the attitude bait. "Right. So, what's up?"

"Had a visit from Carrie's friend."

"Hmm. I see how that could bring up some difficult feelings for you."

Jon shrugged.

"What brought her around?"

"She said Carrie told her if she was ever in trouble to find me and I'd help."

"Sounds like Carrie had a lot of faith in you."

"I guess."

The therapist waited a beat. "Is that all?"

"I'm running low on the meds. I need a refill."

The therapist typed something into her tablet. "Are they still helping?"

"I haven't freaked out in a while if that's what you mean." Jon didn't like the term *PTSD*.

Veterans had earned that diagnosis. He'd never seen war. Despite the shrink telling him there was little difference

15

between combat and what he'd experienced with the college shooting that killed his fiancée and left him with a limp.

"That's good."

Jon left out the part about his recent violent outbursts. Twice he'd erupted, the ire spiking with ferocious speed. He'd held a gun to a suspect's head, later hitting him hard in the face, breaking the man's nose.

"What about the dreams?"

"Still having nightmares."

She took another note. "Maybe we should try another medication. See if that helps."

"You're the doctor."

"I'll call in the prescription to your pharmacy but want your reassurance that you're taking the proper dosage. No more, no less. This medication can be very effective but on rare occasions, patients experience adverse side effects. Poor impulse control, extreme agitation. If we need to, we'll change it."

Jon gave a thumbs up.

"Okay, then. How's work?"

"It's been in a 'hurry up and wait' mode. We had a red-level situation that vanished overnight. It may pick up again but for now it's been quiet."

"And things with Agent Matthews?" She knew Jon's relationship with his boss was frequently volatile.

"Doug's been okay these last few weeks. But he's acting weird."

"Weird how?"

Jon gave the question some thought. "Dressing better, for one. Craig, my coworker says he's dating someone."

"How do you feel about that?"

"Seems kinda rushed. Don't you? His wife just died."

"And that seems disloyal to you?"

Jon bristled. "This isn't about me."

She held Jon's gaze. "Isn't it?"

"Stop that."

Ignoring the plea, she went on. "You've had a hard time committing to anyone since Ashleigh died and that was several years ago. I'm curious if you think doing so would be disloyal to *her*."

"She's dead. It wouldn't be cheating."

The therapist nodded. "I agree. But we both know logic and emotion are two very different things."

There was truth in that. Even with the one real relationship he'd had since Ashleigh's death, he hadn't been fully vested.

"You've had a lot of work stress in recent months. Maybe it's time for a brief vacation."

"I was in Costa Rica not long ago."

"I recall. But from what you told me it was a very active, exhausting trip."

"Yeah, so?"

"So, I'm suggesting something more relaxed. No ziplining, jujitsu classes, whatever. Just a book on a beach."

"With a cocktail?" he smirked.

"Not on those meds," she said, pointing to the iPad, her expression humorless.

"Sienna—that's Carrie's friend—wants me to go with her to Maui to check something out. On her dime." He left out the details.

"Sounds like a perfect solution. If you can get real downtime while you're there, I'd strongly encourage you take her up on the offer."

***

The Bronx

Jon tossed the empty ice cream cups in the trash while keeping an eye on Randy, who was climbing like a monkey in the shop's indoor playground. The boy had wanted to go to the aquarium. It was his favorite outing but the frigid temperatures forced

Jon to decline. His concession was to spend an hour eating raspberry chocolate chip and swinging from the rafters.

Jon smiled to himself amazed at how much he enjoyed the boy. Who would have ever believed Jon a babysitter? *No, it was more than that.* He'd become family. The Santiagos had embraced him as one of their own. The feeling was mutual. Jon had come into Randy's life shortly before the boy's mother was killed in the line of duty. Jon knew some scars would fade while others would remain a lifetime. An only child himself, Jon could count on one hand the people that truly mattered in his life. He wanted something better for Randy.

Jon approached the tubular slide, waiting for the boy to emerge. "Time to go, little man."

Randy pouted. "Five more minutes?"

Jon tried to conjure up a stern demeanor, but it wouldn't come. "Sure, why not?"

On the way out, Jon rinsed Randy's sticky hands, then held one in his own. "Let's get back to Abuela before she starts to worry."

Jon stood in the Santiago's doorway, the aroma of sauteed onions welcoming him.

"Had fun?" Esther asked.

Randy began firing off about the playground, barely coming up for air.

Esther laughed. To Jon, she asked, "Lunch?"

"Can't today."

Esther said to Randy, "Go get cleaned up. I made mac and cheese."

Jon gave Randy a hug. "Bye, buddy. Have a fun week."

Randy ran inside.

"Sienna Lamont came to see me," Jon blurted.

Esther's eyes widened. "I didn't realize you knew her. She and Carrie were close friends. She's a lovely young woman."

Jon glanced at his watch. He wanted to hear more but he was running late. He kissed Esther on the cheek and hurried to the elevator. He'd committed the rest of the afternoon to Matthews. Given what he was considering doing for Sienna, annoying his boss with his tardiness would not be prudent.

CHAPTER 4

SoHo, New York City

J on brought the last of the boxes up to the SoHo loft. The space looked much larger than necessary for one newly widowed man. Doug Matthews was dressed in a way that Jon never got to see. Sweats and high-top sneakers. When he'd called, asking for help with the move, Jon assumed he was desperate, contacting everyone he knew before scraping the bottom of the barrel and recruiting his employees. When he arrived at the loft, Jon was surprised to learn he was the only person Matthews had called.

Doug was a changed man. With the death of his wife, he was starting over in his late fifties. Jon had never met Erica but understood that the couple was perfectly matched —the tough-guy Fed and the workaholic DA. Jon suspected Doug wasn't an easy man to live with. Erica must have been something special.

"This is the last of it," Jon said, placing the box on the kitchen table.

"I owe you a beer," Doug said, grabbing one from the fridge and cracking it open.

Jon made a face. "A beer? How about lunch at Cipriani?"

"Would you settle for a deli sandwich? I think this place has cleared out my bank account."

"I thought you said it was paid for by Erica's life insurance policy."

"Okay, smartass, where do you want to go eat . . . that I can afford?"

"Second Ave Deli. I've been dreaming of an overstuffed pastrami sandwich for the last three hours."

Doug grabbed his jacket and keys. "All right. Let's go."

Jon wiped at his mouth, the napkin coming away stained with brown mustard. He'd shared everything that happened since Sienna showed up at his door. "She wants me to help her."

"That seems somewhat excessive under the circumstances."

"I said the same thing but she's convinced there's more going on over there. She's scared."

Doug took a forkful of his health salad. "Why do I feel like the next thing you're going to say is you want the FBI to get involved?"

"I don't know, Doug. It's why I'm bringing it up." Then, "After hearing her sister's message, I wouldn't be surprised if something more sinister is going on."

"If every time someone shows up asking for your help . . ."

Jon felt his defenses go up. Thoughts of Ed Hernandez came to mind. An LA Times reporter who'd spent much of his adult life eating pastrami sandwiches, Ed had appealed to Jon for assistance in the very delicatessen Jon now found himself in with Doug.

"Ed asked for my help and I didn't give it. At least not initially. And look how that turned out. I won't make that mistake again." Jon was referring to the brutal attack Ed suffered shortly thereafter.

Doug paused, seemingly considering his words. Or maybe he was just eating. "I'll be back in the office tomorrow and I can check out the clinic. Where is it located? Somewhere in Manhattan?"

Jon said something, but his mouth was full.

"How about you swallow first?"

When John finished the bite, he said. "Maui."

Doug looked up. "Huh?"

"The fertility clinic is in Maui."

"You've got to be kidding me!"

Jon did his best to maintain a look of innocence. "Why?"

"Because Maui's a bit out of our territory, Jon." Impatience had crept into his tone. "There's an FBI field office in Honolulu."

"Sienna's a friend of Carrie's. I'll only be gone for the weekend . . . or maybe a couple of days longer. Just enough time to decipher what's going on."

Doug kept his voice steady. "You do realize you have a job here in New York, right? *I* tell you where to be and when."

"Which is why I'm asking permission. In advance. In the past I just took things on and let you know afterward. Isn't this progress?" Jon grinned broadly, showing off his pearly whites, his demeanor now collegial.

Doug's face was contorting, as though trying to hold back a smile. In the end, he just shook his head. "Vacation, right?"

Jon nodded.

"You understand that means until otherwise approved you are helping a friend as a civilian, not as a federal officer."

Jon gave a thumbs up, his mouth full once again. He swallowed, signaled to a passing waiter. "Please pack me another one of these to go."

The waiter nodded. "I'll add it to the bill."

Matthews looked from the waiter to Jon. "Really?"

Jon downed his root beer, addressed the waiter. "What's for dessert?"

Doug let out an exasperated sigh.

Two hours later, Jon stepped into his apartment. The steam whistled loudly from the metal radiators. He opened a window, allowing the cool air inside, pleased with himself. He'd had an epic meal on his boss's dime, convinced him to look into the clinic, and was preparing for a trip to the tropics.

After Sienna's plea for help, Jon had gone back and forth on whether to tell Matthews about it. The relationship with his boss was unconventional from the start. Poorly disguised animosity had evolved into an inflammable mix of respect, codependence and tumult.

Matthews had surprised him. Pleasantly so. In the past, Matthews would have lost his lunch if Jon even hinted at what bordered on an independent investigation. Broaching the subject had felt like walking a tightrope, sharing most of what he was up to with only a few minor tweaks and omissions.

Jon could breathe easier now, ready to make inroads with locating Sienna's sister. Maybe Matthews's new girlfriend was a good idea after all.

Jon assessed his place. Neat as a pin. At two-thirty in the morning, he'd had an urgent out-of-character need to tidy up, even spending twenty minutes mopping the floors. *If Granny could see me now.*

He put the sandwich in the fridge and initiated a video call.

He was about to hang up when Eunice Steadman answered. "Hi honey. Sorry, I had to dig the phone out of my bag."

He was looking at sandy ground. "Can you hold the phone steady?"

Granny's smiling face filled the screen. The image shifted to her pink dry-fit leggings, the ocean behind her. He heard a male voice say, "Who's that?"

Amused, Jon asked, "What are you wearing?"

Her eyes shifted to her left, she smiled. "My, uh, friend bought it for me to wear when we go on our walks."

"Your *friend*?"

She laughed heartily.

Even Granny has someone. While Jon was dying to know

who was standing by her side, he didn't want to put her on the spot. "I wanted you to see my apartment." He flipped the screen slowly panning the room.

"Wow! Did you hire a cleaning service?"

Now it was his turn to laugh. "I did it myself."

"Really? I never thought I'd see the day."

Jon turned the screen back. "Was I really that bad?"

"Let's just say there were a few times I found the remnants of week-old food under your bed."

He smiled at the memory. Granny had brought him up, taking him in after his parents were killed in a car accident when he was eight.

They spoke for several more minutes, catching up on their week's news. When he hung up, he grabbed a Bud Light from the fridge, took a seat on his couch, and reviewed his dinner conversation with Doug.

He inserted his earbuds, took a long draw his beer, then made a call to his co-worker. "Hey, Craig, how's it goin'?" Jon did his best to sound upbeat.

"What do you want, Steadman?" Jon's co-worker asked, the sarcasm overshadowed by his characteristic good-natured tone. He was always so annoyingly cheerful.

"What makes you think I want something?" Jon said, trying to sound offended.

"You're calling me after hours on my cell."

"Well . . . I thought I'd try some small talk first."

"Not your strong suit."

Seemed Craig knew him better than he'd thought. Jon walked into his bedroom, pulled a carryon from the closet, tossing it on the bed beside the freshly washed and folded laundry. He picked out two of the least wrinkled shirts and placed them into the bag.

"True enough. I'll cut to the chase. Can you do a background check for me?"

"Why don't you do it yourself?"

"I'm off the clock. Leaving tomorrow for a short vacay."

"Oh, yeah? Where are you going?"

"Hawaii."

"No kidding. Didn't realize you had that kind of coin."

"Someone's helping me out with it." Before Craig could ask any follow-up questions, Jon added, "So, what do you say?"

"It's for the job, right?"

"Mhmm."

"You know I only ask because of all those pesky privacy laws."

"Sure. So you'll do it?"

A hesitation. "Sure."

"Thanks, buddy. I'll be in touch. And Craig, keep this between us, okay?"

Before Craig could reply, Jon hung up, feeling a twinge of guilt. The Sienna job was a side-gig. At least for now. But Craig was a cog in the FBI wheel, a diehard rule-follower like every other agent Jon had come across. Something Jon would never be.

He stuffed several necessities into his carryon bag, then tossed in his Yankees cap, hoping it wouldn't get crushed on the flight. He set the bag by the door beside his rucksack, wondering if he'd overpacked. No choice. There were things in there he couldn't do without.

He was debating whether to remove some less vital items when through his earbuds he heard, "Call from Gabe Lewis."

It had been a while since he'd caught up with his best friend. "Hey, bro."

"Hi."

The moment he heard his friend's voice, Jon knew something was wrong. "What's going on?"

"Terry left last night and I haven't seen her since."

Jon felt a prickle of fear. "Tell me what happened."

Gabe paused, then said, "We had an argument. A bad one. But you know Terry. She's a passionate woman. I assumed she would blow off some steam and then come back so we could talk things out."

Jon heard the catch in Gabe's voice.

"All she had were the clothes on her back. She didn't even take her purse or phone. It doesn't make any sense. It's not like there's anywhere she could have gone. It's a secluded area."

It wasn't lost on Jon that this was the second missing woman he was being informed about in one day. Only difference was Terry was a close friend and Gabe's fiancée. "Have you asked your neighbors if they've seen her?"

"Yes, of course. So far, nothing." Then, "I was so desperate, I called Terry's mother."

Jon recalled the genealogist, a brilliant woman. "Did Hannah hear from her?"

"No. All I accomplished was worrying her. And letting her know that Terry and I had a falling-out. I know Terry's job comes with secrecy, but this feels off. She wouldn't do this."

Terry had taken on what was the intelligence community's equivalent of a consulting role with the Mossad. Unlike the corporate version of consulting, the job came with the potential for life-threatening danger.

Jon hoped it was all a misunderstanding though he knew that was unlikely. Right now, he needed to keep Gabe calm. "I'll look into this and call you back."

"Jon?"

"Yeah, buddy."

"I can't live without her."

Jon offered some words of encouragement and signed off, hoping he hadn't conveyed his own fears to his best friend. Jon had omitted how he'd caught a prolific hacker responsible for bringing down major American companies. The same person had sold advanced malware to a much bigger fish active in the dark web—an elusive broker of highly classified intel known as the White Knight. In turn, the White Knight had threatened selling it to North Korea. The potentially disastrous consequences were the most dire Jon had seen since starting with the FBI.

The CIA, Interpol, and the Mossad were working hard to track down the broker and destroy the criminal enterprise but the last Jon had heard, leads had slowed to a trickle. The FBI had essentially been left in the dark. As far as Jon knew, the underground broker was still at large. The sale was intended to go through days ago. He'd heard no news about it, but suspected the governments involved were keeping things quiet.

Terry had been tasked with uncovering the White Knight's true identity but was unceremoniously pulled from the case. With no facts about why she'd been discharged, Jon assumed it had something to do with Matthews's stubborn proprietary nature. He'd made it difficult to work with the Israelis on the joint venture, and Terry was the one who took the fall.

Jon made a call he wasn't sure he was supposed to make.

A woman answered speaking rapidly in Hebrew. He didn't understand a word. "Do you speak English?"

"Yes. How can I help you?" Her tone already sounded impatient.

"I'd like to speak with Yosef Kahn."

Hearty laughter came across the line, the condescension palpable from five thousand miles away.

Jon bristled. "What's so funny?"

The woman took a moment to contain herself. "Who are you?" The r came out guttural.

"My name is Jon Steadman. He knows me."

"Do you realize he is the director of the Mossad, Mr. Steadman? You cannot simply call and ask to speak with him. You must make an appointment. He has an opening—"

Jon could hear papers ruffling.

"Three months from tomorrow."

Jon told himself to remain calm. It was hard. "There's no time for an appointment! Tell him it's Agent Steadman on the line. Let him decide if he wants to take the call."

The woman didn't ask him to hold. Jon wasn't even sure

if she had hung up on him.

He was about to click off when he heard the baritone voice. "Jon, shalom. Have you reconsidered our offer?" Kahn was referring to the job offer he'd made, asking Jon to act as liaison between their two countries.

"No, sir. I'm calling for another reason. I just heard from Gabe Lewis, Dr. Lavi's fiancé. Apparently, she's . . . missing."

Silence on the other end. Then, "She went to be with him. For a few days."

"That's correct."

"How long has she been missing?"

Jon explained what he knew.

"Thank you for the call."

Before Kahn could hang up, Jon said, "Gabe's my closest friend. I know we can't tell him details of Terry's work, but he has a right to know if she's okay."

"Understood."

"Will you keep me posted?"

"We'll do our best to find her."

Jon hung up, aware the director had artfully dodged his question.

CHAPTER 5

Somewhere over Colorado

Terry opened her eyes, acutely aware of the pervasive deep hum. She rose, twisted her shoulder-length golden hair into a bun, securing it with the clip she'd left on the nightstand. Dressed only in her underthings, she opened the room's closet, finding a silk kimono, wrapping it around herself and tying the sash tightly around her narrow waist. She opened the shiny lacquered panel doors and let out a yawn.

The last twenty-four hours had been a whirlwind of activity. The pull to tell Charlotte that she'd changed her mind and wouldn't consider her offer, was so strong she nearly capitulated. What sort of woman leaves her fiancé in limbo wondering what had happened to her? If she was dead or alive.

Terry stepped into the main cabin.

"Good morning, doctor."

Charlotte Colbert appeared perfectly coiffed as if she'd just left the salon. Impeccably dressed in a designer skirt suit, white blouse and a string of pearls, she emitted a quiet confidence.

"Did you rest well?"

Terry nodded.

"Why not have a peek out the window?"

Terry opened the small shade and looked out, in awe. Behind them to the east was flat land, massive, neat squares she assumed were farmland. A range of snowcapped mountains lay just ahead to the west. She had spent her teenage years in Boston but never ventured out to the American West. She remained awed by the vastness of a land that could hold several European countries within its borders.

"Where are we?"

"We just entered Colorado. Those are the Rockies. Aren't they magnificent?"

They were. But they reminded Terry how far she now was from South Carolina. Sitting in a leather chair across from Charlotte, she was acutely aware of the surreal circumstances. *I'm on a private plane, sharing morning coffee with an international criminal.*

Despite the veritable ambush on the beach, Terry never once felt threatened. She'd been in a sorry state when Charlotte materialized beside her on the beach, showing authentic concern. But it was obvious Charlotte—or her bodyguard—had been waiting until Terry was alone.

The moment Terry realized the matronly woman was also the White Knight, she shifted into operation mode. Charlotte gave no indication she knew of Terry's connection to the Mossad. As far as the older woman was concerned, Terry was a renowned geneticist with access to some of the most classified scientific breakthroughs. To Charlotte, Terry was someone to court, someone with access to the kind of insider information desired by buyers of cutting-edge scientific intel.

The world was looking for the criminal and the she had come to Terry. It was a one-time-only opportunity, a chance to learn all she could about the woman's criminal enterprise. She would have been a fool not to accept the offer.

Her sole objective was getting word to Yosef Kahn, telling him what she'd learned. He'd taken her off the case but surely this would change things. Now all she could hope for was that her own hidden identity as a Mossad operative remained as secret as Charlotte's once was.

***

Jerusalem, Israel

Yosef Kahn stared out the window of his Knesset office, his eyes barely registering the view of Sacher Park below and the Wolfson Towers beyond it. Though the Israeli parliament building was not his primary office—that location was highly classified—he had a designated suite of rooms in the Knesset's lower level for those times he needed to work out of Jerusalem.

He was deeply concerned for Dr. Terry Lavi's safety. He had recruited her—a scientist, ethicist and patriot. She'd proven her abilities under challenging circumstances. Her involvement in the last mission had gone sour thanks in large part to Special Agent Doug Matthews, head of the New York FBI field office.

Terry's role had been to lure the White Knight out from the shadows. At one point she believed she'd made contact, only to discover her mark was actually an FBI agent on a similar mission. The realization had been deflating, effectively stalling the operation. Matthews took issue with a foreign national's involvement in operations, even those that involved both their countries. It didn't help that U.S.-Israeli political relations were already strained.

Kahn understood it wasn't an equitable relationship. For that reason, he'd shared much of the intel the Mossad had gathered, in hopes of reciprocity. Unfortunately, Matthews chose to put a vise grip on what his own field officers had learned. The result of the bad blood was Terry being pulled from the job.

The White Knight had threatened to sell sophisticated hacking software to North Korea, a threat of global proportions. While the worst case scenario had not yet played out, Kahn presumed it was only a matter of time. Now with Terry's disappearance, he suspected the infamous criminal was involved.

Kahn had already made the call to his cyber team. They confirmed Terry's cover was ironclad, reassuring him that no one would know who she worked for beyond her lab job at the Technion.

Kahn called his assistant to send for his car. He knew better than most that no cover was completely secure.

He needed to find Terry Lavi. Fast.

CHAPTER 6

Mossad Headquarters
Classified Location

A young man barely out of his teens faced a wide bank of blinking computers. A prodigy with AI, he'd been recruited by the Mossad after completing his military service. Yosef Kahn stood behind him, his hands on his hips. The space was no larger than an oversized office, making the proximity to others in the room border on the intimate. Two other people were in the room, the tension thick in the air. Rafi Gonen, the deputy head of cyberterrorism, and Shira, Terry's one-time handler. They waited anxiously while the man typed into his computer.

The smell of tobacco wafting off the techie made Yosef crave a cigarette. Sadly, Israel was being influenced by the Western notion of a smoke-free work environment. How anyone was supposed to get work done running outside every hour for a smoke, was never addressed.

"Sir, we have satellite feed of the beach in South Carolina at the time Gabriel Lewis reported Dr. Lavi missing. I scraped a short video." Given a defined time and specific coordinates, the top-secret software could pinpoint anyone on the planet.

The techie pointed to the screen. A darkened image of a beach at night came up, the waves soundlessly pounding the shore. "Watch closely."

Gonen, Shira and Yosef drew closer to the screen. A

figure sat on the beach, head lowered. Yosef instantly knew it was Terry. She was dressed in a sweater, sandals on the sand by her side. She appeared to be shaking. Crying. Her light hair blew in the wind.

No one in the room spoke as another figure entered the screen to the left, walking slowly along the beach, feet in the surf, then turning toward Terry.

Shira sat in stunned silence as she watched Terry accept the woman's extended hand, speak for a few moments, then go off with her. There was no sign of confrontation or struggle.

"Why can't we get satellite with sound, dammit?" Gonen asked.

Yosef ignored the question, then said, "Zoom in on the older woman."

The screen was filled with a white-haired lady, her features in the shadows, the only light from the moon behind her, creating a silhouette effect. "Get me an ID on that woman, now."

Gonen said, "Looks to me like Dr. Lavi went willingly. What do you make of that, Yosef?"

Yosef Kahn stared at Gonen, Shira looking on. "She's clean, Rafi."

His emphatic words belied what he was thinking. *What the hell was Terry doing walking off with the White Knight?*

***

South Central Colorado

Terry disembarked from the Learjet, descending the stairs onto the tarmac. One runway, automated lights, and two yawning men made up the ground crew. *Crested Butte, CO* was painted on the side of the fuel truck. Given the time difference, the sun had not yet risen, the only illumination coming from the aircraft and the car awaiting them.

A suited man stood beside a black Range Rover, holding

open the backseat door. Terry heard Charlotte say, "Thank you, Simon." Terry recognized him as the same man who'd been protecting the beachside cottage.

Once in the backseat, Charlotte handed Terry a blindfold. "Merely a precaution, dear."

Terry hesitated, noticed Simon peering at her in the rearview mirror, and put it on.

Though she did her best to keep track of the turns, when the car slowed, she was completely disoriented, which of course was the intent.

When instructed, Terry removed the blindfold, taking a moment for her eyes to adjust. A massive lake the size of the Sea of Galilee shimmered in the growing light of dawn. The beauty of it was awe-inspiring. There were no road signs to speak of. They were in the middle of nowhere.

The Range Rover wove through the beautiful landscape, turning onto a narrow road flanked on both sides by soaring evergreens. The surrounding mountains were visible in the distance, the sun's emerging rays glistening off the snow-laden peaks. An iron gate, its black spindles pointing skyward, glided open as they approached.

The house came into view, only moments before obscured by the tree-lined road. A sprawling homestead made of locally-hewn stone and dark wood, was set low in the valley, its earthy hues blended seamlessly with the surrounding landscape. Situated on an inlet of the lake with the sky turning a brilliant blue, the house was a sight to behold. Terry understood the draw of artists who spent their lives capturing nature at its finest.

Charlotte saw the expression on Terry's face. "Welcome to my home. It's beautiful, isn't it?"

Terry said, "Yes, it is. But, why here?"

"The secluded environment allows me a greater deal of freedom. I don't have to worry about prying eyes as I would in a large city. And quite frankly, I love the mountains."

Terry saw no phone lines or satellite dish. "How do you

get a signal out here?"

"We have our own system. It came at exorbitant cost but was worth every penny in the end. Hackers are a dime a dozen nowadays." Charlotte chuckled at her obvious quip. She went on to explain that the house was retrofitted with a powerful scrambler, knocking out all Wi-Fi signals. "It's the only surefire way to fully remain off the grid in today's world."

Not unlike Osama, Terry thought. Granted, a luxury mountain home in the Rockies was an upgrade over a cave in Afghanistan.

Simon pulled up in front of a set of two-story-high weathered pine doors. Terry exited the vehicle, inhaling the fresh smells of the mountains. The air, the wood, the foliage. Divine. To think such a pristine location was housing a vast criminal enterprise was hard to fathom.

Simon retrieved Charlotte's bags from the car's trunk. Terry had nothing with her. And no one knew where she was. Though Charlotte had kept things light throughout the trip, Terry's status was left unclear. Guest or prisoner? Staying in a secluded home in the middle of nowhere without a cellphone added up to something other than 'guest.'

Entering the home, Terry didn't know where to look first. The interior of Charlotte Colbert's home appeared ripped from the pages of *Architectural Digest*. They passed through the foyer into a large sitting area. Wooden beams buttressed cathedral ceilings, massive picture windows looked out on expansive views. A towering balsam fir trimmed with twinkling white lights stood in the corner, several brightly wrapped giftboxes at its base. A Cavalier King Charles Spaniel came up to sniff her.

Terry approached the French doors leading out to a veranda. "May I?"

"Of course."

Terry exited onto the veranda, taking in a lungful of crisp, clean air. It was cold, but not uncomfortably so, different from the coast.

As breathtaking as it was, Terry missed her own country terribly. Her family, the people, her lab. The longing would be bearable if she was with Gabe, but theirs was a complicated relationship.

For months, they'd skirted the issue of their growing feelings. She'd broken up with him once before when she had been unable to get past what they both thought was an unbridgeable gap in their backgrounds and beliefs. Her mother had made a remarkable discovery which removed all barriers. It was nothing short of miraculous. The moment Gabe had proposed to her—the time she'd said yes—would remain with her as the single most meaningful time in her life.

Now, without warning, they were separated once again. She desperately wanted to speak to him and explain what had been weighing on her that led to their argument. The changes, the compromises. Some had seemed too great to even consider.

Standing on the veranda in a foreign land, hundreds of miles away from her beloved, it all seemed so ridiculous. Too bad the revelation only came once she could no longer contact him. Gabe would be terribly worried, wondering what happened to her.

But she had no choice.

When Charlotte found her on the beach, those doors were slammed shut. Terry would have to navigate a dangerous situation alone. No Gabe. No Shira. No Yosef. *Alone.*

Charlotte came up quietly beside her. "Come, let's get settled. Simon will show you to your quarters."

Terry allowed herself a moment of self-pity before steeling herself. *I can do this*, she told herself. *If I succeed, I'll have thwarted one of the greatest crimes in history. If I fail . . . Well, if I fail, the world will never be the same.*

And I'll be dead.

CHAPTER 7

New York City

A blinking neon Miller Lite sign hung above the bar. Framed photos of classic motorcycles hung askew on the cracked walls. The Grease Pit could easily be described as a dive bar.

After twenty-four hours with no news, Gabe became convinced Terry's disappearance was connected to her work for Kahn. He made a spur of the moment decision to go to New York, surprising Jon when he showed up on his doorstep.

Jon paid for the two beers the shaggy-haired bartender placed in front of him and Gabe. "How are you holding up?"

Gabe set his feet on the low bar of his leather-topped stool, took a sip from his glass. "I'm shell-shocked. I called every hospital and the police several times. Nothing. She's vanished. Did you find out anything?"

Jon sized up his friend. He looked disheveled, a perpetual look of worry on his face. "Not yet. I wish I had answers for you."

"The sooner the better. I want to bring my bride home."

A Horse With No Name began playing in the background.

Jon downed most of his lager. "Terry's lucky to have you."

"Thanks, but it's really the other way around. I'll tell you one thing. When you find the right person, the little things don't matter when everything goes to hell. Holding onto anger steals the precious time you have together."

Jon broke eye contact, stared into his glass. Gabe slapped his forehead. "Jeez, sorry. That was insensitive."

Jon had been engaged to Gabe's sister, Ashleigh. Until she was killed in a terrorist attack.

"It's okay. Ash and I were simpatico. We rarely argued. But I know what you mean."

"I'm terrified for Terry."

Jon put a hand on his friend's shoulder. "I know, buddy. I'm with you all the way . . . except for the next few days. I wish I didn't have to leave you, but I took on a job in Hawaii. I'll be gone for a few days."

After another round of beers and a quick bro hug, Gabe and Jon went their separate ways.

***

Gabe walked the half mile to his hotel on Forty-Second Street, past Grand Central Station, taking his time and an unnecessary, longer route. He was trying to clear his head. The air had turned colder, the smell of roasting chestnuts wafted his way. He skirted a sidewalk grate, steam billowing upward from the city's depths, a rumbling of the subway beneath his feet. People walked past in the characteristic New York speed-walk, no one making eye contact.

Gabe needed a plan of action. He'd let his boss know he'd be away for a while. Good thing his boss was also his uncle. Not knowing where he would be this time next week was unsettling. *How does Terry do this?*

Since learning of Terry's extracurricular activities, he'd developed an even deeper appreciation for her and her loyalty to her country.

He was drained and the alcohol hadn't helped. He would go up to his room and crash for the night. After he called Hannah again and booked an overseas ticket.

***

Maui, Hawaii

When Jon woke with the plane's descent, Sienna's head was leaning on his left shoulder, her breath coming in soft puffs. It felt easy, oddly natural. Using his right hand, he squeezed his nose and blew, unclogging his ears.

His head was still spinning from how quickly things had turned around since his conversation with Doug. Shortly after the speech about not taking on cases outside of their jurisdiction, he was thirty minutes from landing in Maui's Kahului Airport.

Sienna lifted her head off his shoulder, her face turning pink. "Sorry about that."

Jon yawned loudly, stretching his arms above him in the cramped space. His legs were numb. The seats weren't designed for anyone over five-foot-nine. He lifted the window shade. Crystalline waters as far as the eye could see. He couldn't fathom where the pilot would land.

Sienna brushed the hair from her face. "You can see the island from the other side." She leaned her seat back, allowing Jon to stretch past her.

Peering out the opposite window, Jon saw there were in fact several tiny islands that speckled the vast Pacific. "Wow."

"Isn't it beautiful?"

"It feels like we're at the end of the world. Maybe we'll find Gilligan down there on one of the small islands."

Sienna raised a brow.

"Didn't you watch reruns of those 70s shows?"

She shook her head. "No. I was singularly focused on my gymnastics."

Jon gave himself a mental pat on the back for nailing it. *Another point for the outstanding Steadman deductive skills.* "What sort of gymnastics?"

"High bar, floor exercises, horse. You name it. My parents seemed to think I had Olympic ability."

"Did you?"

Sienna shrugged. "Hard to say. I worked at it, that's for sure. When my friends were out at the movies, I was at the gym." A pause. "Pretty much my entire childhood."

Jon sensed the ambivalence. "So, what happened? Did you make it to the Olympics?"

Sienna swiped on some lip balm. It smelled like cherry. "Got as far as the world championships. Made the semi-finals. After that I gave up. I wanted so badly to go on dates, throw parties, go to a prom. I tried to create whatever semblance of a social life I could. Between all the travel and my parents' Olympic aspirations, it was a challenge."

"How did your dropping out go over?"

"Let's just say we still don't speak about it."

The plane was now hovering over the water, the shadow of the jet visible on the ocean's surface.

"What can you tell me about your sister?"

"We've had our squabbles, as many siblings do. She is two years older. When you're little, it feels like a significant age difference. While I was the disciplined one, Jen kept getting in trouble. Skipping school, smoking weed, that sort of thing. My mom coddled her but my father, that was a different story."

"Military man."

Sienna nodded. "To the nth degree. He believed in tough love. Still does."

It was the first time since meeting Sienna that Jon felt she was speaking openly, not holding back. "What happened?"

Sienna's face turned sad.

"They had a full-on battle of the wills. My father held his ground. At that point he was doing well, had moved to DC. Said unless she made serious life changes he'd cut her off."

"I guess Jennifer didn't cave to the ultimatum."

"Didn't even blink."

"My kind of gal."

41

"You have a lot in common, actually."

After all the things she'd said about her sister, he wasn't sure he wanted to know what that meant.

"Bottom line, as far as I know, my sister hasn't spoken to my dad in years."

"Does he know she's gone missing?"

"I told him. I had to. He didn't want me to go after her. Said the local police should handle it."

Sounds like a cold sonuvabitch. "Clearly, you don't agree."

"If not for Jen, I'd never know I could have a healthy child. Besides, she's my sister. I'm not going to just sit around and wait for something bad to happen."

Jon could relate to that. He would have done the same. Still, it sounded like Jennifer was a trouble magnet.

"How about you? What's your story?" Sienna asked.

Jon's pulse quickened. His usual defense mechanism kicking in, like he was about to be assaulted. "Not much to tell."

"There must be. You're so young and already being sent on federal missions around the world. Carrie wasn't one to offer false praise. She said you're a talented guy with a bright future ahead."

Jon couldn't help but beam at the words. He could envision Carrie saying them. "Didn't come easy," was all he said.

"Tough upbringing?"

"More like an unfortunate one. My parents died when I was little. I lived with my grandparents. Only Granny is left now. She lives in Pompano Beach."

"I'm so sorry. That must've been hard."

The regular refrain. "Granny's the best. She gave me as uneventful a childhood as she could under the circumstances." He turned to look out the window once again.

"You don't seem to like speaking about yourself."

"That's true. I don't."

Jon heard her speak under her breath. "There's more to you than meets the eye."

You have no idea.

The plane bumped lightly, landing on the tarmac. "We're here," he said.

When the plane came to a stop, they unbuckled their seatbelts. Sienna asked, "You ready for this?"

Beyond the airport's small tarmac, palm trees swayed gently. Jon nodded, his mood instantly improving with the prospect of warm breezes and beautiful surroundings. "You bet." Taking down both of their carry-on bags, Jon turned to his temporary partner. "Aloha, Sienna."

"Aloha, Jon."

CHAPTER 8

Wailea, Maui

J on stood outside his hotel room, a lei of purple orchids around his neck, his bag beside him. Sienna walked past him toward the adjacent room. She looked as tired as he felt.

"Let's get some rest," he said. "I'll meet you at the bar in an hour."

Sienna yawned loudly. "Sounds good."

Jon woke up groggy, taking his time to get out of bed. He dropped to the floor, did fifty pushups, then showered and changed into a white cotton shirt and khaki shorts and stepped out onto the lanai. Below him, dense, colorful landscaping surrounded the hotel's infinity pool, a swim-up bar nestled in the middle of it. The Pacific sat tranquil in the distance.

Jon could hear Matthews's voice in his head. *"There is no such thing as a vacation, Steadman. Get to work, dammit."*

Jon smiled to himself. He hoped Doug was managing well enough. They'd each weathered untold tragedy. Jon probably understood more about the grief his boss would face in coming months than the man did himself. He pulled the phone from his pocket. No missed calls. It was 9:20 in the evening New York time. He grabbed his room key, pocketed his pill bottle, and headed out the door.

Ten minutes later, Jon was seated at a table for two, watching Sienna enter the bar, drawing the attention of several men in the room. She wore a flowing sleeveless sundress accentuating her toned arms. Her streaked blond hair was held back in a fashionable headband, hoops in her ears. She looked tanned. *How's that possible? We've only been here for an hour.* The ways of women would forever remain beyond his grasp.

"You look great."

Sienna offered a carefree smile. "Thanks. You clean up pretty well yourself."

Jon raised a finger, catching the eye of a waitress dressed in an emerald-green shin-length grass skirt. "Aloha," she said with a wide, welcoming smile. "What can I get for you?"

Jon asked, "What's your signature cocktail?"

"The Island Dream. Coconut, pineapple, triple sec."

"Two of those, please."

Sienna peered at him in annoyance.

"What?" Jon asked.

"Did the women's movement pass you by unnoticed."

"Huh?"

"Forget it. I like pineapple, anyway."

Jon pulled out his phone, his pill bottle falling to the floor, rolling under the next table. The woman seated there picked it up, and handed it to Jon. He felt his face heat up and mumbled a thanks, pocketing it. Sienna said nothing.

Jon kept his head down while he tapped his phone's screen. Trying for upbeat, he said, "Let's hit the ground running today."

"Great. Where should we start?"

"By giving me a better sense of your sister." He handed his phone to Sienna. "Can you pull up her social media?"

Sienna took the device, found what she sought. She handed it back, a sad smile on her face. "This is Jen. I always loved those shoes. She bought them in Mexico."

Jon studied the photo of an attractive woman with fine lines around her eyes and mouth. She looked a decade older than Sienna. Unlike her sister's, Jennifer's hair was short, low maintenance. The comparison to Sienna's chic vibe was glaring.

Jennifer was dressed in shorts and a scuffed pair of bright blue hiking boots, a backpack on her shoulder, a mountain in the background. "Are those Lederhosen socks?" Jon asked.

Sienna laughed aloud. "She's a character. She collects hiking paraphernalia from places she's traveled to. She's got quite a collection."

Sienna said, "That was Yosemite, a few years ago."

Jon scrolled through the latest posts, finding nothing within the last week. "I'm confused."

"Hmm?"

"Says her name is Jennifer Cartwright, not Lamont."

"She was married for a short time. Greg was an abusive asshole."

"Why keep his name, then?"

Sienna fiddled with an earring. "Let's just say, the farther away she could get from a connection to my father, the better."

"Ah."

"They're both stubborn. Tough as nails."

Their drinks arrived. Mini paper umbrellas and slices of pineapple hung off the rims. Sienna took a tentative sip. "Ooh. That is good!"

Jon smirked. "No longer deeming me anti-feminist?"

Sienna rolled her eyes. "Anyway, Jen took the whole army brat thing a lot harder than Carrie or I did. To be fair, it can be quite unsettling and I had my gymnastics to keep me busy. Our parents were constantly fighting. They divorced soon after returning to the States. Things went downhill for Jen after that. She had a few brushes with the law. Nothing serious, mostly marijuana possession. She moved around a lot, changing jobs more times than I can count. Met a guy in Minnesota and got married. Too fast, in my opinion. I was relieved when she and Greg split up and she moved to Maui alone. But the move made it harder for us to stay connected."

"Sounds like she's a handful."

"Not really. She's a terrific person. Very giving. It was Jen who told me about the clinic."

"What can you tell me about it?"

"The clinic?"

An overly made up woman standing in the front of the room turned on a mic and began to sing *Shallow*, her sultry timbre a perfect match for the song.

Jon nodded.

Sienna moved in closer to be heard over the music. "Elite, boutiquey, they pay for the best sperm donors. It's in Kihei, about fifteen minutes north of here."

"What was Jennifer's connection to the clinic?"

"She heard about their program. Not sure how. She applied as a surrogate. Apparently, it was an arduous application process. We were both thrilled when they accepted her. Easy money, little work. And they paid for her accommodations."

"Sounds like a good gig."

Sienna nodded. "I was really happy for her. For us. I'm indebted to her for telling me about the clinic. I was so relieved when they accepted us."

"I'd think they'd want anyone who could pay."

Sienna shook her head. "Not at all. Fertility clinics want to keep up their stats. The more successful births, the better their reputation."

"Makes sense, I suppose."

Jon absentmindedly tapped on the table, pursing his lips.

"What?" Sienna asked.

"Nothin'."

"Out with it."

"All right. I'm wondering where all this money is coming from."

"Ah. I've done well with my business."

Craig had not come up with anything yet on Sienna Lamont, which was a red flag in itself. By the look on Sienna's face, she wasn't welcoming more questions. Jon didn't want to turn the chat into an interrogation. He made a mental note to follow up with Craig as soon as possible.

Jon pointed to the phone's screen, still on Jennifer's photo. "Is this what she looked like the last time you saw her?"

Sienna drained her cocktail. "Pretty much."

"Huh."

"What?"

"You look much younger."

"Thanks, I guess. But Jen lives hard. It takes its toll."

Jon scrolled through more photos. "Looks like she traveled quite a bit."

"Whenever she could afford it. Army brats either spend their lives like their parents traveling the world or never go anywhere again. She was in the first camp."

"Most of these pictures are of her hiking."

"It's her passion. If Jen sees a mountain, she needs to scale it."

Jon navigated through Jennifer's favorite online groups, noting the pages she liked. There was little on her politics, no family photos. "She's a member of several hiking groups. There's a hike coming up tomorrow. I say we be there."

"Good idea. But what do we do until then?"

"I want to pay a visit to the clinic. But first we need to follow protocol. Let's stop by the CID office."

"CID?"

"Criminal Investigation Division of the police department."

She turned a paler shade. "Does that mean you think—"

He shook his head vigorously. "Like I said, protocol. If we need the local law enforcement at some point, it's wise to let them know I'm here trying to help you. Maybe it will light a fire under them."

She seemed somewhat appeased. Sienna pointed at Jon's buzzing phone, scooting across the tabletop. "You going to get that?"

Jon read the name on the screen. "It's my boss. I'll call him back."

Sienna raised her glass. "Ōkole maluna."

Jon picked up his drink. "What does that mean?"

She clinked her glass to his. "Bottoms up."

***

Lake San Cristobal

Simon led Terry through a large vestibule, passing several closed doors along the way. She spotted an elaborate dollhouse in the corner of the sole open room, various long-haired Barbie dolls lying beside it.

"This way."

Terry followed the man up a wide, carpeted staircase, taxidermy animal heads leading upward, their lifeless eyes frozen in the past. Simon turned right at the landing, where Terry was shown into a room nearly the size of her Jerusalem apartment. A Western motif was apparent throughout the décor. Stunning photos of local wildlife adorned the walls. A thick woven rug covered the floor, wooden beams crisscrossed the ceiling above a Queen-size bed. A picture window looked out on the shimmering lake, kayaks peeking out of the shed by the shoreline. A small girl wearing a pink puffy coat, her pigtails sticking out from beneath her matching knit cap, came dashing out of the shed. A middle-aged woman carrying a pair of ice skates was trying to keep up with her. The lake had begun to freeze over but it wasn't yet ready for skating.

Terry turned to find Charlotte standing in the doorway, Simon leaving quietly past her.

"My granddaughter. She's come to visit for a few weeks while her parents are in Europe."

"You have grandchildren?" Terry heard her own incredulous tone.

"Is that so hard to believe? I have the same nurturing tendencies as most women. And a desire to pass along my heritage and genes. In my case, there is much more to pass along. An empire, as it were. I'm not getting any younger . . . though *that* is something I've been looking into. Perhaps we can discuss that at some point."

Terry held her tongue. Charlotte was either an innovator or insane.

Charlotte walked to a large ornate armoire. "I've taken the liberty of ordering some basics for you." Hanging in perfect alignment were several long-sleeve shirts, tapered slacks and wool sweaters. Below were three pairs of shoes. They were identical to what she already owned. Same brands and sizes.

"How did—" Terry cut herself off, felt her face flush with anger and forcibly bit her lip. The woman had hacked into her purchase history. At least she hoped that's what it was. The thought of someone rummaging through her closets was too disturbing to consider. "I left my phone on the Isle of Palms. I'm sure my fiancé is terribly worried."

"Why don't you rest a bit? Have a shower. Lunch is called for twelve-thirty. I'm sure you have many questions. I'll do my best to answer them all."

Charlotte hadn't directly addressed her concern, which she'd deliberately kept vague, but the point was made. No phone calls, no communication with the outside world.

Gabe. He'd probably stayed up all night trying to find her, scouring the area looking for her. Did he think she'd drowned? Or worse, left him for good?

She felt sick to her stomach. If there was one thing she would accomplish while in the mountains, it would be to contact him. No matter what the risk.

CHAPTER 9

Washington, DC

Phineas Oberlander sat at the head of the cherry wood conference table, its gleaming veneer reflecting murky silhouettes of the people seated around it. He had it custom made after the one in the White House Situation Room, a place he was intimately familiar with. He'd been one of few seated in the room with the president and Secretary of State when Osama was taken down.

A large man both in height and girth, Oberlander had not reached his position through his looks. His bald head was the shape of an egg, his skin tone perpetually pale. His small eyes, though intelligent, were mostly obscured by sagging lids, the crepey skin extending to his turkey neck.

The emergency meeting took place in a spacious, albeit windowless rectangular room. Located in a concrete-reinforced basement of the Smithsonian American Art Museum, it was a fifteen minute walk from the White House. Built to withstand a nuclear blast, the room, made of non-combustible materials, once stored valuable historical artifacts, and like the adjacent temperature-controlled vaults, was maintained at a cool sixty-five degrees. The space had been made available by the museum's curator, a long-time member of the board.

Established by a core group of fifteen scientists and DC politicos—now referred to as the advisory board— the consortium had since grown to several hundred members.

Two members, both fertility specialists, were seated beside each other. "Did you hear about the woman who died last week in Maui?" one asked the other. "She was one of our surrogates. So sad."

"Did you know her?" the other asked.

"We met a few times when she came in for implantation. Lovely young woman. We expected her to carry to term. Tragic."

"Yes, terribly sad."

A gavel tapped thrice on the table, bringing the room to silence.

Oberlander said, "I call this meeting to order. We have a delicate matter to resolve."

One member, a well-preserved woman in her seventies, wearing a light-weight linen suit spoke up, her Baltimore dialect as prominent as the day she'd left for DC, four decades prior. "It must be quite serious that we've been taken away from out daily responsibilities."

Oberlander looked around in annoyance. "Indeed it is, madam. Each of us has played a significant role in our nation's progress. Every sphere of society is represented in this room. Political, religious, medical, business, tech. Some of you have earned the top prizes in your fields. And yet despite our sacrifices, The United States of America has ventured into territory the Founding Fathers could have never foreseen.

"We are no longer the leader among nations. Our citizens have turned weak. The fabric of our society is frayed, soon beyond repair. The very foundation of our republic faces unprecedented threats. Competition is no longer viewed as a path to success. If we remain docile, our enemies will have no one left to fight. All they'll need to do is walk right in and take over."

One of the members, a man in his early forties and a member of Congress, dressed in a custom-tailored pin-striped suit spoke up. All eyes turned to him, surprised he was daring enough to interrupt the chairman. "It's already happening. Foreign nationals are emboldened, coming here without papers, taking our jobs."

"Agreed, congressman. But this isn't a forum on immigration. Our objectives are significantly more widespread. Ultimately, our focus must remain on the most important factor of all. The coming generations, those of our children and grandchildren. Our work has yielded remarkable results."

Oberlander clicked a remote and all heads turned to the screen creeping down from the ceiling. Aerial views of a building surrounded by palm trees and turquoise waters filled the screen. "Our Kihei clinic is our most successful venture. Despite some setbacks, we remain on schedule. Negotiations with the Pentagon will soon be underway."

A joyful round of applause broke out around the table.

"But I'm getting ahead of myself." Oberlander's face turned grim. "As you are all aware, over the years, a small number of members expressed their concerns with our philosophy. They have resigned, keeping to their original oath to avoid public disclosure at all costs. Which leads us to today's agenda. Unfortunately. . ." he paused, drawing everyone's full attention, "it has recently come to my attention, that one individual threatened to break that golden rule. Nearly two decades of clandestine work are on the line."

Murmurs around the room. One member said, "I thought we had your assurances that Project Codebreaker would remain off the radar until it's been activated."

"Can we contain it?" asked another.

Oberlander said, "We have been monitoring the events closely. We could not have foreseen the current circumstances. The attention of law enforcement was drawn by one of our own."

This time the room became a cacophony of nervous chatter.

"Are you saying one of us has betrayed the project?" one

woman asked, scanning the room.

Oberlander shook his head. "I believe the breach was unintentional. I cannot divulge more at this time." He spoke in a way that would not invite questions. "Suffice it to say, hours ago, an off-duty federal agent landed on the island."

Several board members shifted nervously in their seats.

The congressman said, "Nothing good can come from having a Fed poking around. If our project becomes known, it will threaten our years of work."

"Agreed. Our priority must lie in keeping the project protected. At least until the negotiations are completed. This is a particularly vital juncture. We cannot afford to wait for the inevitable to happen. The project must remain clandestine. I believe this situation can be deemed a clear and present danger. One which requires swift, conclusive action. We are here today to vote on how to handle this unfortunate state of affairs."

Several brows were raised.

Oberlander said, "I know this is a difficult decision. It is for me as well—"

The congressman spoke up once again. "All of us understand what's on the line, sir. We alone stand between a sustainable republic and anarchy. We're ready for the vote."

Heads turned to one another, many nodding silently. The vote would be an unprecedented one.

"Very well." Oberlander lifted his hand high. "All in favor of taking decisive action to protect the sanctity of Project Codebreaker."

Several hands shot up with fervor, others raised with hesitation and dour, regretful expressions. Together, they made up more than half the members. All were aware of what "decisive action" would entail. At least conceptually. None of them wanted the gritty details.

It was understood there would be no debate. Only a quiet vote based on the proffered facts. Like the congressman had said, each member knew what was on the line, and nothing was more paramount than their own hides.

"What's this agent's name?" one asked.

Oberlander clicked on the remote bringing up a photo of a tall, fit man with dark wavy hair, a haunted look in his eyes. "Special Agent Jon Steadman."

***

Sinclair Lamont took a seat on the opposite side of the ornate wooden desk. Framed photos of Oberlander with various heads of state, lined the walls. The man himself sat behind it, his back erect, his gaze firm.

Oberlander pulled out a silver case embossed with his initials. He removed a long, thin cigarette and proceeded to light it, taking a deep inhalation.

Lamont was appalled by his old compatriot's relaxed demeanor. "You've crossed the line with that vote, Finn. The board is sanctioning lethal force only because they believe it's in the interest of national security."

"What would you have me do? Tell them the truth? It's too late."

Lamont stayed silent.

Oberlander tapped his cigarette over the black ash tray. "Project Codebreaker is a raging success, with the power to ensure our national security for decades to come. When Washington decommissioned it, the military made their stance clear. *They* are more concerned with optics than national security. As you know I would have much preferred for our government to make use of the project. They refused."

"I don't disagree, but what you've done . . ."

"We've sunk millions into this venture, Sinc. Our backers want to see the return on their investment. The sale of the project will be finalized in two weeks. The lab's already in the process of relocating. This is not the best time for an attack of conscience. We will pass the baton to the buyers and they will transfer the one-point-five billion to us."

Lamont shook his head. "The board still believes the project will be reintroduced to our military. When they learn the truth, they will bail anyway, point fingers directly at you. At both of us."

Oberlander gave a sardonic smile. "That's why we must keep this to ourselves until the sale goes through. The board consists of savvy businesspeople who will always fall on the side of protecting their own hides. And pockets. I'm simply saving them a bout of conscience. Once they see their money, they'll forget all about the vote and who we sold to."

"Doesn't it bother you that what we're doing is tantamount to treason?"

Oberlander's face turned to stone. "We've been over this before. Times change. You and I know that better than most. I'm no longer a soldier. Neither are you. My idealism vanished when our government decided to befriend the very enemies my troops died fighting against."

Lamont couldn't argue the point. When a government is opportunistic, it's called diplomacy. For the individual, it's treason.

Oberlander eyed his old friend, then set down the cigarette. "Are you having second thoughts?" he asked, a challenge in his tone.

"Will that make any difference in how we proceed?"

Oberlander stood, ushering Lamont to the door. "We've been friends for a long time, Sinc. But no it won't. I suggest you think long and hard about the consequences of stopping now."

It felt to Lamont like a threat.

"I have another meeting now," Oberlander said. "Call me with your decision." He escorted Lamont to the door. "The project must remain safe. We cannot afford to have it derailed in the eleventh hour by a curious agent . . . and your family. Get your house in order, Sinclair. It would be a shame if something happened to your other daughter. Don't you agree?"

Sinclair Lamont left the office, the warning still ringing in his ears.

***

Maui

Jon and Sienna walked into the uninviting anteroom of the two-story stucco building that housed the CID office. Jon whispered to Sienna, "Have a seat out here. Let me handle this." He approached the woman at reception, placing his ID on her desk. If people concluded he was on official business based solely on viewing his badge, so be it. "Agent Steadman to see the chief."

The woman studied the badge, then looked up, raised her brow. Jon got that reaction often enough—surprise at his role. Something about him didn't fit the mold of an FBI agent. He took pride in that. Except when it hindered his access.

"He's not in yet."

"Who can I speak with about a filing a missing person report?"

"Hold on."

She made a call, then said to Jon, "Officer Iona can see you. Follow me."

Jon gave a thumbs up to Sienna who remained seated, then followed the receptionist to the back.

An absurdly muscular Polynesian man of indeterminate age, sat in an office chair too small for his girth. Wearing a navy police uniform with the letters *MPD* on the lapel, he reminded Jon of The Rock.

The officer gestured to the chair across from his mess of a desk. "What can I do for you?"

Jon remained standing, placed a printed photo on the desk beside a crusty bowl of what looked like oatmeal. "Jennifer Cartwright was reported missing three days ago."

He looked from the photo to Jon. "What's this have to do with the FBI?"

"I'd like to see the file."

"Take it up with the chief."

"He's not in."

The man gestured a 'Can't help you,' with his widespread hands.

Jon knew when he was being blown off. Suppressing a familiar angry pit in his stomach, Jon took a risk. He sat. "Full disclosure. All I'm trying to do is help a friend."

The officer looked at Jon askance. "This isn't official business?"

"No."

Iona slowly nodded, then smiled. "So, you want me to share my records with you so you can help your friend find this woman."

Jon returned the smile. Maybe Granny's old refrain is correct. *You attract more bees with honey than with vinegar.* "That's right."

After a moment, Iona said, "Sorry, pal. I don't roll like that. You want the file, you'll need to go through the official channels like everyone else."

"You're stonewalling me."

"Why, no. Of course not."

The smug look on the man's face was infuriating. It took all Jon's self-control not to shout. "You didn't follow up on it. Why?"

Iona's eyes narrowed, "Excuse me?"

"Jennifer Cartwright has been gone nearly a week and..."

"Look, I don't know who the hell you think you are, but this ain't New York effin' City. You have a problem with how I do my job, I suggest you track down the chief."

Several nearby officers stopped what they were doing, taking in the spectacle.

Iona stood. He was tall. Maybe six-three. He held the door open. "Best if you leave now, *Agent.*"

Jon looked around at the belligerent faces staring back at him and stomped out to the lobby. Sienna was there reading

Time magazine. "Let's get out of here," he hissed. "Before I kill someone."

***

Lake San Cristobal

Lunch proved to be an elaborate affair. Fine china, and silverware perfectly aligned atop cloth napkins were set on a twenty-foot unstained wood table, its natural grain setting the tone for the room. A framed oil painting, depicting a bear in a creek with a salmon between its teeth, took up most of one wall. A roaring fire crackled in the hearth.

With barely an appetite, Terry refused the venison, only taking small bites of the scalloped potatoes. Charlotte didn't appear to notice. A waiter who did not appear to speak a word of English, served each course.

Terry waited till they were alone to speak. "On the beach, you said you'd made a spectacular acquisition."

"That's right." She paused. "Would you like to know more?"

The more Terry knew, the more dangerous her position would become. But if she could get the information to Kahn, it would be a coup. "Certainly."

Charlotte dabbed at the corner of her mouth, placing the cloth napkin in her lap. "It's software that can access the most sensitive data in the world, undetected. I'd planned to sell it but have reconsidered."

Terry knew the intended buyer was North Korea. It was the case that brought her attention to the White Knight to begin with. Hearing the transaction never took place was a huge relief. She wondered if Kahn knew it. "May I ask why?"

"It was complicated, given we had a contract. I'll have to pay quite a fee to make things right. I have a reputation to uphold after all."

"You mean the White Knight does."

"Correct. You should consider yourself among a lucky few who know my true identity."

When Terry didn't reply, Charlotte said, "I realized there was a lot more money to be made by keeping the software and selling what it yielded. It will take more work on my end but will be worth it."

Terry felt sick to her stomach. It wasn't the potatoes. Charlotte spoke of wreaking global mayhem as if it were another day at the office.

"It has already yielded more than I paid for it."

"Oh?"

Charlotte stood, leaving the napkin on the table. "It will be much easier if I show you."

CHAPTER 10

Mossad Headquarters

Shira, Gonen, and Kahn were joined by several other higher-ups in what was now deemed a war room. Enhanced images of the woman on the beach were showing on a screen embedded in the wall.

Gonen asked, "Do we have a name?"

Shira shook her head. "They've been working on it for hours. Remarkably, her facial mapping shows up nowhere. Not in any of the intelligence databases or social media. She's a ghost. All traces of the woman have been wiped."

"A monumental feat. All the more validation that she's the White Knight."

Yosef said, "Clearly, Dr. Lavi recognized her. That means they've met before."

Gonen said, "Another proof of my theory. I know you care for her, Kahn. But refusing to consider that Dr. Lavi is a double agent is plain negligent."

Yosef stayed silent, his face a mask of apathy. He never liked Gonen who was the pessimist in every room, always critical with little to offer by way of remedy. Yosef ignored him and directed his question to Shira. "Where was Dr. Lavi recently where she could have met this woman? Somewhere with a large number of people where the White Knight wouldn't stand out."

Shira said, "There is only one possibility I can think of.

The symposium in New York. Her last assignment. Before we pulled her."

Yosef said, "Get me the name and bio of every attendee."

Shira stood. "Yes, sir." As she hurried to the door, Gonen said, "If you find a hint of impropriety on Dr. Lavi's part, I want to hear about it."

Shira looked to Yosef who gave a slight nod. He watched Terry's one-time handler leave, aware she disliked Gonen as much, if not more, than he did.

***

Lake San Cristobal

Charlotte led the way outside just as the wind picked up. She got behind the wheel of a black 4x4 truck retrofitted with snow tires. Terry sat beside her, noting several groundskeepers dressed in long cotton shirts and wool caps, milling near an open garage designed to look like a barn. Inside, the Range Rover was parked beside two more pickup trucks and an enclosed golf cart. The workers were pouring salt on the long driveway. One man waved at them, Charlotte smiling in return.

Terry wondered what the laborers would think if they knew what their employer did for a living.

Hoping she sounded relaxed, Terry said, "Charlotte, I need to get back to my life. I've been patient, not my strongest attribute. Why am I here?"

"You're here for me to court you, of course. I've made my proposal, but thought you'd appreciate seeing that you'll be joining a top-notch operation."

It sounded off to Terry. "I'm one of many scientists you could have recruited. Why me?"

The wind turned blustery, causing the truck to tremble. "Don't play coy, doctor. It doesn't suit you. It's one of several reasons I've taken such a liking to you. You remind me of my younger self."

Terry recalled when she'd first met Charlotte Colbert at a New York symposium, ignorant of her alter ego. Colbert was known in those circles as a pioneer in computer science, one of the first women to achieve notable success in what was—and remains—a male-dominated field.

When Terry didn't reply, Charlotte added, "You are one of the world's up and coming predictive geneticists. And female to boot. You have accomplished great things for a woman of your age and have access to remarkable research."

Terry gestured elaborately. "All this for a job offer? I thought you are in the business of intelligence brokering." She deliberately used the euphemism.

"Indeed, but that is only one of my ventures. I dabble in speculative industries, invest in various start-ups."

"Any of them legal?" Terry couldn't help herself.

Charlotte didn't appear to take offense. "Legality is often subjective, particularly from one country to the next."

"How about here in the United States?"

Charlotte made a dismissive gesture with her hand. "It's in both our interests to avoid such talk. Nothing productive can come of it. I am fully aware of your position as ethical consultant at your institution. Still, I believe you will find my pitch a compelling one."

Terry nearly cried in relief hearing Charlotte refer to the role she had at her Haifa lab at the Technion Institute. Not the one for the Mossad.

They drove past the indoor swimming pool, the cheerful shouts of a child carrying on the wind. The scenery was idyllic, the colors vivid and brilliant. Puffy white clouds hovered over the soaring mountains ringing the ranch, an immaculately maintained expanse of acreage. Charlotte pointed out the stables. "I used to ride. Those days are behind me but I can't bring myself to sell the horses."

"Is this your only home?"

"No, dear, but it's the one I love most. I've done quite

well and have homes around the world. Though none yet in Israel."

The thought of this woman stepping foot in her homeland made Terry cringe.

"I suppose you're wondering why I revealed my alter ego to you."

Before Terry could respond, Charlotte said, "Because you are ethical."

Terry furrowed her brow. "Wouldn't my ethics dictate telling everyone who you are?"

"Not if you believe that keeping my identity a secret is of greater moral value than sharing it."

"What are you talking about?"

"Come, let me show you."

Charlotte pulled up beside an adobe building and the two women exited the vehicle. Thanks to well-designed camouflage, Terry hadn't noticed it until they were practically upon it. The roof and walls blended in perfectly to the surroundings. It wasn't visible from the main house, let alone the road and Terry imagined not even from the sky. "What is this place?"

"One of my command posts."

"*One* of them?"

"On the off chance that this location should be exposed, I can still conduct operations, uninterrupted."

Charlotte opened a pad at the entrance to the building, placed her head against a buffer above it. An eye scanner. She then asked Terry to do the same. "We've already uploaded your eye into the system."

Charlotte saw the look of shock on Terry's face. "Yes, it's a new development. Software that can grab the tiny characteristics of a person's eye. Of course that means scans will soon be replaced by other identifying software. In the meantime, we're ahead of the curve. It's an ever evolving race of staying a step ahead."

They entered an anteroom. No one was there. Terry

asked, "Where is everyone?"

"These days operations are run by AI. It reduces human error and spying."

Terry found it odd. Of all people, the White Knight knew hacking to be the current form of spy craft. Ironically, Charlotte was allowing a spy to enter the inner sanctum. A shrewd woman, Terry knew something wasn't adding up.

"This way, Dr. Lavi."

Terry followed Charlotte into a windowless room. The walls appeared made of concrete. Low ceilings created a cave-like effect. Five large screens faced a wide desk each displaying variations of the same high-definition image. They appeared to be topographical satellite photos with markings highlighting several areas.

Charlotte said, "This is why I trust you'll keep what you learn here to yourself."

Terry sensed something dire. "What am I looking at?"

"Don't you recognize the landscape?"

Now Terry took note of the barren, dry topography. The desert hills appeared ancient. It was Israel.

Terry was shocked, "Is that—"

"Your country's nuclear program has remained under the shroud of secrecy since its inception." Charlotte grinned with pride. "That, my dear, is no longer the case."

CHAPTER 11

Kihei, Maui

The Uber driver dropped off Jon and Sienna in front of a surf shop. Across the street, The Rainbow Clinic was housed in a three-level glass structure. Its modern exterior made a stark contrast to the earthiness of the surrounding swaying palms and yellow hibiscus. Two blocks to the west was the sea.

Inside, several women, some very pregnant sat in a small waiting area, the walls lined with photos of newborns. A young bespectacled Hawaiian woman sat behind the lobby desk. She wore a blousy top with floral print. The place gave off a notably friendlier vibe than the police department.

Jon said, "We're here to speak with someone from management."

"Your names?"

"Jon Steadman and Sienna Lamont."

The woman checked something on the computer. "I don't see an appointment for you."

"We don't have one."

"I'm sorry. We're very busy. I can schedule you . . ."

Jon pulled out his credentials.

"FBI?" The woman looked genuinely distraught.

Jon lifted a finger to his lips. "We're trying to keep that on the down-low. I don't think your boss would want the clients to know we're here. Do you?"

"Uh, I guess not."

"Why don't you call someone and see?"

The woman nodded, lifted the phone. "Please have a seat. Our COO, Dr. Pearson will be right out."

Jon and Sienna sat on a white leather sofa. Three minutes later, a man of approximately forty years old came out to see them. He wore a white lab coat, open-toe sandals, and a tight ponytail.

When he saw Sienna, his tense expression turned curious. "Ms. Lamont, I didn't realize you were in town."

Sienna frowned.

Pearson turned to Jon, a question in his eyes. "How can I help the FBI?"

"I'm investigating Ms. Cartwright's disappearance."

The receptionist said, "Jennifer is missing?" Her face was ashen.

"Perhaps we should speak in my office." He addressed the receptionist. "Please push back my appointments, Darla." Then, "Agent, Ms. Lamont, please follow me."

Jon and Sienna did so. Jon said, "I'd like to know more about what you do here."

The man paused. Then, "That's a loaded question, Agent . . . ?"

"Steadman."

"We provide cutting edge fertility treatments and conduct CRISPR research. Our mission statement is to help women who would otherwise be unlikely to birth healthy children, become mothers.

"CRISPR?"

"Haven't you heard of it?"

"Um, isn't it like a fryer?"

Pearson didn't find it humorous. "Not quite."

Pearson led Jon and Sienna down a long glass-enclosed hallway. Loping by, Jon spotted what looked like an odd-shaped squirrel.

Pearson said, "Mongoose. They're all over the island.

They were brought in to rid us of rats. Unfortunately, whoever made that decision back in the 1800s didn't consider that rats are nocturnal, active while the mongoose are asleep. Now we have both."

They walked past a glass-enclosed laboratory, only two white coats inside. "This facility is primarily a clinic but we keep a small lab to assess the occasional irregularity." Pearson looked at Jon askance, as if debating if he should continue. "CRISPR is an acronym for a type of RNA delivery system that allows genomes to be repaired. The defective gene is essentially edited out."

With a degree in forensics, Jon was comfortable with scientific jargon. Still, he wasn't familiar with the term.

"Never heard of it. How vital can it be?"

Pearson pursed his lips. "CRISPR is the next frontier, the next step in genetic engineering."

"Is it legal?" Jon asked, curious if he'd get a clearer answer than the one Sienna gave when posed with the same question. He noted she had been very quiet since they'd arrived.

Seemingly holding back his irritation, Pearson said, "For research purposes only. But that will change in time."

Jon thought of the operation he'd run in Rome. He and Terry, a geneticist and bioethicist, had acquired the formula for a life reviving elixir which they'd managed to keep hidden. He knew the day would come that such breakthroughs would be impossible to suppress. The world was forging ahead with new technologies. Dangers be damned.

They walked past several widely spaced doors each fitted with a keypad. Pearson said, "Our treatment rooms." A woman who appeared moments from going into labor, left the room, smiling. The door closed behind her with a soft click.

Pearson stopped in front of his office, the only door left ajar. "When applied ethically, the process can help people recover from genetic defects and live healthy lives. We run clinical trials for medical genome editing. Essentially, we can edit out undesirable genes such as those responsible for specific illnesses. For our purposes, it's done at the embryonic stage, though it can be administered to children and adults via inoculation."

"Remarkable." Jon was astounded by the advances in reproductive science. What was once deemed beyond human reach was quickly becoming reality. Pearson gestured for Jon and Sienna to sit.

Jon said, "Who funds all this work?"

"We're fortunate to have had several startup investors. People with vision. The procedures we conduct are quite pricey."

Jon glanced at Sienna. "So, only the wealthiest can access these medical miracles?"

Pearson seemed to take the comment in stride. "No different than any new technology. Starts out prohibitively priced. Once it becomes more mainstream, more members of society benefit."

Jon wasn't sure how he felt about that. It seemed it would be in the self-interest of the top one percent to keep the tech out of reach of the rest of society.

Pearson went on. "Think of the recent privately funded flights into space. A groundbreaking event. Who was on board the spacecraft? CEOs, titans in their fields. Personally, I have no issue with what others would deem a wealth disparity. It's those same people who pay for the tech to begin with."

Jon had no interest in debating the issue, particularly in front of Sienna, who clearly had the means to avail herself of the clinic's services.

Pearson said, "May I ask you a question?"

Jon thought the man's education and speech didn't match his casual appearance. "Go ahead."

"I'm very sorry to hear Ms. Cartwright is unaccounted for. When Ms. Lamont and the police called about her, I knew there was something wrong. She missed a scheduled appointment. But I must ask, do you think the clinic is somehow involved?"

"Not at all. It's standard procedure when investigating a missing person to follow in their footsteps, so to speak."

Pearson gave a nervous smile. "Sure, that makes sense. We take our clients' privacy very seriously. We wouldn't want to draw negative attention to our facility unnecessarily."

"Understood."

Jon asked several additional questions, taking down a few notes. Pearson must have looked at the clock ten times since the meeting began. When Jon finished, Sienna said, "Dr. Pearson, may I speak with you privately?"

"I'm terribly sorry. I have a great deal of work I need to get back to."

Sienna said, "We've come all this way. It's been a tough few days." Jon noted she looked on the brink of tears. Given all she'd been through, he suspected it was authentic.

Pearson hesitated, then smiled. "Of course. Agent Steadman, please return to the lobby and we'll meet you back there."

Jon nodded, exited the office, leaving the door open. He stepped loudly for them to hear his footsteps recede, then heard the door close and slowed his pace.

The same two white coats, one male, one female, walked by deep in conversation, their hair covered in what looked to Jon like shower caps. The man held a pile of folders to his chest. "I'll put these in my office, then let's head to lunch. I'm starving."

Jon feigned interest in something outside and bumped into him, the files scattering about. "Oh, excuse me. Let me help you."

The man appeared flustered as his colleague stood by waiting. "Really sorry," Jon said as he stepped away. Jon waited for them to turn the corner and walked back to the lobby.

**

"Ms. Lamont, can I assume you are here to find a new surrogate?"

It didn't take much for Sienna to turn on the waterworks, full force. She would do her part and give Jon time to investigate. Assuming of course he hadn't already been caught.

When Sienna came through the steel door, Jon was sitting on the lobby couch, his head deep into a *Science Today* magazine. Pearson said, "I hope they find Ms. Cartwright soon . . . and safe."

Sienna sniffled, wiped away a stray tear and mumbled a thanks.

Pearson turned to Jon. He appeared anxious to get back to whatever he was doing before they'd arrived, but to his credit he said, "Godspeed, Agent Steadman."

Jon stood and escorted Sienna out the front door, certain that Pearson was relieved to have her off his hands. "I got some good stuff."

"Really?" She looked behind her at the building as if someone could hear them from that distance away.

"Let's go for a walk."

***

Emerald waters lapped the shore, the foamy surf pulling at Jon's feet as it retreated to the sea. He felt the tug of the wet sand leaving soggy footprints in his wake. Sienna walked silently beside him. The tourist season was in full swing and the beach was busy.

A young girl in a pink swimsuit ran across their path, a filled bucket swaying. "Mommy, look, I'm building a sandcastle!"

A woman lounging nearby lowered the book she was reading. "Ooh, nice job. Will you be the princess that lives there?"

"Of course." The girl plopped down in the sand and got to work. Her mother laughed and went back to reading.

Jon saw Sienna's saddened expression. He was thinking of what to say when she asked, "What did you find out at the clinic?"

"Looks like this Kihei facility is where they do the implantations but the main lab is in Hana."

Sienna looked confused. "Are you sure?"

"Yup. I swiped some documents while you were keeping Pearson occupied."

Sienna bent down, picking up and inspecting a bright orange and white seashell, and placing it in her pocket. "For Randy." Then, "Why aren't the two facilities in the same place? Wouldn't they want the embryos near the carriers? It doesn't make sense."

Jon shrugged. "No idea. Maybe privacy concerns?" But she was right. It sounded like an odd business model. "We should check it out."

"Hana is quite a distance from here, like a three-hour drive. Not so easy to get to."

Jon picked up a conch shell off the sand, pocketing it, searching for more. Maybe he'd start a collection for Randy. Without looking up, he said, "How can that be? We're on a small island."

"The road is windy. It's a slow go."

"Okay, I'll get us a car. We can head there in the morning."

"All right. What now?"

"I want to see Jennifer's apartment."

"I don't have her key."

"I got that covered."

Sienna stopped in her tracks. "What's that supposed to mean?"

Jon turned to face her, a smile emerging. "Let's just say our common friend, Carrie, taught me a thing or two." He winked at Sienna who paused, then laughed.

"Okay, Oliver Twist, let's go."

***

Lake San Cristobal

Terry did all she could to keep her voice steady. "If Israel's enemies ever learned the exact location of their nuclear plant, the consequences would be disastrous."

Charlotte said, "Pinpointing the coordinates required some doing, I must admit. Your government has found a way to make places like this invisible on any satellite. An admirable feat." She grinned broadly. "But we found it. I have the coordinates."

Terry felt the blood drain from her face. "What do you plan to do with them?"

"Well, Dr. Lavi. The answer to that question lies in the hands of one person."

Terry swallowed hard, afraid to ask. Then, "Who?"

Charlotte pointed a manicured finger at Terry. "You."

CHAPTER 12

Wailea, Maui

The Kenolio Apartments had the vibe of a roadside motor inn with a series of bright yellow doors lining an open air corridor. Jennifer Cartwright's unit was located on the ground level of the three-story building. Several banyan trees separated the property from its neighbors, offering a measure of privacy Jon was grateful for. Still, it was the middle of the day and while most tenants were at work, the chances of being seen were high. He would need to do his job quickly.

Scanning both the building and Jennifer's unit, he saw no sign of an alarm system. "You'll be my lookout." Jon handed Sienna a pair of latex gloves and donned his own. "Put these on."

"You're enjoying this way too much," Sienna said, doing as she was told, her eyes darting around. She wore sea blue espadrilles, perfectly matching her summery shift dress. "And you're dressed more for a bar mitzvah than a break-in."

"Explain again why we aren't asking the landlord to let us in."

"You think they'll just hand us a key so we can snoop around your sister's apartment without her permission? I've been down this road. It will take forever to get a warrant and we don't have forever. We'll make this quick."

Jon pulled his lock pick set from his pocket. It was

identical to the one Carrie had used during their mission in Rome. After her death, Jon went down to Costa Rica and learned some very useful skills, lock-picking among them. It was his way to pay homage to his dead partner.

Jon studied the door lock. It was more sophisticated than he would have expected for a residence of this nature.

"What's taking so long?"

"It's not as easy as it looks," he whispered, irritated. Thirty long seconds passed before he got the door open. "Come on."

Sienna followed him inside. A gap between the drawn shades created a wide ray of light, enough to see by. The apartment was decorated in a hodgepodge of brightly-colored floral fabrics, potted plants, and wicker furniture he suspected were mostly second-hand. A book was left open on the sofa. A pass-through from the living room to the kitchen revealed a solitary mug beside the sink.

"Looks like she stepped out moments ago," Sienna said, her voice strained. "It feels like we're violating her privacy."

Jon was in the zone, taking in every detail.

Sienna called out softly from a room in the back. "Her laptop's in here."

"We can't take anything. I'll be there in a minute."

Sienna came up beside him, her arms crossed in righteous indignation. "So breaking and entering is okay, but not theft."

He glared at her. "Seriously? I'm *breaking* every rule in the FBI book for you. We can leave any time you want."

She pouted but stayed put.

Jon was ready to storm out. *What a nerve!* He reminded himself how Carrie had told Sienna to seek him out if she was ever in trouble. And he needed the money. He blew out a lungful of frustration. "That's what I thought. Why don't you see if you can get her recent emails off the computer?"

Sienna seemed to want to say something but took in his expression and turned, heading back to the room.

Jon scanned the books on the wall-mounted shelf. Mostly books on pregnancy, hiking, travel. He pulled several and shook them out. Nothing. The front closet was cluttered with various light jackets, flip flops and umbrellas, and three sets of well-worn hiking boots. Jon didn't see the funky blue ones.

In the kitchen, Jon found a well-stocked refrigerator and small pantry. The bathroom was unremarkable save for a few anti-depressants. He wondered if she could take them when pregnant. He joined Sienna in the bedroom. She was seated at a small desk, typing. The bed was sloppily made, a discarded bra lying atop the gossamer blanket.

Sienna said, "I can't break the password. What do you suggest?"

"Nothing we can do about that now. Look at all this hiking stuff."

"She's been an avid hiker since high school. She even scaled Kilimanjaro. She sold a car to pay for the trip." Jon noted the respect in Sienna's voice.

A car came to a screeching halt outside the building, flashing lights swirling through the gap in the bedroom blinds.

Jon ventured a peek and let out an obscenity.

Sienna rushed to his side. "What is it?"

Jon offered her a look. "Get ready to hear your Miranda rights."

***

Lake San Cristobal

Terry swallowed hard. "Why me?"

"You are in a particularly useful role. Scientists, even the most productive among you, remain out of the limelight, working behind the scenes. Few outside the scientific world would recognize your name."

Terry took no offense. Charlotte was right and it was

how Terry liked it.

"At the same time, as head of the Technion's predictive genetics lab, you have access to some of your country's most vital intelligence."

Terry cleared her throat. "What do you mean?"

"Your lab. You are on the cutting edge of scientific breakthroughs. It's one of several areas your country excels in. You are on the frontlines of what the rest of us will use and know years from now. It's like insider trading. Follow?"

Terry nearly collapsed with relief. Charlotte was not referring to her work for the Mossad. "What do I need to do?"

Charlotte proceeded to explain that Terry would send regular progress reports to Charlotte who would determine what was sellable. In return, Terry's work would be fully funded through a series of legal grants Charlotte had influence over.

Feeling sick to her stomach, Terry asked, "What about the nuclear codes?"

"If you keep your part of the deal, the codes will never be sold."

"How can I be sure?"

Charlotte looked at her with what bordered on compassion. "I could tell you anything, but the truth is, you can't be certain. You'll have no choice but to accept my word as an honorable businesswoman."

As Charlotte escorted her out of the building, Terry understood the offer the White Knight had made wasn't a business proposal. It was clear-cut blackmail.

CHAPTER 13

Maui County Police Department
Kahului

C hief of Police George Akamai sat across from the Fed and his lovely companion, aware the scowl on his face wasn't particularly welcoming. He took issue with mainlanders who came to his island to stir up trouble. "Let me get this straight, you're a Fed with the New York field office but you're here on your own time."

Jon exhaled. He'd repeated himself enough. They were set on giving him a hard time.

"Give me one reason why I shouldn't book you and Ms. Lamont."

"Professional courtesy—for one."

The captain snorted. "Try harder."

An officer entered. "Sir, you have a call on line two."

The captain stared at his blinking phone, then looked at Jon and stood. "I'll be back. Don't go anywhere."

"What a shmuck," Jon whispered to Sienna, who was biting her lip. She'd been silent throughout the interview.

When Akamai returned, he hovered over them. "Consider this a warning. You have no jurisdiction here. If you skirt the law again, you'll pay the same consequences as any civilian."

Working hard to hold back a smirk, Jon stood, Sienna following suit. "Aloha, captain. See ya around."

***

Federal Plaza
New York City

Matthews was going through the daunting pile on his desk when the phone rang. "Matthews."

"Please hold for Deputy Director Lamont."

Stunned, Matthews's papers fell from his hand. *The NSA deputy director?* He didn't know if he should be excited the man knew his name or terrified for the very same reason.

The baritone voice Matthews had heard countless times on CSPAN, came on the line. "Am I speaking with Special Agent Doug Matthews?"

Matthews pictured the man in his mind. Full head of gray hair, military bearing. He knew what everyone else did about the man. Long distinguished career with the army.

"Yessir. How can I help you?"

"Do you have one of your team in Hawaii?" The question sounded more like an accusation.

"No, sir."

A pause. Then, as if he was reading, he said, "Agent Jon Steadman. He isn't yours?"

What the hell did Steadman do now? "Well, sir. Yes sir."

"Is that yes or no?"

What a hardass. "He is on my team. But he's down there on vacation."

"On vacation, you say?"

Matthews would rather spend the weekend in the office than utter another 'yessir.' "Correct."

"Then perhaps you can explain why I just received a call from the Maui police department telling me my daughter was brought in with Agent Steadman charged with B and E?"

Matthews was at a loss for words.

"You there?"

He regained his composure. "Yessir. *Dammit.*

Matthews held the phone away from his ear while the man shouted. When Lamont finally came up for air, he said, "I'll call the department now and square it away."

"Do that, and let me be clear, I expect you to keep your agent on a short leash."

"Pardon?"

"Apparently my daughter hired Agent Steadman for an ill-advised pursuit. I want her to be satisfied with whatever she finds. To a point."

"I'm not sure I understand what you want me to do."

"I want you to get Steadman to throw her a nugget or two. Then get her back to the mainland."

Matthews was lost. *What the hell is going on?*

"Sienna is a headstrong woman. She's after something that may interfere with matters of national security. That's all I can tell you. You need to put a stop to it."

"I see." *I don't see at all.*

"Good. Two more things, Matthews. My daughter does not need to know I'm involved."

"Understood. And the second thing?"

"Sienna's been through a lot in recent years. Last thing she needs is to get mixed up with a G-man. I don't want her getting hurt."

"Sir, I can't . . ."

"Do you follow?"

Matthews hesitated. "Yes." He omitted the 'sir.'

"Good. I'll hold you personally responsible for this situation."

Matthews swallowed hard, trying to keep the disdain undetectable. "Is that all?"

His question was answered with a dial tone.

***

SoHo

Matthews placed a pod in the espresso machine and turned it on. "How do you take your coffee?" He was still learning those little things about Jacqui.

"Black, please." Jacqueline Menard took a seat on the bar stool beside the kitchen island. She was dressed in a short silky robe. Behind her out the window, the streetlamp cast a floodlight on a lazy, steady snowfall. Picture perfect.

Matthews took a mug from the cabinet. It read "Being My Husband is Really The Only Gift You Need." Erica had gifted it to him years before on Valentine's Day. They'd had a good laugh.

He placed the mug back on the shelf, taking a plain one instead, marveling at how much his life had changed. He liked his new place well enough. The loft was far more upscale than the place he'd lived in before. If his wife's premature death had taught him anything, it was to live for the day, checking off as many bucket list items as possible.

The budding relationship with Jacqui offered the first drops to fill the deep crater left behind by Erica's departure. It began as what many would deem a rebound affair. After the hell of watching his wife die from a rapid, ravaging illness, Doug had not been ready for something new. He'd even blurted out as much on their first date. He cringed at the memory. It amazed him that Jacqui hadn't run for the hills.

Matthews poured the coffee, handing her the mug. "Steadman's going to be the death of me."

Jacqui breathed in the aroma, took a tentative sip. "Hon, you've mentioned this agent several times now. If he's a thorn in your side, why not just fire him?"

"I can't, it's complicated." It was several years since Matthews made the disastrous judgment in character resulting in several deaths and an office-wide security breach.

Thanks in large part to Steadman's bravery under Matthews's operative command, a high-profile case was brought to a successful close. As a result, Matthews's boss agreed not to fire him, pending two conditions—reassignment to the New York field office and overseeing Steadman. The latter proved the stricter form of penance.

"Can you have him reassigned?"

"You mean like to New Zealand?"

Jacqui laughed. "That bad?"

"You have no idea."

Jacqui rounded the island and straightened his tie. She took a step back, assessing him, then nodded. "Better." She planted a soft kiss on his lips. Matthews's arms wrapped around her narrow waist. Jacqui was a few inches taller and a few years younger than his dead wife. It took some getting used to. He let her go.

Jacqui seemed to sense the change in atmosphere. "Let's pick this up again tomorrow night. I'm already late. I need to get dressed and head to the office."

Matthews poured himself a coffee. "No problemo." They understood each other's lives which was a big plus at this early stage. Jacqui worked in the DA's office. She'd been a work acquaintance of Erica's. Though not friends, the women had been cordial.

Matthews had a vague memory of meeting Jacqui once before at the annual holiday party. Back then, he and Erica were the next up-and-coming power couple. They'd worked hard at it, sacrificing a great deal to get there. Matthews realized he was no longer in that mindset. He was satisfied with his career as it was. Life circumstances had quickly changed his priorities. But when it came to Jon Steadman, some things unfortunately remained the same.

***

South Street

Matthews collapsed on the shrink's sofa, wondering how many times Jon used his sessions to tear into him.

The therapist fiddled with the window blinds, allowing in the bright winter sunshine. The radiators hissed loudly, forcing them to raise their voices. "Sorry about the noise. Old building."

Her office was located in a red brick building, two blocks west of the pier.

"To what do I owe the honor, Doug?" She and Matthews went back several years since she'd been contracted by the FBI to treat field office personnel who required it, Jon included. They'd developed something between an acquaintanceship and friendship. It was the first time Doug set foot in her office.

Doug sighed. "Like I told you on the phone, this isn't a social call. I'm in dire need of your wisdom."

"Shoot." Then, "Sorry, poor choice of words."

Doug offered a grim smile. "Not really. I'm strongly considering doing just that to Steadman."

"Ah. Few people get to you more than he does. Before we dig into that, how are you doing?"

Doug knew she was asking about his new life without his wife. "Muddling through."

"Anyone special in your life?"

Doug peered at her. "He told you, didn't he?"

The shrink kept a straight face. "You're dressed better than I've seen in years and unless I'm mistaken, you're wearing cologne."

"Okay, Sherlock. Yes, I'm seeing someone, though I have no idea how it got this far. Jacqui's terrific . . . which is a good segue to my dilemma."

"Oh?"

"She claims to be an exceptional judge of character. Probably needs to be for her job with the DA." He breathed in deeply, let it out. "She thinks I should fire Jon. She says insubordination is like a disease. It will spread among my team and then I'll have a much bigger problem to tackle."

"I see. From what I hear you have a reputation of being a top-notch profiler. What do *you* think?"

Doug shook his head, stared out the window as cars bumped lightly over the cobblestones. "I don't know anymore. Kicking Jon out won't be easy given the arrangement with my own boss. That's why I'm here. My equilibrium is off since . . . Erica."

"Very understandable. Your entire life's been turned upside down." She gave him a moment to let that sink in. "What else can you share about Jacqui?"

Doug's eyes returned to her face. "Why do you keep asking about her? That's not why I'm here."

"Humor me."

Doug glanced at the clock on the wall. Twenty-five minutes remained. "Fine. She and Erica used to cross paths at work."

"Were they friends?"

"No. Not really."

The therapist typed something into her iPad. "Anything else?"

"She's a good listener. And a caring lover. It's nice to have something to look forward to at the end of the day." He felt he needed to add, "I told her from the beginning that I wasn't looking for anything serious."

The therapist nodded. "That seems fair. So now, how can I help you?"

"Do you think I should fire Jon?"

"It doesn't matter what I think."

Doug hated it when she was so vague. He must have made a face because she said, "Is he a good agent?"

"Yes, when he isn't breaking the rules."

"Elaborate."

"Jon has great instincts. He picks up new skills quickly.

Bottom line, he's nabbed some of our most wanted."

"Hmm, I see."

"That said, it's only a matter of time till he messes with the wrong person. Lately, he's become more impulsive. He could get himself killed for being a pain in the ass or acting with abandon."

She took another note. "What would you say you're more concerned about—his well-being or if he can be an effective agent?"

Doug was taken aback by the question. Before he could reply, she went on. "Perhaps you're afraid to lose someone else you deeply care about."

Doug stood, his focus once again outside. The early morning snow was sticking to the sidewalks, glistening under the sun's rays. He knew it wouldn't be long before the cars' exhaust would turn the pristine into a muddy mess. "I wouldn't say deeply."

The shrink's voice became softer, barely audible above the hissing of the radiator, forcing his full attention back to her. "You've been through hell and back. As much as you and Jon lock horns, you have a special relationship. But you can't protect him. *He* gets to choose how to live his life."

Doug was silent for a full minute. "I have the power to steer him in another direction."

"You do. Is that a power you want to wield? The price will surely be the relationship."

"He's still wildly insubordinate—"

"What would you do if it was another member of your team who was an outstanding agent but didn't take well to orders?"

Rather than answer directly, he said, "I've tried everything. Reprimands, probation. Nothing works. He's landed in the hospital more than once."

"Isn't it true that some of the best agents are those who think outside the box, try things that aren't found in any rule book? Maybe the reason he is so effective is *because* he's at times insubordinate. Perhaps rather than trying to fit a square into a round hole, you loosen the leash?"

"I work for the FBI, not a ragtag private company. There *are* rules, like it or not."

"You're right. Maybe it's time to have a candid chat with him. When neither of you is on the defensive. If he understands the exact line that cannot be crossed, my guess is he'll push right up to it, but not cross it. You can base your decision how things go from there."

Doug considered her words. Jon wasn't the easiest person with whom to have a calm work-related conversation. Doug had come here in search of direction, not a vague suggestion. Only Jacqui seemed certain of what he should do. For years, he'd taken Erica's counsel on countless quandaries. Maybe it was time he did the same with the new woman in his life. "Thanks for the ear. I'll be in touch." He looked at the time. Fifty minutes on the dot. And nothing to show for it.

CHAPTER 14

Mahana Ridge Trail
Lahaina, Maui

Jon and Sienna joined a small group of twenty- and thirty-somethings congregating at the trailhead. A muscular guy with forearms twice the size of Jon's, wearing a camo cap over his dark hair, hiking pants, and Timberlands, was studying a map. He looked up as they approached.

Jon gestured to the map. "Haven't seen one of those in a while."

"I'm old school. There are some good apps that keep track of your progress without internet, but there's nothing like a compass and paper map to get the bigger picture of where you are. And if your battery dies, you still know where you're going."

Jon had been in some dicey situations and couldn't disagree. "You a veteran?"

The man nodded. "Afghanistan. First battalion out of Camp Lejeune."

Sienna said, "Thanks for your service."

He nodded his acknowledgement. "Name's Mike. Aloha."

Sienna and Jon responded in kind.

Several others introduced themselves.

"Here on vacation?" a young woman with dreadlocks

asked.

Before Sienna could respond, Jon said, "Yeah. We wanted to get in some good hiking."

"Well, you're in the right place, then."

A brute of a man edged his way into the group. Jon wondered what was in the Maui water with so many huge guys around.

The man approached Sienna, gestured at her and Jon. "Are you two together?"

Sienna seemed taken aback by the abrupt inquiry into her personal life. "We're friends."

The man seemed to read her discomfort. "This is a singles group, you know."

Jon hadn't known and by the looks of Sienna, neither had she.

"Right," was all Sienna said.

The man appeared relieved. "Cool. I'm Lee. Where are you from?" He proceeded to engage her in conversation, clueless to her disinterest.

Several more peoples showed up.

Dreadlocks said, "Nice crowd today. Looks like we're all itching to get back on the trails. We had to cancel last week's hike."

Jon's attention was piqued. "Where were you planning to go?"

"Rainbow Falls. A gem of a trail. Not too many people know about it. Amazing views. Sort of in the middle of nowhere."

"Why did you cancel?"

"Pretty heavy rains came through. The ground was too muddy. A trail like that would be a real hazard."

Mike called out, "Let's move, crew." The group made their way onto the trail, Jon and Sienna among them.

Sienna was leading the pack, Lee still pestering her at her side.

She slowed, sidled up to Jon. "Can you get this guy off my back?" she whispered.

Jon sped up. "Hey buddy, you been hiking a long time?"

The guy turned around, searching out Sienna. "Huh? Oh, last coupla years. Mostly, with this group. Decent people, though one or two are arrogant jerks." His eyes shifted to Mike.

"Oh?"

"You know single life. It's survival of the fittest."

"Not sure what you mean. Been outa the scene for a while."

"Took a break, huh? I should too. I met a lady on one of these hikes a few months ago. We really hit it off. Dated her a couple of times. Then she calls, says she met someone else. Really pissed me off."

"It happens."

"Yeah, but she didn't tell me it was one of these guys. Things got a bit awkward after that."

"Is she here now?"

"Nah, she stopped coming. Huge relief. I like this group. Having her around after she dumped me would've been a drag. Guess she felt the same."

"Oh? What was she like?"

"Not the hottest girl I've dated but we had a lot in common. Hiking, photography. She even climbed Mount Kilimanjaro. And she was fun. Up for anything, if you know what I mean." His demeanor was casual. Not a flicker of apprehension.

Whoa. Keeping his voice steady, Jon said, "Sure. What was her name?"

Lee gave him a strange look. "No way you'd know her. She's not a tourist. Jen lives here in Maui."

Bingo!

"Listen, no offense, bro, but I'd much rather hike with that blonde. So, if you don't mind . . ."

Jon wasn't sure how to play interference anymore. He had what he needed. Unless the guy was an Oscar contender, he didn't know Jen was missing . . . or worse. He spoke of her in the present tense. Jon wondered how the man would react once he heard the news, having just spoken of her in disparaging terms.

Jon watched as Lee waited for Sienna to catch up, who was now deep in conversation with Mike. There was no opening for the brute. With a smirk on his lips, Mike gave Lee the thumbs up. Jon heard a string of obscenities.

Not much more Jon could do. Seemed like Sienna had the situation well under control.

***

Downtown Lahaina

Jon and Sienna walked past a series of small shops selling souvenirs, t-shirts and cheap jewelry. They found a small café on Front Street facing the water. Surfers in black wetsuits were doing their best to stay on their boards.

Sienna dug into her Poke bowl. "I had a disturbing conversation with Mike the hike leader."

"What did he say?"

"Not to believe whatever Lee said."

Jon took a swig from the local brewery's lager. "Meaning?"

"Could just be some alpha male competition but he claims Lee would corner Jen on every outing. Mike thinks she stopped coming to get away from him."

Jon thought it over. "Stalker?" he said trying the idea out for size.

Sienna said, "Maybe. The guy wasn't her type. I don't believe for a second that they dated." Then, "What if he has something to do with Jen's disappearance?"

After the Kenolio apartments fiasco, Jon couldn't ask Akamai to check if Jennifer had filed a complaint or restraining order in the last few months. The captain seemed to take a strong dislike to him. He'd need to find another source. "I'll look into it," he said, and stuffed two giant fries into his mouth.

***

Lake San Cristobal

Charlotte stepped behind the mahogany bar, poured two drinks, attaching thin slices of lime to the rims. She handed a glass tumbler to Terry who was warming herself by the crackling fire in the hearth. "Looks like you can use this."

Terry accepted the drink, sniffing the clear liquid. "What is it?" It was the first time she'd spoken since returning to the house from the command center.

"Our finest tequila."

Terry finished it in one swallow just as a little girl pushed open the door, the nanny trying unsuccessfully to corral her. "I'm sorry, Ms. Colbert." The woman's face was bright pink.

The girl, dressed in an equally pink puffy jacket, ran up to Charlotte. "It's too soon to skate, Grand-Mère. Can we take the ponies out for a ride?"

"Sure my darling, as long as Carmen rides with you."

The child cheered, running off, her nanny struggling to keep up.

Charlotte pulled the cart onto the paved road.

Terry said, "One day, that sweet girl will know what her grandmother did for a living."

"I hope she'll be proud. For too long, women haven't had the same entrepreneurial opportunities as men. Forget about seniors. Ageism is now a global scourge. I'm a rare breed. Even if my granddaughter will one day scoff at my projects, she'll surely admire my gumption."

Charlotte continued on as if the interruption hadn't occurred. "Please don't take things personally, dear. Think of what I showed you more as an incentive than a threat. You will be well-compensated for the information you share with us. We want a long business relationship with you. In return, you will become a very wealthy woman. As long as you are sending quality intel without revealing our arrangement to anyone, we will remain in good standing and the reactor's coordinates will stay classified as always."

Despite standing beside the fire, Terry couldn't get warm. Stunned and terrified, she was desperate to get word to Yosef Kahn so he could take evasive action. The fact that Charlotte didn't appear to know of Terry's affiliation to the Mossad was the only card she had left in her hand. She'd need to learn how to bluff. "Why wouldn't you simply sell the coordinates to the highest bidder?"

Charlotte gently placed her glass on a coaster. "I've considered that for some time. But the risks outweigh the rewards."

"What risks?"

"I'm not looking to trigger a nuclear showdown. Selling the coordinates would potentially endanger millions of innocent civilians. I have no incentive or desire to do so. Unless of course, I'm pushed."

"You mean if I don't accept your proposal."

Charlotte took a seat in a high-back chair, gesturing for Terry to do the same. "I gain nothing by sparking the ire of the Israelis. If it's of any consolation, I've become wildly successful because of my honorable business practice. My contacts trust me. In time, I'm confident you will as well. If I give you my word, that's all you'll need."

Terry remained quiet, wondering how much the word of a criminal was worth these days. That Israel's nuclear coordinates would be available to *every* one of their enemies was unfathomable.

"Do we have an agreement, doctor?"

"It seems there isn't much choice."

Charlotte appraised her manicure. "There is always a choice, dear. Only some result in more dire consequences than others."

If the white-haired cyber terrorist called her *dear* one more time . . .

Terry said, "I won't be responsible for an attack on my country."

"Wise decision. Well then, I suggest you get some rest. Dinner will be served at seven with no more talk of business. We will resume tomorrow with a great deal of ground to cover."

***

Lod, Israel

Gabe landed in Ben Gurion airport, noting that it felt like coming home. He'd called Terry's mother before departure. Hannah, a renowned genealogist, was terribly upset, saying that she'd suspected for a long time that her daughter worked for the government, requiring her to be off the radar for weeks at a time. Still, when Gabe told her he was coming to Israel alone, Hannah sounded perplexed. She was worried, and rightfully so.

Gabe exited the terminal just as Hannah was pulling up. He hopped into the passenger seat of the black Hyundai and leaned over to kiss his soon-to-be mother-in-law on the cheek.

"Baruch haba, Gabriel." *Welcome.*

"Toda, Ima." *Thanks, Mom.*

Hannah offered a sad smile, put a hand to his cheek. "You look different."

He was dressed more conservatively than the last time he was in Israel, his hair shorter with more defined sideburns.

Hannah asked, "Any news?"

"I've been in touch with Jon, who contacted Terry's boss."

"Can you tell me who that is?"

Gabe couldn't think of a good reason not to. "Yosef

Kahn."

"*The* Yosef Kahn?"

"That's right." Gabe had learned of Terry's extracurricular work for Israeli intelligence when they were in Israel together months before.

Hannah quickly pulled over, disbelief in her face. "My little girl is working for the Mossad?"

"Hannah . . . Ima, your little girl is a brilliant geneticist and an expert in krav maga. She's a strong woman. Just like her mother. The Mossad is lucky to have her."

Tears filled Hannah's eyes, one brimming over, sliding down her cheek. She swiped it away.

Gabe said, "They can't tell me much, but one thing I know for sure. If Terry is in any danger, Kahn is the best man to get her to safety."

"I don't see how you can possibly get a meeting with him."

"Jon knows him. They've already spoken. If I have to sit outside his office for a week, I'd do it."

Hannah scrunched up her face. "He has to answer for my child's disappearance. I'll join you."

"I agree one hundred percent but we don't want to antagonize him. Stay home with Abba. I promise to tell you everything he shares with me."

That seemed to calm her.

"Do they even know where in the world she is? She could be locked up somewhere. Kidnapped. Who knows? Oy vey."

Gabe had thought all the same things but would never say so aloud. "I wish I had more answers. I'm scared too. But you know your daughter. She can take care of herself. We have to assume the best."

Hannah pulled a tissue from the box between the seats, blew her nose. "Yes, you're right. I'll drop you off at Terry's Jerusalem apartment. There's no sense in you coming to Haifa if you have to be in Jerusalem in the morning."

They drove most of the way in silence, each lost in their own thoughts. An hour later they were climbing the steep road to Jerusalem, its neighborhoods spread across the hills in the distance. Soon they were passing under the lit-up light-rail bridge at the city's entrance. It was now a bright blue.

Hannah stopped the car in front of Terry's building. "Gabe?"

"Yes, Ima?"

"Please pray that my daughter—your bride—comes home safely."

Gabe pulled a small leather-bound prayer book from his pocket. Hannah lifted a brow, extending her hand, which Gabe took and squeezed. "Already on it."

***

Jerusalem

The last time Yosef was inside the prime minister's residence, Terry had been by his side. Today, an aide ushered them into the large office. Small windows retrofitted with bullet-proof glass looked out on a courtyard of fruit-bearing trees.

Yosef Kahn and Rafi Gonen sat across the desk from the prime minister whose distinguished features were set in stone, the blue-and-white flag standing erect behind him. A veteran of Israel's Sayeret Matkal, the army's elite intelligence unit, he'd been voted in and out of office more times than any other politician in the state's history. Both reviled and feared by his opponents, he enjoyed the support of the country's powerbrokers. Reared in Israel and educated in the United States, he was a smooth-talking orator with a firm command of English and American culture. Kahn knew there were secrets his boss was privy to that he wasn't. He also knew that despite his boss's stoic demeanor, he was livid.

When the door closed behind the aide, the prime minister looked back and forth between Kahn and Gonen.

"Explain how this happened."

Yosef passed him a dossier which the prime minister opened. "A black market broker of classified intelligence who goes by the pseudonym the White Knight. Based on video footage, she's a woman in her sixties. Nationality and identity remain unclear. Last seen in South Carolina, U.S.A. She contracts with the world's best hackers. We've been expecting the sale of a particularly virulent software to North Korea. That didn't happen. Yet."

"Are you certain it wasn't a mole in the Office?" he asked, using the Mossad's informal epithet.

Disregarding the slight to his command, Yosef said, "It's something I've considered. I have a team looking into that. If we have a spy in our midst I will personally take care of that. Swiftly. But this was the work of the White Knight. Her modus operandi is to use hackers, not moles, to acquire classified intel then sell it to the highest bidder."

The prime minister rubbed a hand over his balding head. Israelis thought it a nervous tic. But the man was a stalwart of the government and Yosef knew the behavior was an attempt to mitigate his unreported chronic migraines. "All right. Let's get back to how this happened and what is being done about it."

Gonen said, "We are covering all bases to determine the weak spot in our systems. First step is to stem the tide of leaking information. We have our best computer engineers on the job."

"You already had them. It wasn't enough."

There was little to be said that would avoid such critical retorts. The three men had known each other for years. At times, Yosef had found himself in the prime minister's crosshairs, other times on the same side, same political party. Still, underlying it all, respect persevered.

"Tibi," Yosef used the prime minister's nickname. "You know as well as I do that technology changes in the blink of an eye. We are doing our best. Far better than our enemies."

"Until now."

He decided to concede. "Until now."

"What steps are being taken to recover?"

Gonen said, "We have the best assets. Others are being recruited. We will do several things concurrently. As I said, the first order of business is to stop the White Knight—"

Yosef added, "—and get Dr. Lavi out of harm's way."

The prime minister pursed his lips, addressed Gonen. "Rafi, it seems you are concerned for more than her safety."

"The circumstantial evidence would warrant it, no?"

Yosef made a face. "Please, Rafi. Dr. Lavi is an outstanding geneticist and has helped us on more than one occasion, putting her very life on the line."

The prime minister interjected. "Gentlemen, I think we can agree it's a good thing that Dr. Lavi's safety *and* discretion both require locating her. Immediately."

Gonen shrugged, his manner callous. "At which time we will need to determine if Dr. Lavi was successfully recruited by the White Knight."

Yosef looked at Gonen askance. "We've been over this. She's an ethicist for heaven's sake."

"You know full well the sorts of rationalizations people will make when faced with compromising, life threatening situations."

With Yosef and Gonen locking horns, the tension in the room was palpable. The prime minister seemed to turn pensive, his expression recognized around the world as sagacious, contemplative. "I see the dilemma. You do your job well, Kahn. Keep at it. I'll leave the specifics to you."

Yosef allowed himself the win.

"But," the prime minster continued, "Gonen is right. We can't risk Dr. Lavi turning traitor. Even if the likelihood is miniscule. Too much is on the line. She has access to powerful and sensitive scientific data, that if released to our enemies, would prove catastrophic."

Gonen sucked on his teeth, making a squeaking sound,

like a wolf finishing his meal.

"Assess if she's clean."

Yosef didn't want to ask the next question but it needed to happen. Even Gonen appeared sober. "If she isn't?"

"Then you eliminate her."

And with that the prime minister walked out, leaving Yosef and Gonen holding the proverbial bag.

CHAPTER 15

Kahului Resort

Jon balanced two hot lattes nestled in a cardboard holder and tapped softly on Sienna's door. When she didn't answer, he knocked harder. Seconds later, the door swung open. Sienna stood there, her blond mane mussed. She looked groggy. And gorgeous.

Jon entered the room. "Hey."

"Hey, yourself."

She crawled back into bed, reaching out for a cup, which he handed her.

"You're a godsend," she said, breathing in the brew's aroma, then taking a sip. "Mmm." She smiled at him. She glanced at her phone. "Now, that's a brutal hour for a night owl."

"I waited as long as possible to wake you. Thought you could use the beauty sleep."

"Very funny."

"It's going to be a beautiful day. Sun came up about a half hour ago." He walked to the window. "May I?"

"Go ahead."

Jon swung open the curtains, daylight pouring in.

Sienna covered her eyes. "Yikes."

"Rise and shine. We have a long day ahead."

"Why were you up so early?" she asked, letting out a loud yawn.

"I had a few errands to run."

"Like what?"

Jon lifted the plastic cover off his coffee and drank. "You'll see. Get dressed and grab some breakfast. If we can get on the road in a half hour that would be great."

"What about you?" Sienna asked.

"I already ate."

"Sheesh. I just want to lie here."

"You hired me for a job, remember?"

She pouted. "Yeah, I remember. For Jen. You're still a spoil sport." She pushed aside the blanket, emerging from the disheveled bed, and headed to the bathroom. "Make it an hour and we have a deal."

Jon looked at his watch. "Forty-five and it's my final offer. Meet me out front."

Sienna groaned and closed the bathroom door.

An hour later, Sienna eyed the flaming red roadster. "You're kidding."

"What?" Jon couldn't hold back his devilish grin. He patted the Aston Martin affectionately. "I've always wanted to drive one of these."

"I didn't realize they had these cars on the island. You look like Magnum P.I."

Jon knitted his brow. "Who?"

"Now, it's you who doesn't watch old television?"

Grinning, Jon said, "Just kidding. I love that show, though I'm pretty sure he drove a Ferrari. All I need to do is grow the perfect mustache and I'll be indistinguishable from Tom Selleck."

Sienna laughed. "My grandmother had a crush on him."

Jon leaned down and opened the passenger door. "Hop in."

Sienna seemed amused as Jon folded himself into the cramped space behind the wheel and oohed as Jon pressed a button opening the convertible's roof. "Where to?" he asked.

"I'm not so sure this is the best car to drive the Road to Hana," she said. She rummaged through her bag, extracting an elastic band and tied her hair into a ponytail.

"Why not?"

"The road is pretty windy with lots of sharp turns."

"This car is perfect for that. Think *Roman Holiday, To Catch a Thief.*"

"Those were movies, Jon. In real life, didn't Princess Grace die in Monaco on one of these circuitous roads?"

Jon fiddled with some of the dashboard gadgets. "Think this beauty has a seat ejection button?"

"Cute. But I'm serious."

Jon faced Sienna, noting the concern in her eyes. "I've been trained in defensive driving. You have nothing to worry about."

Twenty minutes later, they were on the road, a bag of chips between them. The scenery was spectacular. Waterfalls framed by lush foliage and vibrantly hued tropical flowers ran along sharp switchbacks. Sienna hadn't exaggerated. The roads were twisting, requiring all Jon's attention. He placed a second hand on the steering wheel, silently questioning if he'd been impulsive renting the roadster. He allowed himself a quick glance at Sienna. Her profile was modelesque. She was a beautiful woman.

Sienna must have sensed his eyes on her and turned to face him, a gleam in her eye, her ponytail whipping in the wind. Seemed he'd made the right decision with the car. Despite their current pursuit, she looked happy, carefree. In denial. The likelihood of finding Jennifer safe and sound diminished with each passing day.

The drive was tiring. Unlike highway roads, there were no shoulders to pull onto. Jon realized, with the exception of his meeting at the CID, he'd been in full control of his emotions since arriving in Maui. He hadn't taken a pill in over twelve hours. Maybe he was finally getting better and could stop taking the meds altogether. While they for the most part calmed him, they were a mixed bag.

Months earlier, not far from the shores of Lake Tahoe, Jon had experienced what he since speculated was an adverse reaction to the meds, resulting in a violent outburst. He nearly shot a man he was interrogating. Jon recalled how the pent-up rage erupted so rapidly, his self-control vanishing in a near-fatal instant. He'd intended to ask his shrink about the bizarre episode but it slipped his mind whenever he saw her. For now, he had enough pills to get him through the week if he should need them.

Halfway through the drive to Hana, Jon spotted a roadside kiosk. "Lunch?" he asked Sienna.

"Please."

Jon pulled over, purchased two mango chicken sandwiches and fresh squeezed guava juice, then drove to the first off-ramp they came across, following signs to The Garden of Eden Arboretum. The wind picked up as they paid the entrance fee, gray clouds visible in the distance. They used the facilities and ate their lunch surrounded by thick stalks of orange and blue birds of paradise. The shape of the flowers' feather-like petals were reminiscent of a tropical bird in flight.

"Think we'll find answers today?" Sienna asked.

"Depends if the clinic people are willing to speak to us. But, yeah, I do." He downed the last of his juice still unaccustomed to the Eden-like view. A few other tourists milled nearby, seemingly appreciating the gardens as much as he was.

Sienna said, "I really appreciate you coming with me, Jon."

"Like I said, any friend of Carrie's . . ."

Sienna frowned.

"What?"

"I was hoping by now I'd be a friend regardless."

Jon put an arm around her shoulder. "I don't make friends easily. But I'd say we're getting there." He made a funny face, eliciting her laugh.

"Good," she replied.

They finished their lunch in silence and got back on the road.

***

Gerard sat on a bench, watching Steadman and the woman. There seemed to be an easy familiarity between them. Observing his prey so closely, he felt powerful. Like an owl stalking a rat, savoring the moment before it swooped in for the attack.

The last time he'd crossed paths with Agent Steadman, he'd felt a kinship. Though seemingly reckless, like himself, the Fed had good instincts, managing to apprehend the hacker who sold the sophisticated software. The buyer—the so called White Knight—remained at large.

Steadman hadn't succeeded in catching Gerard, but he'd proven his mettle as a worthy adversary, something Gerard had long been seeking.

The game is afoot, he thought, gratified, thinking himself Moriarty to Steadman's Holmes.

As the couple exited the gardens, Gerard followed at a distance, got into his SUV and waited for them to drive on.

***

Lake San Cristobal

Terry walked by the children's playroom. "Hi." The sweet voice came from inside. A little girl no older than six, with two messy pigtails, sat on the floor surrounded by a mess of toys, brushing a doll's long synthetic hair. It was strange seeing the sweet child under the same roof as Charlotte and Simon, who

Terry now considered her goon.

Terry kneeled down beside the girl. "What's your name?"

"Cosette."

"Oh, like from Les Misérables."

The little girl shrugged. "That's what my mom says. They stayed in *Paree.* I came with Carmen to visit Grand-mère."

Terry smiled at the girl's pronunciation. She approached a built-in bookcase filled with tens of children's books and perused the spines. "You have such a nice room. You're lucky to have so many fun things."

"Yeah, I guess."

The child seemed desperately lonely.

Terry said, "Can I see your teddy bear?"

The girl looked around her room. There were many. "Which one?"

Terry pointed to the toy in the far corner of the room.

"This is Fuzzy," Cosette said, introducing them. "Wanna play with me? Carmen went to make some sandwiches."

The child seemed ripe for a play date. With no other children around, Terry was the next best thing. "Sure." Terry sat on the rug, smiling at the toy. "Hi, Fuzzy."

They spent the next few minutes playing, the little girl teaching Terry the words to *Frere Jacques.*

She was in the best mood she'd been in since lying happily in Gabe's strong arms.

CHAPTER 16

Road to Hana, Maui

Sienna dozed off, her breath coming evenly. Jon stifled a yawn, careful not to wake her. The tediousness of the drive with no one to talk to, brought on a wave of fatigue. To keep alert, he mentally ran through some of the sleight-of-hand maneuvers he'd learned months before in Costa Rica. Jorge, a con man-turned-trainer for hire, had taught him the basics, from pick-pocketing to making 'drops' in the pockets of unsuspecting marks.

Jon glanced in his rearview mirror. Instead of crystal blue skies, a band of heavy clouds was gathering in the distance, rolling eastward. At this speed, he wouldn't outpace it. Last thing he needed was to drive on slick roads. He was about to turn his attention forward when the mirror filled with blinding headlights.

What the hell?

A black BMW SUV was right on his tail. If the jerk wanted to pass him, he could wait for a stretch of straight road and go for it.

Time to teach this asshole a lesson. Applying the same technique he used when New Yorkers rode his bumper, Jon slowed down. He wasn't going to be intimidated into speeding up.

A sudden jolt pitched his body forward against the tense safety belt. Sienna woke with a start. "What happened?"

"The guy back there hit us!" The words were barely out of his mouth when the car rammed into their back bumper propelling the Aston Martin within feet of the cliff's edge.

Sienna screamed.

Jon forced the wheel to the left. The roadster responded to Jon's quick maneuvers, righting itself as Jon sped up, overshooting the lane.

A car flew past in the opposite direction, its horn blaring, missing them by millimeters. Jon let out an expletive. Mere feet ahead of the Beemer, he could only spare milliseconds to eyeball the driver intent on killing them.

A light drizzle began to fall.

"Close the roof!" Jon ordered, flicking on the wipers.

Sienna did as she was told, turned around, and peered out the back window. "It's a man with sunglasses and a hat."

"Do you recognize him?"

"No."

Jon took the curves as fast as possible, perilously steering through the mist. He wouldn't be able to maintain the speed. "There's a case under your seat. Get it."

Sienna felt beneath her seat, extracted the hard black case and put it in her lap. "What are we going to do? You can't outrun him. There's nowhere even to pull off."

"Call it in."

Sienna dialed 911, her voice shaky as she explained what was happening. To Jon, she said, "They'll get someone out here as fast as possible."

She opened the case and gasped at its contents. "You have a gun."

"I'm a federal officer. Of course, I have a gun. Do you know how to use it?"

She exhaled, then answered in the affirmative.

"What's happening back there?" Jon asked.

"He's slowing down, creating a wider gap between us."

Jon grasped the wheel tighter. *He's going to ram us again.* Bracing himself, he slammed the accelerator to the floor.

Sienna grabbed hold of the door handle. "Whoa!"

"Wait for him to take the curve. Aim for his windshield or tires."

Jon was now at speeds hovering near eighty in a twenty-mile zone on slick roads. Several cars raced past, swerving out of their way, honking maniacally. The SUV remained on their tail.

Sienna positioned the gun out the passenger window, and keeping low, she exhaled and fired.

The Beemer swerved. She fired again. This time, Jon heard a loud pop.

"I hit the front tire."

Amazed at her marksmanship, Jon risked a look in his rearview mirror. The driver was struggling to regain control. Sienna took a third shot. As Jon sped away, he caught a glimpse of the Beemer crashing into the guard rail, its back tires on the road, the front ones spinning wildly over the cliff's edge. Sienna sat back, blew out a lungful of air and secured her seatbelt.

"Look out!" she shouted.

Jon shifted his eyes back to the road, caught sight of an oncoming RV and pitched the wheel hard to the right, the roadster tilting on two wheels, then slamming to the ground, coming to an abrupt stop. The RV tore past them with millimeters to spare.

The wind knocked out of him, Jon saw they'd veered clear of the road, perilously close to the broad trunk of a giant eucalyptus. "You okay?"

Sienna was rubbing her arm, nodding. "I think so."

Moments later, they heard one crash followed by another.

***

Gerard watched with a mix of amazement and annoyance. Someone else was tailing Steadman, dead set on running him off the road. If he hadn't been on alert, Gerard would have been caught in the pileup along with the other vehicles. But he'd been watching from his own SUV and within minutes of leaving the botanical park, Gerard spotted the black Beemer SUV. At first he thought it an undercover cop but once it slammed into Steadman's roadster from behind he understood there was more at play.

By the time he reached the accident site, the road was swarming with cop cars that had come from the west. Two ambulances were parked at the side of the road, their lights spinning, casting a blue and red glow across his wet windshield. A cop directed traffic along a narrow makeshift lane intended to accommodate drivers from both directions. Neither ambulance had a patient inside.

Gerard slowed. He saw Steadman speaking to a police officer, a fresh bandage on his forehead. The woman appeared unharmed. The Beemer's front tires were teetering off the edge of the road, the airbags deployed. He didn't see the driver.

Maneuvering past the SUV, Gerard took in the dense surroundings. The wet, untamed jungle-like foliage. Treacherous terrain on foot. The driver had been anything but subtle with his approach, a far cry from Gerard's own ways. Still, there had been premeditation in the attack, something Gerard was expert at. The car spoke of money, its driver of recklessness. It could mean only one thing. The driver was working for someone else. Someone with deep pockets, willing to kill. Someone whose payroll Gerard could tap into.

He watched one of the ambulances leave the scene, its siren silenced. Keeping at a crawl in line with the other cars, Gerard poked at the puzzle. *If I was the driver, where would I go?*

And then it came to him.

***

Maui Police Department

Captain Akamai was past his boiling point. He had four of his officers dealing with the mess on Maui's most dangerous road and a culprit on the loose.

Agent Steadman sported a bandage on his forehead with a few scrapes on his left cheek. Akamai took note of his limp as he entered the office, wondering if it was a result of today's car crash or he'd missed it before.

Akamai pointed to the bandage. "I hear you refused medical care."

"No need. We're both fine."

Ms. Lamont's beauty was unmarred by the large bruise on her upper arm. They were lucky to be alive.

Akamai leaned back in his chair. "This feels like déjà vu. Why are you here, Agent Steadman?"

Steadman met his steely gaze. "One of your officers insisted we stop by."

Sarcastic jerk. "Why are you on my island?"

"As I told you last time, I'm helping Ms. Lamont. It's a private affair." The agent gestured around the room, his face smug. "This is delaying us unnecessarily."

Akamai leaned forward, his abs meeting the edge of the old metal desk. He pointed a stubby finger at the man. "Your so-called private affair continues to become *my* problem. First the B & E at the Kenolio apartments, now this."

Steadman shrugged. "Despite what you think, we're trying to keep a low profile."

Akamai let out a laugh of disgust. "Low profile? I've got seven people in the hospital with serious injuries, and a two-mile backup."

Steadman's face registered dismay but he said nothing. Akamai felt his irritation grow. The Fed was a pompous ass. "I can have you arrested for the stunt you pulled."

He noted the quick glance between Steadman and the Lamont woman. *Did Steadman just wink at her?*

Sienna Lamont spoke up for the first time. "It wasn't a stunt, sir. A man in a hat and sunglasses tried to run us off the road. I'm sure you'll find evidence of that when you check our back bumper." There was a tremor in her voice that Akamai attributed to diminishing adrenaline.

"Do you know what my officers found on the other car, Ms. Lamont? Bullet holes. There are strict and enforceable laws against opening fire on a public road."

Ms. Lamont looked away. "All I want is to find my sister. The driver has to be involved somehow in her disappearance."

Akamai said, "Your description of the driver matches nearly everyone on the island. We have an APB out on him." In anticipation of the next question, he added, "The BMW was stolen." He addressed Steadman. "I'm sure there's more to the story than what you've shared, Agent."

Steadman stared him down, his voice steady. "I'd like to see the file on Jennifer Cartwright."

Akamai offered a toothless smile, shook his head with incredulity. "You want a favor?" Seeing Jon's steely expression, he said, "I'm not at liberty to share it with you, Agent Steadman."

Jon got to his feet, pointing downward for emphasis. "I'm here, dammit. I'm willing to help the case at no expense to you. You're going to allow some old grievances between the PD and FBI to hinder the investigation?"

"This has nothing to do with our relationship with the Feds."

"Then what?"

"I don't like you."

"Maybe your state's commissioner will like me better. You took an oath to uphold the law."

Akamai had heard enough. He gestured to the door. "Go right ahead."

He saw Steadman's face contort, surely forcing down

his ire. For good measure, Akamai added, "Actually, you'll need to stick around for a spell while I contact your superior."

Steadman stood. "Been there, done that." He made for the door.

Akamai nodded to his deputy, standing quietly in the corner. "Please keep an eye on *Mister* Steadman. I need to make a few calls." He hoped the agent caught the slight then instructed the deputy to wait outside with his two agitated charges.

***

New York City

"He did what?" Matthews's knuckles turned white as he tightened his grip on the phone receiver, listening intently to the Maui chief of police explain what had happened. He and the Lamont woman had opened fire on a public road, resulting in several injuries, thousands of dollars in damage, and the diversion of PD personnel.

Jacqui was right. Steadman's playing me for a fool. In the short time Jon had been on the ground in Hawaii, he'd managed to stir up trouble, butting heads with not one, but *two* law enforcement entities.

Being Mr. Nice Guy had accomplished diddly squat. Since being ordered to take Steadman under his wing, Matthews had been pushed to the limit. Independent minds didn't belong in government jobs. And that's precisely what Jon was. From day one, Matthews knew mentoring the survivor of a mass shooting would be an uphill battle. Jon was a damaged soul.

Swallowing his pride for the second time in so many days, Matthews said, "Chief Akamai, on behalf of the FBI, I apologize."

The fact remained his hands were tied. The NSA's deputy chief wanted his daughter to find what she needed to feel vindicated in whatever the hell they were doing, without accessing sensitive information. There were greater things at play than he could possibly piece together. He dreaded his next words but Deputy Director Lamont had been crystal clear. "However, I am sanctioning Agent Steadman's investigation as official until the end of the week . . ."

Matthews listened to more grumbling. "Yes, I understand. I'll make sure he does his job more quietly from here on out. But first, I have one small favor to ask."

He made his request, ending the call, furious. Steadman was up to his old tricks, in trouble once again, rubbing people the wrong way. When would he ever learn? Matthews's boss had inextricably bound his career to that of a loose cannon. It wasn't the first time Matthews was faced with the unfortunate fact. He and Jon would succeed or fail, as one.

Matthews took a moment to cool his anger. Lamont's agenda would have to wait just a little longer. Matthews now had one of his own.

***

Maui Police Department

Akamai beckoned Jon and Sienna back into his office.

Between gritted teeth, Steadman glanced at the guard then addressed Akamai. "I don't get it," he said. "You guys are always complaining about not having enough resources. I'm offering mine for free. What *is* the problem?"

Akamai considered the Fed's assertion. "Well, for one, I don't know what your connection is to all of this. Secondly, you come in here like you own the place. This isn't New York. It's Hawaii. And we don't take well to an in-your-face attitude. I have no incentive to involve you in my investigation. Especially if you're working solo." He felt no need to inform him that moments ago Agent Matthews had given Steadman's case the green light.

Jon peered at the man, "Incentive?"

The chief shook his head in disgust. "Are you insinuating that I'm on the take? *Incentive.* It means a good reason." Akamai stood, making it clear the meeting was over and nodded to the deputy who approached Steadman. The agent's face turned the color of a ripe Macintosh. He looked like he was ready to erupt. The deputy set a hand on his holster.

Ms. Lamont intervened, taking hold of Steadman's arm. "I'll get this squared away."

Steadman said, "I'll call my boss. He'll settle this."

Akamai smirked, handing over the phone receiver. "Funny you should mention that. I just had a pleasant conversation with Agent Matthews."

Steadman appeared startled. "You did?"

"Yup. Seems you're going to be the newest guest of the Maui County jail."

As the door closed behind them, Akamai heard the deputy say "Jon Steadman, you have the right to remain silent . . ."

Satisfied, he faced the woman. "Ms. Lamont, can I offer you some coffee? Seems your friend might be a while."

***

Maui County Jail

After Jon stomped out of Akamai's office, the deputy escorted him to the back of the station where he was booked and shown to a dank, empty holding cell in an adjacent building. A single bulb dangled from the ceiling. The deputy slid closed the barred door and locked it.

It took all of Jon's self-control to keep from exploding. He cursed the deputy for confiscating his personal items including his wallet, phone, and pills—after discovering they weren't needed to keep him alive. He cursed the captain for being an inflexible hard ass. And he cursed his boss. Why hadn't Matthews intervened on his behalf?

Jon took several deep breaths, trying to analyze what had gone wrong with Akamai. So much for burning no bridges. From the beginning, the local law enforcement was giving him the shaft, the belligerence palpable. Even before the B & E incident. It was needling him.

Either way, while Jon had argued for access to whatever info there was on Sienna's sister, without FBI backing, he had no leg to stand on. Jon rolled out the kinks in his neck and did some stretches, noting the deep scratches on the linoleum floor and the ratty gray blanket.

He took a seat on the bolted down bench, made eye contact with the deputy and with a mirthless broad grin, flipped him the bird.

CHAPTER 17

Lake San Cristobal

Terry was desperate. Charlotte had in her detestably polite way given her an ultimatum. Either join her organization, or Israel would pay the price. The heaviest one imaginable.

Little more than a prisoner in a luxurious home, Terry *needed* to reach Yosef. Not only to warn him, but just as vital, to prevent anyone from designating her a traitor. The thought was abominable. She'd rather die than betray her country.

Since arriving at the homestead, she had not seen a single cellphone. The only visible mode of communication appeared to be an internal walkie-talkie system. But Charlotte's criminal enterprise required constant and secure communication. Terry had to consider the possibility that all transmissions were conducted at the control center. The thought was frightening.

Determined to come up with a way to send a distress signal, she got up, paced her room, trying to ignore the thick file awaiting her on the desk. It never once occurred to Terry that prior to her arrival, Charlotte had bypassed the Technion's firewall, mining several classified documents. The theft of her important work was detestable. She was now charged with translating them into layman's terms for potential buyers.

Terry stared out the window. The sun was setting behind the jagged mountains, the rocks turning shades of crimson. So beautiful. So dangerous.

Thoughts of Gabe filled her mind. He must be sick with worry. The way she'd left things would surely lead him to believe all sorts of things. What had she been thinking? He'd been nothing but supportive since the day they'd met.

Terry dropped her head in her hands, the regret building up inside her. If only she could send him a message, let him know what a fool she'd been, how much she loves him.

Focus, Terry. She'd been in tight, dire situations before. With Gabe's closest friend, Jon. Like her, Jon had signed up for government work. She trusted him. He had good instincts. Most of the time. Terry forced her mind to settle. *What would Jon do?*

Like a gear clicking in place, the answer came to her.

***

Jerusalem

The lights turned on as Gabe entered Terry's apartment. A 'smart flat,' the property was designed to sense and accommodate the needs of its occupants.

Since arriving, he had faced nothing but frustration. He'd received one snub after the next. His calls were left unanswered. When he showed up at the Knesset, the man at reception gave him an odd look when he asked to speak with Director Kahn's office. "He has no office here, sir."

It was a never-ending runaround.

He was out of options. Out the window, the walls of the Old City were lit in blue. All the frustrations collided within him. "God, help me!" he shouted.

A cabinet in the kitchen slowly opened, revealing a set of wineglasses. The wine fridge lit up, the temperature displaying on its door. Gabe tore himself away from the window, selected a Tishbi cab and popped the cork, filling his glass. As he heard the water in the shower automatically turn on, he thought, *At least someone is trying to help.*

***

Shira stood at attention, facing Yosef Kahn who was seated at his desk. She had given him the most up-to-date progress report. "Sir, what do we do about Dr. Lavi's fiancé? He has called the Knesset several times and showed there in person, starting a ruckus. I'm concerned he'll decide to go public with Dr. Lavi's disappearance."

Kahn waved dismissively. "Do nothing. He'll eventually tire and go back home."

Shira wasn't so sure of that. On her way out the door, she said, "I'll keep an eye on him just in case."

***

Kahului, Maui

"You okay?" Sienna was standing outside the county jail when Jon exited, blinking against the sun, its rays a charge sparking a fuse. She'd arrived early but was told the paperwork would take a while. Clearly someone had it in for him.

Jon's hair and clothing were disheveled and he was rubbing his wrists. He appeared ready to blow.

"I'm fine," he growled, descending the steps. "I'm ordering an Uber." He fumbled with his phone, a muttered expletive escaping his lips. "Damn cuffs."

Sienna hurried to keep pace. "I'm so sorry. It's all my fault for bringing you into this."

Jon said nothing, though the throbbing vein in his neck spoke volumes.

"I tried to bail you out but they said the judge had left for the day."

"Bullshit. It took me a bit to work it out but this has Matthews written all over it. He's trying to make a point. I can't believe my a-hole boss let me sit in jail all night." A red-hot anger was radiating off him. "And to think I helped the shmuck move into his new place."

"Are you going to quit helping me?" Sienna asked, following him as he paced, emitting a boatload of pent-up negative energy.

"It's all I thought about while staring at the cracked paint on the jail cell's ceiling."

Sienna winced. "Really sorry."

As if speaking to himself, Jon said, "Quitting seems to be exactly what these Keystone Cops want me to do." He pulled a pill bottle from his pocket. "You have water?"

She shook her head. "Back at the hotel." She gestured to the pills. "What are those for? Anything serious?" It was probably not the best time to ask but she couldn't help herself.

Jon ignored the question. "I need a nap, a shower and food."

Sienna exhaled. "Right. Then what?"

"Clearly, there's more to this than meets the eye. All Akamai and Matthews have accomplished is to convince me there's something up with that clinic. I don't know what it is yet but I'm damn well going to find out."

Jaw clenched, Jon stomped off, fuming until the Uber arrived to pick them up.

***

New York City

Matthews spent an equally fitful night. He was well-accustomed to the vagaries of office hierarchy but the whiff of impropriety stemming from Deputy Director Lamont's call had since turned rancid. A life-long public servant, Matthews was a follower. But not a blind one. He would work out what was happening on his own terms.

The decision to make the unusual request of the Maui

PD, left him agitated. Steadman got what he deserved. Initially, it was tempting to subject his subordinate to a week or two in lockup but Matthews knew it wouldn't have mattered. Reprimanding Steadman was akin to scolding an untrainable puppy. A fleeting look of regret, then back to the usual ruckus.

In return for the Maui PD inviting Steadman to spend the night, Matthews agreed to keep the police chief in the loop. Which would entail Jon keeping *him* in the loop. Matthews could only imagine Jon's temperament at the moment. One thing was indisputable. Best to let him cool down before they spoke again.

CHAPTER 18

Kahului Resort

A knock. The moment Sienna opened her hotel room door she noticed the difference in Jon. The shadows were gone from under his eyes, the stubble shaven away and his hair was wet from the shower. There was a small bandage on his forehead above his smiling eyes. He looked . . . hot. She felt a blush creep up her cheeks. "Come in."

Attraction aside, Jon's cheerful mood was a drastic reversal from when she'd seen him last, only a couple of hours before. It was unsettling. *Maybe it's those pills.*

Without asking, Jon took a seat on the edge of her bed.

"Make yourself comfortable." Sienna said, hoping the sarcasm wasn't lost on him.

He didn't budge. "Something's been bothering me. How did the CID know we broke into Jennifer's apartment?"

She said, "I was wondering the same thing. Maybe a neighbor saw us. It did take a while to get inside."

"Maybe, but we didn't see a soul. There must have been an alarm. It would explain how the cops got there only a few minutes after we arrived."

Sienna sat down in the room's desk chair. It was the only remaining available option. "It would have to be a pretty sophisticated alarm system if you missed it."

"Agreed, and from what you said about Jennifer, she couldn't have afforded it."

"True. Maybe the complex pays for it."

Jon shook his head. "I called them. Made it like I was interested in renting one of their units. They don't have a global alarm system . . . wait!"

"What?"

"Didn't you tell me the selected surrogates get free rent?"

Sienna nodded slowly, a light bulb going off. "You think the clinic is monitoring my sister's apartment?"

"I can't come up with any other explanation. Can you?"

She took a moment to consider it. "No. But why would they do that?"

"They're protecting against something. I don't know yet what it is but since we arrived, there have been too many stumbling blocks and we still don't know who was trying to run us off the road to Hana. We need to visit the lab. I'll try to get another car." Jon tapped the address into his phone's GPS. "It will have to wait till the morning."

"Why so long?"

"The clinic will be closed by the time we get there."

Sienna bit her bottom lip, tears welling up in her blue eyes. She'd debated whether or not to wake him, aware the hours were flying by. Thought of his earlier disposition kept her from doing so. "We can't waste another day. Jen's in danger, I can feel it." She stepped out onto the balcony, the air starting to cool off.

Jon followed her, placed a hand on her shoulder. "I understand. I'm sure it's terribly stressful. But it's nearly sunset. We can leave first thing in the morning."

Sienna was taken by the unexpected compassion. "All right. First thing."

"Good. Let's use the time to get some R and R. My shrink keeps telling me to schedule some chill time."

Shrink? Sienna perused the brochures they were given at check-in. "There's a luau at five-thirty on the back lawn. They time it to coincide with sunset."

"Let's do it. I'll meet you there. I have things to take care of."

He left her behind, thinking chill time sounded goddam perfect.

***

Jon exited the lobby's sliding glass doors, awed by the natural beauty before him. The hotel gardens faced the Pacific, the sun slowly sinking below the horizon. The slivered moon and brightest stars began to emerge.

Several tables had been arranged on the lawn surrounded by a manned buffet. Hotel guests milled about, waiters filling their glasses with pineapple-flavored sparkling wine.

Jon spotted Sienna, her back to him. She was leaning over as a diminutive hula-skirted woman placed a lei of purple orchids around her neck and handed Sienna a single flower.

"Place this okika behind your ear," Jon heard the woman say, using the Hawaiian word for the flower. "If you are single, it goes behind your right ear. If you're in a relationship, wear it behind your left."

Jon watched Sienna turn toward him, unaware of his presence. With a slight frown she stared at the flower, then placed it behind her right ear.

Sienna lifted her gaze and saw him, the cloud fading from her face, a sad smile taking its place. She looked stunning, the lei stopping above the waist of her white floor-length sundress. Her hair was loose, its soft waves brushing against her tanned bare shoulders. Her hoop earrings dangled as she approached him. "You look nice," she said, planting a kiss on his cheek, her lips as soft as petals.

He hadn't expected the show of affection. With all the aggravation, he had not picked up on the chemistry between them. Till now.

"Hungry?" she asked.

"Starved."

Jon placed a hand on her elbow, guiding her to the buffet. A soft breeze floated off the water, carrying the saltiness of the sea and the evocative sweet scent of blooming jacaranda.

They filled their plates with poi, poke and chicken long rice, then found their seats.

"Look at that." Sienna pointed to the horizon. Vibrant streaks of indigo and pink painted the sky in the wake of the setting sun. It was the most beautiful sunset Jon had ever seen. "Jen would love this place."

Jon gestured to a passing waiter who filled their glasses. "Here's to finding your sister safe and sound." They clinked glasses and ate in companionable silence.

When the tables were cleared, an elaborate array of guava, passion fruit, and pineapple was spread out. Jon and Sienna helped themselves as a company of hula dancers materialized at the water's edge. Women in bikini tops and hula skirts accompanied a procession of bare-chested muscular men strumming their ukuleles. The women gyrated to the music, their hips and hands swaying in sync with one another.

This is exactly what I needed, Jon thought. He refilled his glass, shoving aside thoughts of the two pills he'd swallowed before leaving his room.

Several couples made their way to the makeshift dance floor. By his third drink, Jon grasped Sienna's hand. "May I have this dance?" he asked in mock formality.

She nodded, following him to the dance floor, her gait unsteady. They mimicked the performers' dance steps, leaning on one another, laughing. Without a sobering thought, Jon brought Sienna close, feeling her head on his chest. He was dancing on a glorious Hawaiian beach, a beautiful woman in his arms. *Doesn't get better than this.*

Sienna took a step back. Their eyes met. Her lids were at half-mast, her pupils dilated. Her perfume, the atmosphere, the music, made for a seductive concoction. She placed her hand behind his head, drawing him downward, slowly closing the gap between them. The fullness of her lips met his. Jon felt something dormant stir inside him, his body responding to the burgeoning passion. She whispered something in his ear. An invitation.

Back in her room, Jon realized he'd been wrong. Things could get better. Much better.

"Ever been in love?" Sienna asked, her voice deep and sultry, her arm draped across Jon's chest. They lay among the twisted sheets, legs intertwined.

"Yes," Jon said.

"What happened?"

"I don't like talking about it."

"Okay." She turned away.

Jon recalled how Sienna's boyfriend left. "She died."

Sienna turned back, her eyes wide, filled with concern. "Oh. I'm so sorry."

The memories brought with them a dull ache. "I know the pain of losing someone you love."

She blinked back tears. "I suppose you do," she whispered. "First Carrie. Now . . ." Her voice drifted off into soft sobs. "I can't lose my sister as well." Then, "Thanks for helping me, Jon. It means the world."

Jon used the edge of the blanket to wipe her damp cheeks then placed her arm back where it had been. "Care to show me?"

Her eyes still glistening, Sienna brought her lips a hair away from his. "You bet."

And she did.

***

Lake San Cristobal

Simon stood in the doorway, cleared his throat. "Ma'am?"

"Yes, Simon. Come in," Charlotte said, a document before her. When he didn't speak, she raised her gaze, looking at the beefy bodyguard. He stood there, shifting nervously, his polished shoes tapping annoyingly on the birch wood floors.

"What's on your mind?" she asked.

"I recommend we increase security."

"Why? Has something happened?"

"No, ma'am."

"Is Cosette all right?

"Yes, ma'am. The nanny has her by the lake. It's frozen over."

Charlotte had a hard time relating to the military types. They made the best bodyguards, were willing to do things other right-hand personnel weren't, but getting them to speak freely was a chore.

"Then what is it? I'm very busy."

"It's about Dr. Lavi. I fear she's of greater value than we may think."

"And that's a bad thing?"

"Only as much as keeping her presence here undetectable."

Charlotte considered Simon's words. "You think we should be further restraining her movements?"

He nodded.

Charlotte looked out the window. Her granddaughter was lacing up her skates, her voice muted by the thick, bullet-proof windows installed around the house. "We are literally in the middle of nowhere. Not another house or business for miles. No internet other than my private server which is more secure than Fort Knox. What am I missing?"

"Someone of her stature in the scientific world may

have resulted in deeper connections than we are aware of."

"I ran a full background check on her. I know everything about the woman, down to her preference in shampoo brands."

"If she's connected to any intelligence service, it may have slipped through our checks."

He'd been with her for years, present when the business skyrocketed. He was overcautious, frequently costing her more than she preferred. But he was good at what he did. Loyal to the nth degree.

"I appreciate your professionalism, Simon. But if we can't rely on the very technology we are trying to sell to our customers as the best in the world, then we will have far greater problems than Dr. Lavi's freedoms. My objective is to recruit her, not imprison her."

Simon shifted in place. "If it's all right, I'd like to investigate further."

"Of her connection to governmental entities?"

"Yes, ma'am."

Charlotte needed to get back to her pile of work. If agreeing would get him out of her office she saw no reason not to. "Go ahead. As long as it doesn't keep you too far from your usual duties."

"Understood."

Charlotte didn't look up as Simon closed the door behind him.

CHAPTER 19

Kahului Resort

J on woke at two a.m., his mouth parched. It took a moment to realize he was in Sienna's room. In her bed. The pills seemed to have so many side effects. Increased libido, suppressed inhibitions, nightmares and sleeplessness among them.

The last few hours were made for the record books, exhausting them both. Despite that, his internal alarm forced him into consciousness. There was something he'd been procrastinating. He couldn't afford to wait any longer.

Jon snuck out of the bed, careful not to disturb Sienna. Five minutes later, he stood barefoot in the hotel hallway, wearing a black tank top and workout shorts, his phone in hand. At least in New York it was an acceptable hour to engage in no-holds-barred verbal warfare.

The call went far better than expected.

Jon was surprised when Matthews announced his decision to make the search for Jennifer Cartwright an official investigation. When he asked why the change, Doug gave him a cryptic answer. "The kingmakers have spoken." He was to report to Matthews who would deal with the local PD. Jon was not to engage with them further.

Both men avoided discussing Akamai, the B & E or Jon's

night in jail, each knowing they'd gone too far. There was an unspoken understanding that being overt would result in a breakdown in communication, neither one achieving what they wanted. Instead, the time was spent with Jon briefing Matthews.

Glad to have his boss's backing to pursue the case, Jon merely grunted his thanks, allowing himself a broad grin only once the call ended.

Jon was about to go back inside Sienna's room when he paused. He couldn't shake off the thought that Sienna was holding back on him. Her seemingly endless funds. Her evasiveness about her vocation. He called Craig who answered on the first ring.

Jon asked, "Any updates on Sienna Lamont?"

"Aloha to you, too."

"Right, hi."

Craig chuckled. "Guess the rainbows and sunshine aren't affecting you."

Jon grunted.

"Okay, then. Down to business. I ran the check. Nothing extraordinary to report. She went to good schools, earned a degree in marketing. Her condo in Manhattan is paid off. Terrific credit score. No arrests. No dependents."

Jon still wondered where her funds came from. She lived in one of the priciest zip codes in the country. "Pretty financially stable for someone her age. What does she do professionally?"

"Something in the fashion business. She probably invested well. I can get her returns if you want them."

It wasn't adding up but Jon was hesitant to push. "I'll think it over. How about her parents?"

"Mother resides in Manhattan."

"And the father?"

"The father?" Craig repeated.

Jon picked up on Craig's hesitancy. "What am I missing?"

"You've been with Sienna all this time. I assumed you knew."

"Knew what?"

"Sienna's father is Sinclair Lamont, the Deputy Advisor for the National Security Administration of the United States."

***

New York City

Matthews studied the exposed pipes spanning the high ceiling, trying not to fidget. He wasn't yet sure how he felt about the loft's industrial vibe. Open concept, exposed duct work, open shelving. He knew it was the latest in design but it felt cold and uninviting. He hoped he hadn't made a mistake with the place. Making huge purchases when grieving was never wise. Too late now.

Jacqui stirred beside him, her brown eyes fluttering open, slowly focusing on his face. "What's the matter?" Her drowsy, throaty voice sounding sultry. She was cozied up next to him beneath the down comforter, the breaking rays of dawn peeking through the slats of the window blinds.

"It's Steadman again. He's in over his head."

Jacqui snuggled closer. "Sounds like he's still making your job harder than it has to be."

"No question about it. He's the most insubordinate agent I've ever had the misfortune to work with."

"I've given our last conversation about him some thought. If you can't fire him or get him reassigned, maybe you can retrain him."

Matthews was pleased to hear she had taken the time to mull over his concern. "I don't have the time for that. I need an agent who can follow the rules."

"If you don't mind my saying so, it sounds like you're part of the problem. Maybe you can offer some help behind the scenes, without him knowing it came from you."

Matthews considered the notion. It was insightful, strategic.

Without his awareness, something shifted in their relationship. Within weeks, their time together began to feel like something substantial. He couldn't have been more surprised. Happily so.

The guilt came in waves, and when it hit, was near crippling. It was a constant battle to force it aside.

Doug pressed his lips on the top of Jacqui's head, the floral scent of her shampoo tickling his nose. "There's more. He's been acting strangely. More impulsive than usual. Angrier. Like when I first met him."

"Didn't you say he's in mandatory therapy?"

He caressed her bare shoulder. "That's right." She was a good listener among other things.

"Then trust his doctor is dealing with it."

It was sound advice. Even as he sensed it may not be enough.

She kissed him then, and all thoughts of Jon Steadman quickly faded away.

***

Kahului Heliport

Jon set an alarm, allowing himself two hours of sleep. Sienna was out cold beside him. Checking his phone, he quickly saw the benefit of having the power of the FBI behind the investigation. Matthews had emailed him, suggesting the most efficient way to reach the Hana lab was by helicopter. He arranged a flight for Jon at dawn.

Jon woke Sienna, telling her to pack an overnight bag, choosing not to ask about her father. He wasn't sure if it was relevant to the investigation, but instinct told him it was. Still, she'd been holding out on him and it felt wrong. Things between them had quickly turned hot and heavy and he needed to keep his wits about him. Perhaps it was time to tap the brakes with Sienna and go back to a cordial, professional relationship.

A slivered moon was still bright in the sky when a car picked them up and brought them to the heliport. Together, they met the pilot who directed them to the helipad. The three ducked under the propellers and boarded the spacious aircraft retrofitted with wraparound windows.

The pilot handed out headsets which they donned. "Let's get this bird in the air."

Within minutes they were gliding over the island, awarded with a view of daybreak, glittering on the Pacific. They flew southward, then turned east over the dense rainforest. The pilot pointed out Haleakala volcano then followed the road toward Hana.

Sienna appeared tired but at ease. Likely, this wasn't the first time she was flying in a helicopter. "Definitely beats driving the Aston Martin."

Jon said, "I liked that car."

"R.I.P."

Jon was glad she could joke about what had been a treacherous experience, especially since there was still no word about who had been pursuing them. "Matthews chewed me out for ten minutes about paying for all the damage."

"Can you blame him?"

Jon grunted. "You never know what you're gonna get with my boss. Sometimes he's a pal, the rest of the time a world-class jerk."

Minutes passed in silence.

Jon broke it. "How did you shoot out the Beemer's tires on the third try?"

"Army brat, remember? Dad made sure Jen and I could handle a firearm."

"Looks like I owe him a debt of gratitude." It was a prime

opportunity to inquire about the man but Jon knew what it was like to have people ask about his parents. He left the questions unasked.

They spent the rest of the flight engrossed in their own thoughts until the pilot announced, "Ten minutes till touchdown."

Sienna chewed her lower lip.

"Nervous?"

"A little. I'm glad you're here with me."

"Me too."

Sienna removed her headset, gesturing for him to do the same. Speaking just above the noise, she said, "How are you going to get into the lab?"

"I have an idea or two."

"I'm scared," she said.

"Of what?"

Her eyes downcast, she said, "That we won't find her."

Jon took her hand. "We *will* find her."

"How can you be sure?"

"Call it professional instinct." Jon lifted Sienna's chin, meeting her gaze and holding it till she seemed convinced. He said, "Okay?"

She squeezed his hand, nodding. "Yes, Jon. Okay."

Jon watched as the ground came up to meet them. *Now all I have to do is keep my word.*

***

Washington, DC

Oberlander finished off the steak and fries his housekeeper had left for him, working hard to forget his cardiologist's reprimands. He'd earned the delicious meal. His virtual meeting had gone smoothly. Oberlander would soon be a considerably richer man.

His personal phone rang. *Unknown Caller.* He set down

his fork and answered it. "Who are you and how did you get this number?"

"You may call me Gerard." The man had a calm, confident voice. "I've had the pleasure of meeting one of your, shall we say, drivers."

Oberlander tapped the phone's screen, opening the tracking app. "I'm intrigued. But I believe you have a wrong number."

"He had an unfortunate accident," the man named Gerard said, ignoring him. "Seems he's succumbed to his wounds."

"Unfortunate, indeed. What can I do for you?"

"Seeing as your previous employee failed to get the job done, I'm offering to do so."

The tracking app was working slowly. He'd need to keep the man on the line. "I'm not sure who you think this is, but I'm not looking to hire anyone."

"I found your man in, of all places, one of the ambulances at the accident scene. Though not where one would expect. He was in the front next to the driver. Clever. Seems he had ample assistance to get away. A bit banged up but functional . . . at the time, anyway. I was waiting for him on arrival at the ER, got him alone for a bit."

Oberlander stared at the screen, momentarily confused. The app identified the caller as his employee, the one he'd sent to deal with Steadman. Gerard had somehow got hold of his phone.

"We had a nice chat," Gerard went on. "At least it was nice for me." He chuckled.

Oberlander said, "Sounds like you're getting yourself involved in other people's business."

"Call it what you will, but I learned you and I have a common cause."

"What happened to the driver in this fascinating story?"

"Let's just say his wounds got the better of him and I put

him out of his misery."

This surprised Oberlander. The man he'd hired had come highly recommended. If what Gerard was claiming was true, he'd managed to dispose of a professional assassin. Oberlander found himself more impressed than horrified. "Shame." Then, dropping all pretense, he said, "You're looking to replace him?"

"There does appear to be a job opening."

Oberlander chuckled. "Well played."

"Thank you. I have various skills you may find are beneficial to the matter at hand. It so happens, I have my sights on a particular federal officer who is closing in on your operation."

"Name, please."

"Agent Steadman with the FBI."

"What do you want?"

"For you to employ my services. I'm not cheap."

"What's in this for you besides money?"

"Very well. Suffice it to say, I have my own reasons. They only serve to benefit you as I will do everything in my power to complete the job."

"How much?"

Gerard told him.

There was nothing to lose. "Call this number when the job's done. I don't care how you do it." Oberlander then gave Gerard instructions for his first assignment. "Get it done by the end of the week or we'll find someone else. And if anything is ever connected to me, you'll find yourself not only without a job, but without a head."

CHAPTER 20

Rainbow Falls
Maui

The body was lying prone in the crystalline pool at the base of the waterfall. Her head tilted away, the woman appeared to be sleeping on her stomach, the pool's rocks serving as her pillows. It was only from the other side that one could see her cracked skull, the frontal lobe slowly washing away.

Officer Peter Kane swallowed a mouthful of bile.

Steering clear of the forensic photographer, Kane cordoned off the area as best he could. The trail, now muddy, was a favorite among hikers in search of a challenge. A nearly two-mile hike to the top, the terrain turned rockier with the increasing elevation.

Kane approached the medical examiner who was hovering over the body, only now noticing the deceased's deep blue hiking boots coated in mud. He wondered if the woman's death could be attributed to something as mundane as poor traction.

He spoke loudly above the roar of the water. "What can you give me, Patty?"

"Not much. But that fall would kill anyone."

Kane looked up at the top of the waterfall, cascading into the pool below, awestruck by its power. The sun was breaking over its edge, creating a spotlight effect on the water's surface.

One of his men volunteered to climb to the top, secure whatever evidence could be salvaged. The environment wasn't conducive to maintaining an intact scene. Birds, insects, moving water, had damaged the integrity of any potential evidence. At least early morning hikers had turned away with the area's closure.

Kane waited patiently as Dr. Patricia Langer swabbed under the victim's nails.

She kept her head down, focused on the task. "It rained yesterday, the ground would've been especially soft and slippery."

"So an accident then?"

The ME scoffed at Kane. "You know I can't answer that now. Let's get her to the morgue. I'll have a report as soon as I can."

***

Hana

The cab pulled up outside the Bamboo Inn, a three-story wooden structure set deep among lush shrubbery. There were several free-standing bungalows nearby. From the car window, Jon could make out a sliver of ocean. *The inn that time forgot*, he mused.

An elderly proprietor stood behind a pale wood counter, a beachside tiki bar visible behind him. "Aloha."

Jon and Sienna returned the greeting.

Jon said, "Hoping we can check in early."

"Got only a one-bedroom cottage ready," the man said, placing an island-shaped key fob onto the countertop.

The man must have picked up on Jon's ambivalence. "I can call Ocean Vista. It's four miles up the road. They might have two rooms available."

Sienna whispered to Jon, "I'm fine with this if you are."

Jon nodded glumly, and she handed over her credit card, accepting the room key.

"You okay?" Sienna asked.

"Yep."

The man looked back and forth between them. "Cottage 108. Happy hour at five. Mai Tais are three bucks. Here are the instructions for the jacuzzi tub."

Jon frowned, taking the slip of paper.

The room was small, decorated in warm colors. A vase of magenta orchids sat beside the Queen-size bed, fresh leis rested on the bedspread. A lanai led directly out onto the beach. The accommodations were dated but clean.

Sienna eyed the bottle of champagne in the ice bucket, the jacuzzi feet from the bed. "Looks like the only room left was the honeymoon suite." She stepped out onto the lanai. "Come look at this."

The sun had just risen. Palm fronds swayed in the warm breeze. Birds sang their morning calls. The air smelled of jasmine and the salty sea. In the distance, backed by a brightening sky, was a helicopter gliding westward.

Jon said, "That's our ride. The pilot said to give him a couple of hours' notice before we need a ride back to Kahului."

Sienna turned to him, her face aglow. "I can tell you're upset."

Jon tried to avoid her gaze.

Sienna placed a hand on his cheek, turning his face toward hers. "Please, Jon, whatever it is, don't be mad at me. I don't think I could bear another loss. I'm asking you to trust me."

For Jon, it was the most challenging of requests. He'd been burned too many times to count.

I have my own secrets, he thought, as Sienna walked back inside. She sat on the edge of the bed, summoning him. She was bewitching.

Jon's senses were heightened by the sounds of the sea, the meds running through his veins. Before he could stop himself, he once again fell under Sienna's spell, all rational thought left behind.

Sienna ran a finger down Jon's toned torso. "I feel like I'm robbing the cradle."

"I'm not *that* young," Jon said, his hand lost in Sienna's golden mane, aware he hadn't felt so relaxed in years. "You're a beautiful woman. Even if you're old."

She pinched him. "Very funny."

"Ouch."

She kissed the spot, craning her neck upward, her expression turning serious.

"What's the matter?" he asked, searching her face.

Sienna scootched upward. "You were right. I've been keeping something from you."

Jon stilled as she positioned herself at eye level.

"It's about my father."

Jon played dumb. "What about him?"

"He's the deputy director of the NSA."

"Seriously?" Jon did his best to appear surprised. "That's impressive. Why keep it a secret?"

Sienna looked away. "Because *I* wanted to look for Jen. If you knew who my father was, you'd tell me to get him to do it."

"Would that have been so bad?"

"He and Jen have been estranged for years."

Jon couldn't understand having a family and willingly living a life without them.

Sienna read the shock on his face. "It's complicated," she said.

Family drama was foreign to Jon. Orphaned at a young age, it was just him and Granny. The relationship was sacrosanct.

"That bad?" Jon asked.

"We've had challenges, we didn't speak for a while after he left my mom. We're in a better place now. He's been supportive of the surrogacy."

"Generous."

"I don't expect you to understand the emotions that come with infertility. But the fact that he was supportive meant the world to me. It's what precipitated our reconciliation."

"If it's any consolation, do you think I would jet off to Maui with a stranger who showed up at my door without checking things out?" Of course, it was quite nearly what he'd done.

Sienna searched his eyes, relief in her own. "You knew?"

Jon nodded, unconcerned about the fib.

"Why didn't you say anything?"

"I assumed you'd tell me when you were ready. Seems you're pretty comfortable right now." He winked, eliciting her suggestive grin. He pulled her close, placing her hand back on his chest.

"Who cares what your father does for a living? Can't imagine how it could ever really matter," he said, his voice petering out as he fell into a dreamless sleep.

***

Jon heard his name called and took the two cappuccinos nestled in a cardboard holder from Hana Joe's pick-up counter, leaving a few coins in the tip jar. Given the recent spike in horizontal exercise, Jon was on a much-needed coffee run. It was nearly eight a.m. He'd been awake since before dawn, flew to Hana and picked up the rental car. He wanted to get to the lab as soon as they opened.

Jon was exiting the shop, when his phone rang. He didn't recognize the number. Careful not to spill the drinks, he tapped the screen's green circle. "Agent Steadman."

"It's Captain Akamai. Aloha."

Jon's defenses rose hearing the unexpected cordiality. "What do you want?"

The chief of police cleared his throat. "I have an update. Consider this a courtesy call."

Must be Matthews's doing. "I'm listening."

"The Hana PD has a Jane Doe at Rainbow Falls. Someone called it in about an hour ago. Body's in bad shape."

Jon placed the drinks on a table outside, gave Akamai his full attention. "What do you know?"

"Not much at this point. You can go to the scene if you want. Look for Detective Kane."

"Tell me how to get there."

Jon memorized the information, tossed one of the coffees in the trash bin, and ran to the car. "I'm on my way."

CHAPTER 21

Rainbow Falls

Detective Kane pointed upward. He spoke loudly, above the pounding sounds of the waterfall. "The woman fell from the top, bounced off the rocks, landing face down in the pool below."

Jon looked up. A rocky narrow promontory protruded from the edge of the cliff. It was a nearly hundred-foot drop. Something the size of a shoe box was flying around up there, buzzing like a giant hornet. "What the hell is that?"

"Media drone. Pain in the ass. Nothing is private anymore. Including death. Been up there since shortly after we arrived. They follow our radio frequency. Means you'll have to wait to eyeball the vic."

Given what he assumed would be the condition of the body, Jon was not going to argue. He had no desire to inspect the deceased.

Several officers milled about, speaking in hushed tones. Jon noted a photographer putting away his equipment. He recalled passing an ambulance parked in the lot, its lights flashing a quarter mile from where he now stood.

The body lay sprawled on the ground ten feet away, a sheet covering it. One shoe was visible. Jon took several deep breaths, trying to keep his heart rate steady, glad he'd downed a couple of pills with the cold coffee before getting out of the car.

Jon asked, "Accident or homicide?"

"ME won't say yet."

"Any ID on her?"

Kane ran a hand down his stubble. "Not exactly." He moved away from the body.

Jon got in step beside him. "What does that mean?"

"Got a tip."

Jon turned to Kane. Speaking to the guy felt like pulling teeth. "A tip?"

Kane crossed his arms, seemingly hesitant to disclose more of what he knew. "This cannot be made public, understood?"

Seriously? "Understood."

Kane led Jon past the medics. They were discussing how best to transfer the woman's remains. When they were out of earshot, Jon directed his attention back to Kane.

"Someone got it on video, sent it to the PD."

"Remarkable."

"Not really. These falls are some of the most photographed in the world. The clip got her face but unfortunately it only starts when she's mid-fall. No footage to show if she slipped . . . or was pushed. At least we can try to get an ID off it. We're low on staff, could take a while."

"I'd like to see it."

"I'll see what I can do."

"Thanks. Any idea who filmed it?"

"There was no accompanying message. Our techies are working on it. They're trying to find where it originated from. Like I said, could be a while till we hear something."

Kane pointed to a small cluster of flowering sugarbush twenty feet away. "Best I can tell, the video was shot from there. Couldn't have been the killer, if there was one, that is."

"Maybe they set up a camera, went to the top and pushed her while being filmed."

"Possible but unlikely. Why go through all that only to risk us tracking them down through the video? Go take a look."

Jon walked over to the spot. Markers had been placed in the soft, muddy ground. If they'd extract distinguishable shoe prints or indentations from a tripod, it would be a miracle. He went back to Kane, watching as two medics expertly lifted the corpse, keeping the sheet in place even as they bagged it, setting it on a gurney. Thanks to the drone he wouldn't have to see it yet.

"Looks like the rain would have washed away any sign of the photographer."

Jon and Kane stepped back, allowing the medics to pass as they carried away the remains. Jon didn't envy their job.

Kane said, "She's off to the ME. I'll get back to you in the next few days with an ID."

Jon swallowed hard. "Unfortunately, I may be able to help you out with that a lot sooner."

***

Bamboo Cottages
Hana

Jon climbed the wood-planked steps onto the porch. A wheel cart with dirty plates sat beside the cabin door. He knocked.

Sienna greeted him with a kiss. She was wearing a white terry robe, the hotel's insignia sewn onto the lapel. Her hair was wrapped in a towel. "I tried to wait for you to eat breakfast but I got too hungry. I guess I built up an appetite." She winked then walked inside.

The Maui News was on the floor beside the door. Sienna picked it up, tossing it on the bed. Jon closed the door behind him.

"No problem."

Sienna pulled the towel off her hair, squeezing out the ends. "I'll be ready to go to the lab in twenty minutes. I just need to dry my hair."

When Jon didn't respond, she asked, "Where were you

143

so long? They give you trouble getting another car?"

Jon rubbed a hand over his face, sat down on the edge of the bed.

"What is it? What's wrong?"

"Captain Akamai called me."

A pause. "They found Jen?"

Jon's eyes cut to the newspaper Sienna had dropped on the bed. The cover story was about a Jane Doe, the color photo likely taken by the drone hovering above the crime scene. Several uniformed individuals surrounded a bulky white sheet. The headline read, "Death on the Falls." They'd gone to print within a matter of hours.

Sienna's eyes raised in surprise, then filled with knowing tears. "It's her, isn't it? The body at the waterfall?"

"She hasn't been identified."

Sienna lifted the paper, scanning the article. "The woman was found in an area popular with avid hikers looking for a challenge. Says it's treacherous in rainy conditions." She looked up at Jon, a flicker of hope in her eyes. "Jen would know better than that. She's been hiking her entire life."

Jon stepped beside Sienna, pointed to the photo, hoping he wouldn't have to say the words aloud. Sienna studied the picture, the spot where Jon's finger rested.

There, protruding from beneath the sheet was the tip of a hiking boot. It was sky blue. He'd seen Jen's trademark shoes in the photos Sienna had shown him.

Sienna shook her head slowly, a strangled groan escaping her lips. "No."

Jon reached out for her. Sienna pulled away, the tears spilling onto her cheeks.

Silently, she turned, went into the bathroom and closed the door. It was seconds later that the heart-wrenching wails began.

Jon opened his eyes. He'd dozed off. The last few days had

been exhausting, the love-making borderline addictive. He was alone in the bed. The crying had ceased.

"Sienna? Are you all right?" he called out.

Sienna came out of the bathroom, her hair half dried, her eyes red and swollen. "You fell asleep."

"Sorry." He made to get out of the bed.

"Please stay. I don't want to be alone right now."

Jon felt an inner conflict. Another glance at Sienna's bereft expression, her silent beseeching. He heard himself say, "All right."

Leaving on the robe, she got in the bed beside him, put her head on his chest, choking away a sob. Jon's heart pounded as he put his arm around her. Softly, he said, "None of what's happened is your fault."

Jon felt her body tremble.

"I-I don't know. If only—" Her voice caught. She snuggled closer, lifting her face, her eyes searching his for the unanswerable. "I wanted a child so badly, I would have done anything."

"There's nothing wrong with that."

"You don't understand. If it weren't for my obsession, none of this would have happened. It's my fault she's dead."

"She's an adult with free will," Jon said, careful to speak in the present tense.

A flood of tears broke through, freely running down her cheeks. "I've lost both my sister and my baby."

Jon moved a stray lock from Sienna's face. Her moist eyes glistened as she craned her neck toward him, offering. He couldn't stop her. Didn't want to. Every nerve of his body was on fire. As if by gravitational pull, Jon lowered his lips to hers. The kiss was gentle, comforting. Then hungry. His hand reached for the robe's belt, when a thought entered his head. Sienna was looking for solace in the most foolhardy of ways.

Something stopped him. Something he'd been missing for a long time when it involved this beautiful, sensual woman. Common sense.

He pulled his mouth away from hers, her eyes searching his.

Sienna sighed, placed her head on his chest and closed her eyes. "Thank you," she said as she dozed off to sleep.

CHAPTER 22

Jerusalem

Gabe woke with a start. The electric blinds were creeping upward, the sun streaming in. The new day brought a much needed change in attitude.

Gabe pushed aside the covers, noting the floor heating had kicked on. The welcome aroma of brewing coffee hit him. *This smart apartment is something else.*

He plodded into the kitchen, poured himself a cup, adding a splash of milk he found in the fridge, wondering if Hannah had arranged for it.

The night's sleep proved restorative. He had a new sense of purpose. Too much time was going by without any action. With each passing hour, Gabe was certain Terry was in serious danger. He was tired of playing by the rules. He took his laptop from his bag, logged in to the home's Wi-Fi. It was time to play hard ball.

***

Hana

The Office of the Medical Examiner was located inside a nondescript building on the edge of town. Due to its remote location, it received few cases, the majority being sent on to Makawao.

Detective Kane had agreed to keep the woman's remains local as a favor to Jon. It was the first break he'd had since arriving on the island.

Jon had seen more than his fair share of dead bodies in recent years and had no inclination to do so again. Unfortunately, it came with the job. He'd updated Matthews while he waited for Sienna to dress.

When they'd pulled into the building's parking lot, Jon told Sienna to wait in the car. He'd call her when necessary.

Jon found the office. An embossed sign bolted onto the steel door read, *Dr. Patricia Langer, Medical Examiner.* He knocked.

"Enter," he heard and walked inside. The room was cool, a bank of stainless steel mortuary cabinet doors lined the far wall.

Jon introduced himself to the silver-haired woman who handed him a clipboard.

"Fill out the form." The words came out abruptly. Most of the MEs he'd crossed paths with were socially awkward. This one was no exception. He filled out the paperwork, signing at the bottom.

Dr. Langer took the clipboard, perused the form and offered him a file folder. "Here's the preliminary report. I'll finish the post-mortem after you make the ID." The entire process had been expedited, so much so that Jon was certain someone of consequence had pulled the strings.

Dr. Langer opened one of the metal doors, pulling out the contents, a sheet-covered, toe-tagged body. An intense odor of disinfectant. He preferred it to the putrid smell that accompanied recently dissected cadavers. He helped himself to a pair of latex gloves, donning them.

With an unexpected look of reverence on her face, the ME removed the sheet, revealing a young Caucasian woman, her features unrecognizable. A Y-shaped incision stretched from shoulders to the sternum. Jon imagined an attractive young woman, starting a new life in Maui. He blinked away the image.

Jon checked the body for puncture marks, finding none. No tattoos or unusual birthmarks. He wanted to hear the relevant info and get out of there. He skimmed the top page of the written report. There were no signs of struggle. No ligature marks, nothing under her nails. He set the file down on the metal table, determined to finish reading it later at the hotel. The quicker he could leave, the better. He'd majored in forensic criminology. He'd have no trouble following the jargon. "Cause of death?"

"Won't know till I finish."

"Were there anti-anxiety meds in her system?"

"No meds, no alcohol, no illicit drugs. Though I did find tiny puncture marks in her left arm that had closed. Signs of a recovering addict."

Jon recalled Jennifer had been mixed up with drugs in her younger years. Maybe there was a recent breakup no one knew about. Regardless, there were too many coincidences. They added up to something bigger. He had learned to look not only at the details of a case but the gestalt. And this one was screaming trouble.

Dr. Langer said, "We need an ID."

Jon stepped away and called Sienna. "It's time. I'll meet you at the entrance."

Five minutes later, Jon escorted Sienna to the morgue. She looked frail but resolute, her jaw set in determination. It was going to be nightmarish.

"You've got this. I'm right here." He opened the door.

The sheet was back in place.

Dr. Langer nodded at Sienna.

Jon said, "This is Sienna Lamont. She'll do her best to make an identification."

The doctor said, "It may be best to do so on an area of her body other than her face."

Sienna turned white, whimpered, "Oh." Then, "She broke her leg when she was nine, falling off a tree she climbed in our backyard. She has a quarter-size scar on her left knee."

Dr. Langer deftly moved the sheet revealing the death-white leg.

Sienna looked like she was going to faint.

"Need a minute?" Jon asked.

Sienna shook her head, seemingly forcing herself to look closely, her face in confusion. "It's not there. The scar. It's not there."

Jon took a close look. She was right. "Maybe it was the other leg?"

"No, I'm sure."

Dr. Langer shifted the sheet. There was no scar on the right leg either.

"Magnifying glass, please."

Without touching the body, Jon studied both legs, inch by inch. No scar. "Maybe she had it surgically repaired."

"It's possible," Sienna's voice was hesitating.

Jon looked to the doctor for guidance. "Any suggestions?"

"ID by next of kin is optimal. If necessary we'll use prints and dental records, DNA." She covered the body, rolled it back inside the fridge, and ripped off her gloves. "I'll show you out."

Sienna walked ahead of Jon, had one foot out the door when she froze.

Fearing she would collapse, Jon took hold of her elbow. "Sienna?"

She turned, her face nearly as pale as the body they'd just viewed. "There's one more thing," she said in a strained whisper. "Jen was nine weeks along."

Dr. Langer said, "Pardon?"

"My sister. She was pregnant."

Jon opened the report, shaking his head, perplexed. It took a moment for him to grasp what he was seeing. What he'd neglected to notice before.

He looked up at the two women eyeing him curiously,

Sienna's lips quivering, her demeanor caught between bereavement and hope.

Jon's lips curved upward. "This woman was not pregnant. The Jane Doe is not your sister."

***

In the hallway, Sienna took shallow breaths, her skin slick from perspiration.

Jon put an arm around her shoulder. "Deep breaths through your nose, slow your heartrate."

She couldn't seem to fill her lungs. The dead woman wasn't her sister.

"You're hyperventilating," Jon said with concern. "Let's get you some fresh air."

***

Jon sat Sienna on a bench by the beach and ran across the street to buy her a bottle of water. When he returned, he found the color had returned to her face.

"Jen could still be dead," she said.

After what they saw in the morgue, Jon could no longer protect Sienna from a potentially harsh reality. "She could be but I don't think she is."

Sienna looked at him through glassy eyes. "Why do you say that?"

"This feels like a set-up," he said.

"Why would someone do something so cruel? And who's that poor woman in there?"

"Million dollar questions. Someone's trying really hard to keep us from getting the answers. We'll hopefully find some at the lab."

Seeing the look on Sienna's face, Jon said, "No, you cannot come. This one's not up for debate."

She closed her mouth, her shoulders dropping in defeat.

Jon's stomach growled.

He led Sienna to the car. "Rule one-oh-one. Can't attempt a second B & E without the proper fuel. Come on, let's find something to eat."

***.

Mossad Headquarters

Yosef Kahn was on the phone with Gonen, running interference for Terry when his office door opened. Nurit stood there, appearing skittish.

"Sir—"

He'd been working round the clock to minimize any fallout from the breach. The military was on full alert, its top commanders coordinating troops and anti-missile strategies. It was something the State was prepared for. Israel was always ready for the worst case scenario.

He held up a finger, letting Nurit know to wait. Gonen let him know that if Terry made it home, a full assessment of her loyalty would follow a lengthy debriefing. It was a process that could take several weeks. Only once the examiners were satisfied would she be allowed to resume her normal life. Yosef had conceded.

"What is it, Nurit?"

"I'm sorry to disturb you. The cyber desk called. Someone's trying to break through our firewall."

It wasn't unusual. Hackers were typically on fishing expeditions or in it for the challenge. "I'm sure our technicians are on top of the situation."

"Someone is searching out specific files."

This got Kahn's attention "Explain."

Nurit placed the printout on the table before him. "Every breach attempt used the same keywords. Theresa Lavi."

Kahn's spine went rigid. "Where did these attempts originate?"

152

Nurit turned animated. "The cyber desk is working hard to figure that out. It's been a challenge. Seems this hacker is far and above anything they've seen so far."

This must be the software the White Knight acquired. It could be another government at this point. "Get everything you can on this and get back to me as soon as you do."

"Yessir."

Thirty minutes later, the head of the cyber desk was on the line. Kahn said, "What have you got?"

"We tried everything to trace the breach. No luck. This malware is smarter than anything we've seen to date. It's amazing."

Kahn was less interested in the impressive level of technology than what it meant. When he was told of the breach, he was hopeful they could use it to trace it back to the White Knight and by extension, Terry. "Cut it off," he said."

"Yes, sir." Then, "I'm sorry, sir."

"Keep at it." Kahn hung up, aware they were no closer to finding Dr. Lavi than from the beginning of the awful mess.

***

Lake San Cristobal

Simon entered the command center's computer room waiting and watching. So far, no hits on Theresa Lavi's name within the Mossad's database. The hacking software Charlotte had purchased worked like a charm.

Still he was surprised the attempt yielded nothing. Simon prided himself on having a nose for trouble and something about Dr. Lavi smelled off. He waited several more minutes. Satisfied, he stood.

The bot's emotionless voice filled the space. "Worm detected and diverted."

What? It wasn't possible. "Shut down now!"

Instantly, all screens went dark. Simon stood frozen in the eerie room. The impenetrable software had just been detected though not traced.

He blew out a sigh of relief, understanding there was only one surefire way to test Dr. Lavi. Then he'd know if his growing suspicions were well-founded.

***

Charlotte tapped on Dr. Lavi's door. She heard footsteps and the door opened. The geneticist stood there, her face pale, the lines around her eyes more pronounced. Past her, Charlotte saw the research papers she'd given Dr. Lavi to interpret. They were in a neat pile on the desk. They appeared untouched.

"I would have thought you'd have something for me by now, Dr. Lavi."

"It's challenging work."

Charlotte considered Simon's suspicions about the geneticist's degree of motivation despite what was on the line. Perhaps he wasn't being overcautious, after all. Lavi was dragging her feet.

"It occurs to me how much you miss your fiancé, Mr. Lewis."

Charlotte immediately saw the reaction. Bold-faced fear.

"I'm sure he's quite concerned for you. And you for him." She glared at Dr. Lavi. "We wouldn't want anything to happen to him, would we?"

In an instant, she altered her demeanor, and offering her most matronly smile, she left Dr. Lavi to her thoughts.

CHAPTER 23

Bamboo Cottages
Hana

J on and Sienna dressed and made their way to the tiki bar where they dined on salmon and rice. The Mai Tais were the best he'd ever had and they imbibed several. Knowing what was coming in the wee hours, Jon doubled up on his meds, gaining an eyeful of curiosity from Sienna. He offered no explanation. By the time they finished their meal, they had a plan.

They'd head to the lab first thing in the morning. Jon would check out the facility and try to learn anything he could relating to Jennifer's whereabouts. He knew the longer she was missing, the greater the danger. Poking the hornet's nest may prove the best way to get quick answers.

On the walk back to the room, Sienna said, "I'll call my father. I didn't want to involve him but we need to find Jen. He has resources available to him."

"You think he'll help?"

"Honestly, I don't know."

Jon fumbled with the key to the room, stepping inside, Sienna behind him.

"What's that?" she asked, pointing to the floor. An envelope had been shoved beneath the door. Her name was scribbled on it.

Jon picked it up, passed it to Sienna who read aloud. "I

know where your sister is. Meet me at Haleakala for the sunrise festival. You and the Fed must come alone. If I see anyone else with you, you'll never find her."

Sienna paled.

"Who would send this?" Jon asked.

"I have no clue."

"It's a trap. Most likely the guy in the Beemer SUV who tried to kill us."

Sienna looked conflicted. "What if it's legit? Someone trying to help me who doesn't want to get into trouble. Like a Good Samaritan."

Jon was amazed at her naivete. "No chance. We already have a plan of action. The lab. It's our safest bet."

"I can't just let go of this lead, Jon."

He peered at her. "You'll be making a huge mistake."

"I'll take precautions." She pointed to the gun on Jon's nightstand.

Jon shook his head. "A surefire way to get yourself killed."

"You saw that I can handle it. Besides, I'm not asking your permission. I'm going. With or without you."

Sienna's jaw was hard set. Jon knew there was no point in arguing.

Begrudgingly, he said, "We'll need to wake up early again, well before daybreak. Where the hell is Haleakala?"

"Don't you remember? The pilot pointed it out on the way here. Haleakala is one of Maui's most famous landmarks."

Realization dawned on Jon. "You've got to be kidding. That's the—"

She nodded. "Active volcano."

Jon?

Jon heard the whisper of his name.

Ashleigh?

156

He felt his fiancée's presence, soothing and pure.

Caught somewhere between slumber and wakefulness, Jon sensed a presence hovering over him. Something ominous. Threatening.

His mind was foggy, still holding on to the dark dream. But someone was there, above him, breathing. Not Ashleigh. She was long dead.

Jon's eyes shot open. The room was pitch-dark.

He sprung up, grabbing the gun from beneath his pillow, estimating where he believed the intruder lurked, he pointed the gun into the darkness.

And fired.

He heard the spurt of the ejected bullet as it erupted from the silenced barrel, followed by a ping of chipped wood. Then the frenzied shuffling of feet.

The intruder moved with lightning speed out of the line of fire.

"Show yourself, asshole!"

Whimpers. "It's me! Sienna!"

Jon shook away the cobwebs. "Wha-?"

He flicked on the bedside lamp.

Sienna was crouched beside the door, her eyes widened in terror.

Jon leapt out of bed. "Oh my God! Are you hurt?"

Sienna was trembling, unable to respond.

Jon placed the gun on the side table. He scanned her clothes. No blood. Thank heavens. "I almost shot you. What the hell were you doing?"

"It's four a.m. I'm waking you to go to the volcano."

Jon collapsed beside her. "I'm so sorry. I-I don't know what happened." Then, "I had a dream about—"

"Ashleigh."

"How do you know?"

"You were shouting her name moments before you fired."

"I don't know what to say."

Sienna's disposition was slowly morphing from fear to anger. "Really? You can start by telling me about those pills you take like candy. You've been acting weird since we got to Hawaii. Carrie never mentioned you were an addict. Guns and pills don't mix."

Jon was stunned by the accusation. "I'm no addict."

"I saw the pills you downed last night. No way your doctor told you to take that many at a time. They're messing with your head. You nearly shot me!"

"That was a defense mechanism!"

Sienna looked at him, her expression incredulous. "You're fired."

"What?"

"You heard me. Pack your bags. Get the hell away from me. I'll send you your pay. I'm safer on my own." She grabbed her bag, tossed her items inside. "Get some help." And with that, Sienna stalked to the door.

"Wait!"

She turned, her face a mask of fear and frustration. "What?"

He closed the gap between them. "I'm so sorry. And you're right. I've been overdoing it with the meds. They were prescribed for PTSD. I don't speak of it often but my shrink thinks they'll help."

"You see a shrink?"

He nodded. "Since starting with the FBI. It started as a job requirement. They didn't want me to do anything . . . like this. The meds help most of the time. They help calm me. When things get dicey, I take more than I probably should." He omitted the part about losing inhibitions, becoming overly aggressive. What would be the point?

Sienna raised her brow. "Have you discussed any of this with the doctor?"

"Not yet. But I plan to."

Sienna broke eye contact, seemingly in thought.

Jon took her hand. "You asked me to trust you and I

have. Now I'm asking the same of you. I think I can help you find your sister and keep you safe."

Sienna chewed her bottom lip, deliberating. She let out a sigh. "Just swear you'll get the meds under control."

"I swear."

"And you'll leave the gun behind."

Jon hesitated. "That wouldn't be—"

Sienna glared at him, the fear still evident in her eyes.

Jon nodded, placed the firearm in his holster and locked it in the safe. He opened the front door. "Grab a jacket, it's chilly."

Sienna did so, then stopped in the bathroom.

When she came out, Jon said, "Let's go. We don't want to be late."

"One more thing," Sienna said.

Jon raised an inquisitive brow.

"Don't take anymore potshots at me."

Jon placed an arm around her shoulders and she leaned into him.

Jon blew out a sigh of relief. "It's a deal."

***

Lake San Cristobal

It was three a.m. when Terry moved the covers aside. Stealthily as a cat burglar, she tiptoed to the closet in the dark. Silently, she rummaged through the neatly hung clothes, still disturbed by the violation of an unseen person knowing the intimate details of her wardrobe.

She found a black turtleneck sweater and blue jeans, the darkest outfit she could find. Now she needed something to cloak her blond hair. Leaving it out would be a beacon to anyone who happened to be awake at this hour in the middle of the night. The best she could find was a navy beanie.

Terry changed out of her nightshirt, putting on the

clothes, and tucking her hair into the hat. There was nothing she could do about the white tennis shoes other than muck them up once she got outside. She'd worry about that later. Surely the house was alarmed. Silent or otherwise. The question was if each individual second floor window was connected. It was one of several variables beyond her control.

A scientist, she would eliminate the random variables to the best of her ability, create a semblance of a controlled environment despite knowing there was no such thing under the circumstances. Getting caught was not an option. The repercussions would be grave. Her country's security. And her own.

Terry opened the window, waited for a reaction. None came. She took a deep breath and climbed out the window and onto the ledge.

CHAPTER 24

Haleakala Crater

The drive up to Haleakala took just under an hour. In the wee hours of the morning, the volcano was a shadowed triangle against a dark sky. Shrouded in mysticism, it emitted strong, ominous vibes.

Sienna had recovered quickly enough from her near-death experience. Jon less so. His instincts were quicker than his mind. If he'd moved his pistol millimeters to the left . . . he couldn't bear to think it. "I'm sorry, Sienna," he said again, keeping the car in low gear as they climbed. "I guess I'm on edge even in my sleep."

"I shouldn't have snuck up on you that way. I woke up early to call my dad. I thought you'd find it easier than an alarm clock."

The guilt and shame hadn't yet lifted but there was little he could say beyond apologies. "How is he handling Jen's disappearance?"

"He was his usual stoic self. But I could tell he's worried. He's coming out here."

"Really?"

Sienna nodded. "He says he has old contacts here in Maui, thinks he can get a proper investigation going. I'm starting to regret not bringing him in earlier."

"You were doing what you thought was best."

"True, but still."

"Will you introduce me?"

Sienna paused. "You want to meet my father?"

"Definitely. We'll have a greater chance of finding Jen if we work as a team."

"I-I don't know if that's such a good idea."

Jon held back from pushing the issue. Clearly, there was lingering tension between Sienna and her father.

When they arrived, the parking lot was close to filled. Jon got out of the car, struck by how cold it was at the top of the volcano at night, and glad he'd remembered to bring his leather gloves. A group of coat-wearing early risers were congregating near the peak. Checking his phone, he said, "There's no reception up here."

Jon and Sienna followed the growing crowd to the spectator platform overlooking the crater. Far below them, smoldering lava crackled from the depths, the heat emanating upward. A woman dressed in colorful traditional garb welcomed them. "Sunrise in twenty minutes. We will begin our ritual then."

Jon whispered to Sienna. "Keep an eye out."

Sienna said, "In this light, it's impossible to see anyone clearly."

"He's probably waiting to see if we were followed."

Sienna squinted in the darkness, shivering. "Surely there were better places to meet us."

"Actually, it's perfect. Cover of darkness, no cell service, a crowd for him to blend into. If he feels threatened, he can easily drive away without us being any the wiser."

They both scanned the area as best they could.

Sienna said, "What should we do?"

"Make it easy for him. Let's find a spot away from the crowd. If he sees us alone he'll show himself. Then we can all sit in our car and talk." *If this isn't a trap,* he thought.

Sienna followed Jon along the crater's edge, holding onto the metal railing as they took the turn away from the group. The paved path soon became loose gravel. Beyond the glowing lava, only a glimmer of golden light was a speck on the horizon. It would be a spectacular sight once the sun came up.

They passed a triangular yellow sign depicting a man slipping on rocks. With no ambient light, it quickly became darker. They turned on their phone flashlights.

Several minutes passed in silence. No one showed. Jon said, "We should split up."

"No way."

"The sun will be up soon and then he'll bolt. It's now or never. Go join the others," Jon said.

"We're here for *my* sister."

"This isn't debatable. I'll wait till sunrise. If he shows, I'll come get you."

Sienna seemed to accept the plan and stepped away. Jon watched her move past a few straggling tourists digging out their phones to film the event. When he lost sight of her, he turned, heading in the opposite direction, grateful for the pistol on his hip. He'd promised he wouldn't bring it, but it was a promise he couldn't keep. He snatched it from the room's safe when Sienna was in the bathroom.

The lava glowed bright orange, a few smoldering loose stones within arm's reach. Despite the heat rising from below, the air chilled Jon's bones. He hoped whoever had sent the note would present himself already. If by some chance this was a legitimate lead, he didn't want to miss it. Whistleblowers tended to be fickle. Jon tried to make his way in the dark, careful to hold on to the metal railing separating him from the roiling crater.

"Steadman?"

It was barely a whisper, the hoarse-sounding voice coming from the far end of the platform. Jon let go of the railing and stepped onto gravel.

"Where are you?" Jon asked in a loud whisper.

"Are you alone?"

"Yes." The mountain's acoustics made it impossible for Jon to pinpoint where the voice was coming from. "You can come out now."

A shadow of a man built like a linebacker, began to emerge from the dark edges of the jagged boulders. All Jon could make out were a pair of scuffed hiking boots.

Sensing movement from behind, he began to turn. Out of the corner of his eye, he caught sight of a man of average height, runner's physique, dressed in a black ski jacket, a dark neck muffler pulled up over his mouth and nose.

Two people!

Before he could react, Jon felt a hard shove, the force propelling him forward toward the railing. Instinctively, he held out his hands, managing to slow his momentum as he hit the ground with immense force.

"You're a hard man to kill."

Sprawled face down on the rocky surface, Jon spat blood from his mouth, an intense heat on his face from the glowing lava mere feet away. The gravel crunched behind him.

Scrambling to get to his feet, he heard a scuffle, and quickly shifted his body. The runner was nearly upon him, the linebacker nowhere to be seen. With his gloved hand, Jon reached out, grasping a burning rock, the smell of smoldering leather stinging his nostrils. With no time to aim, Jon hurled the rock at his attacker, hearing the man's muffled cry as the burning lava fell from his scorched hand. Breathing hard, Jon watched the assailant turn, one hand cradling the opposite wrist as he ran into the darkness.

The second man now came forward, materializing from his hiding place. Jon instantly recognized him. *Mike, the hike leader!*

This time Jon was ready. He aimed his gun at Mike's forehead. "Stop where you are."

Mike raised his meaty hands, his demeanor calmer than it should be with a gun in his face.

"Who *are* you?" Jon barked.

When Mike didn't reply, Jon lunged for him, bringing the pistol down hard on Mike's forehead. The large man dropped to his knees.

Adrenaline ran through Jon's veins. The urge to shoot him was overwhelming. "Who is paying you, asshole?"

Mike cursed, touching the bleeding wound, confusion crossing his face. He muttered something Jon couldn't decipher.

"Louder!"

Mike listed sideways, his eyes now at half-mast, seemingly falling into unconsciousness.

"Who do you work for!" Jon repeated, his angry voice echoing in the dark.

The man's eyes momentarily opened, his pupils dark and enlarged. "The U.S. government," he said. A second later, Mike was out cold.

***

Jon stood, wiping gravel from his face, hoping his voice would come out steady. The man he knew as Mike was at his feet, taking shallow breaths, in and out of consciousness.

"Hello? Who's back here? This area is off-limits." It was the voice of the old shaman woman. The light from a phone lit Jon's face. "Sir, are you all right?" she asked, alarmed.

"My name's Special Agent Jon Steadman. I work for the FBI." He pointed to Mike on the ground. "We need an ambulance, pronto. Another man just tried to kill me. He got away. Call the police to shut down the road."

The old woman appeared distraught. "I have a radio for emergencies. But the nearest police station is miles away. Whoever attacked you will be long gone by then." She hurried off.

Sienna came running, taking in the scene. "Jon, are you okay? What happened?" She looked at Mike on the ground. "Isn't that the guy from the hike?"

Jon filled her in. "I told you it was a trap."

"I'm so sorry. Sienna's tone was filled with despair. "I

thought this would lead us to Jen." Then, "We need to find out what Mike knows."

"He's out cold but I'll be there when he wakes up."

The sun was about to break. A hush fell over the crowd, people clicking on their cameras. The woman returned and began a chant. Slowly, the sun rose up behind her, the brightening sky casting an otherworldly glow upon the fiery depths.

Surrounded by the oohing crowd, Jon and Sienna stood side by side, watching in awe.

Something was nagging at him. "The man who attacked me. I've heard his voice before."

Sienna looked up at him. "Where?"

"I can't place it."

Sienna pointed to Jon's forehead. "You're bleeding."

He touched the spot, his finger coming away red. "I'll live. But the ambulance better get here soon. Mike is in a lot worse shape. We need him coherent. He has a lot of questions to answer."

Jon quieted as the old woman approached him, gesturing for him to bend down. She placed her hand on his head, as if reading an unseen message. Jon could swear her fingers tingled with the volcano's heat. "You have a powerful energy field. Much passion and anger. You must contain it before it engulfs you."

Without another word, the old shaman walked away.

***

Office of The News of Israel
Jerusalem

The newsroom was aflutter with activity. A group of people exited the conference room at the end of the hall, speaking animatedly. Gabe picked up a few snippets from the English speaking journalists.

"Terror attack in Sderot . . . two sirens in ten minutes . . . the prime minister needs to crack down . . ."

He pushed his way through the group, like a salmon swimming upstream.

"Can I help you?" asked a woman, wearing a press lanyard.

"I have an appointment with Caroline Gluck."

The woman pointed to the corner office. "Good luck. She's in a mood today."

Figures. "Thanks."

The office had a small placard on the wall beside it. *Caroline Gluck, Editor-In-Chief.* Below it, Gabe assumed was the Hebrew translation. He knocked.

"Enter."

Gabe let himself in. A woman of approximately forty-five with short dyed blonde hair, her gray roots an inch long, sat behind a wooden desk piled high with papers. She gave him a short glance. "Who are you?"

"Gabe Lewis. I made an appointment."

"What do you want?"

Gabe was no longer put off by the abruptness. "To give you the story of the year."

Caroline let out a sardonic laugh. "If I had a shekel for every such claim."

"My fiancée works for the Mossad. She's missing."

"What's her name?" she said, without looking up.

"Dr. Theresa Lavi."

Caroline let her pen drop from her fingers, onto the desk. She lifted her gaze, now sizing up the man before her. Gabe kept his expression determined.

Caroline sat up straight, pressed a button on her landline. "Rivka, hold all my calls for the next hour." To Gabe, she said. "Mr. Lewis, welcome. Please have a seat."

***

Lake San Cristobal

It was a moonless night. Terry could barely see the hand in front of her face. Carefully, she inched across the window ledge, feeling like a speck of dust on the surface of the moon. So far no alarms had gone off, though a silent one could have alerted Charlotte and Simon. There was no way for Terry to know. Either way, she needed to be quick.

A gutter was to her right. Testing it first, she used it for support. The wood and stone of the home's exterior created a ladder-like descent. Careful with the placement of each step, and fearful of dislodging the gutter, Terry lowered herself to the ground.

Relieved to be on terra firma, she took a moment to listen for any disturbances, prepared to make a speedy retreat back to her room, if warranted.

The silence was profound. She recalled her handler's mantra. Shira's voice was in her head. *Calm yourself.*

Terry breathed in the chilled mountain air and took off into the night.

CHAPTER 25

Maui Memorial Hospital

J on stood at Mike's bedside, still stunned. On the mountain, he had shown his badge to the medics and was given clearance to sit in the ambulance with the semi-conscious linebacker.

Regulation didn't allow for Sienna to escort the injured man. With no choice, she agreed to meet up with Jon later.

By the time Jon arrived, Officer Iona was standing by the doorway giving him the evil eye. Captain Akamai was already in the hospital room, back to emitting a strong whiff of animosity.

Jon's face was slick with antibiotic cream but it didn't compare to the condition of the beefy man in the bed who had not fared well. His head was bandaged with layers of gauze.

"Why aren't there handcuffs on this guy?" Jon asked Akamai, omitting any form of greeting.

Akamai glared at Jon, saying nothing.

Mike sat up, extended a hand to Jon. "No hard feelings, I hope."

Jon looked from him to Akamai and back again. No handcuffs, no arrest. "What is going on? Who are you?"

"Michael Evans. My friends call me Makoa. U.S. Marshals Service. Under cover."

Jon fell silent.

Akamai said to Evans, "Show him some ID."

Evans did.

Jon said, "You were under cover on the hike?"

Evans nodded. "You and Sienna showed up, nosing around. I wanted to get a solid read on both of you."

Akamai said, "And you, Agent Steadman have done a fantastic job at trying to blow his cover."

"For the record, I tried to get the guy off you." Evans said.

Jon's mind was awhirl. "For such a big guy, you did a lousy job."

Evans ignored the jab. "I left you a message at your hotel room. He must've followed me to the volcano."

If it wasn't for Akamai's presence, Jon wouldn't believe a word. "Who was he?"

Jon saw Akamai give Evans a disquieting look.

"I have no idea," Evans said. "But I'm pretty sure who he works for."

It had to be the same person who nearly ran him off the road. Jon gestured for Evans to continue.

Evans and Akamai exchanged glances once again. No one spoke.

Frustrated but desperate for information, Jon said, "The guy who attacked me was familiar. We've crossed paths before."

This seemed to surprise both men.

Jon said, "Get me his name."

Akamai snarled. "You giving orders again?"

Jon ignored him, spoke to Evans, "Where is Jennifer Cartwright?"

Evans looked to Akamai. "I can't tell you that."

Jon felt his anger rise. "Why not?"

"You'll need to speak to someone far above my pay grade. The only reason I left you that message and went to meet you was on Jen's request. We've gone to extreme lengths to make her dead. But she wants her sister to know she's alive and safe. I advised her against it but she was willing to take what she thought was a minimal risk. Proved to be a teachable moment. Even with my caution, I was followed. It's clear they have eyes and ears everywhere."

"Who is *they*?"

Silence.

Jon shook his head in disgust. He had enough of the runaround and half-answers. He'd been attacked on a volcano, run off a treacherous road, and spent a night in jail. "First you nearly get me killed, now you're stonewalling me." He pulled out his phone.

Akamai said, "Who are you calling, Steadman?"

"Someone who can give me answers."

"This is Agent Jon Steadman. I'd like to speak with Deputy Secretary Lamont. I'm a friend of his daughter's."

Akamai reached out, pulling the phone from Jon's ear and ended the call.

"What the f—"

Akamai said, "Sit down, Steadman."

Jon bristled but sat. "You're going to arrest me again?"

"If only I could."

Jon kept on his poker face. The number he'd dialed belonged to his Granny in Florida.

Makoa said, "Jen's in WITSEC."

Jon couldn't hide his surprise. "She's in the witness protection program?"

Makoa nodded. "I can't tell you where. For her safety. You can beat the crap out of me—or try—but I won't. And by the way, if it weren't for me, that guy would have tossed you clear over the side of the volcano."

Jon scowled. "You waiting for a thank you?" Then, "Who is Jennifer supposed to testify against?"

This time Makoa didn't look at Akamai for clearance. Instead, he fixed his gaze on Jon. "She's scheduled to testify against the man you were trying to call. Her own father, Sinclair Lamont."

Maui County Police Department
Kahului

Jon had hoped never to step back into Akamai's precinct. No such luck. He and Sienna sat side-by-side in a closed room, looking through a database of mugshots. None of them were the man who attacked Jon on the volcano. He was a ghost. Someone was hunting them down. Someone no one could yet identify.

Sienna shifted nervously in her seat, biting her lip as she studied the final photos slowly scrolling by. Her elbow brushed against Jon's arm, stimulating him like a spark of electricity. He forced the feeling away. He needed to keep his head on straight.

After meeting with Makoa and Akamai in the hospital, Jon had given Sienna the reassurance that Jennifer was safe, explaining that she was choosing to stay off the radar and would resurface when it was safe to do so. At Mike's request, Jon left out the part that she was in the witness protection program.

Mike had said, "Tell Sienna, if she really wants to keep her sister out of harm's way, she needs to stop looking for her."

At first, Sienna seemed to be greatly relieved. Now, less so. Her sister was alive and if Mike was to be trusted, was well. But Sienna wanted—needed—real answers to where Jen was and why she was hiding. Jon couldn't blame her. He had the same questions and more.

"The attacker isn't in this database," he said, rubbing a hand over his tired eyes. "I'll go tell Captain Akamai." He stood, opened the door, letting in the agitating sounds of a bustling precinct.

"It's not adding up," Sienna said, remaining in her chair, her mind clearly shifting elsewhere.

Jon understood Sienna was speaking of her sister. She'd been preoccupied for hours.

"Jen disappeared but this guy, Mike, knows where she is and won't tell us, to keep her safe. *I* can keep her safe, surely, more so than Mike Evans can. He literally led a killer to the volcano. If things had turned out differently, who knows what would have happened to Jen . . . and the baby."

Or to me. Jon tried to not take the slight personally. Sienna had been on an exhausting quest that was hitting one stumbling block after the next.

Jon felt uneasy keeping a lid on the news about her father being the subject of a clandestine investigation. But tipping her off would mess with whatever probe was underway. One in which her sister was a primary witness. Akamai and Evans were close-lipped about what dirt Jennifer had on her father. Sinclair Lamont was coming to town. Jon could assess the man for himself.

***

Kahului, Maui

Sinclair Lamont's home was impressive both in size and contents. The nearest home was a good distance away. A beachside property, it was fronted by a well-tended lawn, the inground sprinklers coming to life in timed synchrony. Giant palm trees surrounded the house, functioning as a privacy fence. Jon wondered what his primary residence looked like.

Inside, high ceilings, recessed lighting, and upscale furnishing added to the air of affluence. Built-in bookshelves displayed a wide variety of literature. Framed awards and photos of the deputy director shaking hands with various heads of state were dispersed among books on business and finance.

The man stood ramrod straight beside a large oak desk, his graying hair combed back as if he'd made a concession to outgrow a buzz cut and was still uncomfortable with the decision. He wore a perfectly tailored sport jacket over a crisp button-down tailored shirt. He extended a hand. "Agent Steadman, is it?"

"Yessir. I appreciate you making time to see me, privately." Without Sienna's knowledge, Jon had called Craig who with some finesse, acquired the deputy director's personal phone number. Jon needed to see the man whose daughter was prepared to take down. His objective was to shake things up and see what would fall out. Without Sienna's presence.

Lamont was surprisingly accommodating. "I had a few minutes to spare before I see my daughter and then need to get back to DC." Lamont gestured to the chair opposite his desk and took a seat. "How can I help you?"

"As I mentioned on the phone, I've been assisting Sienna. I understand she told you about Jennifer."

Lamont's face turned grim. "It's devastating," he said. "It's why I made a last minute trip out here. I've reached out to my contacts on the island. I'm confident they're doing everything possible to find her."

To Jon, the man appeared less disturbed than one would expect under the circumstances.

Lamont studied Jon's expression and took a seat. "Both my girls grew up with the same parents in the same environment, yet each one turned out differently. You know how it is. I love both my girls equally but Sienna has always been the easier child, more reasonable. Unfortunately, Jen is more like me. Stubborn to the core."

He had only been in Lamont's company for a few minutes and Jon already felt a strong dislike for the man. There was a disingenuity about him. The politician's curse. *Slick Sinclair*, he thought. "Whatever fate Jennifer faces will also apply to Sienna's baby. Your grandchild."

Lamont lowered his gaze, nodding. "Terrible thing. Sienna has wanted to be a mom for as long as I can remember.

Finally, she found a promising solution and it's all gone sideways."

A prim woman in her sixties with a pencil protruding from her tightly wound bun entered. "Sir, your delivery arrived."

"Will you excuse me? This shouldn't take long."

"Of course."

Jon stood up, walked around the room, looking at the photos, books. A picture of Lamont with two teenage girls, posing in front of the Eiffel Tower, sat on the desk. *Sienna and Jennifer*. Pictures with three presidents including the sitting one. One photo in particular drew his attention. Three men in fatigues, mid-twenties at most, one with a cigar dangling from his mouth. *Abuelo*.

Jon used his phone to snap a picture of it and sat back down.

When Lamont returned, he said, "I'm terribly sorry but my assistant tells me I forgot about an important meeting." He glanced at his Rolex. "It starts in a few minutes. It was a pleasure to meet you. I'll be in touch with Sienna with any updates about Jen."

Jon took the cue, stood and shook the man's hand once more. As he left the home, Jon felt like he'd just been in the presence of a very devious man.

***

Federal Plaza
New York City

Doug was nearly out the door when his phone rang. He had thirty minutes to get to the Met where he and Jacqui had tickets to *La Boheme*. "Matthews."

"Rein your boy in or I'll do it for you."

Matthews anger flared. "Who the hell is this?" he asked even as recognition dawned on him. "Deputy Lamont?"

Several agents looked up from what they were doing, distracted by the famed person on the other end of their boss's conversation.

"I told you to give my daughter peace of mind, not to run a full-blown investigation."

Matthews closed his office door, dropped his briefcase on the floor. "What did he do?"

"He just left my home. The Maui police have things under control. Call him today or you'll be out of a job by tomorrow." The call ended in a click.

Matthews had had enough. He no longer cared who Sinclair was. *The guy's dirty.*

He texted Jacqui, apologizing. He'd miss the opera. Several crying emojis came back in reply. He called Jon.

"Sir?"

"Time's up, Steadman. Be back at your desk tomorrow afternoon."

"I'm finally making headway with the case. I need to check out the lab in Hana."

"This is a direct order. We'll discuss where things stand when you're here. You have a new case. And it's urgent."

***

Lake San Cristobal
Colorado

The enclosed golf cart was in an unlocked, detached garage, the key still in the ignition. Terry unscrewed the bulbs on the front and back of the vehicle, placed them in the passenger seat. It was time-consuming but necessary.

This is too easy, Terry thought, as she got behind the wheel, turning the ignition. Thankfully, the vehicle was electric, making virtually no noise or gas emissions. And there was no odometer to assess. She took note of precisely where the golf cart had been parked, the position of the wheels. She would return it the way she found it. *If* she returned.

She'd taken pains to commit to memory the route to the command center. She would stay off the dirt road they'd driven during the day. It would be treacherous in the dark but there was no choice.

Terry tried to focus on the positive. The fact that Charlotte relied solely on artificial intelligence to provide security was in her favor. It was the one thing Terry could exploit.

Terry labored to make out the landscape in front of her. When she squinted, she could keep parallel to the road. The ride took eight agonizing minutes of steering clear of large rocks and gnarled tumbleweed. It seemed like forever.

Relief flooded her when the outline of the building came into view. A single pin of red light was visible beside the entrance. The eye scanner.

Terry got out of the golf cart and ran to the building. She lifted the pad's cover and placed her head against the eye reader.

Nothing happened. *No!*

Charlotte claimed to have mapped the dimensions of her eyes, allowing her earlier entry. It was the foundation of Terry's plan to gain access to the control center. She wouldn't have to break in. Charlotte or Simon must have deactivated her access ability. How stupid could she have been? Didn't it make sense to prevent exactly what she was doing?

A sense of defeat washed over her. There was no way to break into a building made of concrete and steel reinforcements, fitted with motion sensors on the periphery.

She whispered a small prayer and tried once again, this time placing her head gently on the pad. She heard a click. "Thank you," she whispered, and rushed inside.

***

Jerusalem

Gabe felt a wave of relief, praying he was doing the right thing. Caroline assured him they would investigate and if there was enough to run with, an exposé would go out in the morning paper. While she promised to keep his name anonymous, Gabe held no false hopes. Kahn would surely surmise who was behind the piece.

But there had been no alternative. He'd run through all the options in his mind. Contacting the newspaper was the best way to stir up some response. It was his sole recourse. The article was sure to get Kahn's attention. Gabe just hoped it wouldn't result in him being detained in an Israeli prison.

CHAPTER 26

New York City

J on entered his boss's office with a chip on his shoulder. He left Sienna back in Maui, explaining his time was up. She was terribly disappointed but understood. He'd kept to what they'd originally agreed upon. And more. Even if Jennifer hadn't been found, Sienna could rest easy that she was safe.

Crossing his arms, Jon said to Matthews, "I was so close to locating Jennifer Cartwright."

"What you were close to was opening a Pandora's box. If she's in WITSEC, finding her would jeopardize her safety."

Jon fell into a chair, his shoulders slumped. "I get that but I was making progress. I don't like leaving things hanging. Someone clearly wants to get me off the case. There's a lot more to Jennifer's disappearance than it seemed when Sienna showed up at my door." He proceeded to fill in Matthews on his near fatal accident on the Road to Hana and the dangerous altercation at Haleakala.

"There are powerful people involved."

Jon cocked a brow. "That's the second time you referred to higher-ups involved in all this." He prepared his next words for maximum impact. "I met with Deputy Director Lamont. You know, Sienna and Jennifer's father."

"I know. I wish you hadn't done that."

"You knew?"

"He called me."

"What's going on?"

"First answer me. What did you learn?"

Jon said, "That Deputy Lamont is the subject of a classified undercover investigation. Probably why you weren't told about it. I don't know what they're going after him for, but it's big."

Matthews dropped back into his chair, put a hand on his head. "That explains it. Lamont has been using his influence to steer people away from whatever it is he's up to. Even his own daughters."

"So that's it? One man with enough power decides he's had enough and slams the brakes on an active investigation?"

Matthews shook his head. "That's the point, Steadman. It wasn't meant to be a formal investigation. You were on vacation, helping your dead partner's friend. By ramping it up, you sparked a firestorm. You've made him nervous."

"So what now? We simply walk away? Jennifer is still out there somewhere. If Evans is to be believed, she's in WITSEC. Protected so she can testify against the very person trying to stall my progress. He's hiding something major. We need to find out what it is."

"I'm working on it. The man's got secrets. I'm sure he's scared something old will come out and hurt him professionally or otherwise. My question to you is do you think he'd hurt his own child? Even if she is trying to put him away?"

Jon gave the question his full consideration. "He's a tough nut. Barely broke a sweat when we talked about his missing child." Jon thought of the photos he saw in the man's office. They weren't staged. The man loved his daughter. "But no, I don't think he'd go that far."

Matthews nodded, thinking. "I was told," he gestured quotes, "to rein you in."

"Which you've done. So, what's my new urgent case?"

Matthews leaned forward. "To investigate the very man himself. Get me everything you can on Deputy Director Sinclair Lamont."

***

Jon's mind was ablur. Matthews had made it crystal clear that the Lamont investigation should be kept under the radar. Both their jobs would be gone in the blink of an eye if Lamont got word of it. The situation unfortunately would put Jon in an awkward situation with Sienna. He was brought on to look for her sister and she'd paid him in full. Now he was turning things around and going after her father, a man who despite his many flaws, she revered and loved.

***

Jerusalem

Yosef Kahn perused the printout Shira had handed him. It had been taken from *The News of Israel*'s internal mainframe, thanks to a mole at the paper.

"You were right," Kahn said to Shira, his mind elsewhere. Rafi Gonen was ramping up the pressure to get Dr. Lavi placed on a detainee list. If he succeeded, if the geneticist was located alive, she would be treated like a traitor, placed in detention, and cut off from the world until she was either arraigned or deemed harmless. Kahn was fighting Gonen at every turn.

Though he knew Shira was buoyed by his praise, she managed to maintain her stoic demeanor. "Yes, sir."

"Gabriel Lewis has become a particular nuisance. Have you dealt with Gluck?"

"Yes sir. She threw a raging fit."

"And?"

"The piece will not run. Even she had to agree national security preceded the need for public awareness in this matter."

Kahn focused on Lavi's former handler. "You didn't tell

Gluck what was on the line?"

Shira pursed her lips. He'd insulted her.

Yosef added, "Of course you didn't. You gave her just enough to secure her compliance."

A slight nod.

"Well done. It may be time to reach out to Jon Steadman. Press upon him to make sure his close friend doesn't try this again somewhere we have no control."

"Yes sir."

The matter resolved, Kahn's mind went back to Gonen. "Thank you, Shira. That will be all."

***

Lake San Cristobal

The small anteroom pulsed, as if the building itself was a living, breathing entity. Though she had entered the unoccupied building without incident, Terry's urge to maintain a respectful silence was overwhelming. Like being in a library. Or at a funeral. She fought the inclination to cut and run and hurried to the door leading to the command center, once again using the eye scan. The door clicked open.

The interior room gave off an eerie glow in the dark space. Lights from flashing consoles bounced off the desk's reflective surface.

Terry sat in the chair. She was a scientist, not a programmer. The unfamiliar equipment was intimidating. She hadn't noticed a phone the last time she was here, and not seeing one now caused another bout of hopelessness. The thought that all this effort and risking her life had been for naught was crushing.

Terry tried to calm herself. She chose the keyboard closest to her and tapped a few keys. The screen directly above her came to life with the image of a spinning globe.

She typed in the name of her email server. When

nothing happened she tried the same on another keyboard. Nothing. Her fear and despair suddenly turned to anger. No longer caring to keep silent. The room after all, was a vault. She pounded the desk. "I need email!"

"Email initiated."

Terry nearly jumped out of her skin in fear. The robotic voice emerged from unseen speakers. She breathed in deeply, trying to calm her nerves. She'd made an important discovery. All she needed to do was speak her commands! Her heartbeat slowed down.

Terry spoke her request. "Send message from Terry Lavi to Yosef Kahn." Speaking the words and her boss's email aloud terrified her. Who was listening? Did it even matter anymore? Whatever happened to her now, she would at least have shared the vital intel with Kahn, potentially saving a monumental crisis throughout the Middle East.

After several failed attempts at using the speech software, she got the hang of it. Rapidly, Terry spoke a detailed message, conveying the facts as she understood them. And identifying Charlotte Colbert as the White Knight. If anything would get her killed, that was it.

Recalling Charlotte's recent threat. Terry's last words were "Warn Gabe. He may be in danger. Tell him I'm okay, I'm sorry and I love him."

She didn't care that several people would be parsing the words, seeing her private life on display. If Gabe received that message, it would be worth it.

"Engage end-to-end encryption," she said. If it worked as she'd been trained, there would be no trace of the sent email.

A moment before sending it, it occurred to her that Yosef may think she was under duress or that someone had hacked her email, sending a false message. She could only imagine what would be involved to relocate the nuclear site. She needed to prove it was her behind the email.

Wracking her brain for something she could write that would ensure her identity, she spoke, "Love to Claudio."

Claudio was the Italian scientist believed dead or missing. The bearer of powerful, life-changing knowledge, only a handful of people knew he was residing under an assumed name. In Haifa.

She looked at the time on the computer screen. She'd already been gone for twenty-five minutes. Five minutes shy of what she'd allocated. She needed to leave.

Using her sleeve, Terry wiped down the surfaces she'd touched. "Send email."

"Email sent."

"Wipe history and close all screens." She hoped she was using the correct terminology.

"User log has been erased."

The screens fell back into darkness. Terry left the room, praying her message would end up in the right hands.

***

Mossad Headquarters

Yosef Kahn was beginning the third meeting of the day when his assistant, Nurit, came barreling into the room in a panic. The usual mild-mannered woman was not one to barge in on her boss, or on anyone for that matter. A soft-spoken waif in her late-twenties, Yosef knew her to be painfully shy. Which is why he didn't ream her out for interrupting his weekly review meeting.

The four other heads in the room turned to face her.

"What is it, Nurit?"

Nurit waved a paper in her hand. "It's Dr. Lavi."

Yosef said, "Meeting adjourned. Everyone, please excuse us."

The others in the room looked perplexed. When no one moved, he shouted, "Out!"

The two men and two women looked stunned at the ever-stoic director's demeanor. They scurried out.

When the door closed, he said to Nurit, "Tell me."

"She's alive. She sent you a message."

Relief ran through him. What Gonen suspected was true. He had a soft spot for Dr. Lavi.

Given the nature of the profession, Yosef had lost several agents over the years. Those were some of the worst moments of Yosef's life. He felt a deep sense of responsibility. He always did the utmost to keep his agents safe, but there were real dangers inherent in the job.

Yosef had personally recruited Terry. Despite early reservations, she'd stepped up, placing her country before her demanding job and now before her American fiancé. When Agent Steadman had called to report her missing, Yosef understood it was not a lover's quarrel, but the Job. He made a personal vow to track down Terry's abductors and bring them to justice.

Nurit crossed the room and handed him a printout. "Sir, I need to caution you. It is a devastating message."

Yosef reached for the paper, read it over twice and ran for the door.

CHAPTER 27

The Bronx
New York City

The basketball courts in Bronx Park were nearly empty, thanks to the change in weather. The flurries hadn't stuck to the ground but the chill in the air spoke of what was to come.

Jon watched Randy race ahead through the chain link fence, past the brightly graffitied handball court, his child-size ball tucked under his arm. He felt a sense of pride seeing the boy so happy, laughing as Randy began dribbling down the court. The kid was growing like a weed. If he kept it up, he'd soon be ready for a regulation size ball.

Jon missed the sound of the ball pounding the pavement, the exertion and camaraderie that came with a good game. He gave Randy some shooting pointers and was astounded at how quickly the child picked it up, making nearly every basket afterward. "You're a natural," Jon said, ruffling Randy's hair. He got a heart-melting toothless grin in return.

After an hour, Jon said, "It's getting dark. Time to go, little man."

"Five more minutes!" It had become the usual refrain.

Jon laughed. He used to say the same thing to Granny back when he was about the same age as Randy was now. "Okay, five more minutes."

Randy bounced the ball most of the way back to the

apartment. He passed the ball to Jon, who dribbled through his legs, causing Randy to shriek with delight.

Jon put an arm around the boy. "You have fun today?"

Randy nodded, smiling. "Thanks, Papi."

Papi? Randy had said it so casually.

Tears welled up in Jon's eyes. He stayed planted where he was, unsure what to say or do. Correct the child? Randy knew he had a father, as absent as he was. He called him Daddy. Clearly Randy was making a distinction.

Jon opened the building door for Randy. Watching him run to the elevator, Jon wished he had a friend to discuss this situation with. But Gabe had too much on his plate at the moment with Terry's disappearance.

As they approached the apartment door, he decided to run it by Sienna the next time he saw her. Afterall, she was Carrie's long-time friend.

Esther Santiago was sitting at the kitchen table, her calculator app and checkbook in front of her, when Jon gave her a peck on the cheek and took a seat beside her. He'd let himself in with the key they'd given him. "Buenos dias."

"Thanks for taking Randy to the park. It gave me a chance to work on some bills." She glanced at the clock on the wall. "Can you stay for dinner?"

"Not tonight."

"You've been so busy lately. How's work?"

This is work, he thought. "I need to speak with you. It can't wait."

Esther removed the glasses from her eyes, letting them drop to her chest by the lanyard. "Oh?"

"Abuela, do you know who Sienna's father is?"

She seemed relieved with the question. "Of course."

"Why didn't you mention it?"

"Well, we didn't really have much time when you were here last. Besides, I would have assumed you knew."

Jon shook his head. "What can you tell me about her family?"

Esther looked away. "I'm no gossip, Jon."

Jon found her answer curious. "I'm only asking for facts. It could be the thing that keeps Sienna and Jennifer safe."

Esther's eyes widened. "They're in danger?"

"I think so, yes."

"Mis Dios."

Randy came in, took a cookie from the jar and left, unaware of the conversation happening around him.

"We've known the Lamonts for a long time. Sinclair and Raúl went to the academy together. Over time, we made a tight-knit group of young military families, along with another couple, Finn and Ann."

"Have you stayed in touch with the Lamonts?"

"Raúl was better than I was. He did so for a while but it was hard. Each of us went a different way, got stationed in new locations. Eventually, after some health concerns, Raúl decided to leave the military, spend more time with the family." She chuckled. "Or more like *I* decided and he gave in. But we were both happy with that decision.

"Sinclair moved up quickly in the ranks. Finn did as well. But now, it's only holiday cards and the occasional call for life events-births, weddings and so forth. Remembering those times is bittersweet."

Jon knew she meant memories of Carrie. "So you and Abuelo haven't seen Sinclair Lamont for a while?"

Esther shook her head. "Years back we discussed having a reunion, more for the kids than for us. But it never happened. Too complicated with everyone's schedules."

"Can you tell me a bit more about Lamont's job?"

Randy sauntered back into the kitchen, reached for a second cookie. This time Esther stopped him.

Esther whispered to Jon, "Maybe it's time you spoke to Abuelo."

Raúl Santiago sat in his recliner, his reading glasses perched on the tip of his nose, the paper slipping from his hand as he nodded off. Jon took a seat on the sofa, noting that Raúl had lost a good deal of weight in recent months. It was a gradual but stark change from years of rotundity, a result of decades of his wife's exceptional cooking. Perhaps Esther had put her husband on a strict diet.

Esther placed a gentle hand on her husband's arm. "Papi?"

Raúl blinked and snatched the slipping papers. "Si, mi amor."

In his late sixties, Raúl had been a mechanic in the army, serving three tours. Photos of him in uniform were arranged around the home.

Jon recalled that he spoke perfect English, but of late, was frequently reverting to his native Spanish.

"Jon would like to speak with you. Are you up to it now?"

"Of course. Have a seat, young man."

She smiled. "I'll give Randy his dinner and bring you some tea and cookies."

"What's on your mind, son?"

Jon appreciated the endearment. He had no parents of his own and while he adored Granny with all his heart, the Santiagos were the closest he'd come to a traditional family.

Jon asked, "Did you know the Lamonts well?"

Raúl said, "Yes, we served together for several years when the girls were young. Sienna and my Carrie were good friends." He looked off in the distance, lost in his thoughts, the light in his eyes dimming.

Jon couldn't imagine the torture of losing a daughter.

"Did she grow up in a happy home?"

He nodded. "Yes, I believe it was, back then. Never saw signs of major problems. We spent a great deal of time together. Sinc had just finished medical school, wanted to use the degree as part of a military career. After my discharge, I studied engineering. Carrie and Sienna became quite close as I recall."

"You went your separate ways, though it seems."

"It's the nature of the military. Reassignments, lots of relocating. With a demanding job and a young family it can be hard to stay in touch." He smiled as if reminiscing. "But if I saw Sinc today, we'd pick up right where we left off."

Esther placed a tray on the coffee table and left without a word.

Jon helped himself. "After your time together abroad, what did Sinclair end up doing?"

"He became an officer, eventually took a job with the State Department. He's done well for himself."

Jon considered his next question carefully. "Ever regret not taking the same path?"

"Maybe early on. But, as they say, 'happy wife, happy life.' I'm the only one still married."

"You mean the Lamonts' divorced?"

"That's right. As well as other friends. The strain of a high-pressure government job takes its toll."

Esther materialized, setting napkins on the table.

"What happened to Sienna's mother?"

Esther chimed in. "Last we heard, she was living on the Upper West Side. I got the sense the split was a long time coming."

"Do you have her number?"

Esther went to the kitchen and came back with her phone. "I'll send you her contact info."

"Thanks," Jon said, as his phone buzzed. "Abuelo, do you know the sort of job Lamont did for the State Department?"

"Not really. Just that he worked on pretty sensitive projects. He moved around a lot even long after I retired from the army." A pause. "Why aren't you asking these questions to Sienna? She'll know better than I do. My memory isn't what it used to be."

"Papi," she said gently, "I'm sure Jon has his reasons."

"Can you recall where Sienna's family moved to?" Jon asked.

Raúl pursed his lips. "Let's see. We received holiday cards every year. Still do. Germany, then stateside. DC, of course, Hawaii, California. Maybe there were a few other posts, but I don't remember."

Jon sat up straighter. "Hawaii?"

Esther said, "That's right. the Lamonts had spent some time there when their girls were little." She exchanged a glance with Raúl. "They went back from time to time. Sienna invited Carrie to go visit her after graduation, spend a few weeks before college, but the tickets were too expensive." Esther's face fell. "We should have tried harder to find the money."

Raúl took his wife's hand. Jon felt awful for dredging up the memories. These people had gone through hell.

As if reading his mind, Esther said, "We think about her every day. It's the little things. No way around it."

The words did little to absolve him. He got up, kissed Esther's cheek and thanked them both. "Can I say goodnight to Randy?"

"He scarfed down his dinner and went to bed. He was wiped out."

"Then I won't rile him up again."

As Esther walked him to the door, a wave of melancholy fell over him. "Is Abuelo all right?"

Only now Jon noticed the circles under Esther's eyes. "He seems to remember some things like they happened yesterday. Other things, less so. I made an appointment with a gerontologist for next Tuesday."

Jon said, "He's still young. Don't worry."

His words seemed to fall on deaf ears.

On his way out the door, Esther called out, "Wait." She hurried inside, then came back and handed him a small package. "You forgot your cookies."

Jon stepped closer, and noting the pain in her eyes, brought Esther in for a hug, holding her until the tears stopped falling.

Back on the sidewalk, Jon thought of Gabe, left to his own devices. Like the Santiagos, Gabe had lost a loved one. His sister, Ashleigh. Now he was faced with losing his fiancée.

When Shira had called asking Jon to reel Gabe in, it felt like walking a tightrope. If he took a misstep, it would not be only him that would fall. It would be all of them.

***

Jerusalem

Shira closed the office door behind her and took a seat opposite Yosef Kahn.

He didn't beat around the bush. "You're being activated."

"I'm a handler not an asset," Shira replied, confused.

"You've worked with Dr. Lavi. You know how she functions, how she thinks."

"Then, the message has been authenticated?"

Yosef nodded, soberly. "It originated in Central Colorado. Private server. We're working on pinpointing the exact location."

"What do we know about Charlotte Colbert?"

Kahn had received the preliminary report minutes prior. "She's a businesswoman, grandmother, computer science whiz and—" he raised a brow— "aficionado of biogenetics."

"With an unfortunate alter ego."

"Correct," Kahn said. "Dr. Lavi will not sell out to her."

Kahn was being uncharacteristically direct . . . and partial. It was not lost on Shira that he strongly believed in Terry's loyalty. Still, the reality was under such murky circumstances, traitorous behavior could not be ruled out. Shira hoped this wouldn't prove to be the one time Kahn made a disastrous judgment of character. Kahn was known as the shrewdest director to date, dubbed The Mentalist because he seemed to read people's minds and intentions.

He said, "I need you to carry out an extraction. Do whatever is necessary to find her. I want Dr. Lavi back safely where she belongs."

"Understood. I have an idea that should speed things up, but it's unconventional."

"Nu?"

Shira explained her plan. They discussed everything that could go wrong. When they were done, Yosef stood up, his gaze meeting Shira's dark brown eyes. His voice was firm and resolute. "Do it."

***

Shira made a beeline to her car. Her flight to New York was leaving in a couple of hours. They would hold the plane for her if necessary but she didn't want to draw any unwanted attention. Kahn agreed that the trip was warranted. Better to discuss the matter face-to-face.

People found her intimidating and she used that to her advantage. Much of the demeanor was her basic nature. The rest from closely observing her boss, Yosef Kahn. One day she would pursue his job. Optimally his retirement and her rise in the ranks would coincide. She wasn't one to bite the hand that fed her, but she was driven to succeed.

In recent weeks, Shira had concluded that Terry wasn't cut out for clandestine work. To Shira's estimation, the scientist had allowed her personal life to interfere with the job, something that could one day be exploited, endangering her and those around her. As much as Shira was stoic, Terry was emotional. To Shira that equaled volatile.

But after sitting in the small, padded room beside the deputy director on the lower level of the Knesset, Shira's opinion changed completely. Terry had singlehandedly acquired top secret intel discovered in the hands of an enemy of the State and warned her superior. It was nothing short of heroic.

Kahn had immediately set into motion a series of emergency protocols designed to thwart a potential attack on the country's nuclear installations. The IDF's top command would already be alerted. Shira knew very little about Israel's nuclear program, but suspected as most did, that it was well-protected by both human and natural defenses. She could only pray that Israel was prepared, even for the worst.

The fact that Kahn summoned her, Terry's erstwhile handler, soon after receiving Terry's message, spoke volumes. Her boss believed in her and she would live up to his expectations.

***

Lake San Cristobal

Terry sat on the bed, shaking uncontrollably, her heart racing like a locomotive. The realization of what she had pulled off was hitting home. No alarms had blared, no lights burst on in the house when she'd snuck back in through the window. She caught sight of herself in the standing mirror across from the bed. Her hair was still stuffed under the cap, her pants only slightly stained. She'd need to brush the muck off the shoes. But for now, she needed a shower, to decompress. She undressed, tossing the clothes aside.

She set the water as hot as she could tolerate and took her time, regaining her equilibrium. She could now dissect her movements, assess if she'd made a misstep that would alert Charlotte or Simon. Only the coming hours would tell if her derring-do had succeeded.

A mess of questions filled her mind as she stood under the hot stream. Would Kahn send a search and rescue team to Colorado? Terry tried to picture Kahn's people in a tizzy, working to evacuate her. How long would it take for agents to get all the way here?

Or was the focus solely on undoing the damage caused by Israel's security breach? If that were true, an argument could be made to cover their bases and drop a bomb on the entire compound facility, taking out the house and command center in one fell swoop. Collateral damage was against Israel's policy but the stakes could easily be deemed high enough for an exception.

Terry thought of little Cosette. She would be terrified. Maybe she should have mentioned the presence of a child in her message to Yosef.

Terry toweled off, put on a t-shirt she found in the dresser and got under the covers. Exhaustion was taking over. As sleep claimed her, she knew she'd done all she could possibly do.

CHAPTER 28

Upper West Side
New York City

Jon took the subway up to 96th Street and Broadway and walked east toward Amsterdam. He found the building mid-block. A doorman with the nametag, *Larry*, greeted him. "Visiting?"

Jon said, "Yessir. Apartment 4E, please." He gave his name.

Larry sat behind a console and punched in some numbers on a landline phone. "Ms. Lamont, a Mr. Steadman is here to see you."

A moment later, Jon was buzzed in, passing a bank of mailboxes before reaching the elevator that took him to the fourth floor. He had come straight from home and was casually dressed in jeans and sneakers. Showing up on Mrs. Lamont's doorstep looking like a typical Fed would scare the daylights out of her.

Regina Lamont was waiting for him in the doorway. Sinclair's ex-wife was a beautiful woman despite looking fatigued. Light hair, cut short and dark bags under her baby blue eyes. Her casual but expensive-looking attire perfectly fit her slim figure. There was a clear resemblance to Sienna.

Regina invited him in, offering a bottle of water. The apartment was spacious and decorated in high-end minimalist furnishings. She showed him into a living room.

Jon said, "Thanks for seeing me . . . and not mentioning it to Sienna." He'd said the same thing to both of Sienna's parents. It felt hypocritical. Maybe he'd been too harsh on her for keeping some things to herself.

"I assumed it had something to do with my girls' father. Why upset her further, right?"

Jon nodded. "How are you holding up?"

"I haven't had much sleep. Pretty much living on chai lattes. Do you have any updates on Jen's whereabouts?"

He wished he could reveal that her daughter was safe. Jon shook his head. "Still working on it. We're doing all we can."

"I appreciate it."

Unsure how to give the woman peace of mind, Jon changed the subject. "The Santiagos send their best."

Regina seemed generally happy with the regards. "You know Esther and Raúl?"

"Yes, ma'am. I was good friends with their daughter, Carrie."

"Oh, I see. I'm sorry for your loss."

"Thank you." Jon glanced at his watch. "I'm tight on time. If you wouldn't mind answering some questions."

"I'll do my best."

Jon jumped right in. "Can you tell me about your time in Hawaii?"

Regina seemed surprised by the question. "I wondered how long it would take for someone to come knocking."

"How do you mean?"

Regina tilted her head. "How much do you know about what Sinc did back then?"

"Bits and pieces. That's why I'm here."

"Look, I have no desire to get him into trouble."

"I appreciate that. My sole focus is getting information that will lead me to Jennifer." *For now.*

It was almost as if he could say anything to give her an excuse to talk about her ex-husband without being deemed a shrew.

"By the time we moved to Maui, we'd relocated six or seven times. It takes its toll, you know."

"On the kids?"

"Jen, mostly. Sienna sort of rolled with the punches. She was used to challenges, being in competitions and all. And she had Carrie, whose family for years moved with us. It was hardest on me and Jen."

Jon got the sense that both of Sienna's parents were more concerned with themselves than their children's wellbeing. "What sort of work *was* your husband doing back then?"

"He was put in charge of a clinic."

"Is he a doctor?"

"Yes, though as far as I know he wasn't spending much time practicing medicine. It was more about his knowledge base than treating patients."

"What sort of clinic?"

"I never knew exactly what went on over there since it was classified but at one point Sinc wanted Jen to take part in clinical trials. He said it was a once in a lifetime opportunity. That it would help her development."

"What about Sienna?"

"He said she was too young. Anyway, I put my foot down. I wasn't going to allow my daughter to be a guinea pig. Glad I did, especially after that poor child died."

"Oh? What happened?"

"It was so tragic. Sinc came home one day very upset. One of the children in the trial had a bad reaction to the treatment. Jen was good friends with the little boy. He was one of her only friends."

Sienna had not told him any of this. Jon wondered how much of it she even knew.

"Everything was hush hush and my guess is the government paid off the parents—enough to stay quiet and not press charges. Anyhow, the whole affair was the first crack between Jen and her father. They never really got back on track. Not long after, the program was shut down and we were relocated once again. To DC. By then my marriage was on its last legs. The girls were getting older and Jen and Sinc were fighting all the time. It was a challenging time."

"I'm sorry to have to ask this but do you think your husband was directly involved in the boy's death?"

Regina seemed to give it serious thought. "I've wondered that myself over the years. But no. For all his faults, Sinc loves the girls in his own way. He wouldn't suggest subjecting Jen to a treatment that he believed could have such devastating results."

"Maybe he didn't know."

"He was the top dog. I have to assume he knew everything that went on there. That said, the death was an anomaly in my opinion. Something they never foresaw."

Jon wasn't so sure. He'd seen people with ironclad beliefs do awful things, including to family members.

She paused, became pensive. "You know, as much as Sinclair believes Sienna is fragile, it's not the case. Other than her bout of depression after that jackass broke her heart, Sienna has been the stronger of my two girls. When she wants something, she goes after it, hard. Just like her father. Jen was the volatile one, always caught up in some mischief, pushing the boundaries, needing extra attention. Look what good it's done." Her face turned despondent.

Jon sensed it was time to go. "I really appreciate you speaking with me. I'll be in touch when I find out more."

"No matter *what* you find out. All right?"

Jon wasn't sure she really understood what that could mean. "All right," he said, and bid her farewell.

***

Jon left Regina's building, waving to Larry the doorman. He was surprised by the wacky temperate weather, once again warm enough for a run. He was only a few blocks from Central Park, wearing his good sneakers. He crossed into the park, clicked his favorites playlist and picked up his pace. Soon, a woman drew alongside him.

Jon slowed to a jog, pulled the earbud from his ear and turned to face her. Recognition hit him. "Shira?"

She wasted no time with pleasantries. "My boss would like me to speak with you."

Jon had declined the opportunity to work with the Israelis on an official basis. Yet here he was being approached by one of the Mossad's operatives.

His feelings about Shira were complex. The stoic woman had been instrumental in saving his hide on a previous mission. Without her intervention, he'd be dead. And yet, here she was 'pulling a Kahn.' It was the perfect play on words. Like Kahn, Shira was manipulating people and events to skew things her way. Right now, with Terry still missing, none of that mattered.

The consequences of engaging with her any further, could prove as severe as discharge from the FBI, even federal charges. As much as he cared for—loved—Terry, Kahn was asking too much of him.

And yet.

Jon came to a stop. "What do you want, Shira?"

The Israeli seemed to appreciate the bluntness. "We heard from Terry."

The relief was instant. "She's all right?"

"Unclear."

Shira passed along Terry's message for Gabe. She explained that Terry was believed to be in Colorado, though the specific circumstances were unclear. "We need your help to find her."

Terry had saved his life. Back in Rome when he'd been taken captive. She put her own life at risk to help him, along with the hesitant aid of her government. How could he not return the favor?

To keep warm, Jon began jogging in place. "Believe me, I want to help Terry. But like you, my time is not my own. I'm working on an important case. It's hit a vital juncture. I can't just walk away. I need to speak to my boss, get his seal of approval before getting involved again with your service."

Shira said, "Do what you need to do. But do it fast. We are pressed for time. It's possible Dr. Lavi is under duress. I'll need your answer right away."

Jon studied her emotionless face. "Why me?" he asked. "Surely, the Mossad has well-trained agents for this sort of thing."

"The director thought it best to have an American leading the search and rescue," she said. "Israel cannot be seen operating on American soil. We've worked efficiently together in the past, and Dr. Lavi trusts you."

Search and rescue?

"Meet me first thing tomorrow." He told her where. Without another word, Jon picked up his pace, leaving Shira far behind.

***

When Jon reached Central Park West, he walked south toward the subway, deliberating his next move. He knew it was against the rules but he made the call anyway. It's what he would expect in the reverse.

Gabe answered on the first ring as if the phone was already in his hand. "Jon?"

"Terry sent a message," he said, seemingly knowing not to waste a syllable on pleasantries.

"Thank God! What did she say?"

"That she's sorry and loves you."

A choked sob came through the line. "She's alive," Gabe said.

Jon reached the stairwell, taking the steps two at a time. "Yes, bro. But don't stop praying. We still need to bring her home."

***

Jerusalem

Gabe was walking along Emek Refaim Street, a bustling thoroughfare, on his way to evening prayer services when Jon called telling him Terry was okay. Or okay enough to send him a message. It felt as if he'd been held under water, and with only moments left, kicked to the surface, gasping for air.

A group of rowdy teenagers spilled out of Aldo's ice cream shop. He pressed his phone more firmly to his ear. "What else can you tell me?"

"Nothing yet," Jon said. "But—"

Gabe jumped on it. "But what? What do you know?"

A pause. Then, "We have an idea where she is."

"Where?"

"Somewhere in Colorado."

Gabe felt a wave of relief. "I've been sick with worry, trying everything to help her. I haven't made any headway. I came so close but Kahn seems to have influence everywhere."

"Try to hang in there. You still in Jerusalem?"

Gabe let out a strangled breath. "Yeah. I've already missed a few work meetings back in Austin. I probably just lost an important account. I'm a mess. If they know where Terry is, Kahn's people can go and get her, right?"

"It's not that simple," Jon said. "This is foreign territory for the Israelis."

"Then, you get her."

"Believe me, I'm working on it. This is a hot potato, politically."

Gabe couldn't believe what he was hearing. "If you think I'm allowing the love of my life to get caught in a political mess, you're out of your mind! If no one else is going after her, I'll figure out how to do it myself . . . I'll call the *New York Times*, every national radio station, tell them she was kidnapped—"

"Hold your horses. We'll get her. We just need to go through the right channels."

Gabe felt something rise inside him. Anger. And it was directed at his best friend. His brother. "You sound like a Fed. What happened to the 'eff the system' guy I know? Come on, Jon!"

A pause. "I'll try not to take that personally. I am doing everything humanly possible to help you. Trust me. Okay?"

"Not this time, Jon. I need you to convince Kahn to let me come along."

Jon let out a strained laugh. "You must be joking. There's no way."

"Have I ever asked you for anything? All these years I've tried to be a good friend. Even when you kept important information from me, I understood."

"You've always had my back."

"Now I need—no, I'm begging you—to be there for me."

"What you're asking, I can't do. Even if I had the power to involve you, it would be too dangerous. I can't be responsible for another life taken."

Gabe's face fell. "I can't believe it."

"What?"

"I never thought this day would come."

"I don't know what you mean," Jon said, his voice suddenly tentative.

"The day our friendship would end."

***

New York City

Jon entered his apartment, shrugged off his coat, placing it on the back of his kitchen chair and made a beeline for his hidden stash of whisky. He didn't waste time with a glass. He put the bottle to his lips and sucked down a mouthful, impatiently waiting for it to take effect.

After the shared loss of Ashleigh, Jon believed nothing could ever damage his friendship with Gabe. Apparently he'd been wrong.

Jon paced the apartment running through their conversation in his mind. Why wasn't the whiskey working? He rummaged through his coat pockets, found his pill bottle and downed two tablets. Then a third.

Fifteen minutes later he was passed out on the living room floor.

***

FBI Headquarters
New York City

Doug Matthews walked into the office late. He was dressed in a new suit, his shirt collar stiff with starch, his tie perfectly knotted. Jon was still unaccustomed to seeing his once-disheveled boss so well-groomed. He'd made that change since his wife Erica's passing and seemed to be sticking with it.

Matthews passed Jon's desk. "You got a bug, Steadman? You look like hell."

Over the partition, Jon heard Craig snicker.

"Got a lot on my mind."

"The Maui case?"

"No, sir."

Matthews whispered. "Still taking those meds?"

If not for Matthews's look of concern, Jon would have had a hard time containing his irritation. Did his boss ask all his underlings about their private conditions?

Before he could answer, Jon heard the phone ringing from Matthews's office. His boss gave him a curious look and turned away, hurrying into his office and shutting the door behind him.

Jon checked the time. It had been two hours since he'd spoken with Shira. Two more hours that Terry could be fighting for her life. But he now had information he was required to provide to his superiors. If he did so, the relationship between the two countries would be further strained. Despite all his attempts to remain within the lines of his job at the FBI, he kept finding himself drawn outside them. Jon couldn't take it anymore. He jumped to his feet, feeling a sudden desperation.

Craig must've seen something fierce on his face and raised a brow. "Whoa, bro."

Jon burst into his boss's office, catching Matthews by surprise. He had a phone at his ear. "What the—"

Jon said, "Sir, we need to talk. Now."

Matthews studied Jon's face. He spoke softly into the phone. "Something just came up. I'll call you back." Matthews's tone was one Jon had only heard him use with one other person. *Erica.*

"Goddammit, Steadman. What on Ear—"

Jon interrupted his boss once more, grabbed Matthews's suit jacket off the hook on the back of the door. "Let's go for a walk."

Matthews's looked like he would blow a gasket. "Who do you think you are?"

"You asked me what's wrong. Do you want to hear about it or not?"

Matthews stared at Jon, now seeing full-on desperation.

He let out a groan. "You're a piece of work." Angrily he grabbed his jacket from Jon and followed him out the door.

CHAPTER 29

J on sat on a bench in Thomas Paine Park, a short walk from
Federal Plaza, waiting for Doug to join him. Pigeons cooed
as they bobbed their heads in search of breadcrumbs left
behind by the old man slowly making his way out of the park.
The Jenga Building, as it was known due to its resemblance
to the block-stacking game, loomed in the background. A
behemoth of a construction crane moved lazily across the sky
in front of it. Traffic noise competed with drilling from the
road repair a few blocks away. For Doug to hear him, Jon would
need to speak louder than he'd prefer.

"You've dragged me far enough, Jon. What is going on?"
He sounded more in control, his earlier indignation seemingly
taking a back seat to his concern.

"We can't speak in the office."

Doug appeared exasperated. "What are you involved in
now?"

"I met with one of Kahn's handlers."

The surprise was written all over Doug's face. "You met
an Israeli operative?"

Jon nodded. "She reached out to me."

Doug's face turned red. "Kahn's still trying to recruit
you for that liaison job?"

"No. It's about something else. Terry—Dr. Lavi. She's
in trouble and the Israelis think they know where she is."

According to Shira, she'd gone willingly. If he said as much to Doug, the conversation would be over. Either way, Jon was certain Terry was in danger.

Doug sat. "I'm sorry to hear that. Dr. Lavi is an exceptional woman. But why are they involving you, an American federal officer, in their problems? What kind of game is Kahn playing now?"

The question was rhetorical. Jon knew there was no love lost between the two men. He didn't want Terry to pay the price for that. Again. But he couldn't pursue the matter without sharing it with his boss. There was too much for him to lose. His job, for one.

And perhaps even more important—Matthews's trust.

"Here's the thing. The same way they need our help to extract Terry, we can benefit from theirs."

Matthews seemed to immediately grasp what Jon was suggesting. "Keep talking."

"The Lamont case. We need to know what happened at the clinic back when Lamont was in charge. And why someone is willing to kill to keep us from finding out what it is. We've both been sandbagged. You by Lamont and me in Hawaii. Lamont or whoever else is involved, has power. It's why we're being kept in the dark by whichever intelligence branch is after him. The Israelis can help skirt those political landmines."

Matthews, who had been listening intently, said, "If Kahn can get me info to bring Lamont down, I'll help him get Dr. Lavi."

"I'll work on it." As Jon headed out of the park, the seed of an idea began to form in his head. He was still reeling from the call with Gabe, unwilling to accept the end of their decade-long friendship. Maybe, if he played his cards just right, he could assist the Israelis, get their help with Lamont, and maneuver his friendship back on track. There were many moving parts, people to win over. Jon allowed the strategy to grow. If he could pull it off, he'd finally be the one to draw a winning hand.

***

The Lower East Side
Manhattan

Shira allowed Jon to take the lead as they headed west past the storefronts still bearing the names of their original owners. Gus's Pickles, Shalom Dry Goods, Bernstein's Deli. One of the few remaining enclaves of Manhattan retaining its old-world flavor, the Lower East Side refused to fully disappear despite the encroaching gentrification. Still, it was only a matter of time. The brick tenements, once a shtetl, were the latest draw for young professionals with money to burn. Gutted and renovated, those same apartments commanded price tags north of a million dollars. New boutique hotels and galleries popped up each year just blocks from Delancey.

They'd met at the bustling Times Square's red steps, sidestepping ticket scalpers and selfie-sticks and switching subways several times to be sure no one was following them.

It was time to find a quiet, less crowded environment. Jon asked, "Have you ever seen the Highline?"

Shira shook her head. She was a woman of few words, often accused of poor social awareness. She had no problem with that association. It allowed her to get away with more.

"Come, I'll show you."

Jon directed her to a flight of stairs leading up to old train tracks retrofitted into an urban garden that ran from Gansevoort Street north to 34th street. It reminded Shira of Jerusalem's First Station, a reinvented train depot now lined with upscale eateries and an outdoor music venue.

The sun was high in the sky, burning off some of the early winter chill. They sat on a bench overlooking the intersection of 14th St. and 10th Avenue.

She explained most of what she knew regarding

Terry's situation, leaving out the White Knight's true identity and what Colbert was holding over them—Israel's nuclear coordinates. It was Kahn's decision if the Americans should be privy to that information.

Jon's face filled with alarm. "It's true, then? The White Knight has her?"

Shira nodded. "We still don't know under what pretense."

Jon's eyes squinted, seemingly more from skepticism than the sun's glare. "What the hell does that mean?"

"Our investigation indicates she went willingly."

"You must be joking. There's no way Yosef—or you—believe that."

"This job isn't about my beliefs, or the director's. It's about following up on factual evidence."

"Are you telling me that Terry Lavi, a premier ethicist, is engaged in business dealings with one of the world's greatest criminals?"

"No. What I'm saying is we can't rule it out simply because we like her." It was true. She did like Dr. Lavi. While Terry's tenure with Mossad was short, she'd proven herself both competent and brave when it mattered most.

Jon pulled a pair of gloves from his pockets, slipping them on. "I have an idea but I haven't fleshed it out yet. We can use Gabe, Terry's fiancé, as bait."

It took a moment for Shira to grasp what Jon was suggesting. It was ludicrous. They'd spent recent days trying to rid themselves of Gabriel Lewis.

"Not possible. Neither of our agencies will approve that. Bringing him into the mix would both jeopardize the operation and the man's life."

Jon's jaw hardened. "It's non-negotiable."

Shira was impressed, something that didn't happen often. And yet both Terry and Jon had managed to do so. Jon wasn't backing down but this wasn't a decision she could make.

Shira remained quiet for a full minute, then pulled out her phone. "I'll be back. Wait here." She walked along the walkway, made the call. Ten minutes later, Jon was still there, his face red from cold. Shira sat beside him, avoiding his eyes. "My boss wants a word with you. Will your boss allow for it, *now*?"

Jon stood. "Lead the way."

***

Consulate General of Israel
New York City

Jon and Shira sat in a windowless room on the fifth floor of the Israeli consulate facing a large screen affixed to the wall. Yosef Kahn stared back at them. He was seated at a wide laminate desk, the blue and white flag positioned behind him. It felt like a private state of the union. Jon had no doubt it was intentional, staged for optimal effect.

Kahn said, "Thank you for coming, Agent Steadman, despite having refused the liaison job. But the situation has become dire." A pause. "I'm asking a personal favor. One which I am prepared to repay."

Jon understood what Kahn was alluding to. The only reason Jon was now in the room was because Matthews had sanctioned it with the caveat of Kahn agreeing to a quid pro quo.

Kahn said, "You are in a unique position to find her, Agent Steadman. Let me be perfectly frank with you. Dr. Lavi is in terrible danger."

Jon noted the director's stoic veneer was gone.

"She's managed to send us a message but in so doing will surely have alerted the White Knight. We have the ability to exercise a targeted extraction but since our last joint venture, we've had several U.S. intelligence services breathing down our necks. If we attempt a solo clandestine operation on American soil and it comes to the attention of your government, it will spark an international incident we won't soon recover from."

What Kahn was asking of Jon was not an act of treason but if unsanctioned, he'd lose his career and end up in prison. It was an enormous ask. But would serve Jon as a particularly appealing bargaining chip.

Jon took a deep breath. It was time to make the offer.

He spent the next twenty minutes conveying Matthews's proposal. In return for Israeli assistance with the Lamont case, Jon would be allowed to assist with finding Terry. He added his own cherry on top, using the same words that worked on Shira. "You want me, you get Gabe Lewis too. We're a package deal."

Kahn frowned. "What you're suggesting is involving a civilian in a highly classified extraction. The operation is already a significant risk. Why would you make such a request?"

Jon knew this was Kahn's way of negotiating.

"Gabe has been nothing but supportive of Terry's . . . extracurricular activities on behalf of her homeland. He's been left in the dark, only privy to her need to assist you on a moment's notice. Now he's asking to be brought in. His fiancée is missing. He wants—no, he needs—to be proactive. He's tired of waiting for the powers that be to save the day. I can't say I blame him. Taking action to help Terry will keep him grounded and focused. He'll function just fine."

Kahn waved a hand, dismissively. "Surgeons don't operate on family members for a reason, Agent Steadman. Yet, you think a fiancé is the best person to bring into a high-stress mission?"

Jon went on, ready to put it all on the line. "I've known Gabe for the better part of a decade. He's the most mild-mannered person I've ever met. And the kindest. Yesterday, he was prepared to end our friendship over this. I won't risk losing another person I'm close with." When no one spoke, he added, "It's both of us or no one. Your choice."

It was a bold move. Especially since Kahn had helped Jon once, allowing Terry to track him when he'd been abducted along with Carrie. They'd saved his life. Jon appreciated that Kahn didn't mention it. It would have been overkill. And they both knew the reality. America had more power and one favor did not necessarily command its equivalent in recompense.

Kahn said, "Please excuse us, Agent. Shira and I have matters to discuss."

Jon stood, walked out of the room, hoping by some miracle he'd made the sale.

**

With Jon's departure, Shira sat alone in the conference room. Director Kahn's face still filled the screen.

Shira said, "The Americans' proposal is absurd. The last time we worked with them, they did all they could to burn us. Why are you giving Steadman the idea you're entertaining it?"

"If I recall correctly, the fire went both ways," Kahn said, referring to an Italian scientist now living in Haifa, who the Americans wanted to patriate. "I *am* entertaining it."

Shira raised a brow in disbelief. Before she could retort, Kahn continued. "We can use Gabriel Lewis."

Shira shook her head.

"He is the perfect lure for Charlotte Colbert."

Shira peered at her boss. "Explain."

"Terry's message clearly stated that Gabe was in danger. That means Colbert threatened him. My belief is that Terry showed a reluctance for whatever Colbert wants from her. Which means—"

"She's still on our side." Shira said.

"Correct. Colbert resorted to the perfect coercion— threatening a loved one. If Terry can hold out, it's only a matter of time until Gabe will be targeted."

Kahn never failed to amaze Shira.

He went on. "We can easily get Gabe into the devil's lair. Colbert will never suspect he works for us. For the very reason you don't want to use him for the mission. He's a civilian."

The room went silent for a moment.

Kahn said, "You care for Dr. Lavi."

Shira looked away but didn't deny it.

"Despite what you may think, emotion can be a valuable tool in this business. Our country is built on it."

Shira cleared her throat, uncomfortable with the topic at hand. "How will we keep tabs on Gavriel? If he's caught, they will surely confiscate any tech he has on his person."

Yosef said, "That, we can solve."

Shira could see her boss's wheels turning. She'd heard rumors but . . .

She said, "If the Americans ever got wind of this, whatever lingering goodwill remains, will instantly evaporate, the consequences beyond repair."

"We have no choice but to allow Steadman and his superior to manage that. Gavriel is here in Israel now. Come back and train him. Then you can return to the States together for the extraction."

Silence ensued.

Kahn said, "You want my job one day."

Shira's gaze jumped back to her boss. He seemed to read her mind through the screen. The Mentalist.

"Then you must prove you have what it takes to make the tough, at times unconventional, decisions. And be prepared to live with the consequences. As the Americans say, the buck will stop with you. If the mission succeeds you will earn the credit and if it fails you will take the fall. Understood?"

Shira looked into Yosef Kahn's piercing eyes. "*Ken Hamifaked*," she said, using the colloquialism for a soldier to her superior.

"Bring Steadman back in."

***

"Do we have an agreement?" Jon said, trying not to shift nervously in his chair.

Kahn said, "We do. Mr. Lewis will need to be adequately trained. In return for your help extracting Dr. Lavi, we will find out all we can about the clinic's history and Deputy Director Lamont."

The two agencies—two countries—were once again combining forces, even if it was at best a shaky alliance. Jon found it off-putting that a foreign entity could access classified U.S. intelligence when neither he nor Matthews could. Still, there was an odd comfort in knowing Kahn was on the job.

Jon said, "I'll speak to my boss, go over the details with him. As I told Shira, I'm still working the Lamont case. While your help will be appreciated, I need his approval to be diverted to Colorado when the time comes."

Jon couldn't fathom a scenario that would allow for Gabe or himself to partake in such an operation, but it wasn't his problem. It was Matthews's. If he wanted Lamont badly enough, he'd do his best to make it happen.

Kahn said, "Time is of the essence. If Dr. Lavi is still alive, her chances of survival drop with each passing day."

Jon heard Gabe's voice in his head. *I can't live without her.* He stood, bid Shira and Yosef goodbye, feeling a renewed sense of purpose. While sharing the details with his boss might put the kibosh on it all, he'd resigned himself to Matthews's authority on the matter. Now, all he could do is use every tool in his arsenal along with Matthews's virulent animosity for Lamont, to convince his boss to forge ahead.

***

Jaffa Gate
Jerusalem

Gabe passed under the ancient stone archway and into another world. He skirted by an Arab teen dressed in a faded Rolling Stones t-shirt, pushing an empty wheelbarrow over the narrow cobblestone road.

The Tower of David stood to Gabe's right. A two-thousand-year-old fort dating back to the Ottoman era, the complex was one of countless archaeological sites within a compact area spanning less than a half-square mile. Holy to the world's largest religions, one empire after the next made a point to conquer the beleaguered city.

Gabe walked by a deeply wrinkled woman emerging from the souk, deftly balancing a basket of bread on her head. He joined a group of hatted hasids, their swinging white fringes emerging from beneath their button-down shirts, out of sync with their long, curled sidelocks. He figured they would lead him to the Jewish Quarter and the Wailing Wall, where he could pray for Terry's safe return. Turning left into a narrow alley, Gabe sensed a presence beside him.

"May I call you Gavriel?"

Gabe turned to see a dark-haired woman perhaps five years his senior. She was fit and from her strong accent, Israeli. "Who are you?"

"My name is Shira. I'm a friend of Terry's."

He stopped cold, the hasids forced to maneuver around them.

Shira asked, "Do you know where she is?"

As angry as Gabe was at Jon, he wouldn't out him for sharing Terry's location with him off-the-record. He shook his head.

A pause as Shira studied him. Then, in a whisper, she said, "A ranch house in Colorado. Dr. Lavi helps us. You understand?"

Matching Shira's volume. "Yes, I think I do. Is that what this is about? She's not a puppet, you know. Dropping everything the moment Kahn calls." Gabe felt days of pent-up frustration rise to the surface. He hissed, "You've made my search for her an absolute nightmare."

Shira ignored his complaint, gesturing for him to follow her. She guided him silently until they reached the Cardo, the ancient Roman marketplace, its underground tunnel now lined with posh art galleries and souvenir stores. She gestured for Gabe to sit beside her. "You know the director?"

"He's called Terry a few times while I was around."

"Then you know he's an important man."

Gabe nodded.

"Kahn took her off the last assignment. She's not currently on a job."

Gabe was trying to make the pieces fit. "All I care about is Terry's welfare. The last I saw her she had no money. How did she get to Colorado if Kahn had nothing to do with it?"

"There are only a few possibilities. Perhaps she met up with someone who helped her."

Gabe shook his head, interrupted her. "Terry doesn't know anyone on the Isle of Palms. And besides, she would never leave that way." Gabe's face paled. "Someone took her against her will."

Shira stopped him. "I've been in the business long enough not to jump to conclusions. I would advise you to do the same."

"Will you tell me how to reach her? Please?" He knew how he sounded. Pathetic. Lovelorn. He didn't care.

When Shira broke eye contact, he said, "I'm not one to lose my temper, but I'm pretty damn close. Tell Kahn to get her out."

"It's not that simple."

"It is for me. I won't sit idly by while my fiancée's life hangs in the balance."

"That's why I'm here, Gavriel. It's not Kahn, who needs

to get her. It's you."

***

Jerusalem

Yosef was one of an elite group of people in his country who knew the nuclear program had been expanded over a decade ago. For this very purpose.

An underground facility built under a cloak of secrecy, it had been spearheaded by the top echelons of government, his predecessor among them. They'd been charged with maintaining its highly classified status. Like most such programs, it attracted a minority of powerful and vocal critics. Earmarking a chunk of the government's budget for the secondary plant—one that only a handful of people would even know existed—was unpopular when a threat wasn't imminent. The secrecy of using nearly a billion dollars of taxpayer funds on what was deemed by its detractors as a backup plan was challenging, to say the least. A tiny country, Israel's citizens already bore the brunt of exorbitant taxes. Raising them had the potential to impact the economy to a crippling degree.

The prime minister at the time was adamant. The country was frequently at war with its hostile neighbors. A billion dollars to minimize an existential threat was a price he was willing to pay. And Yosef could only be thankful for it now. As unlikely as it was given the clandestine nature of the project, he nevertheless needed to consider the possibility that the White Knight had acquired the coordinates of the backup location as well.

He would never admit it but there was a thrill to the situation. The greatest chess player of all time, Bobby Fischer, once said, "Chess is a matter of delicate judgment, knowing when to punch and how to duck."

Like chess, this too was a battle of wits. Yosef's strategy

was forming in his mind. He'd already set some of his pawns in motion. If he was careful, deliberate, planned his moves out with precise calculation, he would face down the White Knight, until he declared check mate.

CHAPTER 30

Lake San Cristobal

Terry blew into her hands to keep warm as she walked by the horse stable, picking up the distinct smells of hay, leather, and manure. She was glad to get out of the house, finding the brisk air invigorating. Her movements hadn't been restricted whatsoever. Actually, nothing had changed since she'd made the middle-of-the-night excursion to the command center. Whether or not her message had successfully reached Kahn, remained a mystery.

She told Charlotte that without internet she'd need several books to do her work properly. She couldn't stall for much longer. Angering Charlotte would lead to disastrous results.

"Hi, Terry." Cosette stepped out of the stable, holding the reins of a chocolate brown pony. "This is Bella."

"She's a beauty." Terry stroked the horse's mane. It whinnied in response.

"She likes you."

Terry looked around. "Where's Carmen?"

"In the barn with her friend, Luis. They go there a lot."

Oh. "She leaves you alone?"

"It's okay. She told me to knock if I need her."

"Can you teach me how to brush Bella?"

The child brightened. "Sure. Let's go into the stall. I'll show you."

220

Terry imagined the girl was hoping for the same thing she was. To go home as soon as humanly possible.

***

Municipality Office
Jerusalem

Gabe was sitting on a marble bench in the long, narrow hallway, his foot tapping the matching marble floor. The building gave off a cavernous feel. He wanted to scream and let his frustration bounce off the walls. Shira had told him to wait. Over an hour ago.

"Gavriel?"

"Yes!" He jumped to his feet. A mousy woman of slight build stood there.

"I am Nurit. Come with me." She gestured for him to follow her.

Shira was on the phone in a small office, speaking rapidly in Hebrew. Standing at the window was a broad-shouldered man of average height, his back to the door. He turned, made eye contact with Gabe. Shira placed the receiver in its cradle. She looked exhausted.

When Nurit exited, Shira said, "Gavriel Lewis. Director Kahn."

Gabe was floored. After days of trying to meet the man, the director of the Mossad had come to meet him. What was Terry involved in? "Sir."

Kahn wasted no time. "Your friend, Agent Steadman, has made a compelling argument to bring you in to this delicate operation. Let me be very clear. The terms of your involvement will not leave this room. Understood?"

Gabe assented, allowing a slight smile to reach his lips. "Yes, sir."

Seemingly in response to his positive expression, Shira chimed in. "You may not survive this encounter."

Gabe was stunned by the declaration. He studied her. It wasn't hyperbole. He nodded slowly, processing. "Without Terry, it wouldn't matter."

"I see." A moment passed in what Gabe thought of as a silent test of mettle. They were giving him a chance to back out. When he didn't, Shira passed Gabe a file folder, which he opened.

Inside, were satellite photos. "Dr. Lavi is being held in what amounts to a secure compound in Colorado. We will have one and only one chance to extract her. If we fail, you and your beloved will be beyond any help we can provide. Do you understand?"

Gabe didn't hesitate. "I do."

"Have a seat then, Mr. Lewis. There's no time to waste. Let's begin the briefing."

***

Manhattan

Jon assumed he'd been summoned to help Matthews with something in the new place. When he arrived, Matthews was waiting for him when he got off the elevator, looking annoyed, his default persona. He was wearing his coat and boots. "Let's go for a walk."

Jon knew better than to pepper him with questions when he was like this. "Where to?'

"Anywhere but here."

Twenty minutes later, they were seated at a corner table in Frankie's Tavern, a dive bar in the meatpacking district.

Jon quickly realized this wasn't about work.

Doug ordered two beers. "I forgot how insecure people get in new relationships."

Once again, the line between boss and buddy was

blurred.

Jon nodded. "Yeah, can be a tough, especially for a geezer who's been out of the game for a couple of decades."

Doug took a draw from his bottle of Blue Moon. "Yeah," he said, staring at nothing in particular. "I miss Erica."

Surprised at the admission, Jon said, "Maybe you're jumping into something new too fast." His mind flashed to Sienna.

Doug shrugged. "Beats being alone."

"Does it?"

"You sound just like the shrink."

Jon's ears pricked up. "You too?"

Doug nodded. "We're some pair, you and I, huh?"

Jon raised his bottle, clinking it with his boss's. "Any news on Lamont?"

Doug lowered his voice. "It's why we're here. I don't want to discuss it again in the office or even at my place. Call me paranoid, but the guy seems to have tentacles in every law enforcement agency in the country."

Jon had never seen Doug so intimidated. *He must be getting the brunt of the bureaucracy crap.* "I'm all ears."

"I did some digging on his career. Deep digging."

"Find something?"

"More like what I didn't find. Over twenty years ago he was stationed in Maui."

"I already knew that."

"Shut up and let me finish."

Jon took a handful of nuts, popping one in his mouth. "Go on."

"No one can tell me what he did there back then. It's a two-year black hole. Nothing yet from Kahn. I called in a favor at the CIA, a guy I know who owes me. Can't stand him but he's clean. Best he could do was confirm Lamont was working on a classified program."

"I'd think after more than two decades, someone could get access."

"No one I could find. And believe me, I tried." Matthews paused while a couple walked by. "I reached out to Akamai. He had someone pay a visit to the Hana lab. He said it looks like they've closed up shop. He put me in touch with Pearson."

Surprised, Jon said, "The guy from the Kihei clinic?"

Matthews nodded. "Initially, Pearson was hesitant to talk to me. For obvious reasons. He doesn't want to jeopardize his job."

"What did he say?"

"I told him I needed info on Lamont. He recognized the name as an NSA guy but not from the clinic. He sounded surprised about the connection. He explained that all employee records were kept at the lab."

Jon bristled. "I never made it there."

"I'm aware of that. Even if you had, the chances of Lamont's file still being there were slim. Anyhow, Pearson sounded pretty disgruntled. Said he's been at the job for a couple of years and didn't deserve to be treated that way."

"What way?"

"As the head of the clinic he felt he should've been notified about the lab being moved. He was told about a new Maui location at the last minute like everyone else but couldn't find out any details. He ended up tracking down the moving company. He gave me what looks to be a real lead. I'll send it to you."

"Anything else?"

"Yeah, he said, and I quote, "If you have the balls to go after Lamont, you'll have to do so on enemy territory.""

"What the hell does that mean?"

"It means that when you were in Maui, you were on the wrong island."

***

John F. Kennedy Airport

Jon was waiting in the airport lounge for his flight. It had been delayed twice for mechanical problems. Not something passengers liked to hear. The desk agent rebooked him on another flight, this one with a two hour layover in Miami. He still had twenty minutes until boarding. He called Sienna, leaving a message, then made a video call to Esther and asked to speak to Randy. Soon, his face was filling the screen.

"Hey, little man. How was your day?"

Randy proceeded to tell him about his new friend, Sophie. "She's pretty."

"Oh yeah? Is she also nice?"

"I guess so. She shared her Oreos with me."

"Sounds like a keeper." Then, "I'll be away for a bit."

"Where are you going?" Jon thought he saw alarm in the boy's eyes.

"A city that's really far away."

"Will you have somewhere to sleep?"

Jon's smiled. "Sure will."

"Where?"

"It's called the Alahabana Hotel."

"Funny name." Randy repeated it a few times. "You can have my blankey. You just have to bring it back."

Jon kept a straight face. "That's very nice of you but I think I'll use the one the hotel will give me."

Randy seemed to consider that and said, "Well, okay."

"I'll see you when I get back," Jon replied, ever grateful for having little Randy in his life.

He was putting his phone away when he heard the overhead announcement. "Flight 708 is now boarding for Havana." Jon grabbed his bag and made his way to the gate.

CHAPTER 31

Havana, Cuba

Jon stepped out of the airport terminal and into the oppressive heat. A mustard-yellow checkered taxi pulled up to the curb. The driver quickly emerged, scoring the fare before his competitors, keeping his head down as he placed Jon's bag in the car. A slim man, he wore a white guayabera and an old fashioned watch cap low on his brow.

Jon got in the cab, surprised at the man's light skin tone. Intelligent eyes briefly glanced at him in the rearview mirror. "¿Adonde?"

Jon's Spanish was rusty but passable. He gave the hotel address, the driver grunting in response.

Looking out the window, Jon couldn't fathom how this city, lost in time, was a mere ninety miles from the southern coast of Florida. The countries were worlds—and decades— apart. A 1947 Studebaker drove past, its muffler crackling as it scraped the road, tiny sparks flickering from the chassis, fumes spewing from its exhaust pipe. He'd read that Cuba was a retirement home for classic cars, but seeing them in person, Jon thought they were no more than glorified jalopies.

Jon watched in irritation as the meter clicked by. His phone's GPS showed the hotel was only a fifteen-minute ride from the airport and now they'd been in the car without traffic for over twenty. He recalled reading that Cuban taxi drivers had a reputation for taking people "for a ride."

Jon felt his blood pressure rise. "I want to go straight to the hotel."

The driver shrugged his shoulders as if he didn't understand English. Jon would bet otherwise. A taxi driver shuttling tourists on a regular basis, would surely pick up a few words. Even if you had been cut off for decades from your big neighbor to the north.

Jon felt his breast pocket for his pills. They were meant for extreme cases of PTSD, not run-of-the-mill annoyances. He knew the signs and this was not one. It took effort but he left them where they were.

It was dark out now and the lights of Havana were being turned on inside people's homes, shopkeepers locking up for the evening. They reached what appeared to be the center of town. The taxi driver pointed. "El Capitolio," he said, his voice low and gruff.

Jon followed his finger to a stone cupola atop an expansive white building, nearly identical to its counterpart in Washington.

They pulled up to the Alahabana Hotel, a gated, whitewashed two-story hacienda steps from the beach. Jon got out, grabbed his bag from the trunk and tossed thirty pesos into the front seat, leaving no tip.

Bag in hand, he entered the lobby which emitted an old world vibe with contemporary touches. He made for the reception desk.

"Jon?"

He turned, stunned. "Sienna."

"Hey," she said, a nervous smile on her glossy lips. "Looks like I beat you by a couple of hours."

Her nonchalant attitude sparked his ire. "What the hell are you doing here?"

The smile vanished, a grimace taking its place. "The same thing you are. I came to find Jen."

"I'm no longer on your payroll, Sienna. I'm working a new case."

"But it's connected to my sister."

"Why assume that? I have other cases."

"We've spent . . . intimate time together, Jon. I know you won't just leave, knowing my sister and baby are in trouble. We've heard nothing from her or Mike Evans. I need to see her with my own eyes. And so do you." She searched his face. "Am I right? Are you here for her?"

Jon blew out a sigh. "Peripherally." He took hold of her elbow, trying to steer her to the hotel's exit. "You can't stay here."

Sienna crossed her arms. "If anyone has a right to be here, it's me. My child is missing. My *child*, dammit." Her eyes glistened.

Jon softened at her demeanor but he had no intention of telling her he was in Havana to investigate her father. Still, she'd clearly dug in her heels. There'd be no way to shake her. "OK, fine . . . sorry. I was just surprised to see you here. How did you know which hotel I would be at?"

The only person that knew where he was going was Matthews, but that made little sense.

Sienna shook her head, averting her eyes.

"What?" he asked.

"Shouldn't we get you checked in?" She began moving toward the reception desk.

Jon brought her to a stop. "Who told you I'd be here?"

She looked down at his hand, irritated, but didn't pull away. "You have nothing to worry about. Your secret is safe."

Jon's patience was gone. After a long flight and the scamming taxi driver, he didn't want to deal with her dodging every question. "You're not going anywhere until you tell me. This is supposed to be an under-the-radar operation."

Sienna narrowed her eyes, then took out her phone and swiped. She turned it to face Jon, a photo taking up the screen. A grinning Randy was holding a green crayon in one hand and a crude drawing in the other. It looked like a house surrounded by flowers and a rectangular object on the stick-like grass.

"Randy?" Jon was incredulous.

"Abuela—I mean, Esther—said he'd just had a video call with you and wanted to do it with someone else. For some reason, she had me on her mind and called, put him on to talk. He's the spitting image of Carrie at that age." She paused. "He showed me his drawing. I asked him what it was and he told me you went away and he made a picture of your hotel and his blanket."

She put her phone away. "Apparently you said something about a place called Alahabana. He thought the name was funny." Sienna glared at him, a challenge in her eyes. She was right. He *had* told Randy.

Having his plans passed along by a five-year-old was disturbing enough—it never occurred to him the child would spill the beans. Esther had Sienna on the brain because he'd been asking about her. "I won't make that mistake again."

Sienna sighed. "Don't be hard on yourself. Most people think kids don't pay close attention. He's a smart cookie."

"Don't I know it."

"I hear you helped him through a rough patch. The last time I'd seen Randy was before Carrie died. He wasn't speaking, just using gestures. She was really worried he'd be diagnosed with autism. Esther credits you with bringing him out of his shell."

"I don't think autism works that way."

"Maybe not, but now he won't stop talking."

Jon couldn't help but laugh. "I know. Funny kid." It felt good to laugh. "Let's call a truce. I'll get settled in."

"Perfect. I'll find a nice place we can grab some dinner and figure out our next move."

Jon opened his mouth to argue that she wasn't his partner but stopped himself. Sienna had been through the wringer. What harm could come from her tagging along?

***

Gerard pulled the taxicab up to the next corner. His disguise had worked perfectly. He chuckled to himself. He'd become a true man of mystery, a chameleon. Agent Steadman hadn't recognized him even sitting in the back of his taxi!

Of course they'd only met in person on one occasion. At the volcano. Prior to that, they'd spoken only over the phone. Aware his voice could spark Jon's memory, he was careful to keep his words to a minimum.

He'd been tracking Steadman since they'd crossed paths in Lake Tahoe. Tracking the old-fashioned way—not through technology. He'd had enough of that. Once machines came into play, things could go in many unexpected directions and Gerard stayed alive by keeping off the grid.

Smelling his prey in the back of the car had been almost too much to resist. It would have been so easy to rid the world of Steadman. Gerard had gone as far as turning off the main road, heading towards a secluded beach where he could end their game of cat and mouse.

The only problem was it *was* so easy. Taking Steadman out that way would entirely defeat the purpose of a hard-won kill. The playing field needed to be an equitable battle of wits. A hunt of distinction. He'd been seeking a worthy adversary for so long. Since Tahoe, Steadman had piqued his curiosity. Now, he wanted to know what Steadman was doing in Havana. He wanted to know why the Lamont woman was awaiting Steadman's arrival rather than arriving with him.

Observing her through the hotel's front window, it became evident that Steadman was not expecting to see her there. Gerard fired up the engine, feeling a heightened sense of excitement, knowing that a thrilling ride was just around the corner.

CHAPTER 32

Jerusalem

G abe stepped back from the stall and took off his goggles and ear protection, then carefully placed the Beretta down on the table beside him. Shira pressed a button and the paper target depicting a man's torso flew toward them.

Shira was unlike the boisterous, effusive Israelis he'd met before. Emotionless, her English was fluent but monotonous, her affect flat. Despite her manner, Shira came across as competent, well-trained and professional. Both in industry and the military, Israel's women were valued for their intelligence, achieving positions of power not yet seen in the U.S. The fledgling state had elected a female prime minister back in 1969, a glaring cultural distinction in gender perception.

Gabe was gratified to see that every round had hit its mark, creating a zipper down the middle of the target. He owed his appreciation to his Uncle Carl, a gun aficionado, who had taught him about gun use and safety.

Shira studied it. "Meanyen." *Interesting.*

Gabe assumed it was the closest she would get to complimenting him.

"Even better than Dr. Lavi."

"Terry was here?" Gabe asked.

"Of course. All of our recruits need to demonstrate firearm competency."

Gabe knew Terry had completed two years of mandatory service in the IDF. Despite the country's diminutive size, the Israel Defense Forces was known as one of the most advanced militaries in the world. He considered the dangers Terry must have been exposed to. It was sobering. Her devotion to her homeland was unparalleled. Gabe shook his head, trying to clear it. If he was going to succeed and walk out of this nightmare alive with his bride in hand, he would need to regulate himself. Kahn had been openly distrusting of Gabe's lack of military experience, but no one could dispute his marksmanship.

"This mean we're ready to go?"

Shira gave him a strange look. "You have no military experience whatsoever, Gavriel. As much as time is of the essence, your participation in this operation has changed things. So, no, we are not ready to go," she said with disdain. "Your training has only just begun."

**

Lake San Cristobal

Terry put down her pen, yawning loudly. She had run out of excuses. The books she'd requested had arrived. It was only a matter of time before Charlotte would return, asking for results. Terry had gone back and forth whether to sabotage the data. If Charlotte or her buyers got wind of it, all hell would break loose. For now, she was doing the work as slowly as possible, holding on to hope that Kahn would find her soon. She knew her boss well enough. He would be doing everything in his power to bring her home.

She glanced at the large wooden clock on the wall. It was nearly midnight on the coast, seven a.m. in Haifa. Her thoughts turned to her parents in Israel. By now they would have heard about her disappearance from the Isle of Palms. Knowing they were worried brought on a wave of despondency. If this ordeal had taught her anything it was to never again take the ones she loved for granted.

***

Havana

Jon strolled the narrow streets, taking in his surroundings. It was Sunday morning and the city gave off a sluggish vibe. The sun beat down on him and he wished he'd remembered to grab his ball cap. Sienna was still sleeping, offering him an opportunity to get his bearings. They'd agreed that she would stay but he would not share everything he learned unless it pertained to her sister.

Matthews had given Jon the name of a contact, someone well-connected who could direct him where to start. He was to meet the person at the hotel at noon.

Laundry hung from lines far above his head, fluttering in the warm breeze. He passed a wall decorated with street art depicting a beret-wearing Che Guevara, looking off in the distance, yellow sun rays emerging behind him.

The smell of roasting meat wafted from the open windows. A boom box played *No Volveré.*

Yo cuentare a las horas. I will count the hours.

The wistful lyrics brought on a familiar melancholy, quickly dispelled by a car speeding by, raucous music blaring from its open windows.

Jon soon found himself on a bustling avenue of elegant, pastel-colored buildings, a stark change from the down-and-out neighborhood he'd walked through.

The street sign read, *Malecón.* He'd read about the seaside promenade in his guidebook. It stretched from Havana Harbor to the Almendares River, separating the city from the sea. From where he stood he could smell the water and see the seaweed washing ashore, carried by powerful waves fueled by the northerly wind.

The scene stirred up memories of his time in Miami with his then-girlfriend, Melanie. They'd gone for a wedding, the trip ending with him a drunken mess.

Couples strolled past, no one giving him a second look. As Jon crossed the road, he heard a woman shout, tearing him from his reverie. A motorbike, its tires screeching, took the corner, barreling down on him.

Jon jumped out of the way, the bike missing him by inches, he could feel the air swoosh violently against his sleeve. *What the—?*

Shaken to his core, Jon leaned against the seawall, taking a moment to gather himself. Several pedestrians looked on from a distance, oddly impassive.

"Are you okay?"

He turned to see Sienna, hurrying to his side, her face filled with concern. Where had she come from?

"Thank heavens you heard my warning," she said.

Jon's heartrate was still racing. "That guy was crazy. It was almost like—"

"He was aiming for you."

Jon scanned the road. The motorbike was gone. "Exactly."

"Do you think it's the same driver from Hana?" Sienna asked.

"No chance. I checked with the hospitals in Maui. The driver's dead."

The mention of death seemed to hit Sienna like a brick. "Who is behind all this?"

"I'm not sure but whoever it is knows we're in Cuba and doesn't want us here. Has to be someone with eyes and ears everywhere." Jon looked out to sea, his mind awhirl, thinking, *Probably your dear, old dad.*

CHAPTER 33

Jerusalem

G abe sat in the same small office where he received his initial briefing from Shira. Only now he was alone. The training had been rigorous, leaving him sore in places he didn't think could hurt.

Ten minutes elapsed before Nurit entered the office.

"I will escort you to the clinic," she said.

"Clinic?"

Nurit exited, Gabe following behind. They crossed the vast marble lobby, several men gesticulating as they spoke to one another. Everyone seemed to be on a first name basis, the vibe informal and testy, almost family-like. The farthest point of the hallway led to an enclosed bridge, leading to the adjacent building. Traffic flowed smoothly beneath them.

"This way, please." Gabe followed Nurit down an empty corridor till they reached a wide doorway. Nurit scanned her ID tag, allowing them inside a suite of rooms. The interior was all white as if it had been painted the day before. Actually, Gabe smelled lingering fumes.

Nurit said, "This is our new annex for nanotechnology." The pride was evident.

Two lab-coated women, one older, the other closer to his own age, were milling about. The older looked up from what she was doing. "Gavriel Lewis?" she asked, swapping the *b* for a *v*.

"Yes."

"Have a seat in examination room one." Abrupt.

Nurit offered a nervous smile and left him behind.

The door to the examination room opened. The younger woman wheeled in a steel cart. On it, was an oddly-shaped syringe resting on a white cloth. She spoke in a strong accent. It sounded more Russian than Israeli.

"Raise your sleeve."

Gabe raised his hand to stop her. "What is that?"

She raised her brow. "Did they not tell you?"

After days at a snail's pace, everything had been so rushed. Neither Yosef nor Shira said anything about a doctor's visit. "No."

The confused look still on her face, the woman said, "Wait."

She left.

After another ten minutes elapsed, Gabe became increasingly antsy. He tried to analyze his own apprehension. *What did I get myself into?* The self-doubt lasted but a moment. It didn't matter. He'd been more afraid when they'd refused to allow him to participate. If he didn't go along with whatever they expected of him, he'd be out. *Damn!* He shouldn't have protested the inoculation.

Now all he could do was wait. Nurit had confiscated his cellphone and the only things to read were a solitary Hebrew magazine and some signs on the cabinets, ostensibly noting what was stored inside.

Gabe's thoughts turned once again to Terry. She was all that mattered. Was she being held against her will? Imprisoned? Or even worse. *No!*

If he allowed his mind to descend down that rabbit hole, the terror would take hold and he wouldn't be able to do what had to be done.

He pulled the prayer book from his pocket and began to

read from a chapter of *Psalms. I will lift up mine eyes unto the mountains . . .*

A gift from the rabbi he studied with when he'd considered conversion, the book had since provided more comfort than he ever could have imagined.

Gabe was so lost in the powerful words that he didn't hear the door open. "Gavriel."

Shira was standing there, eyeing his prayer book. Something near amusement flickered across her face, then was gone. "I understand there is a problem."

"No problem. The doctor wants to give me a shot. No one mentioned it. What's it for?"

"Questions from someone who said he'd do anything to help."

Gabe held his temper.

"I come from the director's office," Shira said. "He's given me permission to explain." The younger woman returned, and Shira waved her away. She sat, gesturing to the syringe. "It's a new technology that has recently emerged from our biotech labs."

"Terry's?"

"No, but the same institution."

"The Technion."

"Yes."

The Technion, located in the northern city of Haifa, was established in 1912 by three young men, convinced of the need for a university emphasizing studies in technology. It still ranked as one of the world's top academic institutions.

Gabe gestured to the cart. "What does the shot protect against?"

"Losing you. Literally and figuratively."

Gabe furrowed his brow. "I don't understand."

"The shot will deliver a specially-designed nanochip into your system. We will know where you are at all times."

Gabe subconsciously cringed. "You mean like what they use on animals in the wild to study their migration?"

"In part."

"What's the other part?

"It's not an implant. It will enter your blood stream and stay there until it eventually degrades on its own."

"When will that be?"

"Ten or fifteen years."

The words came out so matter-of-factly that Gabe wasn't sure he heard her correctly. "What?" he asked.

Shira shrugged. "It's that or we open you up and look for it."

Gabe swallowed audibly. "Why not use a GPS tracker?"

"Too imprecise. The nanochip will help us keep tabs on your vitals. Heart rate, lung and liver function. Basically anything that could go wrong with your body, we'll know about it."

"Before I do."

"Most definitely."

"And if you find an irregularity, will you inform me?"

"If Kahn—or whoever should succeed him—wishes to."

Gabe shook his head. "This is crazy."

"You ought to be grateful, Mr. Lewis. There are countless people who would give anything to have this nanochip injected. People who fear for their health. It would catch any issue before it became deadly. It's the only reason you're allowed to join us."

Given their tight-lipped policy, Gabe was surprised she was answering so directly. Clearly, Kahn had found a way to mitigate his reservations for including him in the operation. Gabe had unknowingly signed up to be the Technion's newest guinea pig.

***

Hotel Alahabana
Havana

Jon stood in the corner of the hotel's lobby, keeping an eye out for his contact. According to Pearson, the Hana lab and old personnel records were moved to Cuba. Matthews's CIA connection offered a contact in Havana, someone on the ground who could provide logistical support.

A Caucasian man with dark glasses and American style clothing exited the elevator and stepped outside, waiting for a taxi under the striped awning. Jon followed, ready to make a move when he sensed a presence to his left.

"You are looking for someone, señor?"

Jon eyed the fleshy guy. The man's jet black hair was slicked back like Fonzi's from *Happy Days*. He had an unfiltered cigarette sticking out the side of his mouth. A shyster, trying to make a quick buck off a stupid American. "Don't think you can help me."

The man turned his head, spat on the street. Switching to an American accent, he said, "You look better in your picture."

Jon was taken aback. *"You're* Charlie?"

The man laughed, then coughed, sticking out a beefy hand. "Welcome to 1955, Agent."

Jon couldn't help but grin. Charlie had an amiable way about him, reminding him of Craig back at the office. Jon wouldn't ask but the clues were all there. Charlie was CIA.

Jon looked around at the old buildings, the antique cars. "Yeah, thanks."

"How are things back home?"

"As divisive as ever. No offense but I'm tight on time."

"All Americans are the same," he said, his voice picking up in volume, the accent reverting to pure Cubano. In the blink of an eye, Charlie switched personas. "All business, no pleasure."

It took a moment for Jon to realize several people had just entered the lobby of the hotel.

"You are right, señor," Charlie said. "I cannot help you."

Charlie flicked the ash from his cigarette and moseyed away.

Jon knew better than to follow. Moments later his phone lit up with a text. Sender unknown.

Package in your room. Meet me. One hour.

Attached was an address.

Vaya con Dios. Go with God.

Like a modern-day *Mission Impossible*, the text vanished. *This message will self-destruct...*

Jon was ready to get some answers. He would take all the divine intervention he could get.

***

"He's here," Miguel said into his earpiece, his lips barely moving. He was seated on a folding chair to the right of a newspaper stand. Beside him, two other old-timers were drinking café Cubano and playing an excruciatingly slow game of chess.

Miguel had a good view of the Hotel Alahabana's entrance, the tall American, and his informant, a man named Charlie.

Though an expert on a motorbike, Miguel had missed the gringo by a hair. Clearly, the warning had gone unheeded.

Miguel listened attentively to his instructions, then ended the call. He did the math in his head. The windfall from the job would be welcome, allowing for a modest extension to his home. It couldn't come at a better time. With the birth of his first granddaughter, the family needed more room. Maybe he'd even have enough to cover a special gift for Marta. Their anniversary was approaching.

Miguel spoke a silent prayer of thanks for the job. In a city like Havana, it was the hustle that made you successful and he was one of the best hustlers in town.

***

Jon stepped out from under the awning, emerging into the relentless sun, a holster at his back. Charlie had gained access to his and Sienna's room, leaving the Sig Sauer 9mm, a full magazine and a black holster on the bed. A 'No Molestar' tag hung on the doorknob.

At least now, Jon had somewhere to start. If Lamont was dirty, he'd find the evidence here in Havana. A quick Google search told him Charlie wanted to meet in a park, a seventeen-minute walk away.

Jon walked south along the Paseo del Prado, a boulevard of exquisite architecture, keeping an eye out for the motorbike. He passed the magnificent Gran Teatro de la Habana, Havana's opulent theater, its rich neo-baroque style adorned with white marble spires. The expansive grounds of the capitol building were directly ahead. A small park situated across the street housed an old church, painted yellow. The suspended bell inside its brick steeple chimed ten times.

The smell of savory grilling meat reached him and he followed his nose to a small bistro at the end of the street. His stomach grumbled loudly. He had some time before Charlie showed up. The open awning read, "La Cocina Latina."

Through the window, Jon saw cloth tablecloths and contemporary fixtures. He was about to enter when in the window's reflection he spotted a pimply teenager holding an old style flip phone, pointed his way. Despite being only ten feet behind him, the kid took no evasive action, didn't seem to care if he was spotted. That, or he was a complete amateur.

Follow me, son of a bitch. I'm ready for ya.

Jon entered the bistro, keeping his back to the kid and approached the counter. A woman with dark corkscrew curls, close to his own age, smiled at him. "Bienvenidos."

Using broken Spanish and hand gestures, Jon asked for the same grilled chicken sandwich being enjoyed by a seated patron. "To go, please."

While he waited for her to fill the order, Jon had a sense the teen was loitering nearby. He paid for the sandwich and a TropiCola. Keeping his head down, he took his bag outside, walking casually toward the park across the street.

He took a seat on a bench, practically an open invitation. Nothing happened. The kid was gone. Maybe he was scared off by the easy mark. *Damn.*

Jon ate his sandwich and waited.

***

Washington, DC

Oberlander tapped the end of his cigar, deliberating, the acrid smoke rising toward the can lights in the ceiling. The federal agent was still poking around. Only this time too close to the truth.

What the hell was wrong with his employees? His first one, a seasoned contract killer was murdered by the second, who also failed to stop the Fed. Gerard was as creepy as they came. The phrase, *Still waters run deep,* seemed to apply. Deadly depths beneath a calm façade.

When Gerard had contacted him, Oberlander sensed there was an ulterior motive at play. He hadn't heard from Gerard in days but would wager he was close enough to Steadman to touch him.

Even Miguel, his trusted man on the ground in Havana, had failed to take Steadman out with his motorbike. Apparently, Sienna Lamont warned him out of the way in the nick of time.

Seems Agent Steadman has nine lives. He'd escaped three

242

attempts on his life. Oberlander had no intention of waiting for another six tries to achieve success. *No one simply shows up unannounced on my doorstep and expects to walk away unscathed.*

He punched in Miguel's number, gave him instructions. Sometimes the best way to deal with challenging matters was to take care of them yourself.

CHAPTER 34

City Center
Havana

Jon tossed the sandwich wrapper in the bin. Charlie was ten minutes late. From his perch on the park bench, Jon watched as the church doors opened, parishioners spilling out. It was the height of the day and the heat was brutal. Shopkeepers were closing up, heading home for siesta. He waited five more minutes, then typed a text to the number Charlie had used, getting an error message. He crossed the road, once again checking for cars and motorbikes, and the snap-happy kid.

Tired of what seemed like a wild goose chase, Jon returned to the bistro. He needed another drink before heading back to the hotel.

The door was locked, the place dark. Jon got up close to the glass, holding up his hands to keep out the glare. Cursing under his breath, he turned around, coming face-to-face with a phone camera. *Click.*

The kid took off. Jon went after him, hands pumping, sweat rolling down his forehead. The kid was a speed demon. Jon chased him down a set of alleys, snaking between a pair of chain link fences, aware of potential traps, his leg throbbing with the manic pace.

Just as Jon thought he couldn't take the pain any longer, he caught a break. A neat line of metal garbage cans stood at the end of the alley.

Jon saw the collision coming, the kid's impact reverberating off the nearby walls. Jon was on him in an instant, grabbing him by his collar. The kid's eyes were filled with terror.

"Lo siento, señor," the boy managed, attempting to catch his breath.

Jon too, gasped for air. He had a death grip on the kid. "Who are you?"

The boy shook his head. He didn't understand.

"Cuál es tu nombre?"

"Pedro."

"Quién es su jefe?" using the word he knew meant *boss*.

The boys eyes widened. He shook his head.

Jon said, "Quiere morir?" *Do you want to die?*

"No señor. Por favor. Mi mamá . . ." A tear squeezed out of the corner of his eye.

He was really just a kid.

"Su jefe?" Jon repeated, pulling harder on the kid's collar.

The boy whispered "Señor Oberlander."

"Dónde está?" *Where is he?*

The boy vigorously shook his head. "No sé. No sé." Jon believed him. The kid was a mere lackey. Nothing more.

Jon stuck out his free hand. Pedro hesitated, then passed over his phone. Jon erased the photos of him and scrolled for the name *Oberlander*. Nothing. He tried *Jefe*. Nothing. He tossed the device back to the kid.

"Váyase a casa. ¡Ahora! *Go home now!*

The boy scrambled to his feet and hightailed it out of there.

The church bells pealed eleven times. It was time to head back.

Jon was five minutes away from the hotel, sweat soaking through his shirt, when he received a message from Charlie.

Sorry I couldn't make it. Something came up. Another address. *You'll find answers there.*

Jon wasn't a fan of the cryptic but he understood the need for secrecy. He memorized the address moments before it disappeared.

***

"Where have you been?" Sienna asked as Jon entered the hotel room.

His heart rate was back to normal but he desperately needed an aspirin for his leg. Or something stronger. "Walking around town."

"Learn anything about Jen?"

Jon couldn't tell her he was actually looking into her father and his cohorts. "Not much." He'd sent Oberlander's name to Matthews. It was tempting to ask Sienna if the name rang a bell, but it would surely lead to unwanted questions. She'd want to know why he was looking for anyone other than her sister. *Because your father's knee deep in something big.*

Sienna scanned his body. "Why are your pants ripped?"

Jon looked down. Sure enough, there was a tear in his right pant leg. It must have caught on the fence when he chased Pedro. He said, "I got into a bit of a skirmish."

Sienna studied him, clearly itching for more information. "Fine. We have an agreement. Just promise me if you find Jen, you'll tell me right away."

"I promise."

Jon opened a drawer, took out another pair of pants, and changed.

"Going out again?" Sienna asked.

"Yep."

"Can I come?"

"Nope."

"Well, I'm tired of sitting around worrying."

Jon's phone buzzed. Matthews came through.

Oberlander was a high profile dude. A real estate mogul owning property in South Florida, Venezuela, and Cuba, he'd once served as an advisor to President Obama. The message ended with Matthews's typical warnings.

He's a big fish, Steadman. Be goddam sure before you toss your lure in the lake.

Jon put his phone in his pocket and looked up.

Sienna stood there, stripped naked, slowly putting on a blood red bikini and matching sandals. She grabbed a tote. "I'll be at the beach if you need me," she said, and left the room.

Only then did Jon lift his jaw off the floor.

CHAPTER 35

Miramar, Havana

The taxi stopped in front of a two-story pink mansion, set back from the curb, a substantial distance from the other houses on the block. A tall border of trees surrounded the property. Jon double checked the address Charlie had given him. It was the place.

Most of the city's taxis were American classics, referred to locally as *maquinas*. Few had air conditioning, making each breeze that passed through the car a welcome reprieve.

Jon paid the fare, tagging on a tip, and stepped out into the cooling air. Darkness had fallen. It had been difficult to wait for night to come but he had no idea what to expect and preferred to avoid neighborhood busy-bodies.

The place was well-maintained but appeared deserted, as did many of the buildings nearby. The driver had said something in Spanish about the neighborhood encompassing mostly old embassies and homes of wealthy pre-revolution families. It looked more like a very upscale ghost town. His concerns for being seen were unfounded.

Jon had no idea who lived in the house. He hoped the lead was solid and whoever was inside would finally provide some solid answers about Sinclair Lamont. If he was really lucky, he'd also walk away with information about Jennifer Cartwright's whereabouts.

Jon approached the front gate. It was locked with no

evidence of a buzzer. He spotted a camera affixed to the top of a narrow, metal pole to his right, and waved. Nothing happened. He did a three-sixty, noting the scarce number of illuminated homes. No one to ask, if he was so inclined. Also, no one to notice if he took a detour to the back of the property.

Jon lowered the brim of his cap and made his way along the tree line, looking for an alternate entrance. From his vantage point, the tall trees blocked his view of the back of the house. A primal instinct made him feel for the holster at his hip.

Moments later, he was facing a back door. He knocked. "Hello?"

When no reply came, he tried the door. It was locked. He was faced with a choice. Turn around and try again tomorrow or forge ahead. Jon reached into his pocket and took out his set of lock picks and selected the one he needed. He had the door open in ten seconds flat. He was getting faster.

"Thanks, Carrie," he whispered. His former partner had been a magician at opening closed doors, both figurately and literally.

Once inside, he found himself in a kitchen. A single light was illuminated in the hallway to his right. He could hear Simon and Garfunkel's *The Sound of Silence* from somewhere down the hall. He was no longer alone.

"Hello? It's Agent Steadman of the FBI. Anybody here?" He followed the music down the corridor, his gun in hand, passing the stairwell and several closed doors. As he turned the corner, he felt a stunning blow to the back of his head. Jon fell to his knees, the gun slipping from his hand, his vision blurred. Perfectly polished wingtips were the last thing he saw.

"Jon."

The voice was familiar. A no-nonsense baritone.

"Agent."

Jon opened his eyes, inviting a piercing pain into his

skull.

A gray-haired man in his early sixties, wearing an open-collared white linen shirt, pressed slacks over wingtips, stood over him.

Sinclair Lamont.

"Can you sit up?" Lamont asked.

Gingerly, Jon put a hand to the back of his head, his fingers coming away with blood.

"You gave us a good scare."

Jon felt the cool tile of the floor beneath him and pushed himself up to a sitting position, bracing himself against the vertigo. He took in his surroundings. Still in the house, he appeared to be in a large sitting room, a shattered vase at his feet. He stood up unsteadily and took a seat in a rattan armchair.

"I'm sorry I had to do that," Lamont said. He gestured to the Sig Sauer on the desk. "The gun and all. When I heard footsteps in the house, I thought you were one of Finn's numerous thugs." He eyed Jon's head. "You passed out for a few minutes."

Jon was still shaken up. And confused. *What is happening?* "Whose house is this?"

"It belongs to an old colleague of mine who benefitted nicely from Cuba's sugar cane exports." Lamont approached Jon who was feeling queasy. "May I?"

Lamont took a closer look at the gash. "Bad cut. I could put in a few stitches but a ZipStitch will probably do. You'll have a scar but with a head of hair like yours no one will ever see it." Seeing Jon's reaction, he said, "I'm a doctor, Mr. Steadman."

Jon brushed him away, staring at Sienna's and Jennifer's father. "You're under arrest, Lamont."

The man smiled, condescendingly. "For what, Agent Steadman?"

"I know all about Jennifer. She was going to testify against you. What have you done to her?"

Lamont appeared genuinely stung. "You think I'd hurt my own child? I may have a reputation for being ruthless, but even I wouldn't go that far."

He seemed to take note of Jon's reaction. "I had hoped to keep you and Sienna out of all this but she's always been dogged about things. I should have known giving her an inch —"

The door opened behind him.

"Ah, there you are," Lamont said.

Jon wasn't sure he was seeing clearly. He shook his head, blinking to gain clarity. Standing before him was none other than Sinclair's daughter.

Sienna Lamont.

CHAPTER 36

Miramar, Cuba

"Oh my God! What happened?" Sienna asked, rushing to Jon's side, a look of concern on her face. "Are you okay?" She was dressed in a light-blue short-sleeved dress and running shoes. The red bikini was long gone. Jon felt a strange sensation. It took a moment before realizing what it was. *Betrayal.*

His face must have shown something primal. Sienna took a step back, raised a hand. "This must-be a terrible shock. I'm so sorry."

Jon remained silent. He was still processing. Sienna was somehow involved in all this. He cursed his own stupidity. He took pride in his deductive skills, his ability to smell out trouble. And duplicitous con artists.

Coming to his feet, Jon looked her in the eye. "Liar," he croaked.

Sienna bit her lip, nodded.

He made for the door.

"It's not what you think. Please wait."

He didn't stop.

"Don't you at least want to hear what all this is about?"

Jon heard the crack in her voice. "No, not even a little bit." With difficulty, he crossed the threshold, holding onto the wall for support.

Sienna came after him. "What about the children?"

The words had their intended effect, stopping him in his tracks. Against every fiber of his being, Jon turned to face Sienna, forcing his fists to unclench. "What children?"

"Let me show you."

From the doorway, Jon saw Sienna click a small button in her hand. A monitor attached to the wall lit up, displaying a teenage girl dressed in a karate gee, frozen in time.

"This is footage from ten years ago." Sienna said, pressing the play button.

Begrudgingly, Jon walked past Sienna and back into the room

The girl stood in a field surrounded by tall swaying palm trees. "Who is that?"

Sienna stepped around the broken glass and stood beside her father. "Dad will soon explain," she said, somberly. "Just watch."

Jon directed his attention back to the screen. A stretch of sand could be seen in the background. The camera panned to show a round-faced man dressed similarly, a black belt wrapped around his waist, facing the teen. With hands clasped, they bowed to each other. Then the man stepped back.

The girl began what Jon knew was a basic kata. After completing the karate sequence, the man nodded as if inviting the girl to do something. Quicker than the eye, the teenager spun, kicked her leg up and knocked the man down with such force that Jon was left staring slack-jawed at the screen. "Is she some sort of prodigy?"

The video clip ended, and a new one began. The girl now faced the camera, a barbell on the floor before her. The video zoomed in on the equipment. Three-hundred-and fifty pounds. She crouched, placing her hands on the bar. With a deep grunt, she lifted the barbell and in two swift motions, raised it over her head, her neck veins bulging grotesquely. Jon watched silently until the girl let the barbell drop.

A chill ran up Jon's spine. "What *is* this?"

Lamont said, "Carlita is genetically enhanced.

Jon shook his head, baffled. He was glued to the spot. He was concussed. None of this made sense.

"If you still want to leave . . ."

Jon was never more conflicted in his life. Was Sienna playing him yet again, knowing he had a soft spot for traumatized kids? His head began pounding, the bruise pulsating. He closed his eyes and his mind filled with images of Randy at the zoo. Carrie's boy had become a surrogate member of his family. He'd brought Jon more joy than he deserved.

"You need some aspirin. Please, Jon."

Jon opened his eyes. "You've got five minutes."

***

Jerusalem

Kahn read the report one more time. The world was falling apart. On his watch.

Gavriel was back in Texas waiting for the White Knight to make a move. He'd been given the handle, *Black Rook*. In chess, rooks were superior to knights, boasting greater control and mobility on the board.

With the nanochip implantation, Gavriel was a walking beacon, not to mention the most expensive experiment Israel was currently testing. He'd undergone the training and implantation, instructed not speak of the nanochip to anyone including Jon Steadman. That said, now it was time for Kahn to reciprocate. He video-called Special Agent Doug Matthews.

Matthews appeared as weary as Kahn felt. No time was spent on pleasantries.

Kahn jumped in. "Lamont has a mixed history. Nearly two decades ago he was sent to Hawaii to establish a secret program. After the death of a child subject, it was closed down and revamped as an exclusive fertility clinic specializing in medical genetic editing."

"Known intel. What else have you got?"

Kahn closed his eyes, wishing he could hold on to the next piece of data for himself. But a deal's a deal. "Allow me to finish. It's unclear what role Lamont currently plays but the Kihei clinic is a front for what the Hana lab actually does. Which is not limited to embryo selection or medical genome editing."

"Oh?" Matthews said, "If they're not only editing out genetic diseases, then what else *are* they doing?"

"Do you know what CRISPR technology actually does?"

Kahn saw the Fed's passing look of irritation. He had not meant to be condescending, only efficient with their time.

Matthews said, "Enlighten me."

Kahn offered the most rudimentary explanation of gene editing. "In most countries, embryo selection is legal, choosing the most viable one for implantation. However, gene editing is completely different. Traits like IQ and strength can be manipulated. It's a political and ethical quagmire."

Kahn had been easing Matthews into dangerous territory. It was time to cross over the line. "Let me ask you this, Agent. If your country chose to use such technology on human subjects, what would *you* do with it?"

Matthews paused for a few moments in thought. His volume dropped. "We would build an army of enhanced soldiers of war. One that would be virtually unstoppable."

Kahn met Matthews's anxious gaze. "Precisely."

He couldn't have said it better himself.

***

Federal Plaza
New York City

Matthews hung up with Kahn in a state of shock, unsure what his next move should be. He couldn't deny the Israelis had come through on the clinic. It made the quid pro quo for helping them with Dr. Lavi's search and rescue easier to swallow.

If what Kahn had said was true, the situation with Lamont was an international red-level threat. There were powerful people at play. Who could he confide in without risking tipping off the very people behind it?

Matthews dialed Captain Akamai, told him what he needed. Ten minutes later, Mike Evans, the WITSEC guy called.

Matthews said, "I'm Agent Steadman's boss."

"I know," Evans said.

He took a chance. "How's Jennifer Cartwright?"

"Who?"

Asshole.

"I need a straight answer on the next one, Evans. Don't bullshit me. My agent's life is on the line."

When Evans didn't reply, Matthews went on. "All those years ago at the clinic, did Lamont have a partner?"

Matthews heard Evans's soft breathing. He waited.

"He did."

"Who was it?" Matthews asked.

"Listen, Steadman seemed solid, like he's in it for the right reasons. This is all I'll give you, understand?"

"Yes."

"It's a weird name," Mike said. "Phineas—Finn—Oberlander."

Matthews ended the call, his suspicions confirmed. Jon was on the ground with no idea what he was walking into. He was in over his head. Knowing Jon, it wouldn't matter. Once he was dedicated to a case, he stuck with it till the bitter end. For now all Matthews could do was warn him. He dialed Jon's number. It went directly to voicemail. He tried twice more. *Goddammit, Jon, don't get into more trouble than you can safely get out of.*

CHAPTER 37

Miramar, Cuba

Sienna took a seat on a chair opposite Jon. "The project was a speculative but highly classified program originated in 2005 and funded by the U.S. govern—"

"Did you even know Carrie?" Jon interrupted Sienna, his tolerance already waning.

Sienna looked down at her shoes, seemingly fighting an internal battle. "Dad, would you excuse us, please?"

Lamont left the room.

Alone with Sienna, and against his will, Jon's mind reverted to their most recent interlude. Their legs intertwined, Sienna's head on his chest. He felt like the biggest chump.

Sienna puffed her cheeks, letting the air out slowly, "You're right, of course. I should start with Carrie. But you did only give me five minutes." She raised her head, attempting a tentative smile.

Jon glared at her. Her smile vanished.

"Yes, Jon. What I told you was true. Do you think Carrie's parents lied to you? From the time we moved abroad from Hawaii, I grew up with her. She was my closest friend. We were like sisters, confiding all our secrets. There are things I told Carrie I've never shared with another living soul. Her death was a devastating blow."

Jon sighed audibly. He missed her too, dammit.

Sienna searched his eyes, knowingly. "I was there when

Carrie gave birth to Randy. Her dad wasn't well at the time. Abuela was tending to him, so neither of her parents could be there with her in the hospital."

"What about the father?"

"Grade A asshole. Was on a job. Couldn't bother to be around for her due date. Things were already strained. When she went into labor, she didn't call him. She called me."

Jon thought of Randy coming into the world in what must have been a difficult time for Carrie, Sienna there to help. Even when it meant watching another woman giving birth, something she desperately wanted for herself. He felt himself softening. "Did you find it hard given your . . . circumstances?"

Sienna considered the question, seemingly relieved at the direction the conversation was taking. "I never thought of it that way. I was genuinely happy for her. Honestly, it was one of the most special days of my life."

Jon felt the anger ebb, hurt taking its place. "If you knew Carrie trusted in me, why didn't you? Why didn't you tell me the truth about your father's involvement from the beginning instead of letting me believe you're some goddam damsel in distress?"

"My emotional state when I showed up at your door was no act. I was terrified. I still am." A pause. "I needed your protection and help to find Jen and my baby. There was no one I could trust unequivocally. Jen got caught up in something big, that was obvious. She's no shrinking violet. If she went into hiding and told me to watch my back, I knew it was serious. I needed to be sure you were one of the good guys. I was hiring you for a job. I didn't think I owed you more of an explanation. Clearly that was a miscalculation."

"You think? I've been targeted three different times!"

Sienna turned pensive. "Carrie was right about you. She said you're tenacious. Called you the Pit Bull."

The moniker had been something of a joke between Jon and his old partner. His dead partner. He touched the cut on his head. It was no longer bleeding but a bump was growing there.

"Remember the message I played for you from Jen?"

"What about it?"

"There was more. I didn't play the entire thing."

Jon wanted to punch a wall.

Sienna said, "Please just hear me out." A note of desperation seeped into her tone.

Jon felt a strong urge to get up and walk away. He didn't. "What else did she say?" he said, seething.

"That the clinic was a front for an illegal program. She told me to ask our father about it."

"And?"

"I did ask him. He tried to steer me away from looking for Jen. I knew then that he was caught up in this mess. But unlike Jen, I don't want to be party to implicating him."

Jon reached into his pocket for his pills, alarmed that he was running low. He'd promised Sienna he wouldn't take them again while on the job. But she'd lied to him. For days. He took two and dry-swallowed, waiting for her reproach. It didn't come.

Sienna went on. "I was little when we lived in Maui, but I remember my parents arguing about Jen. Dad wanted to take her to the clinic he was running. He said there was a new program that would make her special. I only remember it because I was jealous. I wanted both the time with my father and to be what he considered special. It's probably why I ended up in competitive gymnastics. Anyway, My mother flat out refused, said her girls already were special. She wasn't going to allow Jen to be experimented on."

It was exactly what Regina had told him.

"Over the years, Dad's job and that clinic took on a mysterious aura. When I got older, I asked him about it. He passed it off as a place to help women have healthy babies. I sensed there was more to it but didn't care enough to inquire further.

"Years later, when I learned about my genetic abnormality, I sort of hit rock bottom. I'm not sure why my father didn't tell me about CRISPR back then. Probably because I was in no condition to care for myself, much less a child. Last year, Dad told me more. He said the clinic he once led could help me have a child, if I still wanted one. Guaranteed to not have the genetic issue. The one caveat was to keep him out of it. If word got out that he was helping me, it could ruin his career, possibly land him in jail."

"Somehow that wasn't enough of a red flag?"

"I don't think you can understand how desperate I was. Even a chance at motherhood was like a shot of adrenaline. I already knew carrying a child would be complicated for me. So I called Jen. It helped that she had a different last name than me and my father. Dad could keep his low profile. I told her I'd cover all the expenses. She didn't hesitate. Said if it would make me a mom, she'd do it."

Sienna teared up. "I *need* to find her. Not only for my baby. It's no exaggeration to say she saved my life that day. Now that she's in harm's way, I need to save hers."

Jon knew little about sisterly love. He was an only child. But he could imagine feeling similarly accountable for Gabe. "Enter Jon Steadman, stage left."

Sienna ignored the sarcasm. "When Randy told me where you were going, I suspected you had picked up Jen's trail and I followed you here to Havana."

"I'm not here to find your sister," he reminded her.

She frowned, bit her bottom lip.

"He's here for me," Lamont said, walking back inside.

Sienna's mouth opened in surprise. "Is that true?"

Jon had no intention of explaining himself. He asked Lamont, "If you wanted to keep your distance from the clinic's history, why are you here?"

Lamont turned to Sienna, "Sweetheart, it's my turn to speak to Agent Steadman alone. I encourage you to stay here tonight. It's the safest option."

Sienna looked to Jon, a question in her eyes. Jon said nothing.

"Thanks, Dad, but I'll go back to the hotel."

Lamont sucked in his lips. "Fine. I'll call someone to escort you."

Sienna spoke to Jon, her eyes darting to her father. "Are you okay with this?"

Jon said, "It's fine." Then, "This morning, when I was nearly run over, you were coming from meeting with your father, weren't you?"

Sienna gave a near imperceptible nod.

"You chose not to tell me."

"I'm sorry." With a measure of hope in her tone she asked, "Will I see you back at the hotel?"

Jon shrugged, aware how it appeared. "Don't wait up."

Sienna lowered her head and left.

When the door closed, Lamont said, "She's quite taken with you. I know you owe me nothing, but I beseech you to treat her with kid gloves."

"She's tougher than you think."

Lamont steered Jon toward the opposite end of the room, glancing furtively at the doorway as if Sienna was eavesdropping from the other side. He spoke softly. "I vividly recall the day Sienna learned she likely wouldn't have children. It was horrible. I don't expect you to understand what it's like to see your daughter so despondent. She didn't come out of her apartment for days. It was full-on grief. For a while there, we were very concerned. Then when her fiancé broke up with her she became inconsolable. We had her on suicide watch for nearly a week."

Jon was stunned. Sienna appeared so self-assured. Maybe he'd been too hasty in his judgment. Still, she'd lied to him.

Lamont went on. "She may seem circumspect, even mistrustful but she comes by it honestly. She's been burned repeatedly."

Though he didn't want to give Sienna a pass, Jon could relate.

"Sienna is extremely warm-hearted. She has a maternal nature. Has always been great with kids. She used to babysit for our neighbors, even though she didn't need the money. She just wanted to be around children.

"Her mother and I looked into all sorts of treatments. Of course, I was one of the first to know about the incredible strides made with CRISPR but after some . . . complications, I had washed my hands of it. Seeing my own child in that state, I eventually reconsidered. I told Sienna about the CRISPR clinical trials and contacted Jen. We hadn't spoken in years but we worked it out for her to participate in the program for Sienna's sake."

"After you left Maui, Sienna called me, broke down. She told me Jen's in witness protection, that you'd stopped looking for. She said she couldn't keep her head in the sand any longer. She wanted to know everything that was happening about the clinic, past and present."

"And?"

"That's when I showed her the footage of Carlita."

"Why are you telling me all of this now?"

"Sienna convinced me you are on the up-and-up. She felt guilty for keeping you in the dark. It was clear—to her, at least—that you had no ulterior motives. It was time."

Bullshit. "You expect me to believe you're on board all of a sudden, ready to out the clinic even if you go down in flames? Don't insult me."

"I'm prepared to tell you everything."

Jon said, "Great. You can start by sharing who's been trying to kill me."

Lamont said, "It has to be Oberlander's people." His face darkened. "If there's one thing I've learned, if Finn wants you dead, it's only a matter of time till he'll succeed."

CHAPTER 38

Miramar, Cuba

L amont opened the plantation shutters, allowing in a gentle breeze. He flicked a switch on the wall, causing the overhead fans to pick up speed.

"What I wouldn't do for a working A/C in this city." He took a seat in the chair his daughter had evacuated, Jon following suit on the rattan chair.

Lamont said, "Phineas Oberlander is the mastermind behind what you just saw. He and I originally led the program. My girls called him Uncle Finn when they were children. Raúl Santiago, Finn, and I were best buddies. We were brothers-in-arms. Finn was awarded commendations and served honorably . . . until things went sideways."

Jon recalled the photo of three men he'd seen in Lamont's Maui home. "Are you actually trying to pass Oberlander off as a patriot?"

"He was, initially. But like many veterans he became jaded with time. He'd put his life on the line and when he finally got out of the army, he was left to his own devices. There are more services for veterans now than there were back then. He needed to build a career from the ground up. There's no question he did an impressive job."

Jon was doing the math in his head. "When did Oberlander see combat?"

"You weren't born yet when the U.S. invaded Grenada.

October 1983. The whole episode was over in a matter of days. Finn led troops into a messy situation. He was ordered to secure the safety of over a thousand American nationals living on the island but was provided with little intelligence in advance of the mission. The Cubans were helping the other side and seized control of the airport. Finn's battalion was tasked with bringing it under our authority. Unfortunately, they were ambushed. They drew heavy fire. Five of his men perished. He personally saved two."

Jon didn't want to hear the rationalizations of a self-important blowhard. "What a guy."

Sinclair ignored the scorn. "Years later we were both stationed in Maui, tasked with opening the clinic, intended as a training simulation for enhanced soldiers. The Joint Chiefs of Staff wanted to know what would happen if we enhanced our military using groundbreaking science. Would the edge up against our enemies end all war? No one would ever consider engaging with us once they knew we were superior both physically and cognitively. With the advent of CRISPR, the theoretical became reality. We had the know-how to manipulate the genetics of human beings. We called it Project Codebreaker."

"Isn't that sort of thing strictly regulated?"

"Regulation takes time and is typically a step behind new advances. CRISPR remains in the public domain, the patent privately owned. It's not exclusive to the military. But back then, it was the Wild West."

Lamont turned away, spoke as if to himself. "For the record, we actually helped many women give birth to healthy babies. But after what happened to that little boy—Jennifer's friend—the government ordered the operation closed down. They would no longer fund it. In large part because of the media storm that would surely follow. The U.S. wasn't ready for the unproven, fledgling technology. Finn didn't agree with that decision. He insisted there was too much on the line to stop."

"You went along with it?"

Lamont didn't answer right away. "At first, I told Finn I wanted nothing more to do with Project Codebreaker. If we were caught continuing the work, it would mean an immediate court martial and prison. Finn remained resolute. I eventually agreed. We took it over on our own."

Jon was incredulous. "Why didn't you go straight to the authorities?"

"I had my own issues with the system." He left it at that.

Jon pushed. "You were taking an insane risk."

"Not as great as you'd think. All the logistics were already in place. All we needed was to *act* as though we were shutting it down. We turned the Kihei facility into a fertility clinic. We secretly secured private funding, organized a board, and moved the trials lab to an out of the way location, in Hana."

"What were you planning to do with the hijacked program?"

Lamont ignored the jab. "We were perfecting the technology, significantly minimizing the risks we had faced in early trials. The intent was to reintroduce the project to the military once it was under a new, more hawkish administration."

"Weren't you worried about being indicted then?"

"Enough time would have elapsed. Making a connection to the original defunct program would be near impossible. Negotiations with the military would be initiated by a private company, made to appear like a tech start-up, set up by notable members of our board. Even if the company would be viewed as crossing some hazy ethical lines, once it was viable, who was going to split hairs? We were certain it would be too enticing an offer for the government to pass up."

Jon was desperately trying to put all the pieces together. His head was pounding. He wanted to walk away, fly back to New York, and forget he ever met Sienna Lamont or her father. He'd ask Matthews to be reassigned to another case. It would be so easy. But there were kids being exploited, participating in an experiment they never chose.

Something occurred to him. The reason Lamont didn't go to the authorities, was willing to risk so much. "You had something to do with the child's death."

"No." Lamont's tone was anything but convincing.

"You didn't want to implicate yourself and go to jail. Is that why Jennifer wants to testify against you? About the little boy?"

"No."

It felt like drawing blood from a stone. "What changed, Lamont? Why are you suddenly willing to open the Pandora's box?"

"Finn called me. He said he had an offer on the table to buy the program."

Jon said, "Isn't that what you both wanted?"

Lamont looked to the ceiling, shut his eyes and said, "Not exactly."

***

Lake San Cristobal

The knock was insistent. Charlotte reached for her Rolex in the dark. Three-forty a.m. She flicked on the light switch beside her bed. "What is it?"

Through the door, she heard Simon's voice. "It's Dr. Lavi."

Charlotte got out of bed, put on her robe and took a moment to comb her hair in front of the mirror. "Come in."

Simon stood at the threshold. It was the first time she'd seen him disheveled.

She asked, "What's happened?"

"Dr. Lavi managed to get inside the command center."

"How is that possible?"

Simon appeared to avoid looking directly at her. He was a man of formality, clearly unaccustomed to seeing his employer in her loungewear. "Let's say I made it easy for her."

"Explain."

"I've been convinced she isn't who she says she is. Or better said, she's *more* than she said she is."

Charlotte crossed her arms, waiting for more.

"She took the bait. I didn't update the codes for the building. She used the eye scanner to gain entry."

"Have you confronted her?"

Simon shook his head. "That's why I'm here. How would you like to proceed?"

Charlotte thought a moment. "Where is she now?"

"Back in her room. She climbed up the exterior. I have it all recorded."

Charlotte seemed to take a moment to consider the new circumstances. "Leave things as they are. Let her think we don't know of her subterfuge. Get over there and find out who she contacted."

"I've already done that."

"Who was it? Her fiancé? The police?"

"No, ma'am."

"Who else would she risk contacting?"

Simon paused. "You're not going to like it."

"Well, out with it."

"Dr. Lavi sent a message to her boss."

"At her lab in Israel?"

"No, her other boss. The director of the Mossad, Israel's intelligence service."

CHAPTER 39

Miramar, Cuba

L amont stepped behind the room's oak bar, poured himself a brandy then held up the bottle in offering.

Jon nodded. Lamont handed him a glass tumbler filled with golden liquid, several ice cubes floating inside.

"Enemies become allies and vice versa, often overnight, depending on the political winds of the time."

Jon sensed Lamont was building up to something dire. He was taking too long. "Cut to the chase, Lamont. What happened?"

"Washington didn't buy it."

"Why on Earth not?"

"Finn got cold feet. He didn't want to risk exactly what you suggested—the government figuring out that we had been keeping the program afloat all these years, illegally. Without my or the board's knowledge, Finn sold the program elsewhere. He told me about it after the deed was done."

Lamont took a sip from the snifter.

Jon's mental alarm went off. "Who did he sell it to?"

Lamont's face turned ashen. He looked down into his glass, then in one fell swoop, downed the contents. Speaking barely above a whisper as if afraid someone may be listening in, he said, "Oberlander sold the program to the Russians."

***

Lake San Cristobal

Simon sat silently in Charlotte's office, watching his boss drain the coffee he had brewed for her. She was at her desk, fully dressed. It was well past four in the morning. He knew how her mind worked. She was considering all of her options.

Charlotte said, "I've been playing the strategy over in in my head. This turn of events was unexpected but it will prove to be a cherished opportunity."

Simon believed her. She was the most brilliant employer he'd worked for. "How so?"

"It's not every day we have a chip to play with the Mossad. They know by now that we have their nuclear coordinates. But that doesn't mean we cannot negotiate terms."

Simon wasn't following the logic. "What is there to negotiate? You already have both. The coordinates *and* Dr. Lavi."

"True but I can't very well have her working for me under duress. She hasn't touched the work I've already given her. I need to make the decision easy for her, without any intruding moral dilemmas and without her being deemed a traitor to her country. The only way to do that is with her government's approval."

Simon began to grasp the plan.

Charlotte went on. "In return for not selling the nuclear coordinates, the Israelis will need to let Dr. Lavi go, to become a free agent, so to speak."

"Even if the Israelis agreed to that, Dr. Lavi will not."

"Indeed." Charlotte pursed her lips. "We need insurance."

"Insurance?"

Simon knew Charlotte wasn't one to resort to violence. She was a businesswoman, first and foremost. When she'd hired him, it was made clear. The only time she might require

NELLIE NEEMAN

his special skills, as she referred to them, was if she or her family was in physical danger.

Charlotte told him what she had in mind. "It's the only way to have Dr. Lavi's lasting allegiance."

Simon cocked his head, calculating the potential risk versus reward.

Charlotte smiled at his reaction. "I see you approve."

"Yes, ma'am."

"Then I suggest you get moving."

***

Gulfstream G700
Over the Atlantic Ocean

Gabe rubbed his sore arm, careful not to bump it as he leaned back in the cream leather seat. Shira sat across from him, reading a document in Hebrew. She'd barely said a word since they'd boarded hours earlier. He took in the cabin's décor. An upscale office in the sky.

He'd grown up in privilege but thanks to his parents careful tutelage, neither he nor his sister had been spoiled. They were taught Southern mores of respect, patriotism, and a solid work ethic. It wasn't his first time on a private plane, but it was the first time a foreign government was paying his fare.

The injection had been as painful as expected, the absurdly long needle plunging deep into his skin, propelling the microchip into his bloodstream. Now, he was a walking GPS. More than that, really. Someone, somewhere was monitoring his blood pressure and heart rate. It felt surreal. As much as it was disturbingly invasive, it gave him an odd sense of security. He couldn't simply vanish off the face of the Earth. Like Terry had.

It seemed like a lifetime ago that he'd first laid eyes on Terry Lavi. Back then, he found her sitting in a hotel lobby in Jerusalem, looking nothing like who he'd expected to see. For

270

him, that meeting came close to love at first sight. Since that time, her life—and by extension, his—took many dramatic twists and turns. Through it all, he loved her. Actually, Gabe's feelings for his fiancée had grown deeper with each passing day. Terry was brave, ethical, brilliant and outspoken. A force to be reckoned with.

Gabe took the prayer book from his bag, reading to himself, ending with his own supplication. *Please let Terry come home safe and sound.*

Gabe looked out the window. The ocean seemed endless, Colorado a world away. He closed his eyes. Soon he'd be back in Austin, playing the role of dangling bait.

CHAPTER 40

Miramar, Cuba

T he air had effectively been sucked out of the room. Jon felt light-headed. His last interaction with the Russians had gone south in near-fatal ways. "The Russians?"

Lamont nodded. "They're using CRISPR to build an elite super-army."

What!

Jon took a long drink, the welcome smokey aroma of quality bourbon filling his nose.

Lamont poured a second round. "The Russian president has not been evasive on the matter. He spoke openly about it in an interview with Pravda. He's dead set on getting his hands on the technology before anyone else can."

Jon tried to imagine what an emboldened Russia would do with such technology. The possibilities were horrific.

"In Putin's own words, CRISPR would allow for an army of uber soldiers who are stronger and more resistant to chemical warfare with no interfering morality when faced with an ethically compromised situation. He wants to edit out the genes for muscle deterioration, fear, and pain. It will make them willing to put their lives on the line with greater brazenness."

Jon felt the sweat bead up on his forehead. America had nothing but trouble from the Russians. "CRISPR can do all that?"

"Most definitely," Lamont said. "One has to wonder, is the United States so brazen as to assume they are the sole arbiters of how new technology should be managed? It's laughable. I love my country. I'm a patriot, devoted my life to her. But we behave like a child cheating in a footrace, attempting to slow our competitors with claims of subterfuge when all we are doing is aiming to be the first to the finish line no matter what the means. No different than the space race."

Jon didn't need to hear Lamont's politics. "How is the project implemented?"

"This is where we need to come to an understanding."

Jon had never met a man more cagey. "Spit it out, Lamont."

"I'm prepared to turn state's evidence, if it should come to that."

And, there it is. Jon was disgusted. The man was hedging his bets. When Project Codebreaker seemed to be all systems go, he was there, ready and willing. Now that things were taking a turn, he was ready to rat out his long-time partner if it meant a more lenient sentence.

Jon said, "I have no power to guarantee anything."

"Understood. And there's no time to go through proper channels. I just ask that you mention my cooperation when the time comes."

Jon had no choice. He needed the man's insider knowledge of the facility. Whether or not Lamont was penitent was of no concern to him. "Go ahead."

Lamont didn't press the matter any further. He had clearly already considered all angles. "Finn recruits the carriers from the Maui clinic. It's the perfect cover. Most women are there legitimately, seeking fertility treatments. A minority are brought in as carriers of enhanced embryos, women who are sympathetic to Mother Russia."

"Who are these women?"

"Some are illegal immigrants but most are home-grown communists. They're already here. Marxism is on the rise in the U.S. Not surprising in today's climate."

An entire traitorous operation right under our noses. It was hard to grasp.

"Until recently, the CRISPR process was done exclusively at the Hana lab and the implantations in the Kihei clinic. Finn preferred it over injections. Even young children would draw attention if they showed signs of extraordinary skills. When the babies are born, the mothers are sent with their enhanced children here, to Cuba. The Russians take over after that. Once the final phase of the sale is implemented, the entire operation will be moved here."

"Why here and not Russia?"

"Convenience. Cuba is close and essentially a satellite of the Motherland. Russia and Cuba share similar Marxist philosophy and have maintained strong political relations."

Jon was floored. "What did you say when he told you what the new plan was for Project Codebreaker?"

"I refused to be involved. Told him it was straight up treasonous. He seemed to accept my position, told me I was good to back out. No hard feelings. But he would move ahead."

"You painted Oberlander as a patriot. One would think he would never sell out to his old enemies."

"Quite the opposite. Finn went back to Cuba several times over the years, building new connections. It picked up significantly during the Obama administration when the President was determined to advance diplomatic relations. The war was over, it was time to build bridges. They wanted people who knew the region. Finn used those regular state-funded trips to support the Russian training facility in Cuba."

Jon began pacing. "What was your role in all this?"

"Honestly? To keep my mouth shut."

"Then why spill the beans now? Because he was selling to the Russians? I can't see that being motivation enough for you to grow a conscience and face the consequences. Taking a chance on immunity is too risky."

Sinclair's gaze followed Jon around the room. He

tightened his jaw. "A woman came forward, claiming to have proof about the original classified program. She started making noise about it, said Americans deserved to know what their tax dollars had funded. Finn was alerted to it, determined to quiet her and avoid exposing the current project. She was soon found dead. When Jen went missing, I never imagined Finn had anything to do with it. He was as close to family as my own."

Lamont took a moment to compose himself. "We met. He had the gall to threaten my girls. I began to fear he was behind Jen's disappearance. Things only got worse when she called Sienna, who brought you into all this. I'm speaking up now for one reason only—my daughters' safety."

Jon swallowed what remained of his bourbon. He had so many pressing questions but had no more strength to engage. Everything was foggy.

Lamont said, "The project has long become something of significant value. Something Finn will do anything to protect."

"Valuable enough to kill?"

"We both know the answer to that, Agent. Once the sale goes through Project Codebreaker will belong to the Russians."

Jon didn't want to believe a decorated American war hero would stray so far. "When is the sale scheduled?"

"In three days."

"What?"

Lamont said, "Let me be perfectly clear. Finn has everything on the line. Years of work getting to this point. He's taking no chances. He has eyes and ears all over the island. By now, he knows you're here. If he thinks he's facing an enemy, I can assure you, he won't hesitate to kill you." He paused. "And my girls."

A wave of nausea hit Jon like a hurricane.

"Are you all right?" Lamont asked. He stood, approaching Jon. "Let me have a look at your head."

Jon tried to stand but fell back into the chair.

"Whoa. Take it easy."

Lamont poured him a glass of water. "Drink this. I'll be back in a minute." He returned three minutes later with a small flashlight, an alcohol swab and antibiotic cream. He leaned over Jon, whose eyes were closing. "Stay awake, Agent."

Jon forced his lids open. Lamont flashed the light in each eye. "Your pupils are dilated. You're concussed."

Jon said nothing.

"Are you on any meds?"

Jon took the pill bottle from his pocket. Lamont read the label. "This is strong stuff. I never should have given you alcohol. How many of these did you take today?"

The words roused Jon, a bolt of anger shooting through him. "I'm no addict. They're for anxiety."

"People get hooked on these meds every day. When was the last time you took a pill?"

"Less than an hour ago."

"Finish the water then I'll make us some coffee. You're going to need to stay awake for a while." He pocketed the pills.

Weakly, Jon said, "Hand them over."

"Looks like this prescription was filled a week ago and the bottle is nearly empty. I—and Sienna—need your help to stop the sale of Project Codebreaker."

He helped Jon to stand. "With Oberlander in the way, that is not something you can possibly do stoned."

Ten minutes later, Jon was in the kitchen drinking a high-octane coffee, his hair sticky with antibiotic cream. The water and caffeine were helping. The bump on his head seemed to reach its full size—of an egg. He was lucky not to be spending the night in a Cuban emergency room.

He thought of the White Knight, a trader of secrets who had seemingly vanished into thin air, Terry at her mercy. The Feds were still diligently working the case even while waiting for the other shoe to drop, when classified documents across the globe would be hacked.

So far it hadn't happened and he could only hope it would remain that way. If Doug hadn't agreed for Jon to take Sienna's case, he would be working on the White Knight investigation. Helping Terry and Gabe. Instead of Sienna.

Jon felt his anger flare, realizing his wits could have been better served finding a criminal, rather than being led around by the nose by Sienna. He took a swig of his water, noting the headache was now at a low hum.

Lamont said, "The transition phase is nearly finished. In three days, the baton will be passed completely to the Russians and Finn will bow out. They will transfer the funds and the Hana lab will be relocated here. The transaction will be complete."

Sienna walked in, strode over to the two men, a bag in her hands.

Jon said, "I thought you went back to the hotel."

"We were nearly there when Dad messaged me that you were in a bad way."

"You didn't need to come back."

Sienna seemed more resolute than before. "You can despise me all you want, Jon, but you're still Carrie's old friend and Randy's mentor. And like it or not, you're my friend, too." She handed him the bag. "We made a stop at a cantina. Eat."

Sienna's words had come close to hitting home for Jon. Sitting in an old house on the outskirts of Havana, away from his close friends and grandmother, the loneliness bore down on him. He opened the bag. The smell of spicy chicken made his mouth water. Only then did he realize how hungry he was. He mumbled a thank you and dug in.

She asked, "What's our plan?"

Jon forced down his instinct to argue. If Sienna wanted to risk her life, as long as she didn't slow him down, it was her choice.

Lamont pulled something from his pocket. A neatly folded five-by-five inch paper square. He opened it, flattening it out on the table.

"This is a detailed floor map of the training facility here in Cuba, in a town called Cerro. By now, the contents of the Hana lab should have been moved there. I was there a couple of years ago and drew this from memory. They run training exercises three days a week. Monday, Wednesday and Friday. The other days, the place is buttoned up tight. If this is going to happen," he looked askance at his daughter, "I'd recommend doing this sooner rather than later."

Jon said, "We'll need time to prepare."

Lamont said, "Maybe I haven't made myself clear, Agent. There *is* no time."

Lamont pointed to the map. "The exterior of the property is guarded both by armed patrol and AI, which consists of a high-powered camera and alarm."

Jon and Sienna leaned in for a better view.

"What about inside?" Jon asked.

"Deadbolts. They need the guards to have quick access in case of emergency."

Lamont seemed to consider what he was looking at. "I don't like this, Sienna. It's too dangerous."

Sienna was studying the map. "Go on, Dad."

Lamont cleared his throat. "The alarm is set up to account for unintentional trips."

Jon asked, "What does that mean?"

"Stray dog, a lightning bolt. They can trip the system which without the failsafe would start an elaborate series of unnecessary and expensive actions. If the system is not reset within precisely five minutes—either in person or remotely —all the doors and windows will be locked, trapping inside whoever infiltrated until security personnel arrive."

"I assume you don't mean the police department."

"Correct. They are akin to a paramilitary organization." He left it at that.

Jon stole a glance at Sienna. Her face had gone pale.

Lamont went on. "You will have exactly five minutes to get what you need and get out of there."

Jon whispered to Lamont, "A word, please."

The two men walked into the hallway, Sienna watching as they did so.

Lamont said, "What is it?"

"I left my pills here. Can I have them back?"

Lamont broke eye contact. "They're gone."

A bolt of shock. "Gone?"

Lamont stuffed his hands into his pockets, a smug look on his face. "My daughter's life depends on you keeping your wits about you."

In a split second, Jon had Lamont's collar in his fist, his face a millimeter from Lamont's. "Where. The. Hell. Are. They?"

Lamont was struggling to get Jon off him. "Down the toilet."

"What the hell, Lamont? I need them!"

Lamont glared at him. "You don't *need* them. You want them."

Sienna came running into the hallway, trying to pull Jon off her father. "What is going on out here?" she shouted.

Jon pierced Lamont with his steely stare who patted down his shirt, clearing his throat. "Nothing. We're good. Right, Agent?"

Jon brushed Sienna off him and stomped back inside.

***

Alahabana Hotel
Havana

Though Jon's headache had lessened, his thinking remained clouded. The hotel room had taken on a completely different vibe. What was once a lover's den, now oozed a thick tension.

Sienna sat on the edge of the bed, watching as he packed his things. "I'm sorry for lying to you. For keeping secrets."

"It's too late." The words came out impetuously, child-like. His face turned red, his head began pounding again and he grimaced.

"Here's the thing, Jon. The reason I came to you, not someone else. Carrie told me how honest you are, always trying to do the right thing. As am I. The way I see it, we have a common goal.

"The only difference between us is that you want to go public and I don't. It's true that my father will pay for his actions if we contact the Pentagon, but that's not why we need to keep this quiet for now. Uncle Finn is a powerful man, Jon. He has connections that we cannot imagine. He, along with the Russians, will close ranks. Go underground. Then, we'll never be able to bring them down. Right now we have them in our sights. We have a chance to prevent Project Codebreaker from further exploiting those kids before it's too late. Once Russia's new and improved military reaches critical mass, they will be unstoppable. They'll invade their neighbors' territory, sparking World War Three with their enhanced troops."

Jon said, "That's the point. The stakes are too damn high to keep a lid on this."

"I've already grappled with my conscience. Mine is clear. The question is what is your conscience telling you?"

As angry as he was, Jon was starting to see Sienna in a new light. She was prepared to take on the behemoth. Singlehandedly. He rubbed a hand over his face. "We can't pull that off alone. There's no way. Maybe we can leak the story to the press."

"Who would believe us? We would sound insane. They'd laugh the whole thing off. Which is why we need proof. Hard, irrefutable evidence. Then the U.S. government will be forced to shut them down."

"You're talking about military action on foreign soil."

For a second, they stared at each other. Sienna looked

exhausted, drained of all energy. "We've reached the moment of truth," she said. "Will you help me or not?"

***

Austin, Texas

Gabe glanced at the dashboard's clock. He was late. He was *never* late. The flight back home had been delayed and exhausting.

He parked in the underground lot, grabbed his bag from the back seat and click-locked the doors. From a distance he heard the elevator ding. A suited man holding a leather briefcase was getting in feet ahead of him.

Gabe said, "Can you hold the elevator, please?"

The man did so.

"Thanks."

Gabe pressed the button for the third floor. The doors closed.

Maybe this is it. The guy is going to grab me right here in the garage. Gabe braced himself.

"You okay, man?"

The guy seemed genuinely concerned.

I need to relax. "Yeah, I'm fine. thanks."

"That's my floor, too," the man said. "Don't think I've seen you here. You a rep?"

Gabe nodded.

"Cool."

"Thanks, it's my uncle's business."

"No kiddin'."

The doors opened, and the man gave an off-handed wave. To Gabe, the short exchange seemed bizarre. His fiancée was MIA and he was going about his usual business, chitchatting, meeting with buyers.

But that's exactly what Shira told him to do. Act normal. The problem was, all he could think of was Terry. He prayed every day for her safety. It seemed like a year since she went missing from the Isle of Palms.

What made it even worse was Shira explaining she would not be in contact with him. The moment Gabe got on the El Al flight back to the States, he was considered active, and any association with the Mossad would put both him and Terry in mortal danger.

Gabe checked in with reception. A young, attractive woman was enamored with something on her phone.

Gabe said, "Hi, I'm Gabe Lewis. Sorry for my late arrival."

"They're waiting for you in the conference room, Mr. Lewis," she said, in a perfunctory manner, not bothering to look up.

Gabe knew the way to the glass-enclosed room. A group of people was seated around a table. All eyes were on him. He needed to get into the right frame of mind.

"Good morning," he began. His ten-minute presentation was on auto pilot, proceeding well enough. Until his phone rang.

No name.

"Please excuse me. It's a personal emergency."

Eyebrows were raised around the table, one person mumbling, "What the hell?" as Gabe left the room. The timing couldn't have been worse. Though the account had been with Gabe's uncle for years, a competitor had recently come to town, vying for the same pool of customers.

In the hallway, Gabe answered the call. All he heard were two words, spoken in an emotionless Israeli accent.

"It's time."

***

Shira sat behind the wheel of the Ford Focus, her binoculars set on the office building's door. She had been keeping a close eye on Gabe since they parted ways in Israel. He was an amateur, skittish but motivated. Things were dragging out. The longer Dr. Lavi was in the Colorado house, the greater the risk to her health and Israel's security. But no one had made a move. She hadn't intended to call Gabe but there was no choice.

He would need to make himself an easy target. It was *Espionage 101*. Make it easy for your contact to approach. Of course in this case the contact was the enemy. Five minutes after calling him, Gabe exited the building, pulled a pack of cigarettes and a lighter from his jacket pocket and lit up.

He wasn't a smoker but did a good job making it look otherwise. He lingered, smoking leisurely.

After five more minutes, Gabe scanned the area, found what he was looking for.

Shira saw where he was headed. *Good boy.*

CHAPTER 41

Hotel Alahabana
Havana

Jon and Sienna were seated in the courtyard. Jon spotted Charlie in the far corner, facing the entrance. He was sipping from a demitasse, a copy of *Granma*, the country's daily Commie paper, splayed before him. It crossed Jon's mind that he was under orders to keep an eye on them. Perhaps Matthews had pulled a few strings. He planned to ask him about it during their upcoming phone call.

Last night he and Sienna had hit an impasse, depleting them both. After moving his things to another room, Jon had passed out on the still-made bed, waking up seven hours later, feeling more refreshed than he had since Sienna showed up at his Manhattan walk-up. The bump on his head was still there but was no longer tender to the touch.

An elderly couple finished their breakfast and left. Charlie was now the only other patron in the courtyard and was out of earshot. Jon brought his focus back to Sienna. "Even if we succeed in stopping Project Codebreaker, your father has even more to answer for. A child died under his leadership and there were no consequences."

"He regrets it terribly but if he goes public, he'll go down in flames. Not to mention the danger to my sister."

"Your sister is already in a bind. This has gone far past you or your family's personal challenges. Past saving your own hides. This is a national security issue."

Sienna looked away, put a hand over her face. She remained quiet for a moment. Then, softly, she said, "Don't you think I know that? I'm not making excuses for my father, Jon. What he did—covering it up—was terrible, but he did get out early." Sienna leaned in, whispered, "I know I have no right to ask but please try to keep him out of prison."

"His so-called regret is over a decade late, Sienna. And you're correct. You have no right to ask."

Jon expected an argument. Instead, Sienna asked, "How's your head?"

"Been better."

"Need more aspirin?"

"No, I'm good."

An awkward pause passed.

Jon asked, "What really happened to that boy?"

"When my father was in charge of the project, CRISPR was very new but incredibly promising. They were opening an exciting world of science never explored before. Given the classified nature of the project, they were looking for participants that wouldn't threaten exposure. They had early success with embryonic edits and wanted to explore injections."

"Initially, they approached members of the local communities, indigenous and underprivileged. But the parents were fearful their children would be harmed. Monetary incentives didn't do the trick. They needed a way to unequivocally prove the project was safe."

Jon said, "What happened?"

"Several officers offered up their own children. They wholeheartedly believed in the project, were certain there was nothing to be concerned about. From what Dad said, they were excited to have the first enhanced children. Though I should mention, my mother was against it from the start. My father did his pitch but she wouldn't come around."

Jon was horrified. What sort of parent subjects their

child to an untested experiment?

"The little boy was the son of a new recruit. He had a bad reaction to the CRISPR injection. Seems he had a heart ailment that the parents knew nothing about. His heart literally burst."

Jon couldn't help but picture Randy. What greater evil is there than exploiting an innocent, trusting child?

Sienna's eyes glistened. "When he died, the military offered the family a huge payout. They avoided a drawn out legal affair they would have lost anyway."

A busboy came over. "Tea, coffee?" he asked in English.

They declined and the man left.

Sienna said, "Those kids will be freaks, Jon. Not lauded. They'll be ostracized, have no friends. When they graduate, a new group of children is brought in. And it doesn't stop there. They're being primed as the parents of a new generation."

"What do you mean?"

"Do you know what germline gene editing is?"

Jon shook his head.

"It's possibly the greatest discovery of CRISPR technology. The editing achieved carries down to all its future offspring. Whether CRISPR was administered at the embryonic level or by an injection into a living person. The edits update not only their genetic makeup but also those of their future generations."

"But that would eventually create a whole generation of enhanced people."

"Whether they want it or not."

Jon looked over at Charlie who appeared to be lost in his reading. If he was there for their protection, he was doing a lousy job.

Sienna said, "You can help me shut down the program. Get the kids out of there."

Charlie hadn't moved a muscle, hadn't so much as glanced their way.

"I'm calling Matthews."

Sienna placed a hand on his. "Please don't."

Jon pulled away. "I have no choice. He's my boss."

"I thought you had issues with him."

"I do, but he's as honest as they come and will know better how to navigate this than we do."

Sienna dropped her shoulders, looked away. "All right, do it. If you trust him, I guess I will need to as well."

"Good," he said. "Maybe we're finally getting on the same page."

***

Austin

Gabe entered the alley. An unoccupied black sedan was parked along the wall. He checked his watch repeatedly as if he was late for a meeting.

"Mr. Lewis."

Gabe turned, stunned to find a man of military bearing mere feet behind him. He hadn't heard anyone approach. *Stay cool.*

Looking quizzically at the man, he said, "Do I know you?"

"Your fiancée sent me."

Though he was expecting it, hearing the man refer to Terry was jarring. He didn't need to feign fear. His was genuine. "Is she all right?" he asked.

"Of course. Why think otherwise?" The man's steely demeanor belied his words.

"Where is she?" Gabe made a show of looking over the man's shoulder.

"Somewhere safe. I'm here to bring you to her."

"I don't understand." He did what Shira had told him. "I'm calling the police." He pulled out his phone.

In a flash, the man was at his side, a syringe in his hand.

"All will be clear in due time," he said, as he plunged the

needle into Gabe's arm.

I really hate needles. It was Gabe's last thought before passing out.

CHAPTER 42

Plaza de Armas
Havana

Jon left the hotel, taking extra precautions, fully aware of his surroundings. Maybe it wasn't the smartest idea, given recent events, but after Sienna went back to her room to rest, he badly needed to get outside. He used the opportunity to brief his boss.

He found a secluded and shady corner of the park and shared with Matthews what he had uncovered about Oberlander, Project Codebreaker and Lamont's alleged past involvement. He was expecting a ten-minute diatribe of why breaking into the Cuban facility would be a suicide mission.

Instead, Matthews listened intently, clearly stunned at all Jon had learned. Most surprisingly, Matthews said he planned to quietly contact the NSA Office of the Inspector General. The OIG was responsible for internal investigations of their personnel suspected of misconduct. In the interim, Matthews gave Jon the green light. His instructions were clear. To secure irrefutable evidence of Project Codebreaker's existence and Lamont's and Oberlander's involvement. Once established, a case would be built against them. Along with Lamont's older daughter's testimony, the chances were good both men would go down. Hard.

The bigger concern now was that a project designed to create an enhanced Russian army would warrant U.S. military action on Cuban soil. According to Matthews, that was the CIA's problem. But as Matthews stated, "We'd better be damn sure of the intel before we pull the trigger."

Jon stared at the park's impressive statue of Carlos Manuel de Cespedes. A revolutionary and first president of Cuba, he had one hand casually in his pocket as he looked off into the distance. Jon knew little about Cuban history but the music and food were exceptional.

He was mentally reviewing the logistical details when his phone buzzed.

Meet me in your room in twenty.

Jon looked up. Several women were selling souvenirs, another handing out small bags of roasted peanuts. No one of consequence.

Twenty minutes later, he let himself into his locked room. Charlie was sitting in the desk chair, an unlit cigar in hand.

Irritated, Jon asked, "What are you doing in here?"

"We need to talk."

Jon took a deep breath, not bothering to ask how the spy gained access to his room. "Fine, talk."

"You're going to break into the Russian training facility. I want to come with you."

The only discussions about the break-in were held far from any curious ears. He pierced Charlie with a steely stare. "Did you bug me?"

"No."

"Then how do you know that?"

"My office has been listening in on Sinclair Lamont's dealings for some time."

It made sense. U.S. military action would garner a global outcry. As Matthews stated, the CIA would need as much intel as possible if they were going to put boots on the ground.

Charlie said, "I'll help you get inside, get enough evidence to bring down Lamont and Oberlander and get out."

Charlie must have noticed Jon's skepticism. "Isn't that

why you're here?"

Charlie was affable enough but he was CIA and that usually meant a separate, often conflicting agenda to that of the FBI. Jon didn't know if he could trust the guy.

"What else are *you* after, Charlie?"

Charlie smelled the length of the cigar. "I want the whole operation shut down."

It's what Jon wanted as well, even if his direct orders were to find evidence against Lamont and Oberlander. Jon asked, "You mean by mobilizing troops here?"

Charlie broke eye contact. "The less you know, the better."

Jon considered his options. It *would* be of great benefit to have a pro along. "Let's do it."

Charlie and Jon sat around the small desk, empty paper coffee cups scattered around the room. They'd reviewed Lamont's map, though Jon was evasive about where he'd gotten it from.

The plan would need to be executed after dark. Charlie refused to bring Sienna along. Jon knew she wouldn't like it but it was a deal breaker. The time spent strategizing with Charlie had convinced Jon of the spy's strategic skills.

He walked Charlie to the door. "Midnight, your car, out front."

Charlie stood, patted Jon on the shoulder. "See you then, amigo."

***

Austin Executive Airport

Gabe woke up feeling groggy, alarmed to find that he was slumped in the back of a sedan he had no recollection of entering. He glanced out the window, his gaze falling on a small, white airplane.

The man who'd injected him was opening the passenger door. "Mr. Lewis, I apologize for our earlier scuffle but we're on a tight schedule. I hope you plan to cooperate moving forward. It will be best for both you and Dr. Lavi."

Gabe offered a nod and exited the car.

***

Crested Butte, Colorado

What should have been a two-hour flight turned into a dragged out affair thanks to mechanical issues and a forecasted snowstorm. By the time the private plane landed in Crested Butte, Gabe could only hope the delays weren't a bad omen of what lay ahead. The airplane was no less upscale than the one he took from Israel to Austin with Shira. Like then, he kept the talk to a minimum. Only this time it was out of fear that his nervousness would reveal his true objectives.

Once on the ground, the man he now knew was called Simon, told him to put on the eye mask he handed him. As scared as he was, Gabe's heart pounded in anticipation of seeing Terry after the nightmare of recent days.

It seemed like hours by the time the car came to a stop.

"We've arrived."

Gabe removed the mask, immediately taken by the surrounding beauty. A light snow began to fall as they made their way to the large house on the lake. He wanted to run ahead and kick down the door but he waited for Simon to lead the way.

Simon unlocked the door. As Gabe stepped inside, his eyes scanned the space in desperation.

Two figures emerged from a large room on the right.

Just like that, Gabe's heart was finally whole once again.

CHAPTER 43

Lake San Cristobal

T erry couldn't believe her eyes. Gabe stood before her, his face full of love and longing.

"How?" she said, rushing forward, falling into Gabe's open arms, like two magnets restored to their natural, bound state. She was whole once again.

Gabe kissed her, his lips hard on hers, neither caring about the others present in the room.

He took a step back, holding her shoulders and studying her, as though confirming she was real. He whispered in her ear. "I told you I'd go to the ends of the Earth for you."

He'd come for her. Despite how she'd treated him. Feelings of joy mixed with regret.

"I love you so much," she said. Then, "I'm sorry."

Charlotte, who'd been observing the reunion, said, "Welcome, Mr. Lewis, please come inside and join us."

Terry turned to Charlotte, "Why is Gabe here?"

"Think of him as additional incentive."

"I don't understand."

Charlotte's stare turned icy. "We know about your excursion to the command center."

Stunned, Terry stumbled, Gabe grabbing hold of her.

Charlotte said, "Let's go finish up some business."

Without another word, Terry retreated to the large room, Gabe following her lead.

***

Cerro, Havana

The training facility was a drab four-story building located on the outskirts of an impoverished section of the city, peppered with boarded-up, graffitied factories, the overgrown weeds rapidly reclaiming the land. If not for the guards, it would easily pass as an abandoned warehouse, like those surrounding it, a camouflage Jon assumed was intentional.

Jon and Charlie sat across the road, at the edge of a forest, nothing but woods behind them. Dressed identically, head-to-toe in black, each toting a backpack, they'd been monitoring the facility for the past forty-five minutes.

Jon did a slow scan with his binoculars, noting the facility's six-foot-high fence topped with barbed wire. Posted signs read, *Peligroso*, and what Jon assumed was the Cyrillic equivalent beneath it, warning trespassers away.

The building had one bright lamp above the main entrance, which was fronted by a raised, mechanized overhead gate, its pointed spikes like downward-facing spears. There was a side-door on the eastern wall, and according to Lamont's map, a square training yard in the back. The nearest building was a two-story derelict factory twenty feet away, a downed phone cable bridging the two roofs. If Lamont was accurate, few, if any, employees would be inside the building for the next two days.

Three uniformed guards patrolled the grounds. They were tall, broad shouldered, and armed. One of them was yawning, while another exited the fencing and tossed an apple core into the bushes. The third had recently walked to the back of the property. Other than the guards, Jon saw no one else around. He had to assume the state-of-the-art security system picked up the slack.

Jon had no intention of drawing fire. Or of shooting

the men. The guards were doing a job, and in all likelihood had no idea what they were protecting. Jon could never shoot innocent men regardless of the circumstances. They would need to get past them without detection.

He and Charlie had reviewed the strategy. Charlie would get them inside. Jon would search for evidence against Lamont and Oberlander, while Charlie would photograph whatever he could find to prove what the Russians were up to. They allowed themselves no more than four minutes, keeping one as a buffer. Then they'd leave as quietly as they came.

Silently, they waited among the thick brush. The right moment came when one of the guards went into the bushes to take a leak, leaving the side door momentarily unguarded.

Fifty feet separated them from the building.

"Stay here till I give the signal," Charlie whispered to Jon.

Jon stayed low, watching as Charlie kept to the tree line, only emerging at the last moment, when he rushed toward the side entrance. Light on his feet, he had the door unlocked in under five seconds and raised a gloved hand.

Jon took a last look at the guards' positions. They had timed it perfectly. He had a clear path.

Jon followed Charlie's footsteps, reaching the door in a sprint, his bad leg tolerating the abuse.

"¡Arriba las manos!" *Hands up!*

Jon froze. The guard must have doubled back, spotting him at the worst possible second. Jon slowly turned, facing his captor. Up close, the man was an imposing figure, particularly with a gun pointed at his chest.

Jon was about to fudge an explanation when he heard a soft spit. The guard collapsed to the ground. The two remaining guards turned the corner, saw the felled guard. One shouted into a shoulder radio. Charlie shot them both, his expression impassive.

Shell-shocked, Jon said, "You killed them."

"Would you rather I hadn't?" Charlie looked at Jon. "Get

your shit together. We just lost a full minute. Come on."
They left the men where they were and ran up the stairs.

***

Havana

Oberlander was enroute to Havana when the call came in. It was late but he preferred arriving under the cover of darkness. He allowed himself a moment of excited anticipation. The Russians were already on the island. The many years of hard work were about to pay off handsomely.

He would stay in Havana until the deal was completed and then move on to his new home. He had no intention of stepping back on American soil, at least not for the foreseeable future. The risks were too great.

Gerard had finally proven worthwhile. Two men had infiltrated the facility and shot dead the guards. One was FBI, the other, CIA. Lamont's daughter was not seen.

In Spanish, he told his driver to reroute to the training facility. Agent Steadman had been both persistent and extremely lucky to still be alive. Soon that would no longer be the case. In a matter of minutes, both men would be trapped inside and then he would swiftly dole out the harshest form of justice.

296

CHAPTER 44

Cerro, Cuba

Once inside the facility, Charlie and Jon split up. They'd synchronized their watches to go off every sixty seconds. At the four-minute mark they would book it out of there.

Jon was on autopilot. Three men were down in a matter of seconds. What had Charlie gotten him into? He forced the thought from his mind.

Jon's watch alarm went off. "Three minutes," he heard Charlie shout. "Move fast."

Jon went from room to room, taking photos of everything. He tapped several computer screens, snapping pictures of what came up. Many of the rooms were filled with taped-up boxes. He photographed several labels. *Lab 1 supplies. Glass-Handle With Care.*

As expected, there was no neon sign with Lamont and Oberlander's name on it. With no time to rummage through files, he hoped his photos would suffice.

"Two minutes."

Jon photographed the backyard, set up like a basic training camp with a mix of old and newer fitness equipment and an improvised obstacle course.

He heard Charlie rummaging in the next room.

"One minute," Jon said.

"I'm almost done," Charlie called out.

Almost? If they didn't get out now, the place would shut them in. Jon was ready to bolt with or without Charlie.

"Forty seconds!" Jon couldn't keep the panic out of his voice as he ran for the stairs, Charlie hoofing it behind him.

Jon and Charlie ran past the fallen guards and exited the building. Arms pumping, Jon's bad leg was protesting when they heard loud clicking sounds from behind. Like a vault being shut down. All internal doors and windows were locked. They were twenty feet from the front gate when the overhead spikes began to lower from above.

Jon sped up, clearing the fence with inches to spare. Relief filled him.

"Jon!"

He turned to find Charlie on the ground, the spikes pinning him down by his backpack.

Charlie was trapped inside. Like a bird in a cage.

CHAPTER 45

Cerro, Cuba

Charlie was squirming, trying to get loose. "I can't get free of the pack!"

Jon had a mind to leave him exactly where he was. The extra seconds delayed him just enough to miss the gate closure. Oberlander's guys would be there any minute.

Jon said, "Hold on." He dropped his pack, pulled out a box cutter and got to work.

"I should have given us more time," Charlie said.

Jon said, "What the hell are you talking about? We knew how much time we had."

"I left something inside."

Jon felt a prickle of fear. "What did you do?" he asked, cutting away the pinned strap.

Now free, Charlie stood, lifting the pack by its remaining strap. He glanced at his watch, the first flicker of panic registering in his eyes. "This may not be the best time to tell you but we have five minutes before the whole place blows."

There was no time for explanations. Jon took a look around, forcing his mind to calm, aware they only had minutes until either a team of armed soldiers showed up or the place blew up.

Focus. What would Carrie have done?

Charlie was now looking at him in desperation, like a man on death row. "Jon? I need help."

"I have an idea." He needed to be quick. He reached into his backpack, took out a nylon rope and passed it through a narrow gap in the fence. He pointed to the side of the building and told Charlie what to do.

"Will that work?" Charlie asked.

"Only one way to find out."

Charlie ran back to the building, raced to the ladder attached to the façade and scrambled up to the roof. Jon ran into the adjacent building, taking the steps two at a time. He reached the roof seconds before Charlie, who now stood a floor above him, a gaping twenty feet of air separating them. Jon's end of the downed phone cable was loose. "Wait!"

Below them, two Jeeps sped up to the facility. Six armed men got out, looking around. A Cadillac came to a stop behind them. The back door opened and Jon got a good view of the man. Bald, heavy-set. *Oberlander.* They hadn't yet looked up.

A rusted metal water tank lay on its side. Jon rolled it over, laying it atop the end of the cable. The noise resulted in a fusillade of bullets. He dropped to the ground, realizing Charlie was doomed.

Suddenly, a deafening explosion shattered the night as a fireball shot out from the facility's windows.

"Now!" Jon shouted. Uncertain if Charlie could hear him, he was relieved when Charlie did what he'd told him, tossing one end of the rope over the downed cable. Jon used all his body weight to keep the line taut as Charlie grabbed hold of the rope's loose ends and allowed gravity to take over.

Gerard watched in amazement as Steadman's cohort ziplined over the gate, the building exploding behind him. One of the Jeeps caught fire, and seconds later it exploded, shards of metal and glass shooting upward like July 4th fireworks. As the smoke cleared, he saw several men on the ground. They weren't moving.

Steadman had clearly devised the plan, handing the other man a rope and gesturing to the ladder. The escape wasn't pretty, but it was effective. A matter of basic physics. Ingenious.

Gerard gently massaged his bandaged hand, the lava burn not yet healed. Despite the pain, he smiled. Steadman had once again proven a worthy adversary.

***

Lake San. Cristobal

"Simon, please show Mr. Lewis to his room," Charlotte said. "Dr. Lavi and I have business to conduct." Gabe had undergone a full-body search before Simon allowed the women back inside Colbert's office.

Gabe mouthed *I love you* to Terry and left the office with the bodyguard. A sleepy, barefoot girl in *Frozen* pajamas squeezed past him, her hair mussed. The presence of a child in the criminal's house was off-putting.

"I had a bad dream," the girl said, approaching Colbert, who appeared mildly irritated by the intrusion.

"It's all right sweetheart. Where's Carmen?"

The girl rubbed at her eyes. "Sleeping."

"Of course she is." Charlotte led the girl to the door.

The child looked up at Gabe, pointing. "Who's that?"

Charlotte replied. "Just some friend of Grand-mère's, coming for a visit. You can go back to bed now."

Gabe saw the girl eye the dollhouse, deliberating.

"Now, little one."

The child reluctantly turned and walked away, the house swallowing her up.

Simon gestured to Gabe, leading him to the back of the house. He unlocked a door, motioning for him to go inside.

Creaking wooden stairs led down to a damp, windowless cellar.

Simon flicked on the light, illuminating a wall of wine bottles, each lying flat in its own slot. Along the far wall was a cot, a water bottle on the floor. "Bathroom's over there," Simon said, pointing in the corner.

Without another word, the bodyguard ascended the stairs. Gabe heard the door click shut behind him.

CHAPTER 46

New York City

A fter the events at the Cuban facility, Charlie clammed up, refusing to explain his actions but offering Jon "a ride" back to the States. He didn't ask for Jon's photos and Jon didn't offer them. Both he and Charlie had succeeded in their respective missions. The creation of an enhanced Russian military had been thwarted. It was a coup of significant proportion. And yet neither seemed to feel the need to celebrate.

They drove straight to a landing strip thirty miles east of Havana. From there, Jon sent Sienna a text, saying goodbye, that he needed to get off the island pronto. She would hear about the explosion soon enough.

The flight was awful for Jon. Chills, nausea, and heart palpitations made him listless. Charlie seemed not to notice his discomfort. They made a stop in DC where Charlie alighted, offering only a wordless salute in goodbye.

The plane went on to LaGuardia and five hours after leaving Cuba, Jon was in his own bed. He slept fitfully, unable to recall his dreams when he awoke. By then, the sun was setting.

Jon checked his phone, expecting to find a message from DC requesting a debriefing but there was none. Sienna and her father were still in Havana. He'd agreed to give himself up to the authorities once back on American soil. Oberlander was lost in the wind.

While Jon hadn't processed it at the time, when the bomb detonated, it was as if he'd travelled back in time to that horrific day at his Boston university, watching the explosion that took Ashleigh's life. The fact that he hadn't suffered a full-blown PTSD attack, told him the pills were working.

My life's a train wreck. He'd nearly been killed several times in recent days. It made him think of Randy. The five-year-old had brought him such joy in the short time he'd been in his life. Jon had a brutally difficult decision to make.

Jon showered, his body less feverish. He called Matthews who told him to meet him at his loft.

When he arrived, Jon noticed a lady's silk scarf dangling over a kitchen chair. He didn't ask. He took off his coat, handed his phone to Matthews and dropped onto the sofa. "All the photos are on there."

Matthews pocketed the device and handed Jon a beer. "You okay? You look like hell."

Before leaving his apartment, Jon was surprised to find leftover pills from his previous prescription and took a double dose. "I'm fine," he said, then drained the beer. "The Havana contact–Charlie?"

"What about him?"

"Where did he come from?"

"Why?" Matthews asked, squinting at him.

Jon recalled the long-running feud between Matthews and his CIA counterpart, Carrie's old boss and a professional manipulator. He and Matthews had butted heads more than once. Including when Jon's life was on the line on a case in Rome. If it weren't for Matthews and Terry's intervention, Jon would have perished in an underground cell.

Jon brought Matthews up to speed on everything that happened at the Cuban facility—Charlie killing the guards and blowing the place up, nearly killing them both.

By the time he was done, Matthews's face had turned crimson. "That sunovabitch."

"What?"

"They're covering something up. Something big. Whatever it is, you're now as culpable as they are."

Matthews asked several more questions, and stood, reaching for his coat. "This can't wait till morning. I need to get to the office, go over these pictures. Hopefully there's enough to bring down Oberlander and Lamont."

Jon followed his boss to the door. "It's time I keep my side of the deal with the Israelis."

"We can discuss it another time."

Jon came to a halt. "I'm keeping my word, Doug. I'm going to help Terry Lavi and put the White Knight out of commission."

Matthews pursed his lips, tilted his head in consideration. "All right," he said, and stepped out into the hallway.

***

Gerard wasn't sure he'd heard correctly. Steadman was inside the building, only a few floors up from where he was parked. From what he could gather, the home belonged to a work colleague of Steadman's, perhaps even his boss. Unfortunately, by the time Gerard found a parking spot and set up the device, he only caught the last few bits of the conversation.

Since the great escape from the Cuban facility, Agent Steadman had become somewhat of an obsession. Gerard had been tailing him ever since, curious to know what his next move would be now that Oberlander and his project had been blown to smithereens. It was like watching an action film. Oberlander had exited his vehicle seconds before the place blew up, the explosion dropping the well-armed men like toys. Shame. The old guy owed him money.

Gerard put away the long-range listening device. It was amazing what you could buy at Walmart these days. When the name White Knight came up, he'd nearly dropped the device.

Steadman was still looking for the elusive broker who had purchased the latest in hacking software!

Gerard couldn't believe his good fortune. *The adventure continues.*

CHAPTER 47

South Street
New York City

"How are things with Agent Matthews?" the shrink asked, taking a seat in her usual chair.

Jon was relieved. Anything beat talking about Sienna and how he nearly shot her.

"Manageable," he said. Matthews had given him a hard time with the Israeli mission. As usual, he needed to rant before relenting.

"You want his approval."

Jon's instinct was to deny it. But he didn't. He shrugged. "He has a girlfriend."

"How do you feel about that?"

"Haven't met her yet."

"That's not what I mean."

"If he's easier to be around, then great."

"Hmm. Okay," she said, typing something into her iPad.

Irritation was sneaking up. She was doing it again. Taking him five feet short of the basket then expecting him to make the layup with one second left on the clock.

Jon said, "The nightmares are coming more frequently."

The shrink went along with the change of subject. "Same dreams?"

"Same theme. For those I remember."

"Still debilitating?"

Jon shrugged.

"Have you considered what your subconscious is trying to tell you?"

"What do *you* think they mean?"

"Combined with your complex relationship with Agent Matthews, what do you think?"

"Stop with the mind games and just tell me."

"They aren't mind games, Jon. It's better if you figure it out than for me to suggest something. The power of suggestion is a real thing. I don't want to put something in your head that isn't accurate."

"I'll take that risk."

A pause. "Fair enough. You and Agent Matthews share something unique. You've both been through incredible tragedy."

"That's not so unique."

"I wasn't finished."

Jon frowned.

"You're both loners . . . or, if I may suggest without upsetting you too much, lonely."

Jon wanted to shout that she didn't know what she was talking about. He had friends. *Okay, maybe only Granny, Gabe, and a shaky Terry.*

And Granny was family.

It hit him like a punch to the gut. The shrink was right. How pathetic.

As if reading his mind, she said, "You two understand each other. Deeply. Even if neither of you wants to admit it. There's a respect that comes along with it.

"Neither of you has the luxury of completely throwing out the relationship. Your circles are limited to a few lucky people. When one of those relationships is damaged, you are left with much less."

"I don't need a lot of friends."

"Neither does he. But you need *some* friends. Everyone does. It's not a weakness. Your life has led you to begin with a sense of mistrust, making it a nearly insurmountable challenge to gain it. If your trust is betrayed, it can't be won back. You've already lost too much. No one can blame you for not risking losing more. It's safer to keep people at a distance than get too close and get hurt again."

Jon would pay anything to escape the room. It was too much. And she knew it. Why was she pushing so hard? He looked up at the clock behind him, never more grateful. "Our time is up."

The shrink sucked in her lips, nodded. "Right. We'll pick up where we left off next week. All right?"

There was nothing he could say. His job was dependent on two conditions. One was seeing her every week. The other, to work under Matthews's supposed tutelage. At the moment, both provisos were near unbearable.

"I'll be out of town." His decision was made. Whatever minor reservations he had about going to Colorado, they were now overshadowed. He didn't want to come back next week. Or ever.

"Oh, I see. Let's at least get something on the books." Her phone buzzed an unusual tone. The shrink looked at it, eyes raised. "I'm sorry, I need to take this. It's an ill family member. I'll be right back."

"Of course."

With concern in her eyes, the shrink hurried from the room, leaving her iPad on the table. A minute passed before Jon realized the device was still illuminated. He could hear the shrink's voice on the phone outside. By the sound of it, she would be several more minutes.

Jon leaped to the iPad, ignoring the notes about their session and clicking on the tab titled *Rx*. Quickly, he scrolled through the names of patients till he found his own. It took only seconds to issue a refill of his prescription. He set the iPad back to the notes section, placed it back where he found it, then sat down. The odds of her noticing anything was amiss were slight.

Five more minutes passed before she returned, taking hold of her iPad. "Sorry about that. Where were we?"

Jon smiled. "I believe you were about to wish me a safe trip."

***

New York City.

Jon kneeled down beside Randy. The room was cheerful, filled with toys. "Hey, little man. I have to say goodbye."

Randy looked up from his toy airplane. He eyed the colorful bag in Jon's hand. "Huh?"

Jon sensed Esther's presence behind him in the doorway. "Excuse me, Jon. Can we speak for a moment?"

Jon lifted a finger for Randy to wait, the boy's face showing a mix of confusion, a pout emerging.

Jon followed Esther into the kitchen which smelled divine. She walked to the stove, turned it off, then faced Jon, a look of concern on her face. "Que pasa?" she said.

Jon broke eye contact. "I'm saying goodbye to Randy."

"Goodbye? Are you going on another trip?"

"I am, but that's not what this is about."

Esther gestured to a kitchen chair and took a seat for herself opposite him. "Please explain."

"I can't do it to him. Randy already lost his mother. I know what that's like. I don't want to be the cause of his losing another person in his life. He's so young. He'll forget about me."

"Don't be silly."

When Jon didn't reply, Esther approached him, placed a finger on his chest. "You're walking out on him."

Jon was taken aback by the afront. He had never seen the woman angry. "I'm not walking out."

Esther peered at him.

"Okay, I am I suppose. But it's for his own good. To save him the heartache."

"Eres loco. I don't know what that means."

"My job . . ."

Esther stood, hands on her hips. "Is dangerous. I have a pretty good idea of what you do for a living. We're a military family. I've seen it all. My daughter . . ."

Jon felt like a fool. Of course Esther knew.

She said, "It's far too late for you to save Randy the heartache. He already loves you." Esther sat at the table, slowly shaking her head. "There's always the possibility you'll be taken away against your will. But if you leave on your own volition . . . if you walk out on him . . . that's an absolute. He will lose you. Like you said, he's already lost his mother. He will be further traumatized. He's fighting so hard to overcome his challenges. It will set him back. Don't do this."

Jon tried hard to push down the lump in his throat. "I've come so close to dying. More than once. It's too much of a responsibility. I'm sorry, Abuela." He'd come to call Carrie's parents by the same names Randy used.

Before she could argue further, Jon left the kitchen and found Randy. He opened the gift bag and took out a Spiderman action figure "This is the one you wanted, right?

Randy didn't look at the toy. He was frozen to the spot, his bottom lip now trembling. "You're leaving."

"That's right."

"When are you coming back?"

When Jon didn't reply, Randy said, "You're not coming back. I can't see you anymore?"

Jon tried unsuccessfully to keep his voice steady, looked the boy in the eye. "No matter where I am, you'll be right here." He touched his chest over his heart. Randy rushed to him, sobs tearing from his throat. Jon hugged the boy, kissed his head and walked out. A tearful "Please don't go," was the last thing he heard before the door closed behind him.

CHAPTER 48

S hira escorted the envoy to the door, said something in Hebrew and locked the door behind him. Jon took a seat at a small kitchen table, a duffle bag between them. Shira pulled back the canvas panels, displaying its contents. Night goggles, two tactical weapons, rappelling gear, oxygen masks. They were far more prepared than he was for the Cuba fiasco.

"Looks like you thought of everything," he said.

The two-bedroom house was modest in size with a small kitchen, single bathroom, and an old sofa and computer desk in the communal space. Located in a bedroom community fifteen miles from Manhattan, it was one of Israel's four safe houses on the eastern seaboard. It was also only three miles north of Teterboro Airport.

Shira said, "Right now, all we know for certain is Terry is in the southwestern region of Colorado. The area is enormous but other than ski resorts it's lightly inhabited which helped us narrow down several properties. We believe we have the right one. It fits the profile of where Charlotte Colbert would, how do you say, set up shop?"

Jon nodded.

"Unfortunately, we won't know if we're correct until we're in the air over the territory and can track Gabe's nanochip."

She pulled out her iPad. "These are two satellite maps of

where we believe they're located. One is from several months ago, the other from several hours ago." Jon saw a vast space surrounded by mountains and a house on a lake. Several smaller structures were scattered around the property. The images were identical with the exception of little red dots.

Jon was focused on the first map. "What are those dots along the perimeter?"

"Security."

"You mean guards?"

"No, it's AI. Highly sensitive detectors. There's virtually no way to get to the house undetected on foot. It's completely isolated. They have their own mainframe and infrastructure for utilities. They'll be alerted to any trespassers within seconds."

Jon didn't know what was worse—the armed guards in Cuba, or this.

"Why so many?"

"They are actually laser beams. They're visible here on the map but not on the ground. When activated, they crisscross the property. Once tripped, they sound an alarm, Based on pulled images, the system hasn't been live in recent weeks, ostensibly to allow freedom of movement for the staff. But we can't take any chances. The usual caretakers have left for the holiday, meaning fewer people are milling about at odd hours."

The technology was far more sophisticated than what he'd seen in Cuba. "Maybe this is a military installation."

"It's not." Shira said it so abruptly, Jon understood it was not a matter of opinion. The Israelis had done their homework.

Shira gave Jon a piercing look. "This is a classified mission. Gavriel's presence alone has stretched the boundaries of international propriety. Your friend is on a strictly need-to-know basis. You will only share what is necessary for the success of this mission."

Jon said, "Understood."

Shira gestured back to the maps. "The property

encompasses all this area." Her hand swept along a wide swath of territory. "Twelve square miles. The lasers surround the house. There's no time to locate each one."

The security system went far beyond anything Jon had previously seen. It seemed impenetrable. "How will we bypass it?"

Shira sucked in her lips. "The only logical way, Agent. We turn it off."

***

Teterboro Airport–Colorado

The plane could hold six passengers. Aboard were Jon and Shira, a pilot and co-pilot, both middle-aged men donning starched uniforms, matching caps and aviator glasses. Jon was trying to mentally prepare for what lay ahead, unsure if he would perform when the time came. Shira's was a daring plan.

They would maintain cruising altitudes between eight and ten thousand feet until they could zone in on Gabe. Once on the ground, they'd deactivate the laser security–a highly delicate process that would take hours. Then, they would extract Terry and Gabe and apprehend the White Knight.

Jon looked out the window, The ground was only a few feet below him. Waiting to take off behind gargantuan jets was daunting and dwarfing. Rain pounded the plane's aluminum siding, creating a loud din. It felt like being in a tin can. He sure as hell hoped the pilots knew their business. Shira had checked her phone several times since boarding, seeming to not have a care in the world.

Jon exhaled as the plane lifted off. The relief was short-lived. Within seconds the plane began to shudder. He gripped the armrests, closed his eyes. *Not this way.* He didn't fear death —a discovery he'd made when coming face to face with the prospect. Still, he needed to use the time he had to correct the world's wrongs. Fight the good fight. Take down as many evildoers as he could before he left the planet. He'd seen evil up close and he would be damned if he checked out because of bad weather or faulty mechanics.

Opening his eyes, Jon wiped the sweat from his brow and saw Shira studying him, her expression emotionless. Breaking eye contact, she opened a magazine as if the violent tremors were nonexistent.

Once above the clouds, the plane calmed. Jon and Shira reviewed the plan once more. "Get some rest, if you can," Shira said.

Jon took two pills and closed his eyes.

Jon was jostled awake, aware he hadn't dreamt in several days. Not of Ashleigh or of anything.

Shira went back to checking her phone, this time studying what she saw there, and began typing. She stood, went to the cockpit and said something to the pilots, then passed him, heading to the lavatory.

"We've begun our initial descent," the pilot announced.

Though the shivering had subsided, Jon still felt a chill and kept on his coat and hat. The pills were a godsend, calming him even now. He wondered if the shrink noticed the discrepancy in his prescriptions.

Glancing out the window, he was relieved to see the skies had cleared, a majestic mountain range visible in the distance. The sun reflected off the snow caps, low in the sky.

Not long now.

He unbuckled his seatbelt and stood up to stretch, sensing someone behind him. "Shira—"

A uniform in his peripheral vision.

"Don't turn around."

Shocked, Jon froze in fear. *The co-pilot!*

"Welcome to the friendly skies, Steadman."

Jon *knew* the voice.

Something metal jabbed at his back. It was the barrel

of a handgun. A small one. Good enough to stop a man but unlikely to pierce the plane's siding.

Jon forced away the panic. "Who are you?"

"An ardent fan of yours."

The voice. It was the same as at the volcano. The same voice on the phone in Lake Tahoe.

"Friends don't hold friends at gunpoint . . . Gerard."

A smile snuck into the voice. "Yes, Agent Steadman. We meet again. I've become somewhat of a groupie, following you. Havana was most entertaining. Maui, less so."

"The volcano." Jon searched his memory. "The taxi . . . that was you?"

A chuckle. "Not bad, right?"

Jon wasn't going to indulge the man. Or antagonize him by asking about his burnt hand. "What do you want?"

"Let's just say you intrigue me, Agent Steadman. You're tracking the White Knight. I want to tag along, make the broker's acquaintance."

Jon felt the fire burn in his belly. If there was no gun, he would have pounced. His own was deep in his pack.

Jon felt the plane descend.

"You and your friend will make the introductions."

Jon recalled Gerard's inflated ego. "Not happening."

"Tough guy words from the survivor of a killing spree with a gun at his back."

The man knew who he was. His past.

Gerard waved the gun. "Have a seat."

Jon did so, finally able to see the man. He was lithe with a runner's build. Definitely the man who had attacked him on Haleakala.

Suddenly, a shrieking alarm sounded from the lavatory, startling them both.

The split second was enough. Jon knocked away Gerard's hand. The gun discharged as it spun beneath the rear seats, the bullet hitting the ceiling. The overhead compartment dropped open, its contents spilling to the floor.

As Jon made for the gun, Gerard tackled him from behind, delivering a stunning blow to his kidney. Jon grunted in pain, aware that the only way for Gerard to get to the gun was to get past him. He wouldn't allow that to happen. With great effort Jon pushed Gerard off him, getting as far as the next row, clamoring over oxygen masks and life vests littering the floor.

Over the sound of the alarm came the pilot's voice. "What the hell is going on back there?"

Gerard came at Jon once again, this time knocking the wind out of him. As Jon fell against the rear emergency exit, Gerard scrambled back for the gun. Only seconds till he'd be armed.

Panic coursed through Jon's veins. There was nowhere to go.

Unless.

Jon locked himself into the rear seat and in two swift motions, opened the emergency door.

Instantly, the plane began to list, causing Gerard to lose his footing. With great effort, Jon watched as the man wedged himself between two seats.

The powerful sound of rushing air was deafening, the alarm fading into the background. The remaining bins flew open, their contents falling to the floor, and along with Gerard's gun were sucked out the open door. All except the three parachute packs still firmly attached inside the open bin by their Velcro straps.

Without thinking, Jon unbuckled his belt and lunged for a pack, managing to thread his arms through the straps, struggling to remain on his feet.

The lavatory door flung open. Shira emerged, holding tight to the seats to avoid being sucked out the door.

"Grab one of these!" Jon shouted, gesturing to the open bin.

Strangely calm, Shira did so, deftly putting it on.

Gerard went for the third pack, his gun long gone.

It was too late. Shira was holding it down with her foot.

"Is this what you're looking for?" Without another word, she kicked it into the aisle. Gerard's eyes grew wide as he watched his lifeline tumble out the door.

In an instant, he pounced on Shira.

"He's going for your chute!" Jon yelled.

Shira took a step back as Gerard reached for her, grabbing hold of her harness. The adversaries were held in a life-or-death embrace, pulled toward the vacuum. Gerard headbutted Shira who stumbled backward.

Jon watched in horror as the two fell out of the plane together. Into oblivion.

He took no time to think. There was only one thing he could do. He jumped.

***

Jerusalem

Yosef Kahn and Rafi Gonen met at the cyber desk ten minutes after Shira's message came through. She had finally connected to the nanochip in Gabriel Lewis's bloodstream. As advanced as the technology was—tracking him from ten thousand feet—the wait had been nearly unbearable.

They were looking at an image of a compound surrounded by wilderness. A house was set on a large lake, a smaller structure a half-mile away.

Rafi said, "Take out the whole place, dammit."

Though Yosef's outward demeanor remained unchanged, he was infuriated. Rafi needed to tread more carefully. "Dr. Lavi and the Black Rook are in there. Possibly other innocent parties. We don't allow for collateral damage."

Rafi's face turned crimson. "You're going to put the country's survival on the line for one turncoat scientist. You're through, Kahn." Rafi turned and stormed out.

***

JFK Airport
New York

Sienna wiped away a tear as her father was driven away in an unmarked Chevy. With Jennifer and baby still in hiding and her father's fate unclear, she felt terribly alone.

She tried reaching Jon for the third time to no avail. He was a complex man who had clearly had his share of misery. Maybe it's what drew her to him.

Standing in the taxi line, she observed passengers being picked up by loved ones, the joy on their faces, sparking a twinge of jealousy. She was aware how she appeared from the outside. Like she had it all—looks, money. But what she wanted most—a family of her own—remained out of reach.

A yellow cab pulled up. Sienna handed over her bag and got into the backseat.

"Where to, lady?" the cabbie asked.

It was a jarring question. She didn't want to go home. Alone.

She rattled off her mother's Upper West Side address. Regina had always been supportive, if somewhat distant. But she was family and right now, that's exactly what Sienna needed.

***

SoHo
New York City

Matthews held the door open for Jacqui. She'd spent much of the drive from the airport griping about her job, her co-workers, and surprisingly, about Jon. Clearly, she thought she was being supportive of his own complaints about his subordinate.

To Matthews, it was akin to sibling rivalry. It was fine to denigrate your sibling but it wasn't tolerated coming from someone else. Matthews supposed it was true what they said. You don't really know someone until you've spent three months with them. He and Jacqui were nearly at that milestone and he wasn't liking what he was seeing.

Not that *he* was any bargain to be had. Perhaps it wasn't fair, but he knew what it felt like to be with a soulmate, and this wasn't it.

Jacqui handed him her purse and took off her coat. The loft was still more sterile than lived in. Not the most inviting atmosphere. He'd need to think how to change that.

Jacqui hung her coat in the front closet. "I just don't see why you tolerate such insubordination. If it were anyone else they would be waiting on the unemployment line."

"He has his redeeming qualities."

"Name one."

"He's tenacious, learns quickly, is in it for the right reasons." He laughed thinking how he'd so quickly come up with two bonus attributes.

"If I didn't know better, I'd say you see some of yourself in him."

The remark set something loose in Matthews. It was a nearly identical statement to what Erica had said shortly before she died. His wife knew him better than anyone. Certainly better than Jacqui. And Erica had liked Jon. The fact that Jon and Matthews shared a similar demeanor was appealing to his wife, not a detriment.

Jacqui was in the kitchen, pouring herself a glass of white wine. "Anyway, the clerk sent me the wrong memo—"

"We need to say goodbye, Jacqui."

"—and I couldn't—wait, what?"

"This isn't working out."

Her hand froze inches from her lips. "You mean us, don't you?"

He nodded. "I'm sorry."

She walked over to the sink, poured the contents of her glass down the drain. "I've been too negative."

"That's not it." *Maybe a little.* "It's just too soon for me."

"I'm not asking for much."

"I know." He smiled sadly. "But I am."

CHAPTER 49

Lake San Cristobal

E uphoria replaced the initial feeling of terror. With the
winds keeping him aloft, Jon didn't feel like he was
falling, only flying. A bird, free and easy. Like ziplining.
Only now his life was on the line.

He'd never gone skydiving. Had no idea what to do. All
he knew was his survival came down to pulling the cord at the
right time. Not too early or too late. Unfortunately, he now had
a more pressing problem.

Below him, Shira and Gerard tumbled, spinning
violently. Shira's head was listing to the side, her eyes closed as
Gerard held on to her for dear life, trying to wrest the pack off
of her back.

Adjusting to the sensation, Jon pulled back his arms
and stretched out his legs in an effort to make himself more
aerodynamic.

The ground was rapidly racing up to meet them. If he
was going to help Shira, he had only minutes. He focused all his
energy, miraculously catching up to them.

With the wind howling in his ears, Jon grabbed on
to Gerard's back, trying to pull him off Shira. He was an
immovable rock.

In that moment, Gerard pulled Shira's parachute pack
off her, wove his arm through the straps and with a demented
grin, let go, spinning away. Shira was now in a free fall.

Jon caught up with her once again and facing her, wrapped his arms around her torso. Her eyes flickered open.

"Hold on!" he shouted.

Sluggishly, Shira wove her arms through Jon's straps. "Use my phone to find Gabe!" she forced over the rush of air.

Amazed at her sudden clear-headedness, Jon said, "Ready?"

"Ready."

Jon pulled his cord, the two of them jerking sharply upward. By some miracle he'd kept hold of her.

"We did it!" Jon shouted. He saw her eyes roll back. "Shira!"

Soft puffs of icy breath escaped her parted lips as they slowly floated to the ground.

***

Terry paced her room, fretting over Gabe. Alerted to her message to Kahn, Simon had brought Gabe to Colorado, knowing it would serve to keep her in check. She eyed the pile of paperwork on the desk, finding it distressing.

"Your message to the Mossad has changed things," Charlotte had said. "But not beyond repair. I'm still prepared to move forward and negotiate an agreement with your employer. You and Mr. Lewis will simply need to stay here until then."

Shortly after reuniting, Simon searched Gabe, then placed a firm hand on his arm. "Let's go."

Terry had begged for them to allow Gabe to stay with her. Charlotte gave a small shake of her head, a sign to Simon who led Gabe down the hall toward the far end of the house.

Staring out the window, Terry was terrified Simon would hurt him. *What have I dragged Gabe into?*

Something caught Terry's eye. A tiny, flickering light was trailing down from the sky. It wasn't a shooting star. Something else. Too small to be a helicopter. Maybe a security drone.

Whatever it was, was falling steadily, straight to the ground.

No, not a drone.

Moments later, it was gone. Unsure of what she'd witnessed, Terry put on her coat, hurried out of the room, nearly tripping over Cosette.

"Hi," the little girl said. "Can we play? Carmen was reading me a story and fell asleep on my bed."

"I'm sorry, I can't right now." Terry slid past the frowning child and ran down the stairs.

Charlotte, Simon, and the nanny were nowhere to be seen. With Gabe's arrival there was little concern she would cause more trouble.

Terry opened the door, the cold rushing in. No sign of the falling object. Trying to assess where it would have landed, Terry exited the house.

***

The alarm on Simon's screen sounded. Someone had breached the laser sensors. He shook his head in frustration. Dr. Lavi was on the move. Again.

Five minutes later, Simon was behind the wheel of the 4x4, checking his device. The lasers to the south of the property had been breached but he had yet to come across Dr. Lavi. A momentary doubt crossed his mind. *Perhaps it was a deer.* Didn't matter. His instincts told him otherwise. He had to check it out. Lavi had left the house once before and it likely emboldened her to try again. She was becoming too much trouble. Once he found her, he would deal with it, convince Colbert to stop treating her with kid gloves. In his opinion, his boss was turning soft in her old age.

Simon drove the truck to the periphery of the property,

allowing for a broader vantage point. The topography was thicker here, with more places to hide. As he made the turn toward the back of the house, he spotted a quick movement in the trees. Too tall for a fox. Too slow for a deer. A bear was unlikely this time of year.

Clouds laden with snow had gathered above the surrounding mountains, waiting to drop their load. Chasing down Dr. Lavi under these conditions was not his idea of fun.

Simon got out of the truck, unholstered his weapon. It was always best to be prepared.

***

Cosette wiped away a tear, watching Terry leave the house. The nice lady was her only friend. Cosette stuffed her arms into her pink jacket and placed the wool hat on her doll's head. Carmen said not to go outside today because a storm was coming. But no snow had even fallen yet. She would stay close to the house and away from the frozen lake just like she'd been told. When it got too cold, she'd come back inside. Maybe by then Terry would want to play with her.

***

Terry was nearing the edge of the lawn. Thick wilderness lay just passed the property's evergreens.

Suddenly, she heard a moan. Turning toward the sound, she was startled to see a figure past the first line of trees, carrying something. She called out in her fiercest tone. "Stay where you are. I'm armed."

A strained voice just above a whisper said, "Terry? Is that you?"

The manly figure placed what was in his arms onto the ground and slowly came into view, a distinct limp in his gait.

It was Jon. And an unconscious Shira, groaning at his feet.

"Oh my God." Terry staggered backward, struggling to process what she was seeing—Jon disheveled, his clothing torn, his face scraped and bleeding, hovering over Shira.

"We need your help," Jon whispered.

The words focused her. A nod was all she mustered. The next thing Terry knew, she was sobbing in his arms.

***

Simon detected no more movement. Whoever was out here knew he was being pursued. Simon paused, listening, tuning in to his primal instincts, when he heard the crunch of leaves behind him.

***

Gerard had landed well, despite the calisthenics in the air. The woman he'd wrestled with was surely dead by now. But Jon Steadman was down here somewhere. He'd ditched the parachute under the brush to the west of the huge house, when he spotted the truck. Squinting in the darkness, Gerard made out the shape of a large man walking toward the tree line.

Gerard needed information. He'd put some pieces together already but not all of them. The man in the cart obviously worked here, which meant he could fill in the blanks.

Grateful for the quickly growing cloud cover, Gerard stealthily came up behind the man, careful with his footfalls. The man was armed, meaning he was not here for menial work. He was security. He was holding the gun at his side.

The man said, "Enough games, Dr. Lavi."

As the man spoke, Gerard rushed him from behind, knocking the gun from his grasp. In an instant, Gerard held it in his own, pressing the muzzle against the back of the man's head.

"Your tactical skills are rusty. Who are you?" Gerard asked.

The man's body went rigid. "Who are *you*?"

Gutsy. "I really don't have time for this. Talk or die."

"My name is Simon. I work for Charlotte Colbert."

Gerard noted there was no waver in the man's voice. He was a professional. Likely, post-military. Clearly, the job in the mountains had caused him to lose his edge. He asked, "The White Knight?"

Simon's voice filled with surprise. "How do you know that?"

"A colleague of mine sold the hacking software to her. He's serving a very long sentence at the moment. I'd like to recover what he so unwisely gave away."

No reply.

Gerard asked, "Who else is here besides you?"

"Ms. Colbert and two guests."

He was incredulous. "No one else?"

"Her grandchild."

"You can't possibly be the only security."

"We have the best AI system."

"And yet here I am with a pistol to your head."

Simon said, "Come inside and we'll talk. The staff has been sent home for the holiday. You'll face no opposition."

"Who are the guests?"

"Dr. Theresa Lavi, a geneticist, and her fiancé."

"Why are they here?"

"Business. I'm not privy to the details."

"Hmm. Interesting."

Simon said, "No one has to get hurt. I can assure you Ms. Colbert will offer you an agreeable deal."

Gerard considered this. "Perhaps," he said, "but that's a negotiation I can manage just fine without you."

Simon understood the meaning and spun around, his hand raised, his fist ready. Gerard shot Simon in the face and made his way toward the back of the big house.

CHAPTER 50

Lake San Cristobal

Terry let go of Jon, who stood protectively over a semi-conscious Shira, the vast mountain range at his back.

Yosef had received her message. Somehow, Jon had been recruited to help find her. She had so many questions. But there was no time.

"We can't stay here," she whispered. She knelt, feeling Shira's wrist. "Her pulse is strong." She eyed Jon's scraped face. "You're hurt too. What happened?"

"We jumped out of an airplane. Poor landing."

What?

Terry pointed upward. "That was you?"

Jon nodded.

He had literally fallen from the sky.

Jon squinted, seemingly trying to take in his surroundings. "We need to get out of here," he said, reiterating Terry's words. "Did you see Gabe?"

Terry let out a sob. "He's locked somewhere in the house. I'm not sure where."

The house was enormous.

Jon reached into Shira's pocket, took out a phone. "Shira said something before I pulled the parachute cord. I'll find him." Terry saw a green dot flashing on the locked home screen along with several numbers that looked like blood pressure and heart rate readings.

Jon lifted Shira, wincing as he did so. "Her body's taken a beating. She needs medical attention. Is there someplace safe we can take her? She needs to get out of the cold."

Terry said, "There's a garage. It's not heated but it's shelter."

Staying among the trees, Jon followed Terry until they reached the shed.

Jon said, "Look after her. I'll meet you back here as soon as I can." He turned to leave.

"Jon?"

"Yes?"

"The White Knight. Charlotte Colbert. She looks like a sweet grandmother, but if she feels threatened, she'll destroy you."

***

Charlotte put down her pen, unable to concentrate with the dog's incessant barking. Dusk had settled and the snow began to fall.

The nanny should have already brought Cosette back inside for a bath and supper. They always checked in with her, Cosette giving the rundown of the day in her animated way. The child was both a delight and a handful. Tomorrow, Carmen would be escorting her back to Paris in time for the new school term.

Charlotte thought of her resourceful houseguest. Dr. Lavi was ensconced in her room, her fiancé under lock and key.

The dog stopped yapping. *Finally.*

The house turned quiet. Too quiet.

Charlotte opened her office door. "Carmen?" No response. "Cosette, honey?"

With no cell service, the only means of communication was the internal walkie-talkie system. Charlotte picked up the device off her desk and pressed the button. "Simon, have you seen Cosette?"

No reply.

A flicker of fear passed through her.

Charlotte went to her office window. The sun's dying rays hit the icy surface of the lake. Charlotte shielded her eyes against the glare. The cook and landscapers were gone for the holiday, the homestead feeling deserted.

She squinted, peering into the fading light.

There! In the distance, a man stood out against the dimming background, holding Cosette's hand. He wore dark wraparound sunglasses and a heavy ski jacket. *Simon.* Relief washed over her, followed by annoyance. Why isn't he carrying his walkie-talkie?

Carmen was nowhere to be found. She was paying the nanny double time to work over the holiday. She never liked the meek woman, who always seemed afraid of her own shadow.

Charlotte watched the two holding hands as they passed the small boathouse. Actually, it was more like he was coaxing Cosette along. They were heading toward the frozen lake.

Charlotte wondered why her granddaughter wasn't wearing the new skates she'd received for the holiday. Her hands were empty save the one in Simon's strong grasp.

As the pair reached the edge of the lake, Cosette's small body leaned back as if fearful.

Charlotte opened the window, a jolting wind of cold air hitting her in the face, the snow coming down in thick flakes. "Simon, stop!" she shouted, to no avail.

She tried the walkie-talkie once more. Nothing.

Frantic, she rummaged through her desk drawer, relieved to find the binoculars she'd kept there for bird-watching season. She raised them to her eyes, scanning and refocusing, doing her best to avoid the glare. It took only a couple of seconds to see it. Cosette's doll was on the ground, left behind.

Charlotte readjusted the angle. Simon's back was to her.

Her gaze landed on her granddaughter whose face was wet with tears. He was *pulling* Cosette. *What is he doing!*

Irate, Charlotte moved slightly to focus on her long-time employee. In that moment, he turned. The binoculars slipped from her hands.

The man forcing her granddaughter onto the frozen lake was not Simon. It was a man she'd never seen before.

***

Gerard was sick of kids. They were demanding and unpredictable. His last gig had required him to babysit a child in a dilapidated cabin in Lake Tahoe. That job had gone extremely well. It was also where he'd first set eyes on Agent Steadman. There, in the forested mountains, Gerard learned the value of using children to his advantage. It had paid off handsomely, covering the expenses for a yacht holiday in the Bahamas.

With the girl in tow, he had the upper hand on any future negotiations with the White Knight. After killing Simon, he'd spotted the child, everything falling slowly into place. He was a planner but sometimes special opportunities presented themselves.

Gerard would not underestimate the infamous black market broker. It was why he was going to extreme measures, taking the child onto the lake. It was all about the optics. A performance. The more he made Charlotte Colbert sweat, the more of a windfall it would yield. Today's payoff would be far greater than any he'd previously pursued. If all went well, he would have enough money to *buy* a yacht. And maybe even a small island in the Caribbean where he could dock it.

***

Charlotte hurried as fast as she could, the walkie-talkie in her pocket. The spaniel was trying to keep up, excited to be outside, then running wildly in circles, suddenly aware of the frigid temperatures. She'd hastily donned her coat and boots, regretting the lost seconds, even as the wind picked up. The glare was fading, and she could see her granddaughter and the abductor nearing the middle of the lake. "Cosette!"

Neither could hear her over the howling gusts.

She was twenty feet from the edge of the lake, the wind freezing her face. The man now had Cosette in his arms, carrying her like a baby. He turned, a sneer crossing his lips. Then his eyes widened in surprise.

"Grand-mère!" Cosette's voice was filled with fear.

Charlotte's face paled. "What do you want?" she shouted at the man, not wasting her words to ask who he was. It was irrelevant.

The man tilted his head, in mock confusion. "Your latest hacking software, of course. What else?"

***

The house was lit up when Jon arrived, a small dog barking frantically to be let inside. Quietly, he opened the front door, the dog bolting past him and up the stairs. Silence.

Where is everyone?

Side-stepping a dollhouse, Jon checked Shira's phone and ran toward the back of the house, finding what appeared to be a basement door. He tried the knob. It was locked. He pounded. "Gabe?"

"Jon?"

Jon pulled out his lock pick set from his pocket, the only tools he had left, and got to work. He had the door opened in seconds. Gabe stepped out and gave him a fierce hug. He appeared unharmed. "You're a sight for sore eyes." He looked past Jon. "Where's Terry?"

"She's keeping an eye on Shira. Where's Colbert?"

"She should be in her office." Gabe pointed down the hall. The door was ajar.

"Something's going down." Jon grabbed a throw cover from the bed. "Come on!"

***

Gabe followed Jon through the falling snow to the shed. Terry was sitting on the floor beside Shira, whose face was red from the cold. Her breathing was becoming increasingly regular. Jon placed the throw over her. "I need to find Colbert."

Terry stood. "Shira is stable. Gabe, please stay with her."

Gabe took in the fierce look in Terry's eyes and Jon's filthy clothing. Feeling a deep sense of pride, he said, "Go."

***

Jon and Terry left Gabe with Shira in the shed when they heard a shout from behind the house.

"This way!" Terry said.

An older woman stood near the lake. She had a full head of alabaster hair.

Terry rushed forward. Despite the pain in his leg, Jon kept up the pace "Let's go get her."

CHAPTER 51

Lake San Cristobal

C harlotte watched the man raise a walkie-talkie high above his head, then shake it. He wanted to communicate.

Panic set in as she realized he had taken the device from Simon. He would have had to kill him to do that. She brought the walkie-talkie to her lips. "What are you—"

A crunch of boots sounded on the ground behind her. "Charlotte Colbert. The infamous White Knight. You are under arrest."

Charlotte tore her eyes away from her granddaughter's terrified face. There, in the space between the house and the lake were two people, only one of whom she recognized. Dr. Lavi stood beside a tall, younger man. His clothes were muddy. He had a pronounced limp.

"Who are you? What do you want?" Then, to Terry, "Cosette . . . someone has her."

***

Terry pointed out to the lake. "Oh my God! Cosette!"

Jon saw a bizarre sight. A man holding a young girl in a pink puffy jacket was standing still in the middle of the frozen lake, a good distance from the shore, framed by falling snow. In the foreground was the White Knight, aka Charlotte Colbert.

If Jon didn't know better he'd mistake her for one of Granny's poker friends.

Colbert's walkie-talkie crackled to life.

"Madam, your granddaughter is fussing. Please tell her if she keeps at it, the ice is bound to crack." His voice was eerily calm. They could hear the little girl's whimpers in the background.

Gerard!

"Greetings, Agent Steadman. I must say your antics up in the air were quite impressive."

Charlotte faced Jon, a perplexed look on her face.

Gerard said, "Madam, you went through all that trouble to acquire the hacking software. It would be a crying shame not to use it. As I can."

Charlotte swallowed hard. "Bring Cosette back here and we'll talk."

Jon was impressed with her steady tone, even as her hands trembled.

"No. You will give me access to the software and I will give you the child in return."

The air went dead. For a moment, Jon thought the walkie-talkie had lost power. Then he saw Gerard pull something from his pack. A handgun. But his had fallen out of the plane. Somehow he'd acquired another one.

Jon watched as Gerard raised the weapon.

"No!" Charlotte cried.

She was cut off by the piercing sound of a bullet reverberating off the mountain. A flock of sparrows shot up in the air. Charlotte shrieked. Gerard had fired into the air. Cosette cowered beside him, trembling, her face a mask of terror.

Charlotte cried, "I'll do it! I'll take you to the command center now. Please put away the gun!"

Gerard's voice boomed through the walkie-talkie. "Consider that a warning shot. Any foul play and the next one will hit the girl. Tell Steadman and the doctor to go to the house. You alone will give me the software."

Jon watched Gerard holster the weapon, then grab hold of the girl. Jon heard him say, "Behave or I'll kill your sweet, old granny."

***

Gerard considered that he may have overplayed his hand. Steadman's presence effectively usurped his power, giving Colbert the idea she might prevail. But only temporarily. The warning shot brought him back in control.

He briefly considered leaving with the child, finding a hideout until Colbert begged to give him the software. But he had no interest. The weather was worsening, the terrain challenging. In these conditions, the kid would only slow him down.

A shiver of excitement ran through him, knowing he was minutes from acquiring the most powerful software of the decade. It would allow him to gain access to any computer on the planet, undetected. It was a gold mine.

Gerard would hold on to the child until she was of no further use.

CHAPTER 52

Lake San Cristobal

Heavy snowflakes swirled in the growing wind, coating everything in white. In the distance, Gerard could make out Steadman and Dr. Lavi heading back to the house. Charlotte remained on the shore, fear darkening her features, her eyes following his every step. Holding firmly to the child, Gerard pulled Simon's gun from his waistband with his free hand.

They were fifteen feet from the lake's edge when he slipped, the girl falling from his grasp.

"Run, Cosette!" Charlotte shouted.

The words had the same effect as a marathon starting gun. The child found her footing and with the agility of youth, took off back toward the middle of the lake.

Dammit!

Gerard got to his knees. The girl moved with fierce determination.

He couldn't outrun her. Not on the slick surface.

He had a split-second decision to make.

The snow blurred his target. Still kneeling, Gerard steadied himself, raised the pistol, lining up the sights on the girl's pink jacket. And Fired.

***

Gabe was debating what to do about the gunshots when Shira slowly opened her eyes. Her voice was gravelly as she said, "Ma kara?" *What happened?*

Gabe had picked up enough Hebrew to understand her. "You had a bad fall." It was the understatement of the year.

Shira sat up, wincing. Gabe put a hand on her shoulder. "Don't. You need to rest."

Her gaze shifted to the surroundings. "Where is the White Knight?"

"Terry and Jon went to find her. By the lake, I think."

Shira forced herself to stand. "Show me."

Gabe had spent time with Shira, understood her determined mindset. He wasn't going to argue. Helping her, they headed together out the door.

***

Gerard shut out Charlotte's screams, expecting to see a growing pool of blood. He lost the girl as added leverage. Now he'd have to threaten Colbert directly. It wasn't the same. Adults were far more complicated. But it would have to do.

Squinting past the snowfall, he saw movement. The girl was alive, slowly approaching the western shore. He missed the shot. *Goddam snow!*

He aimed again. This time he wouldn't miss.

He fired. *Click.*

No!

Gerard pulled the trigger again. He cursed his stupid rookie mistake. He assumed Simon was working with a full magazine, never counting the rounds. He was out of ammo.

He dropped the gun in disgust, his mind quickly shifting as he actively searched for an exit strategy.

***

The gunshot reverberated off the mountain and across the expanse between the lake and the house, forcing Jon to a standstill. He spun around in time to see Gerard drop his gun, stepping gingerly along the ice toward the eastern shore. He was making a run for it.

Terry rushed toward the lake, Jon at her heels.

"Look," Terry cried, pointing.

Jon followed her gaze. "Dear God."

The stomach-churning sound of cracking ice reached them. A spiderweb rapidly spread, creating branchy tentacles that snaked along the surface of the lake, shattering the thick ice in its wake. Gerard's bullet had missed Cosette, piercing the ice instead.

Charlotte was slack-jawed, a strangled cry escaping her lips.

"Don't move!" Jon shouted to the child, his voice carrying on the wind.

Jon, Terry and Charlotte watched as Gerard leapt onto solid ground.

"I'll go get her," Terry said, bolting forward.

Jon went after her, grabbing her sleeve. "No way."

"She'll die!"

Charlotte scurried past them. "Cosette, stay still. I'm coming!"

It took only a moment for her to slip and fall. She cried out in frustration. "Help her, please! I'll do anything." Her face streaked with tears, she crawled back to the shore, putting her face in her hands.

Terry said, "Delete all the nuclear coordinates you've stolen. They are never to see the light of day."

Charlotte struggled to a stand, instantly appearing far older than her years. "I can't—"

She was cut off by Cosette's screams. They watched in horror as the ice peeled away, Cosette now stranded on a drifting floe.

Charlotte paled. "I'll delete it all! I swear! Just help her!"
Jon paused, disbelieving the criminal.

Terry grabbed Jon's shoulders. "Please, Jon, we have to save Cosette."

Jon knew Terry was right. They had to help the child regardless of who her grandmother was. With no supplies, he would need to improvise. He asked Charlotte. "Do you have any rope?"

Charlotte hurried to the small boathouse, bringing out a coil of nylon rope. Jon took it from her and said to Terry. "I'll need your help."

***

Jon uncoiled the rope, tying it around the trunk of a thick spruce. He knotted the other end around his waist, testing its strength.

He had one foot on the ice when he saw the child's body plunge into the lake's frozen depths.

***

Jon treated his shoes like skates, never lifting them off the icy surface, the fresh snow allowing for a measure of traction. He'd played ice hockey as a kid in Boston and now managed to stay upright. Terry was holding onto the rope five feet behind him.

Gerard had made it safely to the other side of the lake, seemingly watching the spectacle he'd created with interest. Jon wondered how the man expected to get away. It was freezing, nearly dark, with no civilization for miles. Something told him Gerard never did anything without an escape route. But he couldn't worry about that now.

Jon made it to the edge of the gaping hole, knowing he only had seconds, a minute at most. Beneath him, through the ice, he saw a pink jacket. The girl's body was limp. Jon glanced at Terry, her eyes filled with fear. He took a deep breath and jumped in.

***

Gerard watched Steadman jump into the water without hesitation. If not for the rope, it would be a death sentence.

He was glad he hadn't underestimated the agent. Steadman *was* a worthy adversary, if for no other reason than they were both still alive. It gave Gerard a thrill. Seconds passed in anticipation. He would need to leave soon. But not before seeing how the game would end.

***

The water took Jon's breath away, his body in shock. It was beyond anything he'd ever felt. The child had drifted a few feet, a solid block of ice separating her from the open air. Jon grabbed her jacket and pulled on the rope as hard as he could.

***

Terry knew the phenomenon of superhuman strength in times of life threatening events. Jon had only one hand on the rope, the other holding on to Cosette. Adrenaline shot through her veins as she heaved with all her might, two wet people at the other end of the rope. *A few feet, that's all.*

She couldn't hold on much longer.

"Terry!"

There was Gabe, gripping the makeshift line. He took a position behind her and together they pulled.

It seemed like forever before Jon made it to the edge of the hole.

Terry let go of the rope and grasped the girl's jacket, pulling her out. Her face was blue. Behind her, Jon scrambled out, shivering uncontrollably, unsteadily getting to his feet.

"Get warm! I have her."

Jon nodded, unable to speak. With Gabe's help, he grabbed hold of the rope and glided away.

Terry set the girl on her back and administered CPR. It wasn't lost on her that she and Jon had been in a similar circumstance before. She prayed this time would have a better ending. *Breathe, Cosette. Please, breathe.*

Cosette's body jolted, a lungful of water spewing from her mouth. Terry quickly turned her onto her side.

Her eyes clouded with tears, Terry sobbed. "Okay, baby. You're all right. You're going to be all right."

***

Jon sat in a police vehicle, a Mylar blanket around his shoulders, the heat on full blast. The medic who'd checked him out said he was lucky to be alive. He'd heard those words before. One day, he expected, his luck would run out.

By the time the Feds arrived, the storm had passed, but not before dumping five inches of snow on the ground. Two female Feds out of Denver escorted a cuffed Charlotte Colbert to an unmarked SUV retrofitted with snow tires, a plow attached to its front bumper.

Cosette was medevacked to the nearest hospital. A police helicopter was hovering above, its search light seeking out Gerard. Jon knew they would never find him.

In the hullabaloo, no one noticed where Shira had gone.

***

Terry huddled beside Gabe, the manor overrun with Feds and local police. She would have to wait till she was cleared from the scene and brought somewhere with cell service before calling Yosef.

Gabe placed an arm around her, spoke in a whisper. "Remember when we first met?"

Terry thought back to the transformative moment in the lobby of a Jerusalem hotel, clueless that the man who'd come seeking her advice would play more than a passing role in her life.

Terry said, "You were so apologetic for unintentionally drawing me into a dangerous situation. Now I must ask your forgiveness for the same."

Gabe hugged her close. "Why can't we be like every other couple? Lead normal, boring lives?"

She looked up at him, her eyes imploring, concerned. "Is that what you want?"

Gabe cupped Terry's chin. "In case it's not yet clear, all I want is to be with you. Whatever that will prove to mean."

"Even knowing what my job entails, you still want me?"

Gabe shook his head, laughed softly. "For a genius scientist, you can be really dense sometimes."

Terry's bottom lip trembled. "I love you so much."

Gabe wiped away a wayward tear from her cheek. "I know, my love. That's why I'm here."

CHAPTER 53

T he moment the plane touched the tarmac, Jon turned on his phone. Instantly, it lit up, dinging with an influx of messages from Matthews and Sienna.

Law enforcement in Colorado understood that Jon was required to debrief with his field office before sharing with them all that had happened at Colbert's homestead. He and Matthews had a great deal to discuss. Terry, Shira, and Gabe had remained behind, 'pleading the Fifth.' Jon had no doubt Yosef would manage the situation.

He listened to Sienna's voice message. She sounded like she'd won the lottery.

"Makoa called. Since Uncle Finn's project was derailed, Jen no longer needs to be in witness protection. Seems she and Makoa have been a couple for a while. I'm so excited for her! I just arrived in Maui to see them. They were staying in a farmhouse on the eastern part of the island. Dad's letting us use his place, so we'll move there. Thank you for everything. It's almost as if Project Codebreaker never existed."

Jon hung up, thinking the exact same thing.

***

Six Weeks Later
Soho
New York City

Jon was sitting on Matthews's leather sofa while his boss logged into his laptop.

"Your photos turned up gold," Matthews said.

Thanks to the CIA, the Russian facility was decimated. It was suspected that Oberlander was killed in the blast but they had no way to obtain verification without tipping off the Cuban authorities to their involvement.

Jon heard from Sienna that the reunion with her sister was both celebratory and tearful. They would need time to heal old and new wounds.

Jon put his feet up on the coffee table and scanned the loft. "Where's the girlfriend? I'm starting to think she's a figment of your imagination."

"We broke up." Matthews didn't pause his typing.

"Oh, sorry. I didn't know."

"It wasn't the right fit."

Jon wasn't sure what to say. He'd been traveling so much he hadn't picked up on any change in his boss's life.

"Take a look at this," Matthews said, rescuing him. "I pulled it from your photos of the training facility."

Jon got up, walked over to Matthews's desk. On the screen was an enlargement of a document he'd photographed in Cerro. A list of seemingly random numbers and letters was clearly visible.

"What is that?"

"It's an inventory list of items from the shuttered lab in Hana. Most of the inventory was sent to Cerro and destroyed in the explosion." Matthews tapped the screen. "But these weren't shipped. They're in cold storage." His eyes flashed with excitement.

Jon felt a flutter. "*Cold* storage?"

"The last remaining enhanced embryos."

Jon was incredulous. When he and Charlie left Havana, he'd been sure everything had been destroyed, Project Codebreaker a thing of the past. "Why would they leave them behind?'

"Best I can figure these numbers correspond with the year of gene editing, which would make them from early trials. Perhaps they were intended to be shipped or even destroyed, but neither happened."

A wave of relief washed over him. "They're probably no longer viable."

"Craig is looking into how long they can survive."

"Are you certain they're still in Maui?"

"That's what we need to find out. I spoke to Captain Akamai. He wasn't happy but agreed to send one of his officers to the storage facility and check it out. I'm waiting to hear back."

"He knows about all this?"

"Enough."

"Why not let the CIA deal with this?"

Matthews fixed Jon with a penetrating stare. "First of all, it's domestic now. And second, I've been in this business a long time, Steadman. This case had been buttoned up too neatly. The CIA is holding back. I'm certain of it."

Jon studied his boss, knowing his instincts were usually on target. "Then let's figure out what they've got."

***

Maui

Captain Akamai was pissed off to no end. He was expected to dedicate his resources without being fully informed. It was classic Fed behavior. He would do their bidding one last time. Anything more and he'd claim lack of personnel. He was tired of being an errand boy.

At least they had informed him of Jennifer Cartwright's release from witness protection. Apparently, whoever she was going to testify against was no longer a threat.

When Mike Evans was laid up in the hospital, he'd put Officer Iona on babysitting duty, keeping watch over Jennifer Cartwright. Because of the circumstances, there was no choice but to inform his deputy that the woman who was assumed to have fallen to her death was actually alive and well. As such, they'd learned where she was located—a farmhouse in a secluded area of East Maui. Once Evans was back on the job, Akamai thought his own role in the Feds' affairs was finished. No such luck.

Grumbling, he walked up to Iona's desk, dropped a sticky note with the address of the clinic and told him what to do.

CHAPTER 54

Federal Plaza
New York City

J on sat at his desk, typing up his final report on the
apprehension of Charlotte Colbert, when Matthews called
him into his office. The writing had been challenging
and time-consuming given the various sensitive areas of
international security. He saved his work and closed the page,
reflecting how the entire episode in Colorado had already
taken on a dreamlike feel. Had he actually jumped out of an
airplane and plunged into a frozen lake? *My life is insane.*

Jon entered Matthews's office. Craig was already there, a
printout in his hand.

Matthews said, "I heard from Akamai. My suspicions are
confirmed. The embryos are in a storage facility in Hana." He
gestured to Craig. "Tell us about viability."

Craig read from the printout. "An embryo must be
carefully sealed inside a tank filled with liquid nitrogen
and monitored to keep it at least thirty-one degrees below
zero, Fahrenheit." He looked up. "From all I've read, if that's
done, they can theoretically last indefinitely. It's called cryo-
preservation."

Matthews took the paper and perused it. "Good work."
He dismissed Craig, who walked out whistling.

Jon hoped his boss's pursuit of the matter was nothing
more than overcaution.

Matthews went on. "I still don't know what the CIA is up to, but one thing I'm sure of. Whoever knows these embryos remain will be coming for them."

"What makes you so certain?"

"Project Codebreaker has been in the works for many years with the backing of powerful people. People who are not used to losing. Thanks to the CIA, the whole thing literally blew up in their faces. If they can salvage any of the project, there's no doubt they will." Matthews tapped his chest. "And I want the collars."

Jon had observed Matthews's profiling skills before. He had a gift. "You want to lure them with the remaining embryos?"

Matthews nodded.

Jon liked it. "And we'll be waiting?"

A devilish grin crossed Matthews's lips. "Like hunters in the woods."

Jon remained in Matthews's office until they'd worked out a strategy. Back at his desk, Jon called Sienna.

"Hey, Jon. Thanks for getting back to me. How are you?" She sounded upbeat.

"Busy. How's your sister?"

"Amazing. She and the baby are healthy. I can't believe in a few short months I'll be a mom."

Jon smiled at Sienna's exuberance. "Is Mike Evans still with her?"

"Yes, they're adorable together."

"Good."

Sienna must have heard something in Jon's voice. "Something wrong?"

"No. Send my regards."

She paused, then said, "I was really frightened there for a while. Dad's lawyering up. He's hoping the help he gave with the training facility will lighten his sentence. He's tried reaching out to Jen a few times. She's not ready to talk to him but at least he's trying."

Jon thought Sinclair Lamont had a boatload to answer for but he didn't say so.

Sienna added, "Maybe we can get together at some point when I'm back on the mainland." The suggestion hung in the air for a few moments, the space filled with awkwardness.

"Sure," Jon said, aware the recent distance had broken the spell she had cast over him. "Let's be in touch."

They spoke for a few more minutes. Jon couldn't tell her about the found enhanced embryos. He would lie in wait for whoever came for them and put the whole thing to bed. If all went well, they would never even know Jon was back on the island. As far as Sienna was concerned, the case was closed. Mike was still there, keeping an eye on things, even if unofficially. The sisters were safe.

***

Hana

Jon showed up at the storage facility after ten p.m., grateful the place had twenty-four hour service. He had flown in on a nonstop charter from New York to Hana-Maui Airport, making the journey much easier than the last time. In his bag was a surveillance camera that he could easily install inside the storage unit. As an extra precaution, he brought a GPS tracker to monitor the embryos. He would be notified immediately if anyone came for them and if they were moved.

A young man, wearing a t-shirt with the company logo, was manning the desk. Jon flashed his credentials. "I'm here to view the Hana lab storage unit."

The man studied the badge, seemingly enamored. He looked up at Jon. "Why is it so popular?"

"Can't say."

He nodded slowly. "Right. I'll show you where it is."

Jon followed the man down a long hallway, stopping in front of a mid-sized locker. "This is it?"

"Yep." He fit a key in the lock, lifting the garage-style door above his head.

Jon was surprised to see only a few items. Nothing that looked like it could hold the embryos. "Is this everything?"

"Huh?"

"Something is missing."

The kid seemed nervous. "Sorry. You and the policeman are the only ones to come here."

Jon felt a flicker of worry. "Are you sure there are no other lockers for the clinic?"

"Positive."

"Who else has a key?"

"Only me and the owner, of course."

"Mr. Oberlander?"

The man nodded. "But he's never been here. A delivery service dropped off the items and asked me to mail the key to somewhere in Cuba, believe it or not. It's only been you and the cop."

Jon felt a twinge. "Describe the police officer."

"Guy's a beast. Built like that actor. You know, the one that was a wrestler."

Jon hurried to the exit, leaving the kid behind.

***

"They're not there, Akamai."

Jon was sitting in the car rental, fuming. He was not going to let the captain run him around again.

"The embryos?"

"*Yes*, the embryos. What do you think I'm calling about?" Jon's patience was worn thin. "You said they were there. Where the hell are they?"

"I saw them with my own eyes. I dispatched one of my officers over there and had the watchman send me a photo of the cannister."

Akamai sounded genuinely flustered. Jon wracked his brain. No way the kid took them. "Who did you send over?"

Jon knew the answer before he heard it. The watchman had described the officer accurately.

"My right-hand man. Officer Iona. I'll call you back."

Jon clicked off and called Sienna. The call went directly to voicemail.

***

Akamai rang Jon back on video chat. He explained that Iona had not returned to his desk since being sent to the storage facility. He wasn't answering his radio or personal cellphone. The captain's usual gruff exterior was bordering on the penitent. "I can't believe one of my own is involved in this. Iona's been with me for years."

While Jon waited for Akamai to try Mike's number, he called Sienna's phone again. Still no answer. Akamai had no better luck.

"Did you tell Iona anything about the enhanced embryos?"

"No." Then, "He could have heard my conversation with your boss." Akamai put a hand on his forehead. "Goddammit," he muttered.

Jon recalled the meeting with Mike Evans in the hospital after the volcano attack. Iona was there, standing guard. He would have easily heard what was being said about Jennifer being in witness protection.

The situation had rapidly turned dire. "Do you know where Sinclair Lamont's house is?"

Akamai answered in the affirmative. "I'll meet you there."

***

Kahului

Jon was waiting a half mile up the road from Sinclair Lamont's home, his headlights turned off. The only light came from a multitude of stars in the inky sky.

When the cruiser pulled up beside him, Jon got out of the car. The captain did likewise. He was in uniform, his pistol on one hip, a radio on the other. No sounds but the lapping waves.

Jon nodded his head in lieu of shaking the man's hand. "Any updates?"

"Iona's off the radar. It's not looking good." He pointed a thumb behind him. The house was barely decipherable in the darkness. "What do you think we'll find in there?"

"No idea but we need to be prepared for anything." They had agreed not to bring in the cavalry. In the event there was trouble inside the house, they didn't want to create a hostage situation. Better to run reconnaissance on the place. We can check things out quietly and decide what to do from there."

Jon and Akamai set out at a good clip. They were halfway to the house when gunfire shattered the quiet.

They unholstered their weapons.

Akamai whispered, "I'll cover you. Go."

Staying low, Jon rushed ahead, closing the distance in minutes, his bad leg protesting. Approaching the side door, he nearly fell over a bulky form sprawled at the edge of the driveway. It took a moment for his eyes to adjust and for his brain to compute what he was seeing.

Lying in a heap on the ground was Mike Evans, a black circle burning a hole in his temple.

It took great effort not to hyperventilate.

"Jeez," Akamai said, coming up behind Jon. He reached for the radio on his hip. "I'll call for backup."

"No," Jon whispered. "If the women are here, there's no time. We need to go in now."

Akamai paused then nodded. On instinct, the two men positioned themselves on either side of the door.

Akamai mouthed "One, two, three" and stepping back, kicked down the door.

CHAPTER 55

Kahului

J on led with his gun, and in a swift motion stormed inside. If it was a trap, they'd walked right into it. They were sitting ducks.

No bullets came.

"I'll check the back," Akamai said. Jon turned right into the living room.

Jon risked a loud whisper. "Sienna?"

"Here."

Jon watched as Sienna emerged from the dark corner, her face a mask of fear.

"Jon? Oh my God. What are you doing here?" She went to him. "I heard a shot."

No time to explain. "Where's your sister?"

"A police officer came by. He said Captain Akamai sent him for added protection. That Jennifer was in danger. They went looking for Mike."

"Mike's dead."

Sienna's eyes widened in disbelief. "No."

"Officer Iona was working for Oberlander."

Her face paled as she said, "He has Jen!"

"Stay here. Do not go outside. I'm going after them."

Jon met up with Akamai in the kitchen. "Sienna Lamont is

here. Iona has her sister."

The back door was ajar. Akamai's face was red with anger. "I'm taking him down."

Jon was on Akamai's heels, crossing the threshold, when he heard a soft cry. It came from the beach behind the house.

A bank of clouds parted, revealing a sliver of moon that reflected on the ocean waves. High grass lined a path halfway to the water. Akamai said, "I'll go right, you left." He took off.

Jon ducked out the back door, his senses heightened. Seconds later, he heard Akamai's voice, rage dripping from each word. "What have you got there, Iona?"

Jon crab-crawled behind the brush, the grass creating ample cover. He ventured a look. He had a clear view of Akamai.

Iona stood in the open. He was holding what looked like a metal cannister. Jon had seen them in college. It was a dry shipper, a cryogenic vessel used to transport biological tissue in a deep nitrogen freeze. Akamai's pistol was aimed at Iona's chest.

A car engine started up.

Iona's voice carried on the breeze. "I'm getting paid more for this than I make at the precinct in a year."

Akamai shouted, "Put it down and put your hands behind your back!"

Iona didn't budge. "The WITSEC guy tried to stop me. Don't make the same mistake, captain."

Jon raised his pistol and fired off a round, hitting Iona in the leg and missing Akamai by millimeters. The cannister fell from Iona's hand, dropping to the sand. Akamai was on him in an instant. "Where's the woman?"

Iona was squirming on the ground, letting out a string of curses. Akamai put his pistol to Iona's head.

Iona seethed. "Oberlander has her."

Shocked, Jon came out in the open. "He's alive?"

Jon's mind flashed to Charlie ziplining between the

buildings in Cerro, the training facility blowing up. He never saw Oberlander's body. He was too busy at the time saving Charlie's ass. Somehow Oberlander had survived that explosion.

Akamai grabbed the canister and Iona's pistol. "Where is he?"

A deep, resounding voice came from behind. "I'm right here."

Jon spun around, his pistol raised. There, between the house and the sea, stood a burly man with a beet red face, like he'd been in the sun for several days. He had one hand on the trigger of his gun, the other on the arm of a terrified woman with short blond hair. Jennifer Cartwright.

Phineas Oberlander said, "Lower your weapon, Steadman." His gaze shifted to Akamai. "Captain, step away from Officer Iona."

Akamai didn't move a muscle.

"The embryos." He extended his hand.

It was a standoff. From this angle, attempting a shot at Oberlander would surely end in Jennifer's death.

Jon said, "It's too late. Project Codebreaker is dead."

"If it weren't for you," Oberlander hissed, "and the Lamonts, I'd be an obscenely rich man." His face turned a deeper shade of crimson. "With these embryos I can start over. There will always be a market for them somewhere."

"Maybe so, but you won't be the one providing them."

Oberlander squeezed Jennifer's arm and she winced. "Hand them over."

In that instant, a shot rang out. Jennifer shrieked. Oberlander's hand fell away. Stunned, he looked down at the red stain spreading across his chest. He dropped to his knees, falling face first into the sand.

Jennifer let out a strangled cry, ran past Jon to Sienna who stood there, a smoking gun held firmly in her hand.

CHAPTER 56

Sienna looked out the window at the brightening sky, her arms crossed over her chest. Another magnificent sunrise. As if nothing had changed.

But so much had. Jon sat in the corner chair, earbuds in his ears, his head bopping slightly to whatever tune he was hearing. Without him, Project Codebreaker would still be in operation, the Russians on the brink of establishing an unbeatable army. He'd proven to be an outstanding investigator, helping her in a time of need, just like Carrie had said.

Still, all the lies had hurt them both.

Jennifer stirred behind her in the bed, her arm in a cast, resting awkwardly on the metal bed rail. The bullet had nicked her before entering Uncle Finn's chest. With the increased stress, she'd nearly lost the baby. Thankfully the doctor managed to keep her from going into premature labor.

Their father was in the hallway on the phone. He said the judge had allowed bail but Sienna suspected something else was going on. She knew her father. He was calculating, a survivor.

Jennifer was devastated by Mike's death, even referring to him as her soulmate. Despite all the deception, Sienna's heart broke for her sister.

"I'm so sorry for scaring you." Jennifer spoke to Sienna's

back. "I had no choice but to let people think I was dead. I was sworn to secrecy."

Sienna faced her. The way her sister was positioned, she could make out the contours of her swollen belly. Thank heavens she had the presence of mind to get Mike's gun. When Sienna had seen Uncle Finn holding her sister in a vise grip, a gun in his hand, she didn't flinch. In that moment, she didn't care that he'd been a life-long family friend. All that mattered was saving Jen and her baby.

"Please tell me everything," Sienna said, coolly.

Jon took the earbuds out and sat up straighter.

Jennifer looked down at her hands, seemingly organizing her thoughts. "Shortly after joining the clinic's program, I made a good friend, another surrogate. A couple of months ago, volunteers were asked to help pack up the Hana lab. They were told it was being relocated to a new facility. It was a huge undertaking to organize all the supplies that had accumulated over many years. She agreed to go. They were shown around, told what needed to be done and that two of the offices were to be left untouched. They were kept locked at all times.

"On the last day, after everyone else had left, she noticed one of those offices was left open. Curiosity took over and she looked inside. Everything had been carted away save a shredder with several piles of destroyed documents beside it. Amid the mess, she noticed one page didn't make it through properly. Much of it was illegible but she saw it was an internal memo on DARPA letterhead, dated 2005."

"DARPA?"

Jon chimed in. "Defense Advanced Research Projects Agency. They handle scientific R and D for the U.S. Department of Defense."

Sienna asked, "She took the document?"

"Yes. And the pile of shredded papers around it. The locked rooms, the secrecy, and the letterhead got her going. She treated it like a puzzle. She didn't get it all but was able to piece enough of it back together."

"What was in the memo?"

"A short description of what Project Codebreaker was initially intended to be—a way to CRISPR edits. She was appalled and wanted to know what happened to the project, why the world didn't know about the children being manipulated. Editing out deadly diseases was one thing, but enhancements? She's not the only one to make a clear distinction between the two."

Jen paused a moment to gather herself. "When she told me all this, it brought back a flood of old memories. That little boy who I'd befriended. It was my first experience with death. It shook me to my core."

A silent minute passed. Jennifer placed a hand on her belly. "Baby just moved. Want to feel it?"

Sienna walked over and gently put a hand on her sister's stomach. "Oh." It was an odd sensation, miraculous. Sienna sat down on the edge of the bed. "Please continue."

"My friend started asking questions, got noisy about it around the clinic. One of the scientists at the lab told her to stop pursuing what was old and buried. It only emboldened her. Eventually it seems the wrong people heard about her inquiries."

Sienna sat beside her sister. "The document implicated Uncle Finn and Dad?"

Jennifer nodded. "Both their signatures were there in black and white. She threatened to expose the whole thing to the media. She ended up contacting law enforcement. From what Mike told me, a secret taskforce was established to investigate."

A machine beside the bed beeped, then stopped.

"Of course she had no way of knowing that the project was officially closed down and that Dad and Uncle Finn kept it going."

"She gave you the document, didn't she?"

Jennifer nodded. "I had confided in her long before

about who my family was. That Dad used to work at the clinic and was the one who told me about the surrogacy program. She said she'd gotten nowhere with the memo and maybe I'd have better luck. Two days later she was dead, her apartment ransacked." A pause. "I met Makoa at her funeral."

A silence ensued, each lost in their own thoughts. Sinclair walked into the room, appearing distracted. The tension between him and the others was palpable. Sienna gestured for Jennifer to continue.

"Makoa was sent in to quietly investigate. I confessed that I had the evidence. He told me that I was in serious danger, that a special, covert task force was established. Due to Dad's position, the investigation was to be kept secret. It was so sensitive, only a select few knew about it within the FBI."

Sinclair remained silent, seemingly trying to blend into the background.

"After what happened to my friend, I knew I had to hide. That I'd be targeted next. The task force wasn't satisfied with a document that a future defense could claim was forged. They wanted my testimony, offered me a deal. If I would agree to testify against Dad, I would be given entry into WITSEC. I jumped on it. The whole truth needed to come out."

Sinclair pursed his lips, holding in whatever was on his mind.

"They assigned Makoa to my case." Jennifer sighed. "We started seeing each other." She reached for a tissue and wiped her eyes. "We came up with a plan for me to disappear. Makoa had a connection at the coroner's office. It was risky, his office would never have approved it. But he was convinced it was the best way to prove I was dead."

Sienna was horrified. By the looks of it, Jon felt similarly. She didn't want to hear anymore. But she needed to.

Jennifer looked away. "It took a great deal of negotiating but they gave us a cadaver, a young woman who donated her body to science. Her face and body had been battered in a car accident."

"You *paid* for a dead body?"

Jennifer met her sister's gaze. "Please don't look at me that way. I hated taking advantage of someone's last kindness but it was a matter of life and death."

Sienna took a deep breath. "Go on."

"Makoa put an identical pair of my blue boots on the body. They've become sort of my calling card. We hoped it would stall the identification process. Anyway, we left her in the pool beneath the falls. We hiked up to the top. Makoa set up a camera to video me, made it look like I fell, getting a good look at my face. I used my bungee gear, I jumped. Before we released the video, Makoa doctored out the cables."

Sienna was appalled. Still, the ruse had kept Jennifer and her baby safe for a while.

"It needed to appear as real as possible. I wanted so badly to tell you. I knew you'd be devastated but I had to keep you safe."

Sinclair stood in the corner, leaning against the wall as if it was holding him up. Jen looked at her father askance. She'd said no more than a few words to him since he'd arrived at the hospital. "Tell her, Dad."

"There's more?" Sienna asked, getting to her feet. Jon came up beside her, putting a supportive arm around her shoulders.

Sinclair's eyes shifted from his older daughter to the younger. His voice was strained. "You were so young when we moved to Hawaii. I was leading the clinic back then. Project Codebreaker had full governmental backing."

Sinclair cleared his throat. "As soon as I learned what happened to that little boy, I pulled out. But by then—"

"By then, what?" Sienna heard the panic in her voice.

"It was too late," Sinclair said. "The reason you got on so well with Carrie. You'd met her before. There's no reason you'd remember it. You were so little, the places and faces were blurry. She was there only for a short while. Raúl and Esther had come out to visit. We knew each other from the academy, had kids close in age. Both of them were recent immigrants, trying to succeed in a new country." A pause. "We were desperate for CRISPR subjects."

Sienna shook her head in disbelief. Jon whispered, "Oh God."

Sinclair said, "Back then, CRISPR injections were completely new. It was deemed the next generation in biogenetics. Prior to that, CRISPR was only being used at the embryonic level. We had numerous successful preliminary trials. It was an exciting time."

Sienna didn't want to say the words, as if that would change what she now understood. Finally, she said, "Carrie was injected with CRISPR."

Her father nodded. "It's why she was always so advanced. Multi-lingual, brightest of the bright."

The shock took hold immediately. Everything was suddenly falling into place. How Carrie had far surpassed her peers in academics, sports, even socially. Being accepted to Ivy schools. Excelling at everything she did. She was enhanced.

To think all those years Sienna had felt the occasional twinge of jealousy, assuming Carrie was dealt a winning hand. In the end, none of it was her own accomplishment. "Did she know?"

"I'm not sure, honey. That's a question for the Santiagos." As if reading her mind, he added, "CRISPR is an *enhancement*. Carrie could have chosen to do nothing with it. She put in the work, made something of herself."

Jon asked, "Are you absolutely sure about this?"

Sinclair looked away. "I was there when they injected her. There's no mistake." Then, "To be fair, Carrie had no negative reaction to CRISPR."

Sienna asked in a whisper, "What about my baby?"

Jennifer instinctively placed a hand on her belly.

Sinclair extended a hand to Sienna which she ignored. "Your baby is not enhanced. Only the defective gene was edited out."

The anger suddenly bubbled up. "You encouraged me and Jen to be involved with a corrupt organization. What were you thinking? We were nearly killed."

"Try to understand," he said. "You were desperate, suicidal. As your father, it was terrifying to behold." Sinclair's pain was evident. Almost more than Sienna's own. "I never imagined how far Finn would go to protect the program." Once again, he approached her. "I'm so very sorry."

Unwilling to accept the overture, Sienna took a step back.

"Lamont?" Jon had turned pale.

The others looked up, clearly struck by his tone.

"If Carrie was enhanced, and if what Sienna explained about CRISPR is true . . ."

Lamont put his head in his hands. "Germline mutation would have taken effect."

Sienna froze. "Oh my God, Dad. What are you saying?"

"Carrie's son, Randy, is an enhanced little boy."

CHAPTER 57

Pentagon
Arlington, Virginia

J on and Matthews waited in an office on the third floor
of the Pentagon, both dressed in business suits. They'd
been summoned, told to bring the embryos. An official
limousine met them at Dulles and brought them to DC.

A PFPA guard stood at the door. The Pentagon
Force Protection Agency was charged with safeguarding the
building's occupants and visitors. They seemed more like
prison guards.

"You okay?" Matthews asked. "You look pale."

Since the Cuba mission, Jon had what he guessed was
withdrawal. He'd gone through his prescription in two weeks
instead of four. He couldn't risk asking the shrink for a refill
so soon. The nausea had passed but the shivering and heart
palpitations still came and went. He was irritable, still reeling
from what he'd learned about Carrie and Randy. He was itching
for a fight.

When the door opened, two men walked inside. Charlie
and his boss, Matthews's counterpart at the CIA, the man who
had offered Charlie as a contact for Jon.

"What's going on here, Charlie?" Jon asked.

The CIA guy spoke, Charlie seemingly glad to defer to
his boss. "You did a fine job for us, Agent Steadman."

Jon had come to dislike the man nearly as much as he

knew Matthews did. "There could have been other ways to shut things down in Havana. The death toll was higher than it needed to be. What the hell happened to minimizing collateral damage?"

Matthews was seething. "I never agreed to lethal force."

The CIA men remained standing. Jon was certain it was a not-so-subtle show of dominance. "Sometimes difficult decisions need to be made. U.S.-Cuba relations have been a tinderbox for years, despite the absurd show of renewed diplomacy. Had we not acted as we did, many more lives would have been lost. American lives. Thanks to you, we avoided conducting maneuvers in foreign and hostile territory, which would have quickly sparked a reaction akin to the Cuban missile crisis."

Patronizing sonuvabitch.

Jon addressed the man. "What if we hadn't succeeded?"

"Given what was at stake with the Russian's enhanced army, we were prepared to take care of things in a more public manner. But then you came along, motivated to do exactly what we needed. You saved us the trouble."

Charlie said, "My boss here ordered me to watch you, see how things played out. Smart guy. I got what we needed from the training facility and left no trace behind."

Jon sensed the hate radiating off Matthews. He pondered what sort of retribution would soon be in the works. "And what *did* you get?"

Charlie looked to his boss who hesitated, then nodded.

"Names. The scientists involved, the children already enhanced, the women still in the program, waiting to give birth. When it's the right time, we'll take over operations."

Jon wasn't sure he heard correctly. "What?"

"The subjects are walking superhumans. They'll be studied till the age of majority and their families will continue to be compensated. As far as they're concerned, the only difference will be who signs the check. Instead of Finn Oberlander it will be Uncle Sam. Any experimentation going forward will be done on American soldiers only."

Jon sneered at the CIA men. "All this time we were doing your bidding."

Charlie approached Jon, hand stretched out.

When Jon hesitated, Charlie looked to the guard, who unceremoniously took the dry shipper from Jon and handed it to Charlie.

"And we thank you," Charlie said, as he walked to the far wall, unlocked a safe and placed the case inside.

Jon felt duped, helpless. "You're going to keep the children in the program?"

"Of course." His delivery was emotionless, infuriating.

Jon's chest tightened. All the risks he'd taken to help keep the children safe. It was all for naught.

The CIA guy noted Jon's disposition. "I envy your naivete. This war is no different than the Star Wars program or the race to the moon. Whoever beats the other to the finish line will emerge victorious. Only in this case, the winner stands to gain it all. We'll get things up and running again. The right way. On military land with proper oversight. After all, the program was ours to begin with."

Matthews looked as deceived as Jon felt. "Is that why the charges have been dropped against Sinclair Lamont?" They had only just learned about it. Once again, the CIA honchos were snubbing the rules when it suited them.

The CIA boss's tone was condescending. "He's helped the effort, getting you into the Cerro facility and more recently informing us of the surviving embryos." He pinned Jon with his stare like a disciplining schoolteacher, then cleared his throat. "If we want to take over the program, it would be counterproductive to draw attention to its classified nature with a hearing, wouldn't you agree? For now, Lamont is being put out to pasture. Quietly. Of course, there's little to worry about. Lamont has many incentives to remain silent."

Lamont had once again sold his soul to the devil. This time to save his hide.

Jon fumed. "What will you do with the embryos?"

"I imagine they'll be studied in depth. I'm only a servant of the people, not a scientist."

Jon turned to Charlie. "How do you sleep at night?"

"Each of us had a role to play. This is mine." The spy walked to the door. "I have a flight to catch." He saluted the guard and left.

Matthews shifted in his seat. "We're done here."

The CIA guy held up a hand. "One more thing, Agent." He leaned over in his chair, pointing an accusatory finger inches from Matthews's face. "Don't even think about bringing this up with the OIG or Internal Affairs. You brought foreign operatives onto American soil. Beautiful Colorado, no less. The fact that you collared the White Knight won't make up for that." He offered a wolfish grin. "Don't look so surprised, Matthews. I keep a close eye on my enemies."

Matthews jumped to his feet, his fist primed. Jon stood beside his boss and placed a firm hand on his shoulder.

The CIA man looked from one to the other. "I'll keep your secrets if you keep mine."

***

Washington DC

Jon and Matthews were in the limo on the way back to Dulles, the Potomac flowing on their right. They were still reeling from the meeting at the Pentagon. His heart racing, Jon wiped the sweat from his brow, unbuttoned his collar.

Matthews buzzed up the partition glass. "I don't know how yet but I swear I'm going to take that guy down."

Jon knew how deception felt. The last few weeks had been one deceit after the next.

Matthews said, "Thanks for keeping me from pounding him. It would have made things much worse."

Jon put a hand to his chest. "Something's wrong."

"That's an understatement."

The road outside turned blurry. "No, I mean with me, now." He heard his voice weaken. Seconds later, Matthews's concerned face faded to black.

CHAPTER 58

Asterile room. High-pitched beeping. Matthews couldn't believe he was reliving the same nightmare—someone he cared for lying unconscious in a hospital bed.

Jon's face was covered in two-day stubble, his cheeks gaunt, devoid of their usual vibrancy. The kid had been through the wringer. He'd had a tough life, losing his parents so young, then his fiancée. Why couldn't he catch a break? The same could be said for himself. At least he'd had some good years—great years—with Erica. But she'd been taken too soon. Only recently he'd begun to see a space beyond the pain. Perhaps the time with Jacqui had been beneficial after all.

"Hey, Jon. So here's the thing. Erica said before she died that you and I have more in common than either of us realize. I'm an asshole and so are you. But I'm also a fighter." He got choked up. "And so are you. Push through, Jon. You've faced worse. There are people here who want you around. And you still have a job to do."

No response.

"Don't crap out on me." *You're the closest thing I'll ever have to a son.* Matthews sat quietly for a bit, then realized he needed to pick up the tone. "Here's a secret. Promise you won't tell." *Jeez, Doug.* "I met someone. Not Jacqui. That was an epic fail. Needless to say, I wasn't looking for something new, but there you go. I know it's still too soon. I'll probably break her heart too. But she's something special. We met at a meeting a couple of weeks ago. Smart as a whip. Works in a precinct uptown." He found himself smiling. Then regretted it. "She'll never replace Erica . . . but incredibly, she's into me. It's probably my new, improved look. Anyhow, I'm thinking about seeing where things go. Real slow, you know? Maybe it'll stick this time. As strange as it sounds, I bet Erica would like her."

Aware he was blabbering, Doug's voice trailed off, and he got lost in his thoughts. He stood to leave, placed a hand on Jon's, careful not to touch the IV lines. "Well, thanks for listening." At the door, Doug turned, swallowing the lump in his throat. "Get better, son."

That's when things went crazy.

Jon was convulsing, his head shaking back and forth, the eyes behind his lids rapidly darting from side to side, tears squeezing out.

"Nurse, come fast!" Matthews shouted.

A nurse rushed inside. "He's having a seizure." She pressed a button on the side of the bed. Seconds later a young physician ran into the room. He was carrying a syringe. At that moment, the heart monitor shrieked. "The patient's flatlining," the doctor called out. "Paddles!"

The nurse handed him the defibrillator and stood back.

"Clear!" The doctor shocked Jon's heart.

Nothing.

The seconds it took to recharge seemed to last forever.

***

The scent of lavender.

"Ash?"

"I'm here, Jon."

A sense of peace cloaked him, like none he'd ever known.
"I've missed you so much."

Ashleigh looked resplendent in a purple gown. She twirled as if showing off a new dress. Jon went to her. For the first time since her death he was able to actually touch her. She felt different, lighter.

He kissed her, his whole body shaking as if he'd been holding his breath since she'd left him.

"You can't stay here, Jon. You need to go back."

"No. I'm finally where I belong. With you. It's always been you."

The green of Ashleigh's irises shone like emeralds. "It's not your time. You have so much left to do. So much love still to give."

"I don't want to go."

From his peripheral vision, Jon saw another woman approach, this one with a lovely mocha complexion.

"Hello, Jon," Carrie said.

Jon couldn't hold back his sob. A cry of joy. She looked safe, at peace.

"Please go back. My boy needs you."

Jon vigorously shook his head, even while knowing the truth when he heard it. He cowered, both women enveloping him in a cocoon-like embrace. Tears fell down his cheeks as he felt the kisses on his forehead. Like the wings of a butterfly.

Jon sensed Carrie stepping away.

Only Ashleigh remained. "I love you Jon. I always will."

A blinding light. Jon shielded his eyes. When he opened them, all that remained was a soft glow.

***

"We have a pulse!"

"Give him 10 ccs of epinephrine, stat."

The nurse plunged the needle into the IV. Seconds passed as Jon thrashed. Then he began to settle down, his breathing evening out.

***

Jon forced his eyelids open to find his shrink sitting beside him reading a copy of *Good Housekeeping*. His arm ached from the recently removed IV, the bruising turning a sickly blue. He'd been in the hospital for close to a week. He was told his heart had stopped beating. Granny flew up to be with him and had returned to Florida that morning, only after the doctor's reassurances. Gabe and Terry had called daily from Israel to check on his progress.

"Hey," he croaked. His mouth was parched.

"Good morning."

Jon reached for the cup of water beside his bed and emptied it. "What are you doing here in DC?"

"I'm here to see you."

"You came all the way for me? Don't you have patients to see?"

She smiled. "Priorities. I thought you might want to talk."

He made a face, then blurted out what had been weighing on him since he woke up in the hospital. "I can't be around anyone. Especially not Randy."

"Don't you think that's somewhat extreme?"

Jon asked, "I-I'm an addict, doc."

"Not yet but close enough. I'm partially to blame for that. I should have done a better job monitoring your prescriptions." Then, "We need to get you into rehab. You're on leave until you're clean."

Right now, only one thing mattered. "Randy won't be safe around me."

The shrink kept her voice steady. "You'll get the help you need. I promise you that."

"Don't you see? It doesn't matter. The last thing he needs is another person in his life dying on him. I've had too many close calls. I'm unstable. This is the second probation I've been on with the FBI. I'll be lucky if I'm not chained to a desk for the rest of my career."

"Would that be so bad? You won't be in mortal danger. Randy will know you're here to stay."

"I'm not wired to push papers. I'm a field guy."

The shrink stood, placed her hand on his. "We don't need to find all the answers now. Get better and we'll go from there. Okay?"

Jon offered a near imperceptible nod.

The shrink had one foot out the door when she turned. "Oh, and next time I'll be sure to lock my iPad."

***

"There's someone here to see you." The nurse stood aside as a small head peeked in.

Jon choked up. "Randy?"

The boy stood frozen in the doorway, holding tightly to his Spiderman action figure. He stared at the bed, the tubes and beeping machines.

"You're Randy?" the nurse asked, smiling.

The little boy nodded.

"Jon here told me all about you."

"He did?"

"You can go over to him. Don't be scared."

Randy stayed at the door. "He doesn't want me to."

Jon found his voice. "Hey, little man. How are you?"

Randy didn't say anything.

"Cat got your tongue?"

Randy's curious eyes met Jon's.

Jon smiled. "It just means you're being quiet."

Randy looked down at the floor. "You're not mad?"

"Why would I be mad?"

Randy stared at a crack in the tile. "You said you didn't want to see me and I came anyway." He spoke in a soft, wounded voice.

"I never said that."

Randy looked back up, a challenging look on his face. "I heard you tell Abuela."

The nurse retreated. "I'll be outside if you need me."

When the door closed, Jon said, "What did you hear exactly?"

"That you were going away and didn't want me to be sad if you died. Like Mama."

Jon swallowed hard. "I didn't want to hurt you anymore."

He was met with a confused expression.

Jon felt his voice catch. "I made a big mistake. I thought I was keeping you safe from hurt. But that's not always possible no matter how hard we try." He paused, trying unsuccessfully to contain himself. "I always want to see you."

Randy brightened. "You do?"

"Of course. Do you want to know why?"

"Because I'm good at basketball?"

Jon chuckled. "Sure. But that's not the only reason."

"Then why?"

"Because I love you, Randy. You're the best boy in the whole entire world."

Randy dropped his Spiderman action figure, ran to the bed, and fell into Jon's waiting arms.

CHAPTER 59

Yemin Moshe
Jerusalem

Gabe and Terry sipped their wine on the restaurant's stone terrace overlooking the Old City walls. Montefiore's windmill stood tall behind them. A young man brought over a wooden tray topped with cheeses and seven-grain bread that smelled like it just came out of the oven.

Gabe raised his glass. "To Yosef."

Terry followed suit, still amazed her boss had given her the deed to the Jerusalem apartment. The small, smart-flat was now hers. Theirs. It was a combination of compensation and a wedding gift. Both Yosef and the Prime Minister had expressed their gratitude for her part in safeguarding the country's national security with the takedown of the White Knight.

She hadn't been given all the details but understood that while she and Gabe were pulling Jon and Cosette out of the lake, Shira infiltrated the command center, wiping out all reference of Israel's nuclear coordinates. As backup, new, artificial coordinates were inserted, leading to a different location, thousands of miles from the accurate one. Terry could only suspect where the red herring led.

After debriefing both the FBI and Mossad, Terry and Gabe had come to an easy compromise. They would keep two homes, one in the U.S. and one in Israel. They would do their utmost to coordinate their schedules but were prepared for some time apart, if necessary. They had been through far greater challenges.

They ate and drank in companionable silence until the sun set in hues of crimson and violet.

Gabe asked, "Are you ready to sign on the wedding hall?"

"Are you sure about it?"

"I'm sure," he answered, emphatically. "My parents are excited to come here for a visit and meet your family."

"I'll make up an itinerary. We can show them around the country."

Gabe said, "I'm sure they'd love that."

Terry took her fiancé's hand. "Are you ready for our future together . . . Black Rook?"

Gabe smiled, "You bet. Whatever it may bring." He gently squeezed Terry's hand. "Come on, Dr. Lavi, Let's go home."

EPILOGUE

Manhattan
Six Months Later

J on and Sienna each held one of Randy's hands as he swung between them, giggling hysterically. Jennifer sat on the park bench, rocking little Carrie who was sound asleep in her carriage, her tiny fists raised beside her head like a miniature weightlifter. Jennifer was deep in thought.

The afternoon in Central Park was one for the memory books. A perfect summer day. Randy let go of their hands and ran toward the climbing boulders, trying unsuccessfully to find a way up.

Jon's health gradually improved but he still had some bad days. The shrink put him on a non-addictive anti-depressant. Time would tell if they helped.

Another child came by to play with Randy, gesturing to something he found on the ground, drawing both their interest. Jon felt a deep sense of gratification seeing Randy socialize with confidence. He thought of Cosette, back in France, hoping the child was doing well.

Jon had gone to speak with Esther and Raúl. It was a heart-rending conversation. While Raúl dozed in front of the television, Esther admitted that they'd allowed Carrie to participate in the early CRISPR trials. It explained so much about his old partner, all her special skills. They'd never told her of her enhancement.

Raúl had a long family history of Alzheimer's and decided if given the choice they'd save their daughter from ever suffering from the devastating illness by editing it out of their gene pool. To do so, the clinic had required trial enhancements. The Santiagos viewed the concession as a small price to pay, if at all.

Many tears were shed when Esther revealed what Jon had suspected. Raúl had been diagnosed with the ailment. She didn't regret the decades-old decision that would one day save Randy from a similar fate.

Because of the germline CRISPR treatment Carrie was administered, Randy would also develop a higher than average IQ and grow to be a superior athlete. What else would evolve was still unknown. Before Jon left, he and Esther agreed to keep Randy's enhancement secret from others in the hopes of allowing him as normal a life as possible.

Jon glanced at his watch. He needed to take Raúl to his weekly speech therapy. He was working hard to maintain his vocabulary for as long as possible.

Jon looked inside the carriage at the perfect baby, Carrie's namesake, relieved that she was what one would call normal. Without enhancements. One day, she would likely be in the minority but for now, Jon was comfortable with how the human race had been evolving. At a slow and steady pace.

"Dad's trial is coming up next month," Sienna said.

While Jon was in rehab, Matthews had flouted his nemesis, risking his own career by giving all he knew about the latest plans for Project Codebreaker to the OIG and CIA Internal Affairs. He named names, told them of the CIA's use of excessive force.

Jon knew the CIA guy would retaliate. Matthews was waiting to see if he would be suspended for sanctioning a foreign operation on American soil. Hopefully, his role in apprehending Charlotte Colbert and thwarting the sale of Project Codebreaker to the Russians would weigh in his favor. Jon planned to ask Matthews about it later in the week. They had plans to meet for a Yankees game.

Oberlander's advisory board was still being rounded up. Jon suspected the flurry of early retirements in DC's top circles was related.

Sinclair Lamont was at last facing charges including negligent homicide of a minor. Jon thought about Charlotte Colbert who got twenty-five years. She would be lucky to outlive the sentence.

The fate of a U.S.-led Project Codebreaker was still in limbo. Jon doubted he'd ever be informed of the decision.

Jon asked Jennifer, "Are you still planning to testify?"

Jennifer looked up as if noticing him for the first time. Her hair had grown to shoulder-length, a small scar visible on her arm "I don't know."

Sienna appeared surprised. "Really? I thought it was a done deal."

"He was a lousy father to me but he came to the hospital after I gave birth. He was gentle with Carrie." She shrugged. "Maybe it would be good for her if he's around."

Jon had his own mixed feelings. Lamont should pay for his sins. None greater than a little boy's death.

Jon called out to Randy. "Time to go, buddy."

"Five more minutes, Papi?"

Jon laughed. "Sure."

An old man nearby tossed breadcrumbs to a growing flock of pigeons. Jon and Sienna sat in amicable silence until Sienna spoke. "I have to ask a huge favor."

"Another one?" Jon asked, good-naturedly.

Sienna placed a hand on the carriage's handlebar, peeking lovingly at her daughter. "Will you be Carrie's godfather?"

Jon was taken aback. "I'm not sure that's something you would want."

"I know about your demons," she said.

"Not all of them."

"Fair enough. But I see how you are with Randy. It's

endearing. Your love for each other is deep and pure."

When Jon didn't speak, she added, "If something should happen to me, would you take care of Carrie as your own, keep her safe and loved?"

Jon felt something well up inside him. His eyes watered. "Without a moment's hesitation."

Sienna scooted over, put her arms around Jon and kissed his cheek. "That's what I thought."

Their passion had turned platonic, both at ease with the change.

Sienna leaned back, taking Jon's hand in hers. Gazing straight ahead, they watched Randy play joyfully, then wave goodbye to the other child.

Grinning broadly, Randy ran to Jon, hopping onto his lap. Jon wrapped his arms around the boy and for a moment, all his worries melted away.

THE END

AUTHOR NOTE

Much of what I wrote about CRISPR is factual. As are the Russian leader's aspirations to exploit it. During the writing of this novel, Russia invaded the Ukraine, sparking a global emergency. One can only speculate what would happen if the modern-day Red Army became enhanced. Let's hope the notion will forever remain a work of fiction.

If you are interested in learning more about CRISPR technology, pick up a copy of Walter Isaacson's *The Code Breaker* about Nobel-prize-winning biochemist Jennifer Doudna, one of the early discoverers of CRISPR.

Both life-saving potential and inherent dangers exist within all new technology. From Voltaire to Churchill, and even Spiderman's Uncle Ben, the adage, "With great power comes great responsibility," resonates loudly. We'd do well to heed those words.

Thank you to my outstanding alpha and beta teams who pored over each word of the manuscript, helping me mold it into a far superior story. Deep gratitude to Teri Lubin (The Gentle Suggester), Betty Atlas-Rumelt (The Fabulous Fact-Checker), Tamar Hazout (The POV Queen), Ken Germain (The Comma King), Glenn Bochner (The Great Grammarian), Wes Higaki (The Plot Hole Prince), and of course, the remarkable Karen Sheff aka Eagle Eye, who finds all the mistakes left behind. Sincere appreciation to helpful contributor Naomi Lubin.

A humble thank you to all of you—the loyal thriller lovers, who continue to read, review and support my stories. It never gets old.

Hugs and kisses to my son, mom, and extended family for being proud of me and saying so.

Last but never least, love and thanks to my husband, Glenn, who is always supportive even when I'm incommunicado for long stretches of time. Mountains were moved.

ABOUT THE AUTHOR

Nellie Neeman

Nellie is an avid traveler, swimmer, and hiker who uses her own adventures as inspiration for her stories. She currently resides in Cincinnati and Jerusalem with her husband and Lexi, the wacky Labradoodle. Learn more about her on Facebook and www.nellieneeman.com

BOOKS BY THIS AUTHOR

Spree: An International Adventure Novel (A Jon Steadman Thriller Book 1)

He barely survived a killing spree. Now he's on a mission to prevent the deadliest attack in U.S. history . . .

Jon Steadman is desperate for closure. After the love of his life dies in a campus bombing, his relentless quest for answers reveals bizarre violent incidents involving other unsuspecting students. When copycat blasts add to the tragic body count, he's certain he's stumbled on a lethal conspiracy.

Teaming up with his best friend and pursuing a theory connecting the genetic dots, Steadman finds every avenue blocked by powerful people ready to kill to protect their secrets. As his hunt takes him across the globe, he exposes a sinister terrorist plot known only as The Event.

Can one ordinary man step up and stop ruthless killers from executing a devastating catastrophe?

SPREE is a story of one man's battle to overcome the wounds

of the past and find redemption in fighting for what's right. An action-packed thriller, SPREE takes the reader on a whirlwind ride of unexpected twists and turns until the very last page

Resurrection: An International Adventure Novel (A Jon Steadman Thriller Book 2)

Four powerful men. One terrifying secret. Can FBI rookie Jon Steadman stop them . . . before they bring democracy to a lethal end?

Jon Steadman is back, facing off against a shocking conspiracy of global proportions.

Rookie FBI Agent Jon Steadman is butting heads with his insufferable boss and battling his personal demons, when he is called upon to investigate a radical U.S. congressman. Jon is partnered with Ivy-educated, single mother Agent Carrie Santiago and brilliant Israeli geneticist Dr. Terry Lavi, a woman he prefers to avoid. But, when the FBI, CIA and Mossad combine forces, conflicting allegiances and old resentments begin to flare.

As the mystery unfolds, their pursuit uncovers a decades-old plot, exploiting the far edges of science, aimed at bringing America to its knees. The mission takes them across the globe and face-to-face with an untold evil that will threaten their very survival.

Vengeance: An International Adventure Novel (A Jon Steadman Thriller Book 3)

Can an FBI agent untangle a web of deception before he's caught in its deadly trap?

Agent Jon Steadman is clashing with his no-nonsense boss, and skating on thin ice with his on-again, off-again girlfriend when things only get worse. Jon's friend is brutally attacked while investigating a slew of frightening cases with no common thread. Committed to finding the assailant, Jon picks up the trail in search of answers. With the help of an alluring goth-loving journalist, he begins to put the pieces together, but not fast enough.

People are turning up dead.

Meanwhile, Israeli geneticist Dr. Terry Lavi is planning her marriage to the love of her life. When she's recruited to identify an elusive dealer of classified government documents, she's soon torn between devotion to her fiancé and duty to her country.

A shaky alliance develops when Terry and Jon's missions cross paths. Each is forced to navigate a maze of guile and manipulation. One is tasked with preventing the world's most sensitive intelligence from landing in nefarious hands, the other with stopping a ruthless hacker before innocent victims pay the ultimate price.

Made in United States
North Haven, CT
12 September 2022

24005634R00243